mom

KENSEI

STEVEN SCHLOSSSTEIN, who has spent twenty years in the Orient, knows Japan and the Japanese mind. He did graduate studies in Japanese history and language at the University of Hawaii and Tokyo University, and later served six years as vice president of the Morgan Guaranty Trust Co. in Tokyo. Now president of his own financial consulting firm, he divides his time between Tokyo and New York.

KENSEI

KENSEI

剣
聖

STEVEN SCHLOSSSTEIN

AVON
PUBLISHERS OF BARD, CAMELOT, DISCUS AND FLARE BOOKS

Except for certain public figures and institutions mentioned by name—such as former Prime Ministers Satoh
Eisaku and Tanaka Kakuei of Japan, the Ministry of International Trade and Industry (MITI), and the Japanese Self-
Defense Forces (SDF)—the characters, institutions, and
situations portrayed in this book are fictitious. Any resem-
blance to actual ones, living or dead, past or present, is
purely coincidental.

AVON BOOKS
A division of
The Hearst Corporation
1790 Broadway
New York, New York 10019

The Congdon and Weed edition contains the following Library of
Congress Cataloging in Publication Data:

Schlossstein, Steven.
Kensei.
I. Title.
PS3569.C5144K4   1983   813'.54   83-10093

First Avon Printing, November, 1984

WFH 10 9 8 7 6 5 4 3 2 1

ACKNOWLEDGMENTS

Grateful acknowledgment is made for permission to use the following copyrighted material:

The thoughts and teachings of Musashi, from *A Book of Five Rings*, by Miyamoto Musashi (Victor Harris, tr.). The Overlook Press, Woodstock, N. Y. Reprinted by permission of the publisher.

The lines on pages 162–63 from the poem "Words to a Grandmother, to a Lover," by Susan Tresemer. Copyright 1982 Susan Tresemer. Reprinted by permission of the author.

The lines on page 361 from the poem "Revision of the Seasons," in *Searching the Drowned Man*, by Sydney Lea. University of Illinois Press, Urbana. Copyright 1980 by Sydney Lea. Reprinted by permission of the author and the publisher.

The lines on page 369 from the poem "Song," in *Waiting for My Life*, by Linda Pastan. W. W. Norton & Company, New York. Copyright 1981 by Linda Pastan. Reprinted by permission of the author.

The lines on pages 389, 390, and 458 from *The Way of Life: Lao Tzu*, a translation of the *Tao Te Ching* by R. B. Blakeney. New American Library, New York. Copyright 1955 by Raymond B. Blakeney. Reprinted by permission of the publisher.

CONTENTS

Nations do not have permanent enemies,
Nor do they have permanent friends;
They have only permanent interests.
WILLIAM EVART GLADSTONE,
1809–1898
Former British Prime Minister

We must make our people hate the foreigner
and the foreigner hate us.
TOKUGAWA KINREI-KO
Edict of Tokugawa Japan

KENSEI

PART I

EARTH

地

1

Tsok!

His *keyaki*-wood sword, long and curved and smooth as skin, bounced off his master's weapon with a crack that echoed in the semidarkness of the *dojo*. Master and apprentice changed positions within a split second of their swords having touched. Both waited now, testing, their *tabi*-clad feet inching across the tatami with the soft rasp of silk against grass.

Tsok!

The master attacked, swinging sharply from his right. The student pushed his sword hilt to the left, bringing the wooden blade up and deflecting the master's blow with ease.

Outside, an early April breeze stirred the first soft cherry blossoms of the young spring. Occasionally a petal floated silently to the still-cold ground.

You must achieve oneness with your sword.

The clear, pure words of Musashi echoed in his mind, riveting his concentration, focusing his vision, freeing his soul. Miyamoto Musashi, Japan's most revered samurai warrior, who killed an opponent when he was only thirteen, who spent a lifetime in battle with his swords, who wrote the definitive book of swordfighting strategy.

Musashi. The Sword Master. *Kensei.*

Tsok!

Their blades collided in a blur.

The predawn coldness permeated the *dojo*. The room was unheated, as it had always been, since that first samurai had grasped a crude bamboo rod to begin the development of *kendo* fighting centuries before. Heat dulled the senses and made the mind lazy. Discipline could not be

3

forged if body and mind were comfortable. The cold kept
the mind as sharp as the sword.

Do nothing that is of no use.

Tsok!

He swung low and hard, cutting a swath from right to
left in an attempt to scythe the legs of his master. But all
he heard was the muffled swish of his master's robe as the
sensei sprang quickly away.

He spun around, resuming a defensive position, both
hands gripping his weapon tightly. Perspiration covered
his face, like dew, but his hands were bone-dry and cool.
He had never had problems with slick palms. How many
battles had his opponents lost because they had been ren-
dered defenseless by a weak grip?

The faint light from the backlighted *shoji* silhouetted
the student's lithe figure, isolating high cheekbones into
which pitch-black eyes were set in hollow caverns. His hair
was closely shaven around the entire surface of his head.
Dark fuzz. Not bald, not shiny. A black peach.

Timing is strategy. There is timing in everything.

Tsok!

His master lunged almost directly at him, thrusting
straight at his chest. His hands moved instantly up and to
the right, together, inseparable, forcing the *sensei*'s blade
over his head in a harmless carry.

"Yoshi," gargled the master. "You must put every distraction out of your mind, including your opponent. Only
his sword exists!"

He jumped back effortlessly, crouched in the defensive
position. The *sensei*'s skin was white and smooth. His
short, wiry body disappeared within his quilted robe.

"Shitteru," said the student, his lips frozen in a determined line. "I know." He shifted his sword to the left
hand.

Master and apprentice circled each other, warily. *Sensei*
and *deshi.* A living tradition, as old as Japan. The old
teach the young. Master leads student. *Kendo* embodied
this tradition more than any other cultural form, descending directly from the art of self-defense so essential for the
survival of these proud people from their ancestral begin-

nings on this lonely island thousands of years ago down to the present time.

But survival meant more than defense. It meant victory. Throughout the centuries, han against han, samurai against samurai, Shogun against Emperor, only one would win. Defeat was death. Winning was all that mattered.

Timing of the void is born in timing of the cunning.
Tsok!

He attacked now, breathing in great gulps of the chill air, clearing his lungs of staleness and purifying his mind of every distraction. He swung his sword in a wide arc across the front of his master's body, a slashing blur of *keyaki*. The *sensei* stepped back with his right foot, lifting his blade to foil the blow and spinning quickly to prepare for the next move.

The *deshi*'s calf muscles stood out like apples in his hard lower legs, tight and knotty. His lean body showed evidence of little fat. A strict diet of fish and rice, soybeans, seaweed, and sake helped to accomplish this. A diet he followed religiously. No, not religiously. Militarily.

Know the ways of your opponent.
Tsok!

Shuffling to his left, he brought his sword up and across, as if to slice his *sensei* from right hip to left shoulder. The strength of his effort pulled him slightly off balance, and the master was there in a flash, bringing his own sword down toward the student's left shoulder.

Instinctively he dropped to his right foot, in a crouch, and the *sensei*'s sword whispered harmlessly over his head. He could feel the rush of air across his cropped skull. He rose to his feet, sword ready, circling, *tabi* scratching tatami.

He could hear the blood circulating in his head now, felt a rich tingling in his fingertips, the nerve ends sandpapered to sharpness. His sword was light as a pencil. He surged with confidence.

He could win.

The mind is like a teacup: it must be empty before it can become full.

Tsok!

He twirled his body in a quick, full turn, dropping to a squat position and bringing his sword around in a sweeping motion that clipped the *sensei*'s right heel and flung him to the mats.

The student snapped up like bamboo. His left foot landed on the outstretched sword of his master, pinning it to the tatami, while his own right heel jammed into the *sensei*'s chest, forcing the air from his lungs in a painful cry. He pushed his sword tip against the pulsating vein in his master's throat and felt the rhythmic throb vibrate up the *keyaki* to his fingertips.

And he waited. Waited for the breath to return to his master's lungs. Waited for confirmation of his victorious thrust. Waited for the concession of defeat.

He had achieved oneness with his sword. He *was* his sword.

He thought of the countless hours of discipline and practice. The patience he had endured through the unforgiving criticism of a *sensei* who never admitted to perfection. The perseverance he had forged from the raw ores of his young body and soul. The selflessness, the devotion, the elimination of every external distraction. The flame of his concentration burned like a laser, fusing fighter and weapon into a singularity of purpose.

"*Sensei,*" the student hissed.

"What?" A broken voice, barely audible.

"Say it. I want to hear you say it. For the first time. And for the last time."

"What?" His voice was but a whisper.

"*Shitteru zo!*" said the student. "You know!" His words echoed against the flat walls of the *dojo* as the crack of their swords had earlier.

"I . . . concede," murmured his master.

The student's mind exploded in an orgasm of ecstasy. He could hear the blood pounding through his entire body now, flooding through arms, legs, fingers, toes.

If you can persevere, your opponent will be forced to give in.

How true, Musashi! How sweet the taste of victory!

His eyes were wide as saucers, black pits burning in their sockets. A single sliver of sweat ran down the side of his face.

His mind was empty of every distraction. His entire soul focused on that pulsating vein. Yes, defeat was death. Winning was all that mattered.

Perseverance.

Victory.

Survival.

2

His name was Fukuda Kenji: the Next Sword-Generation of the Prosperous Ricefield.

He lifted his sword from the *sensei*'s neck, edged back several paces on the tatami, and watched his master rise, slowly, painfully, from the mats.

Fukuda Kenji held his wooden weapon stiffly at his side and stood opposite his master, straightening the folds in his quilted robe. His master retrieved his own sword and assumed a similar pose.

Master and apprentice.

Teacher and student.

Sensei and *deshi*.

No more.

The apprentice had absorbed all the master could impart. He was on his own now. He had emerged into a realm where he would have to make his own rules, fight his own opponents, on the strength of his own cunning and character. His face reflected a newly won confidence.

Deshi bowed first, a short, respectful ducking of the head. *Sensei* followed with an equally abrupt nod and turned swiftly on the balls of his feet, disappearing from the *dojo* with a swish of his padded robe.

Fukuda walked to the *shoji*-covered doors and shot them back along their wooden moorings. Out on the small balcony he sucked the cold air into his lungs and felt the chill of it knife into his chest. His exhilaration had nothing to do with ego. He had simply achieved that oneness with his sword, as Musashi had preached. He looked across the dark courtyard. Blossoms from the lone cherry tree continued their silent descent to the ground.

Darkness. Invisibility. *Invincibility.* The essence of Japan.

As he stood quietly, he thought about his great-grandfather, Kenichi, First with the Sword, a loyal *daimyo* in the final years of the Tokugawa Shogunate, one of many feudal lords who had fought to the death opposing the opening of Japan to the west. The epic cry stuck to his lips like the caked blood on his enemy's sword.

Sonno Jo-i! Revere the Emperor, and expel the barbarians!

Then under the guidance of the new Emperor Meiji, beginning in 1868, came the Era of Enlightened Peace. Fresh capital was created and new institutions established, with the government as major shareholder. Building railroad systems and unifying the country. Igniting blast furnaces for steel mills which, a century later, would be the world's largest and most efficient. Orchestrating a chain of shipbuilding berths along the gentle, protected coastline of the Inland Sea that would catapult Japan into a position of unrivaled supremacy.

Then, as now, Fukuda thought, the Japanese bureaucracy focused its attention on strategic industries: those essential for national defense and those crucial to exports.

He lifted his sword above his head and stretched. Yes, it was a continuous link. His paternal grandfather, Kenjiro, Second with the Sword, had been born in the year Meiji-3. He was the first Fukuda to attend Tokyo Imperial University. Graduating with honors from the Department of Economics, he proudly entered the ranks of the elite bureaucracy in the Ministry of Finance, bringing great respect and prestige to the Fukuda family as the new century opened.

Fukuda Kenji rested his *keyaki* sword against the iron railing as his eyes adjusted to the dark courtyard. His grandfather had learned early on never to trust the *gaijin.* Outside people. Foreigners who provided Japan's leaders with the technology, training, and organizational structure necessary to modernize.

"We will borrow, if we must, from the *gaijin,* " his grandfather had said. "But we will borrow to improve, to perfect, and to win." Japan had borrowed from the West, not because their institutions and ideas were to be imitated. But because they had power. Military power. Yet their cultures were incomplete, unfinished, inferior. They lacked the depth, the tradition, the perfection that the Japanese would add.

Fukuda's thoughts turned to his late father. Kensaburo. Third with the Sword. Born just before the Russo-Japanese War in 1905, when Japan's overwhelming naval victory gained for the country major power status. After graduation from Tokyo University, he entered the Imperial War College for military training at a time when the army assumed supreme command of the country's domestic and foreign affairs. Among prisoners of war under his overseas command, Kensaburo was known as the Fanatic. His hatred of things foreign was exceeded only by his glorification of things Japanese.

Fukuda Kenji reached down for his sword. He remembered his father's command, at an early age, to honor and preserve the uniqueness of his culture, above everything else. All the great spiritual qualities and values in life, he had said, were Japanese in origin and gave Japan its greatness as a nation. Keenness of intellect. Appreciation of beauty. Social harmony. Discipline, perseverance, and spartan simplicity. Enduring loyalty to the family, to the country, to the Emperor. Fukuda Kenji knew that his people, the Japanese, were far superior to any other. He felt it in his blood.

He turned now and reentered the *dojo,* feeling the soft texture of tatami under his feet. At the door to the stairs that led down to the soaking bath he paused to remove his *tabi,* easing his feet into the straw slippers worn outside. Holding his sword proudly by his side, he cast a final glance about the room. It was completely still now, unmarred by signs of struggle. On the opposite wall, a scroll of Musashi's calligraphy hung in the darkness.

Thunder is good, thunder is impressive, but it is lightning that does the work.

Fukuda Kenji bowed to that scroll, silently, deeply. He bowed to his invisible master, to his training, to his discipline. To perseverance. To victory. To survival.

His slippers slapped at the cold concrete steps as he descended into the changing room. The attendants had readied the bath, and wisps of white steam trailed through the thin slats that covered the sweet-smelling cedar tub. It would be hot, he thought. Inhumanly hot. He stopped to remove his robe and viewed himself in the full-length mirror, clouded with steam.

His body was short, but not squat. His shoulders and thighs were stonehard, and he could see the muscles ripple from waist to knee as he flexed a leg. He could absorb a blow to the midsection without pain, and his taut mid-body muscles enabled him to sit erect, cross-legged, semilotus, for hours. His weight was a perfect 138 pounds.

As he wiped his towel across the fogged mirror, he saw not just himself but an unbroken line of Fukudas stretching back and forward in time. He was responsible for his generation, as his father had been for his and his grandfather for his. And, he hoped, as his son would also be for his. Kenshin. The fifth generation. The Spirit of the Sword.

He slapped his cheeks hard, twice, and turned to enter the bath. Once submerged, he sat motionless and let the intense heat sting deeply into his body. Spires of steam rose from the water's surface, forming droplets of perspiration at his hairline. He closed his eyes and reflected again on his skill in defeating the *sensei*. His discipline was nearly perfect, he thought, but he still felt less than satisfied. Musashi expected more.

Perceive those things that cannot be seen.

When he stepped out to towel off, steam leapt from his skin in the cold air. His body glowed a deep red.

Like all Japanese businessmen, Fukuda Kenji dressed to disappear. A simple white shirt under a gray worsted suit. The invisible uniform. He tied his black, plain-toed shoes and picked up his small black briefcase, stuffed with office papers.

Moving toward the door he paused to reflect again on his victory. The match was behind him now, and he looked ahead, keen to apply his confidence and superiority to business battles. From the outside, he appeared perfectly ordinary. That was just fine, he thought. He was invisible.

He was *invincible.*

Japan was invincible!

The old door creaked on its rusty hinges as he pushed it open and bounded up the stairs, stirring swirls of dust in the entryway. He glanced at his wristwatch. It was barely five o'clock. Ample time to meet the Major.

Ample time.

Timing is strategy. There is timing in everything.

Standing on the deserted platform of Shinagawa station, he blew short puffs of smoke from his Hi-Lite cigarette into the dark void over the tracks as he waited for the 5:09.

"Chikusho!" he muttered. "Damn!" He glanced up at the lighted schedule. The trains always seemed to run less frequently on Saturdays, even though it was a workday like all the rest.

He stopped. He puffed. He thought. The success of the project depended on him.

Fukuda Kenji was forty-eight years old. He headed the entire planning division of Matsuzaka Electric Industries, Ltd. *Matsuzaka Denki Kogyo.* His formal title was *Keika-ku-bu, Bucho.* Division Head, Planning. His colleagues, both senior and junior, simply called him Bucho-san. His immediate superior was the Board Director responsible for Planning—in the Bucho's case, Matsuzaka Yukio, the chairman. Like all Japanese companies, Matsuzaka had no outside directors. Everyone rose through the ranks at Matsuzaka Electric, from the chairman on down. One-company careers fostered discipline. And loyalty.

The mint-green Yamate Line train slid silently into the station. Flicking his Hi-Lite onto the tracks, Fukuda Kenji stepped into the nearest car, settled down on the red velvet cushions, and smiled. As Bucho, he was near the top of Japan's business hierarchy. All Japanese organizations, from the Imperial family to the smallest shop functioned solely on the basis of hierarchy. Position. Rank. And as Bucho, of course, he had his own company car and driver. But that particular Saturday morning was different. He had a meeting with the Major.

Matsuzaka Electric, together with two other Matsuzaka companies, Matsuzaka Trading and the Matsuzaka Bank, formed the core of the Matsuzaka *keiretsu:* the Matsuzaka Industrial Group. The Matsuzaka *keiretsu* had become the largest industrial conglomerate in postwar Japan, more powerful than Mitsui, larger than Mitsubishi, far outweighing Sumitomo. It ranked number one in Japan.

Number one in total revenues. Number one in gross assets. Number one in taxes paid to the Japanese government. Number one in recruitment of the elite.

Matsuzaka Electric had its origins early in the Meiji period, in the 1870s, as had the other Matsuzaka core companies. Founded by Matsuzaka Seiichi, Chairman Yukio's grandfather, the company began as a manufacturer of power systems for the blast furnaces of Matsuzaka Steel, buying coal from Matsuzaka Trading and selling electricity to other *keiretsu* companies.

By the end of the nineteenth century, as the use of electricity grew, Matsuzaka Electric began manufacturing large power systems, transmission cables, voltage regulators—anything that used electric current. In the new century, the company began producing radios and radically new electric appliances for the home, and Matsuzaka quickly became a household name in Japan.

Matsu. Pine tree.

Saka. Hill.

Osaka. The great hill.

Matsuzaka.

Hill of Pine.

"Tamaki. Tamaki degozaimasu."

Fukuda Kenji glanced up at the sound of the conductor's voice. Tamaki station. Not yet. A row of advertising posters were strung along the top of the car. On one was Chairman Matsuzaka's picture with the company's motto: *Foreign trade is nothing but war. Both exporter and importer try to extract wealth from the other.*

During the Pacific War, Matsuzaka was the largest manufacturer of electrical systems for the Japanese military government and became known around the world as the General Electric of Japan.

After Japan's demilitarization and defeat, Matsuzaka pioneered the development of television and miniaturized component parts, following the invention of the transistor by Bell Labs. Then came its videotape recorder in the 1950s while the Zaka-I and Zaka-II palm-sized transistor radios, which became such a consumer hit in the West, launched the company on its way to becoming Japan's leading exporter of electronic equipment.

In the 1970s Matsuzaka spurred the growth of semiconductor research as it formed, with the cooperation of the Japanese government through the Ministry of International Trade and Industry—the famed MITI—a visionary committee whose principal objective was to set strategic priorities for the nation during the latter decades of the twentieth century. This industrial strategy was based on preeminent Japanese accomplishments in the knowledge, information, and computer industries. The group was known as the Committee for Development Policies of the Twenty-first Century. *Hasseikai.* The control group. Japan's cutting edge.

"Shimbashi. Shimbashi degozaimasu," the conductor called.

Fukuda Kenji, who could relax now knowing that he would not be late, thought back to his early days on the Hasseikai. He had pushed aggressively for the establishment of the electronics and computer industries as targets for Japanese dominance and superiority in the years to come. Primarily because of the strategies he had developed for his Chairman, Matsuzaka now ranked third in the world behind IBM and Phillips, well ahead of Hitachi and its other Japanese competitors, NEC and Fujitsu.

Closing his eyes, he leaned back on the cushioned seats and recalled the three key steps.

Calculation. The selection of a strategic plan.

Domination. Culminating in victory over his competitors.

Elimination. Darwin at work in the Japanese market. Survival of the fittest.

The Matsuzaka *keiretsu* consisted of ten companies. In addition to the core companies—Matsuzaka Electric, the

Trading Company and the Bank—there were seven others.
Matsuzaka Steel, the world's largest producer. Matsuzaka
Heavy Industries, a leading manufacturer of ships, loco-
motives, jet aircraft and military transport equipment.
Matsuzaka Shipping and Transportation, with total gross
tonnage greater than any ocean carrier in the world. Matsuzaka Mining, a major exploration company, the overwhelming majority of whose assets were outside Japan in
resource-rich countries which supplied Japan's insatiable
appetite for iron ore, coal, oil and precious metals. Matsuzaka Light Metals, one of the largest aluminum makers in
the world. Matsuzaka Agricultural and Forest Product Industries, Japan's largest landholder and the most significant producer of rice, as well as the dominant importer of
wood and pulp products for housing and public works. Matsuzaka Chemicals, after DuPont the largest integrated
chemical company in the world.

The chairmen of these key companies, all graduates of
Tokyo University, met once a month to set Group policy.
Although each unit in the Matsuzaka *keiretsu* was listed
on both the Tokyo and Osaka Stock Exchanges, none was
controlled by the public. This was prevented through a
unique system of interlocking stock ownership. At least
five percent of the common stock of every Matsuzaka company was owned by one of the other Group companies, putting at least fifty percent of the equity of each key
company under Group control.

By the early 1980s, the Matsuzaka *keiretsu* had more
than a thousand domestic and overseas affiliates, subsidiaries, or joint ventures, situated in every major industrialized or resource-rich country of the world. Group assets
were over $500 billion, and annual revenues exceeded $2
trillion, in one of the greatest concentrations of industrial
wealth and power the world had ever seen.

"Kanda. Kanda degozaimasu." In a voice as cool as the
early April air, the conductor announced Fukuda's stop.

The station seemed deserted, a ghost of its cramped,
rush-hour fullness. Fukuda's footsteps echoed softly in the
dim light as he handed his ticket stub in at the empty

wicket. On leaving the station, he glanced up at the tower clock.

He was right on time.

During the late 1970s, the Matsuzaka Group had decided to push ahead with its own 256K semiconductor research project in a calculated attempt to wrest leadership in the computer chip market away from the Americans.

The 256K. A silicon chip with the computing capacity of 256,000 bits of information. The entire capacity of the early Univac, which had filled a large room, would soon be on a piece of silicon no larger than the human fingernail.

Fukuda Kenji, as Bucho of the Planning Division of Matsuzaka Electric Industries, was responsible for overseeing the 256K project, with one special and purposeful twist. His 256K must have eyes, it had to see. A computer chip with optical properties had never been achieved by a Japanese electronics company. So far, only one American firm had the technology. And the Bucho had to get Matsuzaka's optical chip into production.

It was his obligation to do so. An obligation to his company, of course. But primarily an obligation to his country.

Fukuda Kenji stood on the footbridge looking across at the black-tiled rooftops of Honganji Temple. He buttoned his suitcoat against the chill. The warming effect of his bath had worn off now, and he could feel the cold.

Drifting through the morning stillness the centuries-old Buddhist chants of the Honganji monks echoed like a baritone chorus of cicadas. He listened for a moment, without moving, his eyes clear and wide. Then tightening his grip on his briefcase, he proceeded across the bridge.

He didn't want to keep the Major waiting.

4

"Well?" asked Major Nakamura Hideo. In his younger days Nakamura had been a whiz kid, tops in his class at Tokyo University, honors graduate of the Military Institute. He was now a respected force in the hierarchy of the *Jieitai,* Japan's Self-Defense Forces. The SDF was equivalent to the Ministry of Defense in a country unable to possess offensive weapons. A country not permitted to go nuclear. A country constitutionally lame.

They walked slowly along the inland bank of the Sumida River, near the Tsukiji market, hands jammed stiffly into trouser pockets, necks submerged, like turtles, to protect against the predawn cold.

"Almost," Fukuda replied. He held a thumb and forefinger millimeters apart.

Tsukiji, Tokyo's central wholesale fish market, was about to explode with surrealistic theater, an unorchestrated but harmonious unloading, weighing, grading, sawing, hacking, icing, packing, and crating of countless varieties of fish for the thousands of *sushiya* who depended on fresh fish every day.

Major Nakamura removed his black knit watch cap and wiped his skull with a handkerchief. He was completely bald. The cool, white fluorescence of the lights under the enormous steel-and-wood shed shimmered faintly on his pink skin.

"Almost won't do, Bucho-san. You know that."

Fukuda nodded, eyes ahead, an expression of serious intent crinkling his brow. "The process is nearly complete," he said. "We lack only the prototype. Everything checks out but the visual sensor."

Nakamura gazed across the river to the opposite bank. The first thin twinge of daylight was on the horizon, silhouetting the gray concrete buildings like cardboard cutouts on the waterway.

"You realize, of course, that everything is scheduled for May 15," the Major said. "Not only must a prototype be ready, but a reliable optical sensor has to be tested, and installed, and then tested again, to make the demonstration practical. That schedule cannot be delayed." Nakamura's eyes flickered with eagerness.

"I am well aware of that," Fukuda said solemnly, as they made their way down the long, narrow wharf. "The deadline will be met."

Row upon row of giant tuna stretched ahead for the morning's auction, filling the entire pier several hundred yards in length. The two men threaded their way through the frozen hulks, absorbed in thought.

Nakamura stopped, turned abruptly toward the river, and began to relieve himself; his urine arched quietly into the murkiness below.

"You have a contingency, of course?" he asked over his shoulder.

Fukuda withdrew a cigarette from his coat pocket, sucked it against a match until the end glowed, and exhaled. The smoke disappeared into the cold air with the soft white vapors of his breath.

"*Mochiron,*" said the Bucho. "Of course. My man will be in Kamakura on Monday. If the delay lies with us, or with one of our suppliers, we have no alternative but to put the option plan into effect immediately. That plan is under my control."

The Major turned his head as the wind picked up the raw, putrid stench of the river and flailed it across his nostrils.

"The Russians are pressing us on the northern islands," he said. "They think they can offer us huge quantities of Siberian gas and oil in exchange for dropping demands on the return of the Kuriles." He coughed abruptly and spit a glob of phlegm into the river. He wiped his mouth on the

sleeve of his beige jacket, which was devoid of either affiliation or rank.

"But the Russians are so stupid!" he roared. "First of
all, they forget 1905, and second, they think we're so cor-
ruptible as to exchange material goods for a claim on our
own homeland! They know nothing about our concept of
time, about perseverance. They are truly barbaric!" He
hurled his last words out through lips stretched thin across
clinched teeth. Hate leapt from his eyes.

"Exactly," Fukuda agreed. "The only reason they have
any clout at all is because of their military power. Industri-
ally they are nothing." He took a final puff and flicked the
glowing remains of his cigarette into the river. It disappeared with a hiss.

"The same with the damn Americans," the Bucho said,
stooping to examine a frosted tuna. Its head had been
hacked off on the boat's return from the sea, and a small
chunk had been removed from the tail so the buyers could
check the grain and thickness of the meat.

"With the decline of their industrial base, their power,
too, rests solely in their military capability. We are far superior in most industries, and we are poised to take over
their role of economic leadership in the world."

The Major shook his head. "Except for military
strength. We are nothing, not even a shadow of our former
greatness."

Fukuda rose and looked his friend straight in the eye.
"That is why the Security Treaty with the Americans
must not be renewed," he said.

Nakamura nodded. "We were honored to be chosen for
this great mission, my friend. And we need that optical
chip if we are to justify the trust they place in us."

There was no debate, no need for explanations, between
the two men. For more than half their lives they had
shared the same ideologies, the same goals. They had met
at the National Institute for Competition, the Kokunai
Kyoso Gakuin, founded in the late 1950s by Chairman
Matsuzaka Yukio. Participants were selected by the government from a cross-section of business and industry.

The KKG's principal aim was competition: how to

achieve it, how to encourage it, how to manage it. Chairman Matsuzaka believed that Japanese industry should develop a competitive intensity within its own protected boundaries, sharpening its strategic skills and manufacturing talents, until it was ready to dominate the world markets.

Strategy, that was the key. Protect the home market first and defend it from foreign imports. Then attack the overseas markets with a vengeance.

Foreign trade is a war . . .

Two sessions were held at the KKG each year, lasting six months apiece. Fukuda Kenji had joined the first group, representing Matsuzaka. Nakamura had been nominated by the SDF to attend, and the two established a strong bond immediately because of their common interest in *kendo.*

Classes at the KKG met seven days a week, beginning at dawn and lasting until midnight. Discipline was forged through the absence of heat and hot water at the training facility, coupled with a strict diet of fish and vegetables and spartan living conditions. Traditional martial arts were emphasized, and Zen meditation was part of the daily regimen. Computer science was pushed to new levels of achievement. National pride was fostered through immersion in Japanese history and myth. Organizational theories were analyzed, picked apart, studied in detail. Geopolitical strategy was formulated, especially from the historical perspective of Asian dominance in world affairs.

At the end of six months, fifty Japanese industrial giants and government agencies would receive their participants back, as another fifty took their place. One hundred zealous, intensely motivated, rigorously trained graduates of the KKG each year. A thousand in a decade. One thousand disciplined, dedicated young managers who would lead their organizations into battle with America and Europe. *Calculating* competitive strategy. *Dominating* key industry sectors. *Eliminating* the competition. And raising the *Hi-no-Maru,* the Rising Sun, to greater heights, on more flagstaffs, in more countries than ever before.

And they would win.

"Pin maru go! Pin maru go!"

The strident voice of an auctioneer brought the Bucho back to Tsukiji.

"Point five! Point five! Do I hear six?"

A hand rose above the crowd.

"What about seven, who'll take seven?"

Another hand went up.

"Yoshi. Where's eight, point eight, let's hear eight!"

The auctioneer looked out over the gathered wholesalers, his grease pencil sweeping across their heads in a wide arc, like a priest administering baptismal rites.

"Pin maru nana! Point seven."

The auctioneer wrote the name and number of the buyer on a clipboard in bright red, obtaining this information from the large waterproof pin clipped to the buyer's cap. A huge tuna had just been sold for a thousand seven hundred yen per kilogram to Ofuna Trading, one of a dozen wholesalers who bought and distributed $100 million worth of fresh fish every day of the week. For Tokyo alone.

Fukuda and Nakamura pushed through the growing mass of bodies in the open shed. The whine of electric hacksaws pierced the air. Fires crackled and popped in small iron buckets dotting the floor. Workers wearing hip-length rubber boots scurried about dragging wooden packing crates, chopping ice onto packed fish, hammering crates shut.

The Major kicked a hunk of fish carcass across the cold concrete floor. "We're too far along to turn back now, Bucho-san. You realize that."

The head of Matsuzaka Electric's Planning Division nodded. "Of course. We will see it through."

Suddenly a fight broke out to their left. One of the buyers shoved the auctioneer off his pedestal, shouting in disgust. Caps flew and shoes slipped on ice. The auctioneer's bell dropped to the floor with a muffled clang.

Nakamura and Fukuda watched the disturbance briefly, then sidestepped their way toward the center of the shed.

The Bucho smiled. Competition. Hard, intense competition. It was good for the soul, kept the spirit strong, sharpened the mind.

Stopping at a seaweed stand, Fukuda flipped the owner a small coin and took a handful of nori-wrapped rice crackers, which he shared with the Major. It was nearly time for breakfast, and he was getting hungry.

"You're certain no one else at the SDF knows of our plan?" Fukuda asked.

"Just get the prototype finished," the Major replied.

The two picked their way through the brightly lit stalls. Row after row of sea bream, salmon roe, shellfish, eel, flounder, squid, shrimp, octopus, sparkled in the bright overhead lights. Crushed ice in the stainless steel stalls glistened with a cold, crisp radiance.

What was it about the first time they had met? Fukuda wondered, frowning at the floor. Ah, yes, he remembered now. That round, shining skull. An affectation, to be sure, and highly unusual in a society marked by strict social codes. But evidence of a keen commitment to discipline, to perseverance, that would unite them forever.

They had fought together, their brown *keyaki* swords clashing in an endless daily ritual. They had run together, long, exhausting marathons in the hills of Kyoto. And they had bathed together at night, soaking in the scalding hot water of their common wooden *ofuro*, massaging, kneading, caressing, every inch of their tired flesh.

The early morning sky had turned from black to gray by the time they reached the far entrance and exited the bedlam of Tsukiji.

"Keep me informed."

The Bucho smiled. *"Mochiron."*

5

The Bucho glanced at his watch as he cut down an alleyway, sandwiched between rows of small shops that slowly yawned open. Time for some fruit, he thought, and he'd still make the office before his staff arrived.

The fragile glass and wood doors of the shops squeaked and groaned across their moorings. Some merchants pulled their storefront displays to positions immediately outside. Others, with bamboo and straw brooms, swept the areas directly in front, continuing a tradition as old as Japan. If everyone cleans and cares for his own, then it becomes unnecessary for the city to do it for all.

The black asphalt pavement blended harmoniously with the wooden and concrete structures, their unpainted facades testimony to Japan's tradition of spartan simplicity. The only vivid dots of color were the public telephones, lipstick-red on their waist-high stands.

Fukuda Kenji paused at a fruit stall.

"Ohayo gozaimasu," the old lady nodded from behind a rack of shiny mandarin oranges. *Mikan.* Smaller and juicier than Western oranges, they were more like tangerines.

"Ohayo," said the Bucho in the abbreviated form used to address inferiors. "Morning. Five mikan. Don't bother with a bag, I'll carry them in my satchel."

"Arigato gozaimasu," she replied bowing. "Thank you very much."

Fukuda watched her select five oranges with care, stooping as if permanently bent from the waist. Five, Fukuda thought. For the five Buddhist elements: Earth. Sky. Water, Wind. Fire. The old woman's face was etched with

the lines of a lifetime, her skin as gnarled as the *mikan*.
She used the polite form when addressing her customers,
mindful of the importance of position. Rank. Although the
Bucho was a stranger, he was a customer, and in Japan the
customer was god.

"Here you are," she said, bowing again as she placed the
five small oranges in his black bag. Fukuda shoved a coin
into her hand and nodded curtly.

As he walked on, he reached into his bag and tore into a
tender *mikan*. Tossing the peel aside, he popped an entire
quadrant into his mouth and chewed it quickly.

Why would the Americans try to export citrus fruit to
Japan? With these luscious *mikan* so plentiful and so
cheap . . .

He shook his head. We Japanese have the best of everything, he thought. No need to import inferior products
from abroad. His eyes narrowed as he spat out a seed. Foreigners. Outside people. They had little sense of history, no
appreciation for the proper hierarchy of society, less cultural depth, few traditional institutions, no permanent relationships.

He spat out another seed. Japan gained nothing by im-
porting their goods, the Bucho thought, other than the
gaijin's slothful inefficiency and decadent values. His people were perceived by the foreigners as polite. He laughed.
Of course they were polite to *gaijin*. *Gaijin* were guests.
Customers. But that didn't mean the Japanese respected
them. Or even liked them. Quite the contrary. Most Japanese despised them. Because tradition dictated Japanese
behavior. And obligation. Those were the rules.

Fukuda threaded his way down a narrow path alongside
Honganji Temple. Entering the path, he had choked on the
stench of human excrement; now, cupping a palm over his
mouth to ward off the odor, his eyes darted to a cloud of
flies buzzing around the entrance to a nearby public conve-
nience.

A young man, still full of the previous night's sake, staggered out the door, through the black curtain of flies,
lurching from side to side while tugging unsuccessfully at
a reluctant zipper.

Fukuda lengthened his gait. When he reached Hong-anji, a more poignant smell of burning trash pricked his nostrils. A tiny stream of smoke curled out from behind the temple in his direction. The acrid odor brought back an indelible memory of 1945 when his father had dragged him through the war-torn streets of Tokyo.

The Bucho closed his eyes and breathed deeply, once, twice, three times. He would never forget that day.

He had lived most of the war with his mother and grandmother in the country, beyond the Tama River to the west, cradled safely in the hills, beyond the reach of the black bombers that unleashed their firebombs on a defenseless capital, its wooden buildings igniting like matchsticks and blazing with the intensity of hell on earth.

At the end of the war, his father had brought young Kenji to see the rubble and destruction of their capital, reminding him sternly of his country's proud heritage. Of its descendance from Amaterasu Omikami, the Sun Goddess, Creator of Japan, whose spear dipped into the chaos beneath the heavens millennia ago and formed the most majestic islands in the world, the Japanese archipelago. His father had evoked the memory of the divine protective wind, the *kamikaze,* which had saved their country from destruction by the invading barbarians centuries before. Of the sacredness of the Imperial tradition, and of the *bakufu,* the military government, headed by the Shogun for a millennium. Of the preeminent years of isolation from the outside world during Tokugawa, when Japan's finest achievements in its long cultural history had been produced. Of the victories over China and Russia following the Meiji Restoration and return to Imperial rule.

Fukuda Kenji, the Next Sword-Generation of the Prosperous Ricefield, remembered that day, the smell of defeat, destruction, and death. He would never forget it—etched as it was in his memory with the acid of personal sacrifice and suffering.

Only determination will subdue the enemy.

These precious words of Musashi echoed in his mind

as he left the temple and made his way toward the busy street ahead. He glanced at his watch. No more time to dawdle. He raised his hand, and a taxi swerved to the curb.

6

Fukuda Kenji's jacket hung open as he climbed out of the cab in the congested Marunouchi business district. It was distinctly warmer. A cloud cover that hung low and heavy over the city was beginning to darken as the morning's gaseous pollution rose to meet it.

Rain unlikely, Fukuda thought, as he sniffed the air. He would not need the umbrella he had left at home.

Rounding the corner into Nakadori, the Bucho was swept into a river of undulating black heads, the steady stream of commuters pouring into Tokyo's business center, hurrying, sprinting, hustling to their jobs. *Gaijin* dragged themselves to work, he thought; our people can't wait to get there.

As he neared the Matsuzaka Electric Building, his eyes caught a government *kanji* banner flapping against the Central Post Office tower. He stopped to read the month's new message.

We will encourage and protect the people at home, and wait patiently for the confusion that will eventually destroy the unity of purpose and action among the Western powers.

"Ohayo gozaimasu," the security guard said as he recognized the Bucho.

"Ohayo," Fukuda replied.

The Bucho wore a twenty-five-year service pin in his lapel. A solitary pine tree, in gold and jade, perched atop a hill. Like all Japanese companies, Matsuzaka acknowledged seniority with symbolic awards. After five years, a small silver and ceramic "M." At ten years, a gold-leafed, green ceramic "MZ." At twenty-five years, the jade pin. Fukuda had joined Matsuzaka Electric right out of Tokyo

University. It was his second home. He wore the jade pin
proudly.

Matsu, the pine tree, sign of purity and strength
throughout Japanese history. *Saka,* the hill. Hill of pine.

Symbol of the Matsuzaka *keiretsu* for over a century.
More feared than the three diamonds of Mitsubishi. More
honored than Mt. Fuji, badge of the Fuyo Group. More
powerful than the crossed bars of Mitsui.

Fukuda entered the spotless elevator and watched the
indicator lights blink toward thirteen. His floor. Foreigners told him his office was on an unlucky floor. But the
number thirteen was neutral in Japan, had no significance
whatever. Four was the number to be avoided at all costs.
The *kanji* rhymed with death.

Getting off at thirteen, he strode quickly down the hall
to the Planning Department and to his desk at the rear of
the open, bullpen-style room. There were no offices. Everyone sat at identical, steel-gray desks. Fukuda's was different only in its angle and position at the back of the room, to
set off the Bucho from the rest of his staff.

As he flung his briefcase onto the floor beside his desk,
he began to leaf through the accumulation of telexes that
had arrived from affiliates and subsidiaries throughout
the night. He reached into a desk drawer and withdrew a
new pack of Hi-Lites.

Behind his desk hung the Matsuzaka motto, in vertical
kanji the shade of pine.

*Being forced to work, and work hard, will breed self-
control and discipline, perseverance and loyalty, virtues the
idle foreigner can never have.*

"Ohayo gozaimasu."

His Overseas Development Section Chief, Sakamoto
Ryuji, strode briskly forward and bowed his usual good
morning. Small for a Japanese, Sakamoto barely cleared
five feet. He wore his hair long, almost over the ears, and
always watched for Fukuda's upraised eyebrow when it
was time to get it cut. Severely myopic, he wore such thick
lenses that his eyes retreated to fine points behind them.
Bulky, black plastic frames rested snugly on the bridge of

a wide, short nose. Like all the others, he dressed to disappear. Yet he radiated intensity. His job was his life.

Fukuda looked up from his reading and blinked.

"Ah, Sakamoto-kun. *Ohayo.*" He remained seated, addressing his *kacho* in the informal *kun,* rather than the more polite *san,* as was customary in señior-junior relationships. "How are you?"

"Maa-maa," Sakamoto replied, tossing his raincoat onto a chair. "So-so."

The Bucho pulled out a Hi-Lite and puffed it alive. He blew a cloud of smoke over Sakamoto's head. "We need to talk about the 256K optical chip at Kamakura," he said, gesturing with his cigarette. "Right away."

"Hai." The *kacho* retreated to his desk for the Kamakura file.

Sakamoto Ryuji was also Fukuda's *kobun* at Matsuzaka. The *oyabun-kobun* relationship was a very close one. More than master to apprentice or teacher to student, it was like father to son or parent to child.

Sakamoto had first worked for Fukuda in the Department of Subsidiaries and Affiliates, when he had joined the company after graduation from Tokyo University. At that time, Fukuda had had the difficult assignment of bringing a small affiliate, Aoki Denki, under the Matsuzaka umbrella. Matsuzaka owned twenty-five percent of Aoki and wanted fifty-one percent, or control. Fukuda ordered Sakamoto to prepare a full report on Aoki's principal customers, so Sakamoto drank tea with Aoki's bankers, took Aoki's key salesmen out for sake, and put together a complete dossier on the company.

Fukuda was pleased, not just with Sakamoto's thoroughness but with his eagerness to accept an assignment that bordered on the unethical. As a result of Sakamoto's findings, Fukuda instructed Matsuzaka's sales department to cut prices on competitive products so that Aoki's customers had no choice but to buy from Matsuzaka. Squeezed by falling sales, Aoki was forced to sell out to Matsuzaka.

Fukuda was ecstatic. His judgment had been vindicated. And Sakamoto's loyalty had been forged in the heat of a difficult assignment. Their *oyabun-kobun* relationship was sealed for life.

Sakamoto took the Kamakura file and lowered himself into a chair next to Fukuda's desk. He brushed back his dense, dark hair with a short sweeping motion and opened the file.

"Design, on schedule," he began, scanning the performance chart, updated, on the inside cover. "Testing, in process. Bonding equipment, error-free." He was absorbed in the plant reports, never looking up at the Bucho. "Prototype production . . . prototype production . . ."

He paused as he suddenly realized he had no figures. *"Nashi,"* he said flipping rapidly through the various reports. "Nothing." He squinted at Fukuda through his thick frames.

"Exactly," said the Bucho. "There appear to be production delays for the prototype and we need to know why." He drummed his fingers nervously on the desktop. "The Americans have developed the optical chip technology, and we have not." He blew a lungful of smoke across his desk. "It is more than exasperating. It is intolerable."

Sakamoto watched the expression on Fukuda's face harden. He nodded slowly.

The Bucho looked out over the room, watching other members of his department go about their tasks. Telephones began to ring now, and telex machines to clatter. Another *kacho* bowed his good morning.

Fukuda's eyes flicked back and forth. "When were you last at Kamakura?" he asked.

"Two weeks ago Tuesday," Sakamoto replied. "It's been almost three weeks." He cracked a knuckle nervously.

Fukuda took the file and leafed through it. Nothing new.

Handing it back to his *kobun,* he jammed out his cigarette in the ashtray. "I want you to get back down there immediately. Talk to plant manager Sumiyoshi, go through that factory inch by inch, see if we've overlooked anything. Tell Sumiyoshi—no, put a little Aoki fear into him. Let him know that I'm unhappy with his progress. Talk to the engineers about the equipment. Check it all out yourself!" Fukuda slammed his fist down on the desktop.

Sakamoto took the file, making a note or two on the inside cover. "I'm due in Osaka Monday for meetings on foreign market development," he said, checking his calendar. "I'll take the late train back Monday night and be in Kamakura first thing Tuesday morning."

Fukuda's eyes narrowed. "I said I want you there immediately! Cancel the Osaka meetings or send one of your assistants. This has priority."

"Understood. Kamakura Monday," Sakamoto said, popping his index knuckles. "I'll have a full report for you Tuesday morning."

Fukuda smiled a thin, straight, humorless smile. "Unless of course, you have something for me late Monday, in which case I will expect it then."

Sakamoto stood, folding the file.

"Of course," he said.

7

The Chestnut Room of the Hotel Okura overflowed with guests attending the annual U.S. Trade Mission, packed like commuters in a subway car. A gentle roar rose in the large hall as small groups, in twos and threes and fours, stood and chattered, louder and louder as the room filled.

Fukuda Kenji pressed closer to the bar to order a drink. His eyes scanned the room for acquaintances and contacts. Where could he be? the Bucho wondered. Saturday evening was no different than any other.

Japanese bartenders, clad in the Okura's distinctive maroon and gold, made a blur of bottles as they scurried to take drink orders and refills. Along the near side of the room stood a row of small wooden carts serving an array of Japanese delicacies.

Sushi. Yakitori. Tempura. Sashimi.

A train of tables with Western food along the far wall, waited for the *gaijin*. Smoked salmon. Sliced roast beef. Fried chicken legs. Baked ham and potato salad. Fukuda glanced over at it and scowled. Animal fats, he thought. Not for us.

"Osake kudasai."

He took the small bottle of sake in one hand and a thimble-sized cup in the other and pushed his way out of the tight throng around the bar.

He filled the cup, drained it, and filled it again. He walked over to one of the wooden carts, its polished pine gleaming under the hot ceiling lights. Holding bottle and cup in one hand, he deftly maneuvered a pair of chopsticks and sampled the raw fish.

Tuna. Squid. Octopus.

Cold and fresh, straight from Tsukiji, soaked in soy sauce and *wasabi*. How fortunate Japan was to be an island country the Bucho thought. To have a diet free of animal fats, based on fish and vegetables, giving his people the longest life expectancies in the world!

At the entrance, a line of dignitaries greeted the guests as they continued to pour in. Bureaucrats from the American Embassy stood stiffly, shaking hands with the new arrivals, bowing uncomfortably and unskillfully, like ventriloquists' puppets.

"Where *is* he?" Fukuda muttered, edging slowly across the room, his eyes bounding from group to group.

Heavy crystal chandeliers sparkled above his head like floating mirrors. Rich gold-leaf wallpaper reflected the brightness, made the room seem smaller. And louder.

"Of course, we can sell in the Japanese market!" Fukuda heard a voice say as he passed by a cluster of American businessmen. "The problem is not price, it's accessibility. If the Japanese government would only relax its restrictions, we could double our sales here in a year."

Fukuda put the comment out of his mind as he downed another cup of sake. The Tokyo press was full of criticism by Americans that the Japanese market was closed to foreign goods. He shook his head. That was not his battle to fight, even if the criticism was unjustified. It was just another excuse for American laziness.

"Ah, *yatto.*" He smiled as he broke through to the far side of the room. "Finally." He stabbed out his cigarette in a nearby ashtray and downed the remainder of his sake.

"Katoh-kun. *Chotto.*"

Katoh Shohei, Bureau Chief, Special Industries, Ministry of International Trade and Industry, turned to greet the familiar voice.

MITI. Famous and feared.

The government agency that set and controlled industrial strategy after the war, to get the Japanese economy moving again.

The same government agency that set and controlled export and import policies, established quotas, determined tariffs.

The same government agency that set and controlled the pace at which Japanese domestic industries would be allowed to expand, approving capital investment projects, deciding priorities for new plants, as well as when, and where.

The same government agency that set and controlled the flow of foreign exchange earnings from precious exports sold abroad, how much to be retained in special deposit accounts, how much reinvested by the exporter in export promotion, how much given to the exporter in profit.

The same government agency that set and controlled relationships between Japanese companies and foreign corporations. Patents and royalties. Licensing agreements. Joint ventures.

In a word, MITI was control. It had achieved oneness with Japanese economy.

It *was* the Japanese economy.

Katoh Shohei excused himself from the triangle of identically clad Japanese businessmen and turned to greet his friend.

The two men bowed, deeply, silently.

"You're not drinking?" Fukuda asked, seeing his empty hands.

Katoh shook his head. "I'll have another."

They retreated to the bar, shouldering their way through the crowd. Katoh raised two fingers. The bartender instantly handed him a pair of sake bottles and two cups.

They lifted their refilled cups in a silent toast, and drank.

Katoh's round face glowed and perspiration streamed down his broad forehead in tiny rivers, steaming his thick lenses. He was a *dohai* of Fukuda Kenji, a classmate when they were students together at Tokyo University years ago. Their allegiance had been forged during the time Fukuda was active as a political reactionary, and each still supported the most conservative faction of the Liberal Democratic Party. Japan's majority party. The LDP.

They had drunk together, studied together, participated

in political demonstrations together. The latter for pay, of course, since the major parties in Japan all encouraged the students to demonstrate on their behalf. It was a quick and easy way for a young man to make a few thousand yen. And to show his loyalty.

Katoh was heavy, unusual for a Japanese. He stood out like a cask of sake in a grove of bamboo. Intensely nervous, he perspired profusely, giving the impression of doubt and uncertainty.

"Have you spoken to the Major?" Fukuda asked, edging the two of them into a vacant spot behind one of the wooden food carts.

Katoh nodded. "He told me we're in danger of running behind schedule. That worries me." He blinked away a drop of sweat.

"Everything worries you, Katoh-kun. Why should this be any different?" The Bucho drained his sake cup and refilled it. He thought of the many times Katoh had doubted the wisdom of a Matsuzaka project, only to be reassured by Fukuda's repeated successes.

Katoh's hand shook slightly as he raised his cup. "This is hardly your normal MITI assignment," he replied, taking a sip. "I mean, if we fail, you realize the consequences."

Fukuda shook his head. "We will not fail. That's your problem, Katoh-kun. Doubt eats into your mind, like acid. One day you will be so full of negative thoughts, you won't be able to roll off your *futon* in the morning without fear of hurting yourself on the tatami."

"I don't know. This project worries me." He removed his fogged lenses and waved them gently in the air to clear the glass. "I mean, *really* worries me." He placed the frames back on his nose.

"In the first place, the optical chip is not ready. In the second place, even if we get a prototype soon, it will take time to put into production, which means less time for adequate testing. And in the third place, if we push ahead with the test flight and fail, then we not only look like fools but we may embarrass our government."

Fukuda scowled. *"Chikusho,"* he muttered. "This government deserves to be embarrassed, you know that! How much longer are we going to kowtow to the Americans? How can we possibly give in to their unreasonable demands?"

"I know, but—"

"Look at the *gaijin*. Just look at them!"

Fukuda jerked Katoh's elbow, spinning him around. "Look at these fat fools," he hissed. "Their world leadership today is based on one thing, and one thing alone!"

"I know, military power. But—"

"But their economy is rotting! America has lost direction, it's drifting. The people have no leadership, they lack motivation, their machinery and equipment is worn out, antiquated!"

Fukuda filled his cup. He was shouting to make himself heard over the crowd.

Katoh pushed his glasses back up on the ridge of his nose. "Everything you say is true, Bucho-san. That is why we must dominate the information industry. Our computer companies will lead the world in another year or two. We'll outsell IBM, Texas Instruments, Digital Equipment, all the American companies put together. This is our chance!"

"Baka! Who cares? All the integrated circuits in the world count for nothing if there's no military to back them up."

Fukuda moved closer. He lowered his voice. "There is a stalemate now between the Americans and the Russians. No other country in the world has the advanced economy, the discipline, the tradition, the depth of culture that we have."

As Katoh nodded, perspiration flowed down his face. "But the Americans have limitless natural resources. We are so vulnerable."

"Nonsense! Vulnerability is a matter of control. You, more than anyone else in this room, understand what control means. We have few raw materials, that is true. But we can *control* them. *Dominate* them. And the only way for us to dominate is to push ahead with the missile program."

"I don't know," Katoh said, shaking his head. "It's so—"

"So risky?" the Bucho asked. He grabbed Katoh by the lapel and pulled him closer. "Think about it, Katoh-kun! Their society is coming apart at the seams. Social structure eroding. Crime out of control. Divorce rate soaring, families crumbling, *everybody* on drugs. Is that the power that should be leading the world?"

"No," Katoh replied softly.

"And you know the stature of those who have given us this responsibility?"

"Yes."

"Then you'll continue to grant the construction permits for Ise," the Bucho said.

"Of course," said Katoh, his eyes fixed.

"Yoshi." Fukuda produced a cigarette and lit it. "It's for Nippon," he said, exhaling.

"I know."

"For our future."

Katoh nodded. "Let's press on."

They parted as surreptitiously as they had met, corks floating on the surface of the sea.

Yet Fukuda frowned as he knifed his way through the packed crowd. Was Katoh folding? He would advise him of Sakamoto's report on the optical chip, once he returned. Get the optical chip and dangle it in front of Katoh's face. Then Katoh would see that failure was impossible.

Winning was all that mattered.

Perseverance.

Victory.

Survival.

8

"Tadaima."

Fukuda Kenji stepped into the entryway of his small suburban house and tossed his briefcase into a corner. Kicking off his street shoes, he slid into a pair of straw slippers. "I'm home."

"Okaenasai."

His wife, Michiko, was in the kitchen, adjusting the automatic rice cooker. Drying her hands, she came to the foyer and greeted her husband. "Welcome back," she said. She bowed.

The Bucho padded across the tatami to the squat table which was set for dinner. Kicking a *zabuton* into position, he lowered himself onto the quilted sitting cushion, dropping his legs into the *kotatsu* beneath the table. He stretched out his legs in the soothing warmth of the footwell, which contained a small heating element.

"Everything all right?" Michiko asked, bringing in the covered aluminum rice bowl. She kneeled beside the table to serve. "You're getting home so late these nights."

"The Kamakura plant," he said gruffly. "Some production problems, that's all." He pried his chopsticks apart with a quick twist of the fingers.

"Ken-chan! Your father's home." Michiko yelled upstairs, calling him to dinner.

Kenshin bounded down the narrow wooden stairs two at a time and shuffled over to join his parents.

Michiko sat with her legs folded under her, in the traditional style. Kenshin, like his father, swung his into the *kotatsu.*

Michiko poured her son a cup of *misoshiru,* a soybean-

and-seaweed soup. "You'd better not waste any more time," she said. "You've got to prep for your exams." She passed a cup of soup to her husband.

At seventeen, Kenshin was in his final year of high school and had begun to prepare for the only tests that would ever matter in his life, the entrance exams to Tokyo University. *Shiken jigoku:* examination hell. These separated the elite from the common, and the Bucho wanted nothing more than for his son to follow in the Fukuda tradition. The fifth generation at Todai. This would ensure his future success in either business or government. The only two paths that mattered.

"No rush, Mother. Doesn't matter if I'm late. Only nonsense subjects next week—politics and history." Kenshin sipped the steaming soup from its lacquered container.

His father stopped sipping, chopsticks poised in mid-air. *"Baka!"* he said. "That's terrible, what you say. All your preparations are important, especially history. That's the whole genesis of our heritage." Fukuda glared at his son across the table. "Don't let me hear you say that again."

"But it's true," Kenshin persisted, pinching a piece of *tofu* with his chopsticks. "The teachers and exam staff emphasize the importance of our cultural background, Father, just as you say. But what has that to do with computers? Or music? Or art?"

The Bucho reached over to pluck a pickle from the table. "It has everything to do with it. Tradition is the bedrock of your future."

Michiko ate quietly, staring at her rice bowl. She spooned rice into another pair of bowls, then passed them across the table. She knew that her son was dangerously close to driving a wedge between himself and his father. She wondered if she could play a buffer role much longer.

Kenshin munched on a lotus root. "But we've already had history and politics," he said. "How much do we have to do? Our teachers emphasize our past and our treasured cultural history. Fine. But what does that have to do with us now?

"I mean," Kenshin went on, "my generation has different needs than yours. Our country is now well ahead of the

West in most areas. There is no longer the need to push, to drive, to consume ourselves with growth for the sake of growth as we did in the past."

"Baka!" Fukuda growled, his eyes widening. "Where do you learn this rubbish? If that's what your teachers are saying, then your mother better have a talk with them."

Michiko glanced furtively at the flower arrangement she had placed on the *tokonoma,* the honored place, a slightly elevated platform of pine along the wall behind her husband. The other walls in their living room were bare, testimony to a spartan life.

As her husband had so often said, "We live for tomorrow."

"Yes, but we are alive today," she had dared think to herself.

Kenshin crunched another lotus root and wondered if western sons had similar run-ins with their fathers. Were they so tradition-bound, so . . . *predestined?* He had no foreign friends—his father hated *gaijin,* of course—but he knew they were more creative, freer to decide, less . . . *obligated* than his own people.

He scratched an eyebrow with a chopstick. His black hair was long, not as long as he wanted it to be, but longer than his father would prefer. His face was slightly pockmarked with adolescent acne. When he smiled, a rare occasion these days, his teeth hid behind thin, tight lips. His friends called him *Majime-san.* Mr. Serious.

"It's not our teachers, it's what we read, what we see, what we experience." He scooped more rice into his mouth.

"Your family," his father said sternly, "has established a reputation for achievement, for prominence, for excellence, that reaches back generations. Tradition, once established, has to be continued. Otherwise, we will wind up like the *gaijin:* chaotic, purposeless, without direction. That is why we are superior."

"Superior?" Kenshin asked. His cheeks reddened. "Because we build more ships than any other country in the world? So what? Because we manufacture more cars now than America? Our roads are jammed and our air is filthy. So we outproduce everybody in TVs and cameras and watches. We're the leading producer of consumer junk in the world! Where are our great artists now, our writers, where is our superiority in philosophy, in music, in—"

He never saw his father's hand fly across the table as it came in a blur, like his sword. The pop of skin against skin brought tears to his eyes. His chopsticks quivered in his hand. He stopped dead.

"*Baka!*" shouted the Bucho. "Utter nonsense! How many times must I tell you there will be no deviation from the path set by our forefathers? No deviation *whatever*, is that clear?"

Fukuda held his chopsticks vertically, in a fist, as he pounded the small table for emphasis. Kenshin nodded, his head lowered. His mouth drew into a tight line. He knew he could never tell his father about his music. He had played the piano brilliantly for years, shielded by a protective, loving mother who saw precious little of her husband in any event. She aided and encouraged his only son, knowing full well the wrath she would incur if the truth came out too soon.

"Are you preparing adequately for your entrance exams?" his father asked, his voice more normal, his eating resumed.

"*Mochiron,*" Kenshin said as he stared at his rice bowl. He knew it was futile to continue the conversation.

"All right," said his father. "Persevere."

Michiko reached down by her side and poured *sencha* from a small glazed teapot into three identical cups, watching the solitary curl of steam float upward out of the spout. She passed them across the table in silence.

Sipping his tea, Kenshin reflected on the Fukuda family tradition. That's why discipline and perseverance were so important to his father. He must be ready to serve in a new world, characterized by Japanese domination and leadership, and to help establish a global empire the likes of which the world had never seen! To continue the cultural tradition. To persevere. To win.

To survive.

He tasted the words with disgust. His smooth delicate hands extended from the sleeves of his black school uniform, its gold trim contrasting vividly with the funereal cloth. How he hated that uniform, detested the inability to choose what he wanted to wear to school. Its stiff, narrow collar clamped tightly around the throat. The future. To him, without his music, there could be no future.

"Excuse me," he said.

Kenshin drained the contents of his teacup, rose from the table and bowed politely to his parents before disappearing upstairs.

Michiko covered the rice bowl, its contents cold and hard now and unmanageably stiff. The remnants would be scattered, later, to the carp in their small garden pond.

The Bucho poked into his pocket and pulled out a Hi-Lite. Striking a match, he held it for an instant, watching the flame dance and glow, before putting it up to his cigarette.

Michiko sipped her tea. "He's only seventeen," she said, hesitantly. "Give him a little leeway."

"Chikusho!" he grumbled. "Ken-chan's got to learn. He can't discard centuries of tradition with a casual flip of the hand."

"Of course not," she reassured him. "But don't bully him so. You have said yourself—what was it?—something from Musashi, I think."

The point of greatest pressure is the point of least resistance.

Of course, Musashi had said that, he thought. But Musashi had been referring to swordsmen, to physical battle.

Fukuda Kenji pushed himself back from the *kotatsu*. "His exams begin soon," he said.

"I know," she replied.

A thin strand of hair curled down across her forehead. She stroked it back into place with an effortless gesture. Tall for a Japanese woman, Michiko stood just an inch under her husband. Her coal-black hair was swept back and tied in a knot behind her head. Her cheeks glowed with color, like *mikan*. Her skin was smooth and unblemished.

"How are his marks?" the Bucho asked.

"Upper quartile."

"And his motivation?"

"Unswerving," she lied.

"Yoshi," he said. "I just wish I knew where he gets those ridiculous ideas."

"It's nothing more than idle chatter among schoolboys. I wouldn't take it seriously."

"I hope you're right."

"Weren't you excited at his age, about things *your* father thought were unacceptable, irreverent, or wasteful?"

She closed her eyes, hoping his anger would subside.

"Of course not," he muttered, blowing on his tea to cool it. He paused. "Well, maybe. I remember wanting a bicycle more than anything in the world. My father refused to let me have one. He said his generation walked, and walked everywhere, and so would mine."

Michiko sighed inwardly. "There, you see?" she said. "Try to put Kenshin's loose talk out of your mind. He'll do well on his exams. You'll be proud of him. He's a Fukuda. Wait and see."

Fukuda drained his cup. *"Yoshi.* He'd better. He's the future head of the clan."

Michiko collected the dishes and carried them out to the kitchen. The Bucho sucked on his cigarette, staring blankly into space, preoccupied now with the optical chip. Sakamoto had to find the problem with the prototype. He took a final puff, stabbed out the remains, and exhaled resolutely.

Michiko rested her arms on the kitchen counter, a damp apron clenched tightly in the fingers of one hand. A tear rolled down her cheek and dropped, silently, on the countertop as she prayed for her son. He was her hope for the future. Her sole offspring.

Her happiness.

Her life.

9

Monday dawned with a bright spirit. The April skies were clear, and the sun rose with brilliance. Southerly winds, sweeping up from Kyushu, had dissipated the cloud cover and with it the despondent mood prevailing before.

Horizontal shafts of sunlight hacked at Sakamoto Ryuji's eyes as he shifted and turned on his *futon.* He kicked off the covers in a desperate attempt to gain an extra moment's sleep. His head, pulsating from the vast quantities of sake of the night before, hammered and pounded as he slowly adjusted to the new day.

"Chikusho," he muttered, struggling to an upright position and running his stubby fingers through a mass of snarled hair.

Dimly Sakamoto realized he had much to do that day. He glanced at his watch. Just after six. Plenty of time to catch the 7:05 out of Shinagawa for Kita-Kamakura. Plugging in his Matsuzaka coffeemaker, he punched the pressure-sensitive touchplate for two cups, and ordered up "Extra Strong."

The Gotanda platform bristled with commuters. Sakamoto squeezed through the crowd, pulled a *Nikkei,* the *Nihon Keizai Shimbun,* Japan's Wall Street Journal, from the newsstand, and stepped aboard the bright-green Yamate shuttle that circled the Tokyo loop.

Minutes later he exited at Shinagawa, ran up the stairs to the Kamakura-bound platform, and slid into a packed car just as the doors sighed shut. It was a smoker, but he didn't care. With discipline and self-control, he could ignore anything.

Holding onto a plastic handgrip to steady himself, he

glanced at the morning headlines. The *Nikkei*'s Monday message was splashed across the top of the front page in bright red *kanji:*

It is always better to sell to foreigners than to buy from them. Exports bring a definite advantage; imports inevitable damage.

Out of Yokohama, as the sleek commuter train sped noiselessly south, the countryside began opening up with vivid cherry blossoms lining the tracks, dotting hillsides, arching over country lanes. Their soft white petals sparkled in the sunlight, giving the drab landscape its first touch of spring color.

As the conductor's voice announcing his stop crackled sharply in the packed car, Sakamoto stuck the *Nikkei* into his briefcase and shouldered his way toward the door. When he stepped off onto the platform, he looked up and down the tree-lined embankment for the Matsuzaka driver.

"Sakamoto-san! Kochira!"

He looked to his left and saw Hayashi running toward him, darting through the mass of people on the platform. Clad in the traditional light-green Matsuzaka uniform, Hayashi waved a hand in the air.

"Sorry to keep you waiting," he apologized, as he removed his driver's cap and bowed deeply, repeatedly, before the *kacho.*

Sakamoto ducked his head in response. "Never mind. Let's go."

Outside the station exit, hundreds of bicycles stood in a long, neat line. There were no locks on any of them. There was no need for locks—not one would be stolen.

As Hayashi drove into the Matsuzaka parking lot, Sakamoto saw the employees grouped on the athletic field about to begin their morning calisthenics. He hurried to join them, bowing from the shoulders as he recognized familiar faces.

He took a position near the front of the group, standing at attention with plant manager Sumiyoshi and his assistants. They began by singing the Japanese national anthem, a daily ritual. As their voices rose in unison, the

Hi-no-Maru ascended slowly up the flagpole near the front of the building, the bright red circular spot in its center exploding in a burst of glory in the pure white background.

They sang the Matsuzaka Electric company song next, proudly, louder and with greater spirit than the national anthem.

> Oh, Matsuzaka, we stand so proudly here;
> Oh, Matsuzaka, to thee we owe our lives!
> We'll work, we'll work, we'll never stop
> Making these precious products
> That unite ourselves, our families, as one!
> Oh, Matsuzaka, you've given us our identity,
> To thee we dedicate our spirits, our lives;
> Help us, Matsuzaka, to work better, longer, happier,
> Each day we bring our lives to thee!
> Oh, Matsuzaka! Oh, Matsuzaka! Oh, Matsuzaka!

With the final refrain, each worker, male and female, removed his cap and pushed it proudly into the air, three times, in cadence with the words. How many times had he sung these words, Sakamoto wondered. Hundreds? Thousands? Each time, whether at the corporate headquarters or at an outlying factory or affiliate, he felt the same swelling in his throat, the same rapid quickening of his heart, the same tearing in his eyes, as he rededicated himself to the company.

The workers all wore the identical, light-green Matsuzaka uniform: a pair of loosely fitting trousers, and matching short, zip-front jacket, buttoned at the wrist. The pocket on the left breast, over the heart, was emblazoned with the solitary pine tree symbolizing the Matsuzaka *keiretsu*. The same emblem adorned the front of the cap, which resembled the old military cap worn by front-line troops during the Pacific War.

Next the workers bent, bowed, stretched, twirled, touched toes, entwined arms, kicked out and kneed down, following their leader, with such precision that even Sakamoto was awed every time he saw it.

Following the calisthenics, they marched, again in pre-

cision, up and then back down the soccer field, turning on
the whistled signals of their plant manager. Black, gritty
dust from the practice field billowed up from their feet in
clouds as they stamped out their drills. It rose slowly as
one vast, misty veil and hung over their heads in the still
April air.

Finally, they jogged, a dozen rows of a dozen workers
each, again in cadence and again with a uniform step.
From the side, it appeared as if each row were one man,
arms and legs moving with harmony, in unity, with military precision. As their left feet hit the ground, every
worker shouted, *"Yoshi!"* This they did repeatedly as they
marched crisply up the field and back.

Right foot landing: silent.

Left foot landing: *"Yoshi!"*

Right foot: silent.

Left foot: *"Yoshi!"*

"Yoshi! . . . Yoshi! . . . Yoshi!"

When they returned to their original starting position
near the flagpole, plant manager Sumiyoshi stepped
smartly forward, spun around on heel and toe, and addressed his troops.

"We are the proud workers of Matsuzaka!" he roared,
his face red, his cheeks puffed out like small balloons. His
voice surged as he proceeded through his daily drill. "For
our customers, we must do everything possible!"

Without cue, every Matsuzaka worker repeated Sumiyoshi's words, verbatim, in voices deep and full and soaring with pride.

"For our customers, we must be creative and responsive!" Sumiyoshi cried.

"For our customers, we must be creative and responsive!" his workers shouted back.

"For our customers, we must devote ourselves with
every ounce of effort!"

The troops replied word for word, a hundred and fifty
voices as one.

Sakamoto reached up with a handkerchief to dab at the
pearls of sweat that had formed at his hairline. A speck of
dust caught in his eye, and he gently eased it out with a

fingertip, streaking his cheek with gray as he drew his finger across the layer of grit on his face.

"We must never forget our customers—they are our only chance for survival!"

Again, the response, louder and with even more depth.

"Today," Sumiyoshi roared, "we will make our production targets! For we do not simply manufacture electronic products . . ."

". . . we do not simply manufacture electronic products . . ."

"We create dreams for the world!"

"We create dreams for the world!"

"Ryokai?" Sumiyoshi's voice boomed. "Understood?"

Plant manager Sumiyoshi stood stiffly at attention while waiting for the chorus of voices to respond in unison.

"Hai!" they shouted, the single word of harmony and unity carrying far beyond their building into the wooded hills nearby.

"Ryokai?" he implored again.

"Hai!" the group yelled back fiercely, the intensity of their response forcing plant manager Sumiyoshi to wince with the pleasure of pain.

"Ryokai?" Sumiyoshi shouted for a final time, raising his right hand rigidly to the bill of his military cap in solemn salute.

"Hai!"

They roared as with one voice, a hundred and fifty hands responding simultaneously to return the salute with a crisp flick of outstretched fingers.

Their final roar echoed in the hills, rolling over the flat white stucco factory, dissipating in the clear, cloudless, windless sky.

10

Sakamoto walked up to Sumiyoshi as the workers dispersed. He bowed politely, deeply, in deference to the older man's more senior position.

"I am Sakamoto," he said. "Despatched by Fukuda."

"Sumiyoshi desu." The plant manager bowed in return. *"Domo."*

Sakamoto wiped his sweaty neck with his handkerchief as they walked slowly back to the plant—one of the oldest Matsuzaka structures. The thin, whitewashed veneer was peeled and chipped in places, revealing the bare, gray concrete beneath. But it was in immaculate condition.

The single-pane windows were spotless, gleaming in the early morning sun. In front of the main entrance was a miniature garden, neat and trim and sparkling like jewels with drops of fresh spray. A far cry from the chrome-and-glass campus buildings of many American companies, Sakamoto thought. No opulence, no wastefulness, no fat, at Matsuzaka. It was results, not looks, that counted.

Sumiyoshi stopped before an oversized all-weather poster, positioned just to the side of the main entrance. It showed two lone pine trees, one about twice the size of the other. Black, cursive Japanese *kanji* above read, from right to left, *"Go-Nen-Ni-Bai."*

Double in five years.

"That's our long-range production target," Sumiyoshi explained. "It reminds the workers each morning when they come to work that we expect to meet our targets every day, every week, every month. In five years, we will double our existing output."

"Very good," he nodded, his eyes scanning the board.

Sumiyoshi smiled.

"But that assumes a successful prototype," Sakamoto said softly. "For the 256K optical chip."

Sumiyoshi's smile disappeared. He stood still, hands on hips.

"The 256K optical," Sakamoto repeated. "The Bucho needs to know why the prototype is behind schedule."

The plant manager's eyes narrowed when he heard Fukuda's name invoked a second time. True, Fukuda was a Bucho, but in Sumiyoshi's mind, as Plant Manager at Kamakura, they were equals. But Fukuda was Chairman Matsuzaka's *kobun.*

"It's a prototype, that's why," he said, stiffening in defense of his performance. "All of the products currently in commercial production are at, or ahead of, schedule."

"Shall we go in?" Sakamoto asked, a wry smile nicked into the corner of his mouth. "I'd like a chance to look at the prototype progress myself." He used the less polite, more informal mode of expression now as a reminder to Sumiyoshi that he came from headquarters as the Bucho's personal delegate.

As they entered Sumiyoshi's office, Sakamoto was handed a hot *oshibori.* His face disappeared into the clean, moist cloth as he rubbed off the accumulated grit from their morning routine.

Sumiyoshi sat behind an uncluttered steel desk in a stiff wooden chair. Production charts covered the wall behind him, with target lines in blue and actual performance in red. The red line either covered or soared high above the blue.

"As I was saying earlier," the plant manager said, "the 256K chip is not yet in commercial production. We are doing our best to bring it along. And we are redoubling our efforts on the 256K optical."

His coarse black hair was parted in the middle and flew out toward either side, in the style of a kabuki actor. He wore no glasses. His face was clean-cut and smooth.

Sakamoto cracked the first two knuckles in his right hand, bending them sharply under his thumb. "You know that our Planning Department needs this optical chip badly?" he asked, pushing his black frames up the bridge of his nose.

"Mochiron," Sumiyoshi replied. "The problem, as we see it, is not in the front end, but in assembly and bonding. Mask design, wafer fabrication, and photoetching all seem to be on track. At least, our tests at each state confirm the accuracy and precision of our production techniques. That is, up to assembly and bonding."

The door to Sumiyoshi's office opened quietly, and a young woman clad in a Matsuzaka smock brought in two cups of green tea. Bowing silently, she placed the teacups on the desk, bowed again, and left.

Sakamoto took a sip of tea, slurping audibly to cool it as he drew the liquid into his mouth. "What happens at assembly?" he asked. "Why can't they phase in the optical sensor?"

"We don't know yet. We have a special team working to try to get an answer."

Sumiyoshi blew on his tea, watching the steam fly off the surface. He took a sip. "Besides," he continued, "the more complicated phase is the link-in with the visual sensor. You know yourself there's only one company in the world that has the optical chip in commercial production."

"Micro Optix?"

"Exactly. Even IBM and Texas Instruments are scrambling to catch up. And we know our principal domestic competitors—NEC and Hitachi—are pushing ahead madly to beat us into domestic production. That's why we've put such a priority on it."

"Then why can't you get some action out of assembly and bonding?" Sakamoto demanded. He punched his knee with a clenched fist.

"We're trying, Sakamoto-san. Why don't you come with me so you can see for yourself?"

He nodded, cracking the knuckles of both thumbs. "Let's go," he said. "The Bucho is expecting a full report."

They started in design. A team of green-coated technicians sat at a large, flat table in the center of a windowless room. In front of them lay a huge master sheet of thick drafting paper, grid-lined, fully ten feet square.

"They are just now working up new designs for the logic—the computing—side of the chip," Sumiyoshi explained. "Once they lay the basic chart, they transfer it to computer." He pointed to the Matsuden ZAK-III CADCAM screen on the wall. "The computer-aided design program incorporates their requirements into the overall electronic circuitry."

One of the young electrical engineers looked up briefly, bowed his head in deference to the visitor, and returned to his work.

"The ZAK-III has a built-in error-seeking test-probe," Sumiyoshi continued. "It is preprogrammed to self-correct. There cannot possibly be any weakness at this stage."

Sakamoto nodded. He was impressed. More than that, he knew the reliability of the Matsuzaka CAD-CAM computers.

In the next room an automatic drafting machine spun and danced along another oversized sheet of graph paper. Four needlelike nibs jutted out from a single knob, suspended vertically from an overhead device into which four thin black hoses converged. They spit ink into the computer-controlled diagram in black, blue, red, and green, in a whirling, spinning maze of colored streaks, circles, squares, and diagonal connectors.

Sakamoto whistled quietly. "How can you be sure that thing doesn't make mistakes?"

Sumiyoshi laughed. "That machine—the AccuWriter—is also linked to the preprogrammed ZAK-III," he said. "Once the design elements are locked in, the AccuWriter simply takes the electronic signals from the computer and translates them into final copy on this permanent drafting paper."

"Our machine?"

"Not this one. Designed originally by IBM. We bought a prototype several years ago and improved it. Now, IBM doesn't even have a model this sophisticated."

"What happens to the finished design?"

Sumiyoshi walked over to the machine. "Once the design is complete, the drafting sheet is taken to be downsized. That, again, is done by computer. The design on this

three-meter-square sheet of paper, for example, is transferred onto a plastic mask no larger than your little fingernail."

Sumiyoshi held up his little finger to dramatize the reduction. "About a quarter-inch on a side. Two hundred and
fifty-six thousand binary digits of memory and logic capacity. It used to take a whole room to house a computer with
that kind of power."

"What's the next step?"

"Once the plastic mask is ready for photoetching, the
wafers are prepared," Sumiyoshi replied. He led them
down a right-angled turn, up a staircase and along a second floor corridor to the dust-free photoetching room.

"The wafers—thin, circular slices of silicon, roughly five
inches in diameter—are brought into this room and inserted into these machines to be etched with the plastic
mask design you just saw. The wafers are exposed to ultra-
violet light in automatic intervals, and electrically
charged chemicals soak into the wafers, etching the intricate pattern of lines and channels."

Sumiyoshi turned and looked Fukuda's *kobun* in the
eye. "The process is known as photoresist," he said.

Sakamoto nodded. "I know what the process is called,"
he said coldly. He looked through the duo-pane glass at the
antiseptic machinery. "There's no way we can verify the
accuracy of these photoresist machines?"

"No need to. The probes do that automatically. These
machines, by the way, were built originally by Teledyne."

"The American company?"

"Hai. We bought several of them some years ago, broke
them down and reverse-engineered them, so we could
build our own advanced models." Sumiyoshi pointed to the
gleaming equipment. "Nobody in America has photoetching machines as efficient or as accurate as ours."

"What about Micro Optix?" Sakamoto asked, jamming
his hands into his pockets and following Sumiyoshi down
the hall.

"Micro Optix did the same thing we did—bought the old
Teledyne models and then rebuilt them. But don't worry.

Micro Optix is such a small company, they will be no competition for us."

Sakamoto grabbed the plant manager by the elbow and stopped him. "Then why do they have the 256K optical chip and not we?" he asked.

Sumiyoshi's neck tinged with redness. Silence was his answer. They walked back down the stairs.

Sakamoto shoved his glasses back up his nose as they moved through a series of thick double doors into the probe section. He frowned as he looked down a long row of wafer-testers. The machines looked like large mechanical beetles, with short, black angular microscopes jutting out sharply from a rounded head. Here there was no movement, only sound.

They listened as the machines responded with clicks, pings, squeaks, and snaps as the tiny electronic leads moved successively from one prototype chip to the next across the entire surface of the circular wafer.

Attached to each wafer-tester was an automatic digital readout, its neon numbers glowing softly in red. As the chips were probed, or "scored," by the electronic taps, the readout machines verified the accuracy of the etching process.

Sakamoto saw now that Sumiyoshi had been correct. The numbers in each digital readout spun silently, slowly, through 50, 60, 80, 90, 100. Then the counter would stop, and an automatic ejection device would carefully remove the tested wafer, placing it to the side in an insulated storage rack.

Sakamoto pulled out his handkerchief and wiped his forehead. 100. Perfect scoring. Even the Bucho would be impressed, he thought. He glanced back at Sumiyoshi, whose eyes were riveted on the readouts. Each time a meter clicked 100 and the digits flashed perfection in red, he blinked. Another confirmation.

And another.

And another.

We do not simply make electronic products . . . we create dreams for the world!

The words echoed in Sakamoto's mind.

Perfection.

"So you see, Sakamoto-san . . . Sakamoto-san!"

Sakamoto turned slowly toward the plant manager. His eyes were wide with fascination and pride. His face reflected the superiority that was the essence of Matsuzaka.

"So the fault cannot possibly lie in the front-end stage, which we have just completed," Sumiyoshi said. Sakamoto nodded numbly, transfixed by the red neon readouts. "And that is why I have a crash team studying the assembly and bonding process, to see if the error creeps in there."

Sumiyoshi guided Sakamoto back down the hall. "Our analysis so far has led us to the conclusion that the bonding process is as error-free as the front-end stage," he said. "So we are concentrating on assembly. Once bonding is complete, there are two final steps. One is the insertion of the optical sensor, which is crucial to the successful performance of the chip, and the other—the last stage—is when the entire chip, with sensor, is mounted and fixed into its ceramic mould. Asahi Optical supplies us with the visual sensors. KyoCera—Kyoto Ceramics—with the moulds."

Sumiyoshi led them to a packing box, reached in and withdrew one of the mounted assemblies. It looked like a dead roach.

"This is a standard 16K leadframe assembly," he said, holding it between thumb and forefinger. "Until recently, the industry standard. Today, it's the 64K, with four times the computing power. Tomorrow . . ."

Sakamoto took it in his fingers and turned it over. It looked so useless, detached from a computer plugboard. Like a toy, he thought. He realized that he held in the fingers of one hand the entire computing power of the first vacuum-tube computer produced by Remington Rand in the late 1940s. That bulky, medieval machine had used over 18,000 vacuum tubes and generated enough heat to warm the whole Kamakura plant. Of course, the entire Matsuzaka *keiretsu* had been buried under the crumbled remains of its prewar plants at that time.

"So, somewhere in assembly, you think?" he asked, handing the device back to Sumiyoshi.

"Yes. We are examining each step of this final process carefully."

"When will you have a report available?"

"That I cannot say. My technicians have removed one of the assembly machines, to check for malfunction. The 16Ks—and the 64Ks too, for that matter—emerge in perfect operating condition. The chips check, the leads are flawless, and the mounts are error-free."

Sumiyoshi led Sakamoto back out into the narrow corridor.

"About the optical sensors," Sakamoto asked. "You are testing them individually as they come in?"

"Of course. We have also sent a team to Asahi Optical to work with them on quality inspection at their plant. The problem is not with the sensor. It checks, when tested alone. Asahi's quality control methods are as thorough as ours. But it does not check once it is in the prototype chip."

It was nearly one o'clock by the time they returned to Sumiyoshi's office. They lunched briefly, downing bowls of *oden*, a soup of fish paste, seaweed, and *konnyaku*, a jellylike substance made into different shapes by blending the potatolike root with milk of lime.

Sakamoto was asking Sumiyoshi more questions about the assembly process when the phone rang.

"Moshi, moshi. Sumiyoshi desu."

He looked up at Sakamoto. "It's the Bucho. He wants you."

Sakamoto took the phone.

"Moshi, moshi? Ah, domo. We have just finished the tour. I will have a detailed report for you tomorrow morning, first thing."

He held the receiver an inch away from his ear and winced. "All right," he said, bowing automatically to the phone, "your office at six." He cradled the receiver, then looked at Sumiyoshi.

"Fukuda wants an oral report from me this evening. I need copies of three files: the last analysis your team did on the assembly machine, the results of tests on the moulding process, and the quality control figures on the sensors." He pulled a small notebook from his coat pocket and made a few notations.

Sakamoto spent the rest of the afternoon poring over the files. He drew no conclusions, made no guesses, offered no explanations. He simply summarized the findings. Fukuda would come up with the answers.

He bowed his polite goodbyes, and Hayashi drove him back to the station. On the train to Tokyo, he went over his notes on the three reports. Everything seemed to be working perfectly well.

He was puzzled. The Bucho would not be pleased. He would expect more than this. But where was the flaw? It was in there somewhere, like an upside-down jigsaw piece, inserted out of place.

And why was the Bucho in such a hurry for the report? Was there something Sakamoto didn't know—something he wasn't supposed to know—about the 256K project?

The smooth, cream-and-blue cars of the Yokosuka line train shot silently along the rails. Sakamoto shaded his eyes as the train leaned into a curve near the Tamagawa River, just outside Tokyo. The warm April sun drenched the train in a golden bath, the skies still cloudless, the *sakura* soft against the parched brown riverbank.

He watched as the Tamagawa Practice Links dropped from view, empty and deserted. Yesterday there would have been a thousand would-be golfers propelling a million white pellets into the air. Today those thousand Sunday golfers were back in their factories, creating dreams for the world.

11

"Tokyo. Tokyo degozaimasu. Shuten degozaimasu."

As the conductor announced the last stop, Sakamoto grabbed his briefcase and fought through the crush of homeward-bound commuters pouring into the station.

He glanced up at the clock on the front of the station tower. 5:58. Good, he thought. He would not have to keep the Bucho waiting. Beyond the tower, the sky glowed pink.

When Sakamoto arrived, Fukuda was waiting at the main entrance to the Matsuzaka Building, puffing nervously on a cigarette. He flicked the remains aside when he saw his *kacho* stride through the door.

"Yoshi," he said. "Let's go."

"Go?" Sakamoto asked, shifting his heavy briefcase to his other hand. "Go where?"

"Shimbashi," said the Bucho. "It'll be easier to talk."

They hailed a cab outside the main entrance.

"Let me see the reports."

Sakamoto dug them out of his briefcase and watched as Fukuda scanned them hurriedly, nodding as he read.

Shortly the taxi deposited them outside the famed *sushi* restaurant, its name emblazoned across the gray-tiled rooftop in small, blue neon characters. Edogawa. The River of Edo. Tokyo's historical name. Fukuda had known this restaurant since his student days. He was still a frequent and popular visitor.

Fukuda and Sakamoto settled themselves at one end of the long wooden counter. The master of the *sushiya*, recognizing Fukuda instantly, came over and bowed.

The Bucho nodded in response. He was the customer. And the customer was god.

They ordered two bottles of hot sake. Within minutes, the small, white earthenware bottles were placed beside them. Fukuda filled Sakamoto's thimble-size cup, and his kacho returned the favor.

"How long did you spend with Sumiyoshi touring the production areas?" Fukuda asked.

Sakamoto paused, letting the smooth, syrupy sake slide down his throat. "Nearly half the day," he replied.

"And you covered each section thoroughly?"

"We went through every step. Painstakingly thorough," he said. "Why?"

Fukuda took a sip of sake.

"Because everything seems to make sense, that's why. The technical reports on the assembly equipment check out. The quality control analysis on the optical sensors from Asahi checks out. And the moulding test results are perfect."

Sakamoto nodded. "I know. We're no closer now than we were last week."

"Exactly. And Sumiyoshi's as thorough a plant manager as we have in the system."

"A little sashimi?"

An apprentice behind the counter stood before them, his clean white jacket yet unmarred by fish flesh, the *kanji* for Edogawa sewn neatly above the left breast pocket. He bowed to the Bucho, palms turned inward on the wooden cutting surface, elbows slightly bent.

Fukuda nodded curtly. He ran his fingers along the unblemished surface of the wooden counter before him, felt the soft smooth caress of the wood.

The *deshi* placed a large cryptomeria frond down on the wooden surface, squeezed a pinch of raw ginger and then of *wasabi*, and dropped them onto the fresh green leaf. He wore his hair closely cropped, like bristles on a flat, black brush. His face was round and full, and when he smiled, his eyes clicked shut. His name was Fujita.

With a flash of his sharp knife, he deftly sliced off several thin strips of red snapper. Lifting the knife across the glass-enclosed canopy in front of him, he slid the raw delicacies off onto the leaf.

Fukuda pinched a slice with his chopsticks, slapped it hurriedly into a dish of soy sauce and *wasabi,* and popped it into his mouth. He closed his eyes as he tasted the piquant freshness on his tongue.

"Exquisite!" he exclaimed. "Fresh catch?"

Fujita nodded, beaming with pride. "Early morning, first out of Tsukiji. Best of the batch."

He drained his sake cup, washing down the fish.

Fujita smiled. His eyes disappeared. "Something with a little rice?"

"Squid," Fukuda said.

Sakamoto shook his head. "Tuna."

In seconds, Fujita had formed a small rice ball in the palm of his left hand, slipped a streak of *wasabi* across its surface, and laid a sliver of fresh squid along the top, squeezing the sushi gently together. Repeating this swift hand motion, he duplicated its mate and placed the pair in front of Fukuda. He did the same with the pink slices of tuna for Sakamoto.

They finished off the sake and ordered another pair of bottles, which appeared instantly, warm and steaming. Fukuda took a thimbleful and drank it down immediately, letting the smooth, clear liquid caress his throat.

He could feel the warmth in his stomach, as the alcohol began to take effect. His face glowed a soft red. His neck tingled with the addictive pleasure of the national drink.

The Bucho turned to Sakamoto. "If you've read those reports, you know there's nothing there. On the surface, everything's functioning perfectly."

Sakamoto nodded, draining his sake cup. He refilled his own this time. He, too, could feel the softening effects.

"The problem is, we can only pick apart the prototypes one by one, trial and error, until we run a thousand different tests over a thousand different circuits to see where the fault is."

"So?" Sakamoto asked, taking another sip of sake.

Fukuda drained his own, then refilled it. "So? *So?*" He glared at his kacho. "That will take weeks, perhaps months, until we have an answer. We can't afford to wait that long."

Sakamoto stopped chewing momentarily. There was that funny feeling again. He *knew* there was a reason for Fukuda's urgency, but he still didn't know why.

"Why not?" he asked, simply.

Fukuda's impatience bubbled to the surface. *"Baka!"* he shouted. "Because Matsuzaka Electric has promised to have a perfectly functioning prototype ready by the end of the month."

Fukuda drained another cup of sake, sloppily spilling half of it down his chin. He dabbed at it clumsily with a cloth napkin.

"So tell the customer we need another month," Sakamoto said. "Push the delivery date out to May."

Fujita stood before them, his eyebrows raised.

"Shellfish," Fukuda said gruffly.

"The same."

"Baka!" Fukuda hissed. "You know well enough that we cannot tell a customer that we will miss a promised delivery date. Think of our reputation! Think of our competition! Any excuse we give them—"

"But why not? Nobody's even near us with the optical chip," Sakamoto interrupted. "NEC and Hitachi are weeks, perhaps months, behind us."

Fukuda downed another cupful of sake. Sakamoto followed. Their bottles again empty, they reordered for a fourth time. Fukuda felt his lips begin to thicken as his tongue swelled against his teeth.

"Wouldn't matter," he slurred through swollen lips. "Once the customer learns Matsuzaka can't deliver, he would reset a date in line with a competitor's own expectations, cutting us off for good."

Fukuda slipped the shellfish into his mouth with thumb and forefinger, washing it down with more sake as the roof of his mouth exploded from the spicy *wasabi.*

Sakamoto filled Fukuda's cup and his own. With arms entwined they drained the cups.

"Must be a pretty important customer if they're that intent on meeting the original delivery date," Sakamoto said, weaving now on his stool. "Who is it?"

Fukuda tossed down another cupful of sake. He looked

up and down the counter. He had decided that Sakamoto simply had to know.

"Jieitai," he whispered, mumbling badly.

Sakamoto sat bolt upright, as if stung by an electric shock. "The SDF? What do they want . . . ? What possible use could they . . . ?"

Fukuda clamped a hand over Sakamoto's mouth. "No questions," he hissed. "More sake."

He began humming. He picked up a clump of octopus with his chopsticks and placed it in his mouth, waving the chopsticks in cadence with the tune.

Sakamoto was confused but knew better than to press the Bucho, recognized the song and hummed along. He refilled their cups. They drank again, swallowing the contents with a single slurp.

Fukuda started to sing, not softly, but full-voiced. Others began staring in their direction.

Sakamoto joined in. Their voices rose as the words came automatically to their lips.

"Oh, Matsuzaka, to thee we owe our lives!
"We'll work, we'll work, we'll never stop . . .
"Oh, Matsuzaka! Oh, Matsuzaka! Oh, Matsuzaka!"

The final words flew out of their mouths with an almost violent frenzy. Fujita stood back and watched, uncertain. Company songs were sung frequently in the Edogawa, but rarely with this ferocity.

Other customers stopped, and watched, in silence.

"More sake!" yelled Fukuda.

They took the new bottles and drank straight from the lips of the *tokkuri*, consuming the contents in one long gulp.

"The bill!" Sakamoto shouted. As he stood, he kicked his stool over. It fell to the floor with a crash.

Fujita ripped off the form on which he had kept track of their orders and presented it to the kacho. Sakamoto tossed a handful of bills onto the counter and stuffed the stamped receipt into a pocket.

Outside, they drew in lungsful of air.

"So what's your idea, Bucho-san?" Sakamoto slurred, weaving unsteadily from foot to foot.

Standing to one side, Fukuda unzipped his trousers and began urinating against the building. "No idea yet," he mumbled unintelligibly, his back turned. "But we have to come up with something. The deadline is staring us in the face, and the Matsuzaka name must be protected at all costs."

Sakamoto wondered again about the end-user. *The SDF?*

He bowed his good night, stumbling forward as he did so. He belched slightly, tasting the rancid flavor of digested fish.

Fukuda waved a hand in the air and stopped a passing cab. Nodding curtly to his *kobun,* he disappeared inside.

"Kawasaki chodai," he said as the automatic door clicked shut.

Perseverance, he thought. We must win. To survive.

The words of Musashi echoed dimly in his swollen skull.

Be aware of your enemy's every move.

1 2

The cab lurched to a halt. Fukuda clumsily fished a handful of change out of his pants pocket. He dropped it uncounted into the driver's hand.

Inside the darkened building, he turned slowly to the elderly woman dressed in an old, frayed kimono and asked for Kiku.

"Kiku desu ka?" She checked the board. "Kiku's busy."

Fukuda stared her down, weaving in front of her and breathing a sweet, syrupy smell in her face.

"Tell her the Bucho is here. And do it *now.*" He thumped her desk.

She rang Kiku's number on the house phone. "Kiku? *Chotto sumimasen. Ano, Bucho da so desu.*" Her eyebrows rose, then dropped. She nodded curtly, cradling the receiver.

"Coming," she murmured, averting his eyes.

Fukuda Kenji walked over to the wooden hibachi. Its coals glowed softly in the dark. He warmed his hands for a moment, then sat down, massaging his burr head with his fingertips. He lit up a Hi-Lite.

He jiggled his legs impatiently, kicking off the straw slippers. He tapped the ash of his cigarette against the rim of the enormous steel ashtray, took two quick puffs and blew smoke at the tiny fluorescent light on the ceiling.

"Ano, Bucho-san?" It was Kiku.

She stood before him, her small, graceful figure silhouetted against the dim light.

"Yoshi," he said, stabbing out the remains of his Hi-Lite and moving slowly behind her. They padded down the dark, carpeted hallway. Halfway down the hall, he heard a

slap behind a door to his left, followed by a sharp, muffled cry and a quick second hit. A half-smile etched itself into his face.

Kiku led him into her room. He thrust the door open heavily, banging the knob against the adjoining wall. She flinched when she heard it hit.

"Bucho-san," she said softly. *"Daijobu?* Are you all right?"

"Daijobu," he replied. He closed the door gently behind him.

She dropped to her knees in the small, tatami-matted entryway, bowing deeply. Her hands were in front of her, fingers clasped, fan-shaped, as her forehead touched the floor.

"Welcome," she whispered.

"Domo," he said, kicking off his slippers.

"Let me do it," she said softly, unbuckling his belt and dropping his pants to the floor. He stepped aside as she folded them neatly over a hanger.

He watched through blurred, bloodshot eyes, as she undressed him. He touched the smooth white skin inside her thighs when she stood on tiptoe to take off his shirt.

She wore a skimpy haltertop and a pair of light-blue, tight-fitting shorts. Braless, her nipples crested against the blouse in the cool, unheated night air. The shorts came down just to the curvature of her buttocks, revealing a sliver of white cotton panty.

Her skin was as soft as the down on a doe's antler. Unlike most Japanese women, she had shapely legs. Thin, tapered calves rose from small, narrow feet; her toenails were painted cherry red and sparkled in the dim light. The muscles of her upper legs flexed visibly when she moved, suggesting a regimen of regular exercise. Her stomach was firm and flat; when she stooped down, the folds of skin fit snugly together like a young child's.

"Haven't seen you in a while," she said.

"Busy," he said. "Lots to do."

She rolled down his socks and slipped them off his feet. A pastel lamp in the corner bathed her face in a soft shade of blue, revealing ebony eyes that sat in shallow sockets on either side of a gentle nose. Her cheekbones glowed with deep color. When she smiled, she displayed a set of even white teeth, neat and squared off, like tiny tablets. Her lips bore just a hint of redness, suggesting, beckoning, and ready.

She walked to the *ofuro* to start the bath. Hot, steaming water cascaded down from an ornately carved wooden spout, filling the cedar tub quickly. When she raised a smooth slat from its top, clouds of billowy steam leapt up to caress her face.

"You like it hot, don't you?" she asked, turning to face him.

He nodded, his expression unchanged. "The hotter the better."

She removed the remaining slats and swirled the stream of fresh, hot water with a large wooden paddle. *"Yoshi,"* she said. "It feels hot enough."

Kneeling down, she slowly withdrew the bath towel from around his waist. "Looks delicious," she whispered, kissing his flaccid penis.

Fukuda grunted. His mind was elsewhere. He had a problem to solve, and not much time to solve it.

He squat down on a small stool, farting audibly. Kiku took a wooden scoop and spooned out a bucketful of hot water, pouring it quickly and expertly over his body.

He shuddered as the heat penetrated his sake-saturated frame. He sat with his hands clenched at his side, his toes curled inward, pressed tightly against the tiles. The Bucho said nothing, made no noise, scarcely breathed. His eyes were closed. His mind raced ahead.

Like a teacup, the mind must become empty before it can become full.

She poured a second ladle of steaming water over his head, watching it cascade down his rigid body. He neither flinched nor jumped.

The reverse side of pain is pleasure.

With the third drenching, his hands unclenched. The water rolled down his body in waves, curling in under his arms, splashing off his knees, disappearing into the black bush around his penis.

Kiku drew him up off the stool and helped him into the

bath now. He stepped in slowly, painfully, inch by scalding inch, adjusting himself to the water as he eased his body in.

She had never known his real name. Bucho. That's all she knew. He never carried any identification, always removed his company pin before entering the building, never spoke about his job, never mentioned his personal interests, if he had any, said nothing of friends or family.

He had been rough from the beginning. Not so rough that she sustained injury, of course, but harsh enough to raise the threshold of pain to a new level for her. Somehow he raised that level slightly higher each time, but he always seemed to know when to stop, when to let her down from that sanctuary of pain called pleasure.

Fukuda sat with his eyes closed, off in a dark world, a world filled with competitive pressures, optical sensors, and foreign hate, the thrust and power of the Matsuzaka Group behind him. His body absorbed the incredible heat of the water, forcing his blood to circulate in saturated arteries, bringing oxygen to his starved brain.

She touched his shoulder. He flinched slightly at the unexpected touch of her soft hand. His eyes blinked open, and he rose, in slow motion, from the water.

Seated again on the stool, he waited for her to soap his body. In an instant, he was covered, neck to foot, with a layer of white suds.

Kiku took the large, natural sea sponge and began massaging his skin. She rubbed and squeezed his muscles back to life.

Lathering just her hands, she reached up to massage his face with her fingertips. She pressed lightly, but firmly, on his temples, smoothed his closed eyes, pinched his cheeks through the soft, filmy soap. The pungent aroma of pine pierced his nostrils as he breathed in the familiar scent.

Matsuzaka pine.

His eyes were closed again. He had returned to his familiar universe.

The rain has ended, the clouds have parted, the sky is clear.

With a tremendous splash, Kiku doused the Bucho's

body with fresh water. The suds vanished, coursing down his body in a slippery trail of white, disappearing down the circular bamboo drain.

She retrieved the bar of soap and again lathered both hands. Kneeling down, she reached between his legs and caressed his penis. Her hands massaged and soothed, soon bringing it to attention with her expert strokes.

She slipped her left hand under his buttocks and up between his cheeks. With her right hand stroking and pulling his erect penis, the little finger of her left hand slipped smoothly into his rectum as she alternately stroked and rubbed, pushed and pulled.

She could feel her own wetness now as she stroked, felt the keen drive of desire penetrate deeply. Gently she rubbed and pulled, his firmness rising and falling in tandem with her strokes.

He entered the tub a second time, breathing in the heady mixture of cedar and steam that knifed into his lungs. The heat stung his body with tiny, piercing pinpricks of pain.

While he soaked, Kiku took a bucketful of water and spread it uniformly over the surface of the massage mat, to warm the rubber cover. She smoothed her soft hand across its sensuous texture, testing the temperature.

Kneeling again, she checked the vat of coconut oil and camphor heating slowly on a small burner nearby. Testing it with a fingertip, she judged it ready.

"Ready when you are," she whispered in his ear.

He said nothing.

She paused.

"Ano—"

Suddenly, his fists rose up out of the water and chopped angrily at the surface. His eyes flashed open and burned with intensity. The pupils were fully dilated. His thrashing splattered her skimpy costume, darkening it where it had become wet. The outline of her nipples pressed clearly against the water-soaked cloth. She slipped slightly on the wet tile as she jumped back to avoid the spray flying from Fukuda's blows.

Slowly, methodically, he rose from the water. Where had he been? she wondered. Who is he? *What* is he?

His body was entirely out of the water now. Quickly, he slashed his left hand across his front in an imaginary thrust at an imaginary opponent. His right hand grasped the handle of his invisible sword as both hands soared above his head and came whipping down, splitting the head of a powerless foe.

This spring belongs to no ordinary season.

"Bucho-san! Bucho-san!"

He stopped as suddenly as he had begun. Shaking his head rapidly, he slapped his cheeks with both hands, sharply. His body glowed a deep red, baked, like crayfish. Steam rose from his skin in lazy white trails as he reached out for a towel, his eyes closed.

Then he lay on the mat, exhausted and limp, face down, eyes shut. His breathing was imperceptible again. Small slivers of steam still escaped from his hot body, despite the thorough towelling Kiku gave it.

She poured a ladleful of camphor oil onto his back, criss-crossing his shoulders and buttocks with the soothing balm. He tensed abruptly as he felt the hot, oily substance penetrate the pores of his skin. Then he relaxed his lower back as he felt the heat of the oil sear into his spine.

The peak of honor comes from fighting to the death.

Kiku spread the oil as she worked, smoothing it in a curving, pulling motion. She slid her hands down the small of his back, and massaged his lower spine, digging her hands into the muscles protecting his kidneys, now rubbing, now squeezing, with fingers more powerful than those of most men.

She again found his rectum with the middle finger of her right hand. She guided it into the opening, which had widened from the heat of the oil.

Moving her right hand down between his legs, she brought his genitals into her oily grasp, squeezing them lightly as she coated them with smoothness. She grazed a finger across the tip of his penis, teasingly, with a touch lighter than air.

Placing both of her knees on his back, she steadied herself with a hand on each of his shoulders, driving her knees into his muscles with force and power. She could hear him grunt as she drove the air from his lungs with her punctuated strokes.

Then she flipped him onto his back, coated his chest with oil, and caressed his stomach. His eyes remained closed, his face expressionless.

Nothing is impossible to perseverance and self-control.

Fukuda Kenji was entirely preoccupied with the optical chip. He knew it would be fruitless to analyze the Kamakura prototypes further. There was simply not enough time. The Major would be furious if there was even the hint of a delay. And assuming they could find the source of the problem, they would need sufficient time to test a completed prototype adequately to ensure it met Matsuzaka's stringent standards of reliability and performance before it could be handed over for the . . .

No, that approach would have to be scrapped, he decided. His eyes darted back and forth in random patterns as he relaxed under Kiku's practiced hands.

The situation called for more dramatic action, he thought, a plan that would telescope time and circumvent the technical delays. He had to be bold! This was not a time for thorough planning, for patient research. This was a time for a quick strike. A key blow.

There are two kinds of opportunities: one which we chance upon, the other which we create. In time of great difficulty, one must not fail to create his opportunity.

Kiku ladled out a final spoonful of oil and camphor, coating Fukuda's torso a second time. She massaged his chest with firm, strong strokes, and moved her hands slowly down the sides of his body, her fingers light as a feather.

She stepped back now and unzipped shorts, slipping them down her hips. She rolled her white briefs down her legs and kicked them aside. One by one, she undid the diagonal line of buttons across her halter front and shucked it off, standing totally nude before the Bucho.

Squeezing her nipples lightly, she caressed her young breasts with experienced hands. She let her hands slide down the sides of her delicate figure, closing her eyes and relishing the feel of her own soft, smooth touch. Spreading her legs slightly, she slid a hand slowly up the silkiness of her inner thighs. Pressing a thumb gently into her wetness, she shuddered with a spasm of pleasure.

She was ready.

Kneeling now, she pried Fukuda's legs apart and massaged his testicles, slowly, gently, her hands coated with the sweet-scented oil. As she worked expertly with her fingers, her eyes widened in expectation as she watched his fullness rise, throbbing upward and outward from his body.

She smiled as she watched its slow ascent. She kneeled down to take him into her waiting mouth, curling her soft lips around his hardness. He was immense. She reached down with her left hand and caressed his shrunken scrotum, compact and tight with desire.

The heavier our bodies, the higher our spirit rises above them.

Fukuda Kenji thought back to his ancestral past, to his great grandfather, respected Tokugawa *daimyo;* to his paternal grandfather and the victories over China and Russia; to his father, Kensaburo, and how hard he had worked to turn the young Kenji into an expert swordsman.

His mind burned with the knowledge that it was his turn now, his duty to carry on the great traditions of his past. Failure was unacceptable. Perseverance was the only option.

Because perseverance meant victory!

And victory meant survival!

In his mind, he was in the *dojo,* his *keyaki*-wood sword held at the ready as he danced and spun before an imaginary opponent. His sword became invisible as he twirled it through the air above, below, behind his body, whirling in a magical blur. He was invincible, in eight places at once, confounding and confusing the enemy, achieving oneness with his sword!

Perseverance and discipline are the virtues that will lift us to greatness.

Was Matsuzaka Electric built on timidity? Had the Matsuzaka *keiretsu* expanded to a position of power and dominance through inaction? He had to move quickly, and with boldness. He focused on supply: who had the optical chip, where it could be gotten. But his Japanese competitors were even further behind than they. It was inconceivable that he could tap a domestic source, even assuming some friendly but underhanded competitive tactics. Using a dummy order, for example, from a Matsuzaka subsidiary buried so far within the group that its affiliation could never be discovered.

He stirred with restlessness, feeling now the warm, soft embrace of Kiku's caresses. His body and mind were uniting in a fusion of flesh and spirit. The entire force of his spiritual energy focused on this immediate problem. His mind raced ahead tirelessly.

Loyalty is only another name for love.

His right hand flexed as he felt for Kiku's thighs. He slid the fingers of his right hand smoothly up her inner legs until they found her hot wetness. He drove his entire hand sharply into her with a single, powerful stroke.

Kiku's head snapped back instantly and her eyes grew wide with shock. She reached down and slapped at his hand, rising off her knees.

As he felt his hand withdrawing, he grabbed for her clitoris with thumb and forefinger and squeezed. Hard. She yelled and tried to stand but slipped instead on the oil that had drained onto the floor.

His left hand reached across and caught her right arm at the shoulder. His right took her left hip and with one upward, sweeping motion, he lifted her up onto his erect penis.

His eyes were wide with anticipation as he relished the look of shock, of surprise on her face. Her legs hung limply as he positioned her body atop his fullness. With a sharp, downward thrust, he jammed her body onto his. His penis found its wet-hot target with ease and rammed inside her. He came almost instantly, feeling the semen rocket from him in explosive thrusts.

Just as one man can beat ten, ten can defeat a hundred, a hundred can overwhelm ten thousand.

Kiku moaned, feeling her insides being ripped apart.

"Itai, itai!" she cried. "That hurts!" She was stretched to the fullest, felt the wrenching pain each time Fukuda pulled her down sharply on his insatiable staff.

His right hand released its grip and swept up in a blur, slapping her hard across the face. As her head snapped back, he pressed forcefully with his left hand and pushed her off to his right, pulling his body out from underneath.

Fukuda Kenji's eyes were ablaze with competitive desire. Perspiration hung in pockets at the base of his neck. His face was red with passion, his mind alive, on fire, consuming him.

As he flipped her over onto the side, he spun her around with both hands and turned her onto her stomach, pulling her right arm behind her back toward her shoulder blades, so she could not resist. He pushed her onto her knees, her head and shoulders against the mat, her round buttocks arched high into the air.

Sliding his body into position and guiding his hard erectness with his left hand, he found her anal opening and rammed it in with a powerful surge that seemed to split her in half, like bamboo, ripped apart down the center.

"Iya . . ." she whimpered, half dazed, half afraid. *"Iya da."* She struggled weakly, in vain.

The room seemed to shake with the violence of his thrusts. He disappeared into her, hammering her repeatedly, delaying his final orgasm until the last possible moment, bringing body and mind to that fusion of harmonious unity called perfection.

When he erupted, his body convulsed and shook with a hundred spasms of pleasure become pain, his mind exploding in an ecstasy of total concentration. The solution came to him in a clear, cold instant, enveloping his mind in unfiltered joy. It all made sense now! Why hadn't he thought of it before? It was magic! It was mystery! And it would ensure his victory!

Japan's victory!

Japan's survival!

Only determination can subdue the enemy.

He tossed her ragged body aside, like a tumble of tangled clothes, and left her lying at the edge of the mat. His hands had gripped her with such force that his thumbs and fingertips had left deep canyons in her white skin. But they were invisible to him. His mind and his spirit were focused on other targets.

Fukuda Kenji soaped and rinsed quickly, dressing without thinking. He had already forgotten the violence that had shattered the room moments ago. His mind raced ahead in a blur as he began to sort out, step by intractible step, what he had to do.

It all fell into place. His vision was now clear, his spirit void of every distraction.

It would work!

It could not fail!

Victory belonged to him! To Japan!

Shouldering his coat, he withdrew a small brown envelope, and without glancing in Kiku's direction, he flicked it at her shapeless form and turned to leave. It dropped onto the tatami near her blue-black thighs, a final, automatic gesture born of tradition.

He strode calmly but purposefully back down the long, dark hall. His body felt light as air. No, he was walking on air. No, he *was* air, oneness with the void, simultaneously past and future, heaven and hell, god and . . .

Fukuda Kenji, Bucho of Matsuzaka Electric, number one among *keiretsu,* flung open the swinging door at the *genkan* with such force that it banged the old woman out of her late night sleep.

"Itte'rasshai," she murmured, lifting up from the desk, her eyelids sagging. "Come again."

He said nothing, heard nothing, as he kneeled to lace his shoes.

Timing is strategy. There is timing in everything.

It was in the palm of his hand. He was unaware of the falling rain as he strode out the door. He *was* the rain . . . and the sun . . . and the earth. His leap of brilliance was not his own personal effort, it was the result of generations, of centuries, of tradition.

Perceive those things that cannot be seen.

Yes!

Was nothing impossible? Failure was impossible! He recognized no alternative but victory.

Japan would survive.

He stood in the murky darkness as he puffed a cigarette alive. His eyes darted and danced in the flame.

13

"Sakamoto-kun! Sakamoto-kun!"

Fukuda's shrill voice echoed across the rows of gray steel desks.

Sakamoto's head snapped up from his papers. *"Hai?"*

"Chotto!" The Bucho waved to him with a curt hand motion.

Sakamoto sprinted quickly over to his desk. *"Nan desu ka?"*

Fukuda looked him in the eye. Lowering his voice, he spoke rapidly, with agitation.

"I have the solution to the optical chip problem," he growled. An angry, determined expression crossed his face.

Sakamoto looked him straight in the eye, unblinking. He popped one knuckle, then another. "What is it?" he asked. He fiddled nervously with his necktie as he saw the frenzy in Fukuda's eyes.

The Bucho sat board-straight in his chair. "We know the Americans still have the edge on us with the optical chip," he said. He picked up his ruler and grasped it like a small sword. "We need a working prototype before the end of this month, and there's only one company in the world that has it."

"Yes," Sakamoto nodded. "Micro Optix. Small, but intensely competitive. Known as a market breaker."

"Exactly. They patented their photoetching process and were the first to perfect it. Unfortunately, they patented it as a trade secret and it cannot be licensed. No doubt because they complained to their government about our so-called unfair trade practices."

"And Washington agreed because they wanted to prevent Japanese companies from getting access to the technology through normal licensing channels," Sakamoto interrupted. "A typical response by the Americans in time of trade friction."

The Bucho nodded. "Precisely. Two or three years ago, perhaps even last year, we could have arranged a plant visit to Micro Optix and toured their entire facility as 'interested Japanese businessmen.' Our engineers could have pretended to be administrative staff or finance department representatives, and they could have seen the whole show."

He paused, flexing the plastic ruler.

"Under those circumstances, they would have been able to see what kind of machinery the Americans were using. Without even breaking the equipment down, they would have known what process was being used, because our engineers are so familiar with the entire setup. And their noses are so sensitive, they could have just sniffed the air in the plant to determine what chemicals the Americans were using."

Sakamoto stood in front of his Bucho's desk, arms folded across his chest. "We could try to arrange a visit now," he said. "Represent a fictitious affiliate, or a joint venture. Surely Micro Optix would never know."

Fukuda flipped the ruler back onto his desk. He leaned forward and took a sip of tea.

"Impossible," he said. "In the first place, MITI and the Department of Commerce are negotiating too many sensitive issues right now. We could never get something like that cleared, even with our size and influence at MITI."

He stretched back, hands behind his head.

"Second," he said, his eyes on the ceiling, "the Americans are increasingly suspicious of Japanese motives. Micro Optix, especially now that they have the optical chip, doesn't allow *any* outsiders in. They give the excuse that it's disruptive to production, but they may suspect industrial espionage even from other American competitors. They're smarter now. They keep their doors shut, just like we've done all along."

Sakamoto popped another pair of knuckles.

"So?"

"So there's only one way we can even hope to get a look inside their plant and get data on their optical chip back here in time to meet our deadline."

"And that is?"

"Smuggle one of our people into their plant."

Sakamoto whistled softly.

"But that's next to impossible," he said, frowning. "The security there would be as tight as ours. We'd never get anyone in, especially a Japanese."

Fukuda nodded. He retrieved the plastic ruler. His eyes were wide. "Of course not," he said, "if we go in by the front door. But that's not what I had in mind." He smiled.

Sakamoto froze. "Breaking and entering? That's suicidal! Besides, that would turn Tokyo on its ear."

"Baka!" Fukuda shouted. "Don't be so stupid."

The tea lady, dressed in a faded green smock and wearing plastic slippers, approached the Bucho's desk. Bowing deeply, she refilled his small teacup. A faint wisp of steam rose from the hot tea. Then she bowed again, and with a soft, white cloth, wiped a drop that had fallen on his desk.

The Bucho lowered his voice. "My idea is, we infiltrate from within, not from the outside."

Sakamoto thought for a moment. "Great," he said. "We get one of our junior engineers to apply for a job with Micro Optix as a business school graduate." He lowered himself into the chair by Fukuda's desk. "But instead of asking for a position in production or design, he requests an assignment in public relations or personnel? Ridiculous!"

"Baka!" Fukuda exploded again with impatience. A few heads turned around now. "Nothing so stupidly obvious! I had in mind a less visible position, something quite simple and harmless, on the surface."

Sakamoto took a deep breath. He was not about to make a fool of himself again. "Like a mailroom clerk?"

"Even more harmless than that."

Sakamoto crossed his arms and frowned. "Messenger?" He shrugged his shoulders.

"Even lower on the scale. The lowest."

"Driver?"

Fukuda leaned forward and pushed the plastic ruler against Sakamoto's chest.

"Janitor," he hissed.

"Janitor?" Sakamoto's eyes blinked, unbelieving.

"Mochiron," Fukuda said, with a smile. "Employee turnover is highest in this category. It's the dregs of American employment. Nobody wants the job, and when they have it, they want to get out of it as soon as possible. Americans understand that philosophy instinctively. They have not yet learned our superior system, where everybody has a place and is expected to keep it."

"But Americans hire Mexicans and blacks for those demeaning jobs, not Japanese. And you can't disguise a Japanese as a Latino."

"Wrong again, Sakamoto-kun," Fukuda said, still smiling. "It's not just Latin Americans who apply for such jobs. There's another minority group I had in mind."

Sakamoto thought for a moment, then shrugged his shoulders again. "No idea."

"Boat people," Fukuda whispered.

Sakamoto's eyes widened. He understood immediately. "Vietnamese!"

"Exactly," Fukuda beamed. "The Americans can never tell the difference between Chinese and Korean, Japanese and Filipino, Vietnamese and Thai. *'They all look alike.'* How many times have you heard that expression when you visited the United States? How many times have you been mistaken for a lowly Korean or Chinese?"

Sakamoto smiled. "Countless."

"So you see," said the Bucho, "Americans would never expect a Japanese to apply for a position as janitor in a high-technology company. They know Japan is an advanced, industrialized country. They know of our successes in autos, TVs, electronics, watches, cameras, ships." He drummed the strategic sectors on his desktop.

"A Japanese as janitor?" he continued. "So incredible, it will never even enter their minds." Fukuda's eyes darted eagerly now as he unfolded his plan.

"We know the Vietnamese are now the second largest

body of immigrants into the United States, after Mexicans," he said. "Larger than any other nationality. Larger, even, than the refugee groups streaming in from Cuba. And where is their principal point of entry?"

Sakamoto gazed out the window behind Fukuda's desk. "California," he said.

"Yes. Mostly southern California, because the climate is closer to that of Indochina, but a growing number in northern California where large groups have settled. San Francisco. Oakland." He paused. "Silicon Valley."

Sakamoto nodded. "They are kept in camps until their papers are processed. Easy to maneuver in society, assuming the papers can be arranged." He ticked off the points on outstretched fingers. "And with the right papers, they can apply for jobs."

Sakamoto was following the Bucho step for step now.

"Exactly," Fukuda Kenji said. "And there's a boatload of Vietnamese in Yokohama right now, under pressure to depart for the U.S. Our government has always maintained that the Vietnamese people are not welcome in Japan because they would never fit into our superior society. They would displace our own people from jobs that are necessary to keep them in their lower social strata."

The kacho frowned. "I thought we had been coerced into accepting a quota for humanitarian reasons."

Fukuda smiled that cunning, humorless smile. "Washington and the UN both tried to pressure us into doing so. But our government generously increased the amount of financial aid we were willing to contribute to the UN resettlement fund, and simultaneously stonewalled Washington on the issue of quotas. Washington gave in—another example of the gullibility and impatience of the American *gaijin*—and persuaded the UN to drop its pressure on us to accept the Vietnamese."

"But they still keep coming here."

"Only for food, fuel, and blankets. The expatriation is very well organized by the North Vietnamese now. They are getting rid of their social critics and social misfits, just as we did in the late nineteenth century when we sent our dissidents to Hawaii and California." He pulled a cigarette from his desk drawer and lit it. "The emigrants are usually willing to pay just to be able to get out of the country. When they stop here, our government provides them with temporary shelter, giving them sufficient food and medicine to make their onward trip to America. And we always make sure we get proper press coverage when we do."

Fukuda exhaled audibly, flipping the ruler back onto his desk. He stood up and walked to the window, watching the morning rush hour traffic thirteen flights below, snarled in the light spring rain. A taxi waited to turn at a distant corner, its indicator light winking steadily, patiently, impervious to the flow of oncoming traffic. His horn never honked. Patience. Perseverance. How well the Japanese could endure!

He turned back to face his *kobun*.

Sakamoto was almost afraid to ask the obvious. "Who do you have in mind to . . . to send over from Matsuzaka on this mission?" His eyebrows arched upward.

"Do we have a choice?" Fukuda asked in return. He dragged on his cigarette and exhaled. "You will go."

"Me?" Sakamoto yelped. He squirmed in the chair. Other heads now spun around in surprise.

Fukuda placed a finger to his lips. "Yes," he said. "You're the only one I can trust to keep this project completely confidential. I doubt that the engineering groups would be willing to spare one of their people for such an assignment, and anyway they would not have the breadth of experience necessary to do the job skillfully. You would have a much better feeling for the overall organization of a company like Micro Optix. You could get to the right optical chips more quickly. Plus you are directly under me, so we can avoid any leaks." The Bucho sucked on his cigarette and blew a cloud above his kacho's head. "I'm afraid it's the only way."

Sakamoto swallowed. He twisted his fingers nervously, the knuckles all played out. They responded noiselessly.

"I understand," he said, stiffening proudly. "How do we proceed?" He knew he had no choice. His thoughts turned to his company. He would do anything for Matsuzaka.

Anything.

Fukuda opened the top drawer of his desk and pulled out a large, sealed envelope.

"Yoshi," he said, breaking the seal. He held the cigarette in his lips as he opened the package. The smoke curled up into his eyes, causing him to wink back the sting. "This is the rest of the plan."

He piled the contents of the envelope on top of his desk. Taking a final drag on his cigarette, he crushed out the remains.

"Your new name will be Le Duc Pho," he said, lifting up a small card with Sakamoto's photo attached. "This is called a White Card. With it, you can go anywhere, do anything—except get a job. It's evidence of your status as a Resettled Refugee."

He handed the postcard-size document to Sakamoto, who fingered it, glancing quickly at both sides.

Fukuda eagerly lit another cigarette and exhaled. He was soaring now, his sword flashing through the air.

Sakamoto frowned. "There is no address on the card," he pointed out, staring at his picture. It was a recent photo, no doubt from Matsuzaka's personnel department. No one would ask any questions. Fukuda was a Bucho.

Fukuda reached over and took the card from Sakamoto's hand. "The address is missing, and so is your signature," he said. "Once you find a room to rent, you fill in the address and sign the card on the other side."

"Wakatta," he said. "But how can I go about getting a job? Won't somebody be suspicious?" He placed the White Card down on the edge of the Bucho's desk.

Fukuda picked up another, smaller card and handed it to Sakamoto. "This is a Social Security card," he said, flicking an ash onto the floor. "Resettled refugees usually get this card when they leave the settlement camp so they can apply for a job." A single trail of smoke rose from the glowing end of his cigarette.

"Is it like our National Identity Card?" Sakamoto asked. He scratched his head. "No, on second thought, obviously not. Only my name and a number. No picture, no thumb print, no address, no record of leaving and reentering the country, no personal history summary, no record of arrests or offenses."

Fukuda smiled. "Exactly. The Americans have still not recognized the benefit of our superior national ID card. They think it is undemocratic and totalitarian to keep track of their population in this way. We have had such an advanced system in place for centuries." He drew on his cigarette, exhaling twin streams of smoke through his nose.

Sakamoto held the Social Security card up to the light. "These are easy to get?" he asked.

Fukuda laughed. "Of course." He leaned forward. "This card is all you need in order to get a job. Anyone asks, you just shrug your shoulders and explain in broken English, 'No understand.' "

Fukuda threw his hands in the air, palms up, scrunching his shoulders together in a dramatized shrug.

Sakamoto grinned. *"Yoshi.* I can use my White Card to find a place to live. Then I can present my Social Security card when I apply for a job."

"Exactly. But sew both cards into your *haramaki.* We want to take no chances of their being discovered," he said, tugging at the band which he wore around his waist. For generations, the Japanese had worn a wide strip of wool around their abdomens as a stomach band, a mid-layer of insulation between underwear and outer clothing.

They both laughed.

The Bucho reached into the pile of materials on his desk. He grasped a handful of paper currency.

"Piastres," he said. "Vietnamese money, about five hundred dollars' worth. For all intents and purposes, worthless, but stuff it in your pocket. Take enough yen and dollars with you in the *haramaki,* but keep everything in cash, pay for everything in cash, even your rent."

Sakamoto nodded, taking the worn bills from his *oyabun.* They were split, torn, and filthy dirty.

"I can change the money easily, at one of the Japanese banks in California," he said, tucking it into a pocket. "And then I can convert an electric wall socket into a hiding place. No problem."

He frowned suddenly. "What about birth certificates? Passports? Official papers?"

"Nonsense," Fukuda replied, shaking his head. "You are a Vietnamese peasant, right out of the rice fields. You have *nothing,* except for the piastres in your pocket and the clothes on your back. That's all."

The Bucho then reached into a deep bottom drawer and pulled out a small bundle, wrapped in brown paper and tied with string.

"This is the extent of your personal possessions," he said, tossing the bundle to Sakamoto. "A pair of straw sandals, some old pants and a tattered shirt. You can buy other things after you have safely arrived."

Sakamoto juggled the pack of clothing in his hands. It was very light. He looked at Fukuda without smiling now and swallowed again.

He rose and walked to the window behind Fukuda's desk, watching the rain come down in sheets and concentrating on his obligation to his company, and to his *oyabun.* What was it? Yes, teamwork. That was it. Self-denial. Sacrifice by one for the good of all. Had to be. How would Japan survive otherwise? This country could never tolerate a free, egocentric society.

We Japanese *need* each other, Sakamoto thought, *depend* on each other, *support* each other. So we can reach the collective goal, the supreme test, of what's best for all. Personal desires, individual preferences, have to be sublimated to the group.

Survival.

Yes, that was it. Was it really so difficult to understand?

He turned back to face the Bucho. His chest swelled with pride as he realized that his *oyabun* had chosen him for this difficult task. The obligation to succeed was his, and the weight of a generation's generation was on his shoulders.

Fukuda pulled out another cigarette and ignited it, tossing the match aside. He cast a quick glance across the room to make sure their conversation was being ignored.

"One final item," he said, taking a drag on his cigarette. "And key." He picked up a small, flat device and held it between a thumb and forefinger. "This is how you will communicate the optical chip circuit patterns to me." He handed it to his *kobun.*

Sakamoto's eyes widened. "A microimagizer," he said, his voice barely audible. "That's in limited use by the SDF. It's classified!"

"Correct," Fukuda intoned, his cigarette dangling between his lips. "We make them for the SDF. Look at the top, where it's indented. No, the other side."

Sakamoto held the device in the palm of his right hand. It was no larger than the face of a wristwatch, and no thicker. He picked it up and held it to the natural light.

"At specified intervals," the Bucho instructed, "you can transmit signals by tapping the top with a small, pointed metallic object, like a pin, or a needle, or a tiny nail. It contains a microscopic mercury battery with sufficient power for six weeks—much more time than you will need. The base is built around our most powerful ZAK-80 microprocessor. It will translate your taps into coded signals and automatically relay them to my facsimile receiver at home."

Sakamoto was transfixed by the device. "How will I know when to transmit?" he asked.

Fukuda handed him a small slip of paper, handwritten, with specific dates and times of the day, in *kanji.* "During certain hours of each day, one of our commercial satellites will be in position over the Pacific Ocean to receive signals from North America and relay them to Japan," he said. He tapped away an ash. "Memorize these times and destroy this sheet—burn it—before you leave here today."

Sakamoto took the list and read over the dates and times. Simple, he thought. He would memorize it mnemonically. Break the dates and times down into phonetic counterparts and string them together in a simple proverb, a catchy *kotowaza.*

The Bucho took a deep drag on his cigarette. "We will need circuit patterns of the 256K optical chip that Micro Optix has designed and produced. It will fit on the back side of the microimagizer. When you transmit, you will be sending me coordinates of the intricate internal construction of the chip, which will print out automatically on my high-speed printer. We can translate the computer language into design coordinates later, on the machines at Kamakura, like the ZAK-III. That way, we can compare the design of the Micro Optix chip with our own to see where we need to make the corrections."

Sakamoto listened to Fukuda's instructions, but his eyes were fixed on the tiny electronic device he held in the palm of his hand. He cupped the palm. It practically disappeared. What couldn't Matsuzaka do in the field of miniaturization? Performance. Achievement. Excellence. He felt that he, too, was on a new threshold, a higher level of loyalty.

Sakamoto placed the microimagizer in a deep front pocket and tucked the two identification cards into the folds of his *haramaki*. He pocketed the piastres, and rolled the clothing into a small bundle.

He looked up at the Bucho. He was ready.

Matsuzaka was depending on *him*.

"Remember," said Fukuda Kenji, crushing out his cigarette. "Regular reports. Memorize the transmission times and destroy the grid. Any problems arise, I want to know about them immediately."

"Yoshi," said the kacho, nodding.

"Oh, and one more thing."

"Nan desu ka?"

"Absolute secrecy."

"Of course."

14

Tsok!

Calculation!

His legs glided across the tatami in smooth, effortless strides. He was weightless, floating on a cloud of confidence, in himself, in Matsuzaka, in Sakamoto, in his country. His sword felt invisible in his hands.

Perseverance and discipline are the virtues that will lift us to greatness.

He traded blows with his master, their swords echoing off the flat walls of the *dojo*. His silken *tabi* moved soundlessly across the straw matting.

His mind was there and it was not there, simultaneously moving his sword and projecting ahead to the 256K optical chip at Micro Optix. He had made his bold move, taken the initiative, bent the rules of the game to favor Japan.

Japan, his country, a poor country, devoid of natural resources, completely dependent upon the outside world for raw materials and export earnings, strong because it knows how to persevere.

To win.

To survive!

Tsok!

Domination!

He swung his sword over his head so fast it disappeared in a blur. He was coming and going, rising and falling, moving and stopping, alternately visible and invisible to his opponent.

His *sensei* struggled to pinpoint his target, but he knew it was useless now. The *deshi* had far outpaced him, surpassed all he could teach. He tried to maintain a simple, effective defense, but he knew it was in vain, like trying to catch rainwater in a bamboo basket.

The peak of honor comes from fighting to the death.

Fukuda Kenji whirled and spun on the toes of one foot, twirling his brown, *keyaki*-wood sword in a circular arc in front of him, catching his *sensei*'s weapon in an inferior defensive position. The master's sword flipped up and out of his hands, landing harmlessly on the tatami, out of reach.

His ego was totally submerged now. He had achieved oneness with his sword. His confidence merged with his spirit, his soul combined with his flesh, to yield a superhuman force. He was invincible. He *was* his sword.

He would persevere.

Japan would win.

Japan would survive!

Tsok!

Elimination!

Only determination will subdue the enemy.

PART II

SKY

穴
工

1

"Shit."

The ball just nicked the end of his racquet and squirted into a corner, dead, scoring a point for his opponent.

"Eight-all, your serve," he said as he retrieved the ball. He flipped it against the white, scuffed wall with his racquet and watched it carom off in a perfect line toward the server.

Arthur Garrett, forty-three-year-old president of Micro Optix, Inc., took up the receiver's position in the backhand court against his opponent who bounced the black ball twice to steady his serve. Roger Harris, thirty-eight, was Garrett's partner, responsible for R&D. The two semiconductor specialists played squash together on Garrett's basement court about twice a week, early in the morning. Very early.

Harris swatted the ball against the front wall. It slowly arched over Garrett's head into the back corner and bounced just enough for him to slash a backhand down the side.

A split second later, Harris's return whistled past Garrett's right ear, hit the front wall, and shot diagonally to his right. Garrett chipped a drop shot into the front corner, hoping it would catch Harris too far back, but Harris lunged forward quickly, in anticipation, and smashed a hard, straight shot through Garrett's legs for a winner.

"Nine-eight," Harris puffed, breathing heavily as he reached for the ball. He strode to the opposite serving court. Six inches shorter and some thirty pounds lighter than Garrett, he could still not match the older man's depth of experience.

The windowless court sparkled a pristine white in the brightness of the overhead lights. Outside a fine mist shrouded the countryside in a silent veil of gray, delaying the onset of dawn. The mid-April air was cold and seemed more like late fall than early spring.

Garrett balanced himself on the balls of his feet, shifting his six-foot, three-inch, 185-pound frame as he waited for the next serve. He loved the game of squash, felt he could play every day if he just had the time. But time was as scarce as honest politicians when you ran your own business.

Harris slammed a screamer off the front wall. Garrett's forehand crosscourt caromed back along the left side. Harris sliced a return to the right which dropped sharply.

Garret raced forward, his racquet ready. He picked the ball up on the bounce and smashed a backhand deep into the corner. Harris had to hustle to get the rebound. He banked it against the rear wall and watched it rise in a high arch as it touched the red foul line along the right side.

"Out," Garrett exhaled. He caught the ball with his left hand as it dropped from the side wall. "Nine-all."

Garrett's muscles rippled in his torso and legs, evidence of his fine athletic condition. His legs were lean and compact, his stomach flat and smooth. His arms were not especially strong, but he had good control, exceptional control, with his hands, which, coupled with his anticipatory skills, enabled him to retrieve well. He could disguise a stroke until the last moment, making his opponent wonder whether he would go for a drop shot or slam the ball long.

His handsome, angular features were softened by an easy smile. He kept his fine blond hair stylishly long and let it brush the tops of his ears. Clear blue eyes gazed out from deep, carved sockets, framing a slim nose, and a crisp moustache arched over both corners of his mouth.

Roger wiped his eyebrows with his wristband, pulling his arm across his face with a quick, easy motion. His moist hair glistened in the bright lights. Although the early morning air was still cool, it had not taken the two men long to drench their thin cotton clothing. The sweet stench of sweat hung over the court like a cloud.

Harris stuck the cotton terrycloth grip of his racquet under his shirttail and tried to squeeze it dry. It was still slick to the touch. He wondered which was wetter, his shirt or the sweaty grip.

The remaining points went to Garrett as he continued his mastery over the R&D specialist. The game, and the match, were his.

"I'll be damned if I know how you do it," Roger said, breathing heavily as he snatched his towel off the floor at the head of the court.

Art smiled, exhaling. "A little luck," he confessed, walking over to shake his opponent's hand. "Somebody once said that luck is a by-product of design. Not far off the mark."

Harris buried his face in his towel, temporarily stopping the rivers of sweat that flowed from his hairline like tiny waterfalls. "Yeah, but God gave some of us more ability in the design department than others," he said, looking at his boss out of the corner of one eye.

Art Garrett threw a sweaty arm around Roger's neck, still wet with perspiration. "Nonsense. You played well."

"Thanks."

"Stay for breakfast?"

"Thought you'd never ask."

Roger led the way off court. At five-nine, he was not especially small. His 155 pounds were well distributed over a lean, wiry body, and his arms and legs were strong. His coarse black hair, still slick with sweat, curled down over his forehead and ears. Dark brown eyes peered out from behind tortoiseshell glasses. His whiskers were dark and heavy; his cheeks, chin, and throat seemed masked by the previous day's growth.

Garrett shut the undersized, narrow door, flipping off the ceiling lights as they left. Outside the door was a circular steel staircase that led to the paneled den of his reconditioned farmhouse.

As they clambered up the stairs, Garrett ran a hand along the railing. How many coats of bright orange primer had he given it? Two? Three? How many hours had he scraped and brushed and skinned and prepped the surface to take the two finish coats of dark brown enamel?

He had forgotten now. When he went to work with his hands, he disappeared into a world where there were no corporate problems and time had no meaning.

They surfaced through the wooden hatch at the top of the stairs, their sneakers silent on the black iron steps. Art cleared the opening and kicked the cover with his heel. It thunked shut with the precision of a bank vault. He looked at the hatch and thought back now to those absorbing days. He knew he couldn't change the past, of course. It was useless to wonder how different things might have been had he not been so absorbed by starting his own company and refurbishing the old farmhouse.

But when Jane died, half of him had died with her, and he had immediately cut back on his work, delegating more to his division heads, and taking a month's leave of absence to reexamine his life.

He had been tempted to give up, chuck it all and live off his investments, tuned out, withdrawn. But his memory of Jane in their brighter days helped him pull it all back together: it was for her that he committed himself to restoring that precious balance between work and play, involvement and detachment, commitment and isolation.

He had not been certain then, and he still could not say for sure, when he began to slip into that overcommitment to his work. But he remembered the beginning of the end of Jane's sense of humor, her withdrawal from community activities, her lack of attention to him, her waning interest in life.

And then it had happened.

He closed his eyes and tried to push it out of his mind. It still surfaced, five years after the fact. Sometimes it just floated back, like memories of acute embarrassment as a kid, and he had to struggle to keep it from dragging him down. He could never forget the sound of the siren, the orange lights flashing, flashing . . .

"Great workout," Harris said as he tossed his squash gear into a corner.

He drew no immediate response.

"I said, great workout. Feels good." Perspiration still flowed down his face. He wiped his forehead on a soaked shirtsleeve.

"Sorry," Garrett said at last, turning his head slowly and refocusing his attention. "Absolutely. The exercise alone makes it irrelevant who wins or loses."

He blinked away the past temporatily and set his squash racquet down on the oval bar that stood in the center of the spacious room. Opposite the bar, a large brick fireplace yawned its seasonal retirement in muted tones. Natural reds and browns. Used bricks, with texture.

Stained mahogany bookshelves, crammed floor to ceiling with everything from binary calculus to Browning, lined the far wall. Sliding glass doors at the outside end opened onto a broad redwood deck from which one could view a small garden and beyond, into the rolling hills. The floor was parqueted in hardwood. African ebony. Indestructible.

"Easy for you to say, since you win all the time." Roger's sneakers squeaked on the black wooden squares as he walked to the far wall and switched on the recessed overhead lights that bathed the bar in a soft glow.

"But you're right. Ever since I've known you—what? fifteen years now?—I've never seen you hung up on that Vince Lombardi stuff. You know, winning is all that matters, you're nothing if you're not number one."

Garrett edged behind the polished pine bar and pulled a bottle of orange juice from a camouflaged icebox.

"Can't afford to," he said, popping the lid and pouring two glasses. "Once you get into a winning-is-everything mode, the pieces get out of balance. They're both impostors, winning and losing."

"Kipling?"

Garrett smiled, and handed Harris a glass.

"Very good," he said. "I thought you were just a retread in electrical engineering."

They took long swallows, starting the replenishment of fluids lost in the heat of battle. Art held the cold glass against his forehead, felt its soothing relief.

Then he heard it, a long, low, deep-throated yowl. Gar-

rett drained the remainder of his juice and moved across to
unlatch the glass doors. An orange-and-white striped cat
scooted in, rubbing himself with a loud purr against Art's
legs. He was soaking wet.

"Good morning, Captain. Ready to call the SPCA?"

In response, Captain shook his taut, muscular body and
sprayed the Micro Optix chief executive with a shower of
April mist.

"You know where your food is. No special favors on
Tuesday."

He shut the door and turned back to Roger.

"Quick shower?" he asked "Then I'll cook us some
eggs."

"Perfect."

Later, they resumed their positions at the bar, their
glasses replenished, their souls refreshed. Garrett wore a
pair of faded Levi's and an old maroon sweatshirt that said
"MIT^2." Roger Harris had on beige cords with a dark green
turtleneck.

"Did you have a chance to complete those market share
figures yet?" Art asked, glancing at his watch. It was only
seven-thirty. He reached into the mini-fridge, pulled out a
bowl of eggs, some bacon, and thick rye bread.

Harris shook his head. "Finish, no. Make headway, yes.
I'll have the final numbers for you tomorrow." He poured
himself another glass of juice.

"How do they look at this stage?"

"Not good. The Japanese now have a stranglehold on the
64K market with a global share of over 80 percent. And
they've dominated the 16K market for so long now that
American companies simply aren't price competitive."

Garrett frowned. Eighty percent. That was higher than
he had guessed, based on earlier industry statistics. It was
sobering.

He looked across at his R&D expert. "Hitachi?"

Harris nodded. "*And* Fujitsu *and* Matsuzaka *and*
NEC."

"Component share breakdown?"

"Can't give you those until tomorrow." He drained his
glass a second time, refilled it and Art's.

Garrett slipped back behind the bar to start the bacon and put some water on to boil. As he pried the strips loose, he thought about the battles Micro Optix had fought with its numerous Japanese competitors. The continued push toward downsizing—more and more powerful computing capacity on the same small silicon chip—had taken its toll. How many of his former American competitors were still in business?

The industry standard, until recently, had been the 16K. Sixteen thousand binary digits capable of being stored and accessed on a tiny piece of silicon. The 16K had powered hand-held calculators, driven the tiny microprocessors in programmable videotape recorders, served as memory storage units in video games. Once the domain of American semiconductor makers, the 16K market was now totally controlled by the Japanese.

And then Texas Instruments had broken through with the 64K, which became the industry norm. Like the four-minute mile, once it had been achieved, everybody started doing it. Four times the computing power—64,000 bits—on the same size chip.

But now the Japanese dominated the 64K market, as well.

"What about the 256K?" Garrett asked. He came out from behind the bar to retrieve his glass and leaned on the polished pine top.

Harris smiled. "Still ours, Art. The Japanese are all busting ass to get a 256K into commercial production. But so far none of them even has a prototype ready. MITI is upping the ante."

"How much this time?"

"For R&D alone, $350 million last year, $500 million budgeted this year. The Electronics Industry Association thinks Matsuzaka will have a 256K prototype within nine months, possibly before the end of the calendar year."

Garrett sipped his orange juice thoughtfully, licking the ends of his blond moustache. Nine months. Not much time, he thought, but enough for us to preserve our thin lead.

Micro Optix had gotten the jump on everybody else because of it entrepreneurial, innovative nature. First with the 256K. Ahead of both its Japanese and its American competitors. Art and Roger had pushed the company into early 256K development when practically everyone in the industry thought that further downsizing would be impossible.

Micro Optix had shown that the 256K was not only not impossible, it was destined to become the new industry yardstick.

The 256K—*256,000* bits of information capable of storage and retrieval on a silicon chip no larger than a human thumbnail.

And Micro Optix had done it first.

Then they followed it with their optical sensor, the 256K optical, as they called it. The chip that could see. It offered radically new industrial applications, effectively replacing the laser, and equally dramatic advances in defense weaponry, giving guided missiles an accuracy that made the smart bombs of the past look dumb.

Of course, Texas Instruments and Motorola were right on their heels, but Garrett was more concerned about the Japanese. He figured his company's small size and innovative ability could keep him ahead of his American competitors. But the Japanese were something else. It was their drive, their relentlessness, their persistence, that clearly worried him now.

He first became acquainted with Japan as a young student in music, after his undergraduate years at Indiana but before his specialization in electrical engineering at MIT. He had studied for a summer with a brilliant pianist in Kyoto, in 1964. The year of the Tokyo Olympiad. Symbol of Japan's having rejoined the modern world.

Art Garrett would never forget the intensity with which the Japanese people threw themselves into their work, their play, everything they did. The discipline, the motivation, the perseverance impressed him vividly as a young man, impressed him still as a competitor.

He thought he knew something about discipline and hard work before he went to Japan; he knew he knew something about discipline and hard work when he came back. "A cultural boot camp," was what he told his friends it had been like.

Garrett edged back to the small grill behind the bar, flipped the bacon and switched on a small exhaust fan mounted in the countertop. The aroma magnified his appetite.

"Coffee?" he asked, kneeling down to search for the paper filters.

"Tea, if it's handy."

Art played checkers with the food staples beneath the bar, shifting bottles and jars from front to back to front again, in search of the coffee filters. "Tea it is," he said, and pulled two Earl Gray bags from a tin. "I'm out of filters. Have to leave a note for Bea to get more." He set two mugs on the counter and dropped a tea bag in each.

Beatrice was Garrett's housekeeper, cook, and social secretary. Black as anthracite and every bit as solid, she had been with him since he cranked up Micro Optix five years before. She worked days, after Art left for the office, cleaning and cooking and answering the phone. They communicated with each other by means of handwritten notes left pinned to a corkboard in the kitchen. Bea's kitchen. Art used the grill behind the bar.

"I need those component figures as soon as you finish them," he said, pinching the bacon free with a pair of chopsticks. He drained the grease and dropped four eggs into the pan.

"You're still testifying next week in Washington?" Harris collected the empty juice glasses and arranged two place settings at the bar.

Garrett nodded. "Senator Hobson Mitchell's Subcommittee on Trade and Investment. The Boston Brahmin. I'm told his initials stand for 'His Majesty.' The guy's apparently got a pedigree as long as your squash racquet."

He stood over the pan now, shaking the eggs with his left hand, expertly flipping them with his right. One by one their yellow eyes winked out. He lifted them onto waiting plates, extracted two slices of rye from the toaster, poured hot water into the mugs.

Captain jumped up on the bar, having smoothed out his

fur, and began pawing at the bacon. "You know the rules, my friend," Art said, and pushed him off with an elbow.

"Glad you don't treat us like you treat the Captain," Harris said, reaching down to stroke the cat's ears. His purr-box rattled alive in response. "You were saying, about the Senator?" He took a fork and began eating.

Garrett came out and sat down beside him. "The EIA is sponsoring legislation that will enable us all to improve cash flow with a more aggressive depreciation allowance, higher tax credits on capital investments, and increased deductibility of R&D expenditures."

Harris snorted. "I'll believe it when I see it," he said, chewing on a strip of bacon.

"No doubt. But we've got to make a case for industrial policy. If your numbers are right, it looks like the Japanese will be killing us in chips just like they killed us in automobiles, TVs, and textiles. So far, Congress thinks it's just a matter of trade policy and protectionism. They still don't understand how crucial the electronics industry is to national security." Garrett paused, blowing on his tea to cool it.

Roger grew serious. "The Japanese really seem to have their ducks lined up, don't they?"

"Much better than we. Under the MITI budget, the government has allocated significant sums to sponsor research in all of their key industries, not just electronics. They allow companies in these industries extraordinary depreciation allowances on capital investment in new machinery and equipment, which helps them write off the expenditures faster and more efficiently, giving them greater access to state of the art production techniques."

He dipped a piece of rye toast into a waiting yolk.

"This has meant lower earnings on a much smaller equity base, of course, but has ensured the support of their commercial banks, who continue to provide low-cost, long-term financing, interest on which is naturally tax-deductible. And with the newest plant and equipment, they are better able to ride the experience curve. And ride it faster." He sipped some tea. "Eggs OK?"

"Perfect," Harris said, crunching on another strip of

crisp bacon. "And the ability the Japanese have to write off all their development expenses in the current operating year gives them another leg up on us."

Garrett nodded. "We're still in the middle ages, still deferring expenses over product development time."

"How can Washington think of protectionism for the electronics industry, as if we were highly unionized and based in Detroit?"

"That's their mentality. We protect our industries when they become old and inefficient. The Japanese protect theirs when they are young and vulnerable."

"Hell, we're young and vulnerable."

Garrett laughed. "Of course we are. And we're not looking for protection, either. We're trying to grow stronger and tougher. But we can't do it with one hand tied behind our back."

Harris drained his teacup, then glanced at his watch. "I better get going. More number crunching to do. You're off to St. Louis today?"

Garrett nodded. "Big meeting with McDonnell Douglas."

Roger Harris paused as he picked up his squash gear. "On the 256K optical chip? Jesus, that one company alone is responsible for fifteen percent of our annual sales."

"Damn right they are. And they're worried because our deliveries have dropped off from the original contract specification."

Harris looked his boss in the eye. "But the reliability factor is up."

"I know that, and you know that, and once we can increase production of the opticals to a higher yield, we'll be all right. But Frank Martin says he's worried, so I've got to go out and hold his hand." He stacked the breakfast plates in the shallow stainless steel sink and submerged them in water.

"Well, who do they think they're going to get as an alternative supplier? TI won't have an optical ready for months, maybe not until next year. And the Pentagon won't let us license the technology to any foreign firms. Too sensitive."

"That's what I intend to find out. All I know is, Martin's howling."

Roger moved toward the door, scratching his wiry, black hair. "Anybody else outside this country gets their hands on the 256K optical—the Krauts, the Russians, some banana republic—look out World War III. See you tomorrow."

Art waved as Roger headed down the pebbled drive toward his waiting car. He looked at his watch. It was just after eight. He had to get moving if he wanted to make the TWA flight out of Newark on time.

He thought about Roger's comment as he walked back through the den to get his jacket and pick up his briefcase. Could Micro Optix continue to protect this sensitive technology and keep it from falling into unfriendly hands? What would the Pentagon do if another country somehow acquired the optical chip and incorporated it into their own sophisticated weaponry?

Art Garrett shuddered when he thought of the possibility of yet another escalation in the arms race. The world was uncertain and insecure enough as it was.

2

"I don't care whether my name's in your damn computer, or not," Art Garrett said, looking anxiously at his watch. He had ten minutes to make the St. Louis flight.

"I'm sorry, Mr. Garrett, but we show no record of your reservation." The prim attendant, her eyes focused on the computer screen in front of her, showed no sympathy. "We'll be glad to give you a standby card."

Garrett shook his head. "Unfortunately, that won't do me any good." He set his ticket down in front of her, putting the thought of a canceled meeting with McDonnell Douglas out of his mind. "My ticket shows I have a confirmed reservation on this flight, whether your electronic genius here knows it or not." He took off his windbreaker and piled it on top of his briefcase. The passengers behind him began to bristle with impatience.

The agent still refused to meet his glance. She spoke as if on the telephone, at a distance, unemotional, cold. "Your travel agent must have canceled the reservation after they issued the ticket." She paused. "Human error, not uncommon."

She looked up at him now, folding her hands on top of the tube. Her eyes were red-lined and strained from fatigue, like cracks in porcelain. Baggage rumbled behind her on a conveyor belt. Outside, another jet roared into flight.

Art leaned forward and spoke to her in quiet tones. "Miss"—he glanced at her nametag—"Townsend. I run a computer company. These little boxes make mistakes, too. Nobody's perfect. But if you don't give me a boarding pass for this flight, you'll put me in a very awkward position."

He then did something he didn't really like to do, wished
he could avoid, but did when he had to. Reaching into his
hip pocket, he withdrew a small leather case and set one of
his business cards atop the screen, next to his ticket. The
Micro Optix logo on the card matched the symbol on the
machine.

"We do a lot of business with Fred Perry," he said.
"That's one of our machines you're leaning on."

She froze at the mention of the senior executive's name.
She had never met the man, of course, never set eyes on
him. But she knew the name, knew he was very senior.

"Well, Mr. Garrett," she said, staring at the title on his
card, "let's just assume Mr. Perry receives no unfriendly
letters, shall we?" She punched his name into the keyboard and his boarding pass chattered out.

"Thank you, Miss Townsend. But I'm sure he'll be glad
to hear what a fine job you're doing." He watched her eyes
soften as he took the stiff card, then picked up his briefcase
and dashed for the gate.

Later, safely on board and airborne, Garrett unbuckled
his seat belt and pulled out the McDonnell Douglas file. He
skimmed through copies of recent correspondence and internal memoranda, reviewing more thoroughly a summary of their optical chip development that led to
formation of Micro Optix relationships with the aerospace
industry.

Beginning in the early eighties, Micro Optix had made
optical chips in various sizes—up to 64K—for sophisticated
inspection of delicate or sensitive manufacturing processes. Welds, specialty steels, joints, fusions, castings,
strength tests, porcelain "skins" for aircraft and spaceship
bodies, piston and camshaft borings for engines—products
that used to be inspected by hand, then by caliper and later
by laser, were now carefully and more accurately scruti-
nized by electronic machines using the Micro Optix optical
chip.

When Art Garrett had committed Micro Optix to the development of the 256K, he pushed ahead on a parallel
route with the 256K optical. This chip changed the Pentagon's concept of electronic warfare almost overnight.

The principal application of the Micro Optix 256K optical chip was in military TerCom devices. TerCom was Pentagon shorthand for Terrain Comparison, an electronic guidance system developed by McDonnell Douglas that incorporated the 256K optical chip. The Boeing Company was a primary buyer of TerCom systems for use in its ALCM—the Air-Launched Cruise Missile, popularly known as the Cruise.

The Cruise was programmed to strike a predetermined surface target. TerCom kept the missile on course through an optically sensitive microprocessor—the Micro Optix 256K optical chip. This chip compared preprogrammed geographical features in its computer flight plan with the actual geography "seen" by the visual sensor during flight. When the two overlapped in an identical mode, the missile would fix unerringly on its target and speed to destroy it.

Boeing's Cruise utilized an airframe developed under the Pentagon's Subsonic Cruise Armed Decoy program—SCAD, as it was known. Launched in large numbers, each Cruise missile would have to be countered individually, making defense against them both difficult and costly. The Cruise was designed to dilute enemy defenses and to penetrate enemy targets more accurately. It had what the Pentagon called a hard target kill capability and was used for decoy and reconnaisance as well as other nonnuclear missions.

But the Cruise normally carried a nuclear warhead.

Art looked up as a stewardess shoved a plastic tray in front of him. "No, thanks," he said. She moved ahead to the next passenger. He returned his attention to a memo from Jim Masters summarizing the latest production figures from Sunnyvale for the 256K.

The first calendar quarter, January through March, showed a record of over ninety percent pass scores on the standard chip's probe tests. A great improvement, he noted, over the initial scores of fifty to sixty percent during the early runs last year, when the Sunnyvale plant first committed a full production line to the 256K.

Art smiled, simultaneously pressing his moustache. Those figures were the best in the industry. Nobody got

probes of ninety percent or better, even on the smaller
chips. And that was not just reliability of the chip circuitry, but total performance of the semiconductor device after assembly and bonding. A clear vindication of his
decision to automate production.

The problem, Art knew, was with the optical sensor. It
had to be built into the standard 256K circuitry, which
meant a slower production run because of the more sensitive assembly process for the optical element. Production
volume was still about half the standard 256K run. While
Sunnyvale produced around 500 standard 256K chips an-
nually, they could turn out only a maximum of 300 opticals a year.

But the reliability tests of performance after assembly
and bonding for the opticals yielded scores in the low seventies. That meant Sunnyvale couldn't speed up production without risking a further weakening of the reliability
factor.

As the seatbelt sign blinked on, Garrett buckled himself
in for the slow descent into St. Louis. He scribbled a few
marginal notes before returning the file to his briefcase. (1)
Delivery timely? (2) Customer satisfied with performance
after installation in TerCom? (3) Alternative sources of
supply?

That was the crucial question, Art thought, as he
snapped his briefcase shut and secured it under his feet.
He watched the clouds envelop the aircraft, like packing
cotton around a small toy, as its landing gear grumbled
into position.

Micro Optix was the only company in the country—so
far, in the world—that had the 256K optical technology.
Where did McDonnell Douglas think they would get their
optical chips if Micro Optix couldn't make them fast
enough, or dependably enough, for TerCom?

That question continued to nag him as he stepped out of
the dark limousine at the entrance to the McDonnell
Douglas building. The weather in St. Louis was considerably worse than Newark. The mist he had left three hours
earlier had turned into a steady drizzle, and the wind

whipped pockets of water across the concrete drive as he ran into the building.

Art signed in at the receptionist's desk, got a visitor's badge, and was immediately escorted to the third floor. The small, neatly printed sign on the door read, F. Martin, Executive Vice President, Electronic Systems.

"Art, come in. Good to see you," Martin said with a smile as Garrett was shown into the spacious suite. He held a half-smoked cigar in his left hand. A heavy man, taller than Art, older, and out of shape, he wore a gray pin-striped suit with a maroon tie. His lace-up shoes were black, and shone like small mirrors.

"Frank," Art said, offering a hand. His grip was firm, his face serious.

They shook hands. Art was introduced to Martin's assistant, a young, pale-faced junior executive with wire-rimmed glasses and a recent haircut. Charles Cotten, his badge read.

The three men moved to overstuffed chairs near the wide, duopane windows that kept out the airport noise. The auxiliary runway doubled as a McDonnell Douglas test site for jet fighters it developed for the Pentagon.

"We appreciate your coming all the way out here, Art," Martin said, chewing on his cigar and lowering his large frame into one of the blue velvet-and-chrome chairs. The cushion sighed as he settled in.

Art sat down and crossed his legs. "When a major customer of ours gets anxious about supply, we don't resort to polite telephone calls." He looked across at Cotten, who stared at a spiral notebook in his lap. "You've been good clients since we first developed the 64K optical almost five years ago. And you're the major buyer for our 256K opticals."

Martin nodded, offering Art a cigar. He declined. "Micro Optix has done a superb job. Small, loyal, dependable. And strictly first-class products. That's what we like in a supplier, right Charlie?"

Cotten nodded, mirroring his boss. He clicked a ball-point pen and scribbled something in his notebook. His crisply pressed Haspel suit and shiny Cordovans with the smooth soles were straight from the pages of a Brooks Brothers catalog. Another B-school hotshot, no doubt: strong on standardized tests, zilch on judgment.

He looked back at Martin. "But you're not happy, Frank," he said. "Roger's reports indicate a serious dissatisfaction with delivery." He massaged his moustache.

The rotund man hooked a thumb under his belt, giving support to his protruding stomach, and glanced out the window. With the wet weather, the auxiliary runway was quiet, like a church parking lot on Monday. He pulled a three-by-five card out of a coat pocket.

"Late last year," he said, shifting his gaze to Garrett, "when you started commercial production of the 256K opticals, you shipped us twenty a month with sixty percent reliability factor. Last quarter, we received fifteen a month, with a reliability factor of seventy percent. That's a net reduction."

Garrett's expression remained serious. "You know as well as I do that early production runs with these sophisticated optical chips are subject to erratic behavior. It takes time to perfect the process. The supply contract recognizes that fact."

"It wasn't that way with the standard chips."

"Sure it was. You just started ordering from us after we were well down the experience curve. I'll put our standard chip figures up against anybody's in the business."

"Even the Japs?" Martin asked, his voice rasping.

Art clenched his jaw. "Even the Japs, Frank. Hell, they don't even have the opticals—the Pentagon won't let us license the technology and for good reason. But our standard chips are the best in the business. Higher probes, better performance after assembly and bonding, stronger reliability factors."

"Then why can't you get your valley boys in Sunnyvale to step up the runs on the opticals?"

"I spoke to Masters about that last week. Roger Harris is going out there next Monday to make sure we're doing all we can to bring these opticals out with as high a reliability factor as possible. But it can't be done overnight. Besides, you've had TerCom, and Boeing's had the Cruise, a full year before the Pentagon said it could be done. And at a tremendous cost savings, thanks to our optical chip."

Martin paused to relight his cigar, chewing it in a corner of his mouth. A gray cloud of smoke momentarily obscured his head. He fanned the match in the air, watched it go out, and tossed it into an ashtray.

"Correct," he said, exhaling. "But if the figures for May and June show no improvement, we've got no alternative but to develop an alternative source of supply. We need at least twenty opticals a month for the TerCom project alone."

Art shook his head for emphasis. "Believe me, Frank, we're going to make every effort to get those figures up. But don't forget, without Micro Optix you'd still have no optical chip, and no TerCom." He couldn't resist hammering that nail again. Big companies, he recalled from his IBM days, always negotiated with a heavy hand, and he was so insignificant in this David and Goliath relationship.

"But I don't understand your thinking about alternative sources of supply," he continued. "TI and Motorola are the closest to having the 256K optical, and everybody agrees it'll be next year before they can get it into commercial production."

"My friends at Lockheed tell me otherwise. There's another company that'll beat them."

"Who?"

"Amdahl."

"Amdahl?"

Martin nodded.

"Christ, Frank, they're owned by the Japanese now. Fujitsu took them over years ago. The Pentagon'll never approve them as a supplier for this sensitive component, even assuming they can develop it, which is doubtful."

Martin shook his head. "Amdahl is an American corporation, registered in Delaware, regardless of the ultimate foreign ownership. They've applied for permission to supply 256K opticals to American defense contractors as soon as they have the chip in commercial production."

Garrett stood and walked to the window. The rain was

sweeping across the runways in great vertical sheets, like
a curtain of water on a black stage. Be just his luck to get
stuck in the airport, he thought.

"An American subsidiary of a Japanese company sup-
plying one of the most sensitive electronic devices for our
most sophisticated missile guidance system?" Art asked,
turning back to face the portly McDonnell Douglas man.
"It can't happen."

"Can't it? Charlie, remind Mr. Garrett about the Magic
Pantry case."

Young Cotten sat upright in his chair and cleared his
throat. "About a year ago," he said in a squeaky, nervous
voice, "a Canadian company sued the Pentagon to permit
foreign companies in allied countries to compete with
American suppliers for specified defense materials." He
looked up from his notes.

Art smiled for the first time that day. "Mr. Cotten, that
was a food industry case. Magic Pantry. We know it well.
But the jury's still out on this one, and even if they decide
in favor of the plaintiff, does anybody really care where the
Pentagon gets its freeze-dried potatoes?"

Cotten's face turned red. He looked over at Martin,
whose face remained stern.

"We're talking about the most sensitive piece of hardware in the entire defense arsenal, not K-rations," Garrett
said.

"And we're talking letter of intent with Amdahl," Martin said, unblinking.

The telephone rang. Cotten got up to answer it. Holding
a hand over the receiver, he said, "Mr. Garrett, you'll join
us for lunch, of course?"

His eyes fixed on Martin, Art said, "Providing your coat-
and-tie policy in the officers' dining room has changed."
He glanced over at Cotten. "Of course."

Martin's assistant hung up and excused himself as he
stepped from the room.

"You know, you could just wait a year, Frank. Then you
can import the opticals straight from Japan, if that's the
route you want to take."

Now it was Martin's turn to smile. "They'll no doubt be cheaper, too." He wasn't joking.

"You encourage the Pentagon, even covertly, to allow Amdahl to supply opticals to you for TerCom and you're essentially inviting the Japanese to dominate production." Garret rattled off the Japanese market share figures for the 64K.

Martin's face turned pale. He chewed on the cigar, rolling it from one side of his mouth to the other.

"Which means what?" he asked.

"Which means a year from now the Pentagon might as well import the goddam Cruise right from Japan. Because once they get the optical chips, the Japs'll have everything they need to make the entire thing."

Martin sucked on his cigar stub. "And?"

"And then all they'll need to do is stamp Made in Japan on the tail fins. We'll be out of business."

So they adjourned quietly for lunch.

3

"Morning, Mr. Garrett."

"Good morning, Sam."

Art Garrett pulled into the Micro Optix lot the next morning as the guard pushed a button that raised the metal barrier. He drove through the safety check and eased his maroon Rabbit into its place near the entrance to the building.

The clouds had lifted, and a thin April sun covered the green landscape with the softness of a flannel blanket. As Art got out of his car, he filled his lungs with the fresh, cool air. He wore his faded Levi's and a blue cotton workshirt, freshly starched, with a light wool sweater to keep out the chill.

Micro Optix had begun in a suitcase and a garage, but soon Art and Roger had to look for a headquarters site. Art wanted to avoid both Massachusetts and California, although he realized he would have to locate some of his manufacturing capacity in either state if he were to tap available talent in Waltham and in Silicon Valley.

They picked Basking Ridge in south Jersey because it had only a small number of corporate headquarters. The next problem had been suitable space. Cost estimates had been prepared for 10,000 square feet of new office space, but Art's own background as a craftsman convinced him they could do better. So he decided to search for an existing building they could renovate, and stirred up a truckload of dust tromping through a half-dozen sites before they made their final choice.

They finally found an old textbook warehouse, abandoned by a publishing company that had switched from hardcovers to paperbacks and no longer needed the space. Spacious, with high ceilings and a completely open work area, it was tailor-made for renovation. It also had an open, paved area formerly used for shipping and receiving that would easily provide space for employee parking.

When it was finished, and the exterior brick sandblasted to restore its original color and brightness, the building had a shine and polish the new company could be proud of. The renovation won a state award from the Historical Preservation Society because the building's exterior quality, which dated from the late nineteenth century, had been so tastefully restored.

As he walked up the brick pathway, Art remembered that hectic, sweat-filled period—people hired, but no place to put them. Equipment ordered, but no place to store it. And a thousand legal forms had to be filled out for local, state, and federal bureaucracies, which kept the company's lawyers busy for six months and had Art so scared he thought they would run through their initial capital just getting Micro Optix registered to do business.

Pushing through the double-glass door, he came into the antechamber that cleared all people into the building. On the left wall hung a large sign, brightly lettered in red, which announced, clearly and succinctly, to all who entered:

BADGES MUST BE

1. Worn at all times.
2. Worn above the waist.
3. Visible at all times.
4. Presented to Security upon request.

"Morning, Harold."

"Good morning, Art."

The security guard showed Art the sign-in list for the previous day's visitors. Names down the left-hand side, columnar data across the right.

Company affiliation and title. Purpose of visit. Date. Former Micro Optix employee (yes or no). Briefcase (yes or

no). Person to see. Telephone extension. Salesmen's samples (yes or no). Time in. Time out. Other accompanying articles (coat, umbrella, etc.).

The sign-in sheet was one of the most thorough in the industry. The front guard knew the whereabouts of every
visitor at all times. Once the total number of visitors at
any one time reached ten, no one else not affiliated with
the company could enter the premises until another visitor, already clocked in, had come out.

"Busy day yesterday, Harold. Thirty-two visitors, over a
dozen from government agencies. I tell you, they're either
going to overregulate us or buy the hell out of our small
machines."

"Or both?" The guard smiled.

Art nodded and handed the clipboard back.

"No unusual events yesterday?"

The guard shook his head. "Clean as your mother's
laundry."

Plant security was a top priority for Micro Optix, as it
was for all the major computer companies. Everybody was
on guard against the loss of proprietary information such
as computer software. And last year the industry had experienced thefts, or losses, of hardware—the actual chips
themselves—exceeding $50 million. More than the annual
sales of Micro Optix for its entire product line.

In the center of the passageway stood the Micro Optix
fingerprint scanner. For corporations concerned about security, Micro Optix had developed an optically sensitive
16K chip that could "read" fingerprints. Its scanner would
compare the thumbprint on an employee ID card with the
actual fingertip pressed against a glass screen. If the contours of the scanned finger matched the print sealed under
plastic, the machine would automatically open the access
door. If the prints did not match, the machine would instantly flash a warning light to security and simultaneously seal off the chamber, until security guards either
cleared the person after a further check or ejected him
from the premises.

Art Garrett inserted his card into the Micro Optix
scanner and heard the door lock click as he put his finger

on the glass reader. He removed his card and pushed his way through the door.

Telephones rang and telex machines clattered as he mounted the angled staircase up to the second-floor offices. Heads nodded in recognition.

Although it was early—shortly after eight o'clock—the office was already buzzing with activity. Most of the support staff—finance, corporate planning, legal, research—were there. People in marketing and sales tended to come in late and stay late, since customers in earlier time zones wouldn't open until later, local time.

The technicians in design and testing seemed always to be there. Art could never tell, when he came in and saw them in the early mornings, whether they had just begun or were still working on problems that had kept them there through the night. The "red eye" crew, as they were called, would work thirty-six, forty-eight, seventy-two hours at a stretch, and then crash. It was that kind of business.

"Morning, Barbara."

"Oh, good morning, Art."

Barbara Tompkins, Art's secretary, was a renegade from Semiconductor Arrays, a small West Coast–based company that specialized in advanced integrated circuitry where Art had worked before starting Micro Optix. For a woman of fifty, she looked ten or fifteen years younger. A wisp of reddish blond hair fell across her forehead and rested on the rims of oversized, tortoise-shell glasses. Her body was exceptionally fit and trim, a testimony to her regimen as a swimmer.

"They were calling for you again late yesterday afternoon, from Washington," she said, turning in her chair. "Senator Mitchell's staff." She combed her hair back with a bright yellow pencil.

"LaCoste," he said, nodding. "Bea left me a note that he had also called me at home."

"Want me to try him for you now?"

He shook his head. "Too early. We'd never reach anybody in Washington at this hour." He paused. "Oh, tell

Roger when he comes in I need to talk to him about Mc-
Donnell Douglas."

Nodding, she pushed her glasses onto the bridge of her
nose with the pencil tip. Her deep azure eyes were clear,
bright with spirit. Art often wondered if she wore those
outsized glasses to accentuate her attractive features. It
was not the first time he had thought about how different
things might have been had they been closer in age and
had met earlier on.

"What else have we got going for us today?" he asked,
glancing down at the small, pocket-size, typewritten
agenda with the day's events, which she typed out for him
each morning.

"Freddie wants to see you at eleven," Barbara said.
"Something about the figures you want for Washington.
Lunch with Ted Quinn to discuss the annual meeting, and
that's it. A less hectic day for a change."

He stuck the agenda in his hip pocket. "Let's try the
Washington call around ten." She nodded, and swung her
chair back to her desk.

As usual, Garrett's desktop was cluttered with random
patterns of documents spread across in multicolored plastic file envelopes, each representing a different function:
green for finance, red for production, blue for legal, cream
for personnel, orange for planning. Barbara had long ago
learned not to keep these folders in order; Art had his own
filing system.

Art spent the next hour reading the morning mail,
dictating brief responses into his hand-held Miniature Re-
porter, a palm-size cassette recorder designed and manufactured by Micro Optix. Some of the incoming items were
delegated to appropriate departments, others chucked out
immediately.

A small world map hung on the wall behind Art's desk,
next to a window, with five simple push-pins stuck in strategic locations. Bright red at Basking Ridge, the corporate
headquarters. Navy blue at Sunnyvale, California, where
the semiconductor plant was situated, and at Waltham,
Massachusetts, where Micro Optix made its microcomput-

ers. Clear pins marked Brussels and Hong Kong as the company's overseas sales offices.

From design to assembly, everything technical was done in the United States. Art insisted on it, said there was nothing Americans couldn't do. Micro Optix had fully automated its production processes in both silicon chip production and minicomputer assembly so that it had not been necessary to use low-cost, people-intensive labor in Taiwan or South Korea, as their American competitors had done. The only other electronics companies to automate were the Japanese.

Art swiveled around in his chair and propped a Levi's-clad leg on the credenza behind him. Dress was casual at Micro Optix, as it was throughout the electronics industry. Jeans. Loafers. Tie or no tie, up to you. Long hair, short hair, mutton chops, beards. Amazing how people could concentrate on real priorities if they were given control over how they wanted to dress. Art couldn't remember the last time he had worn a coat and tie.

Flex time. People could come when they wanted and leave at any time, provided they were in the office during the core hours of ten to three. Given that freedom, most chose to come early and leave late. Everybody liked the policy, and productivity was high.

The enforced air of informality was not really a conscious choice, as Art enjoyed explaining to visitors. His view was that without it, creativity would be stifled, innovation would suffer, and people would think they worked for a bank or an insurance company. And when was the last time a bank was known for being innovative?

Art attacked his pending file now and pulled out a short report on the Japanese competition in *Business Week*, shaking his head. Amazing, he thought, how the mass market magazines never seem to take the Japanese seriously. They make great motorcycles, excellent cars, superb cameras, fine color TVs. But when it comes to sophisticated electronics, or aerospace equipment, suddenly all the American experts turn defensive and can't admit that the Japanese are—or soon will be—formidable competitors in industry sectors that used to be the exclusive domain of American manufacturers.

A bright red cardinal, full of the freshness and vibrance of spring, fluttered onto Art's windowsill, temporarily distracting his attention. He watched it preen itself, using the glass pane as a mirror, poking a crisp, yellow beak into its fiery feathers.

Barbara broke his concentration.

"Jack LaCoste for you on line one," she said, peering over the shoulder-high cloth partition that separated their desks. It had been Roger's idea to use partitions throughout the building rather than fixed, individual offices. And it had worked well.

"Garrett speaking." He swiveled back to his desk.

"John LaCoste. Of Senator Mitchell's office?"

They exchanged obligatory greetings.

"I was calling yesterday with regard to our hearings on trade and investment," LaCoste said. His voice was high and squeaky, like a tenor in a boy's choir.

"So I understand." Art frowned.

"The Senator would like to confirm your availability next week to appear before his committee."

"When, exactly, Mr. LaCoste?" Art jerked his calendar toward him and flipped it open. He walked to the partition and waved the calendar at Barbara. She opened hers.

"Wednesday afternoon, April 20?"

"Wednesday is a rough day," Art said, glancing down. "Finance committee. Final preparations for our annual meeting."

"I see," LaCoste said. He paused. "How's Thursday morning?"

It was clean. "Thursday looks fine," he said. He glanced at Barbara. She nodded.

"Fine. Thursday, the twenty-first, then, at ten. Can we ink that in?"

'Ink that in.' Art wondered why people in Washington used so many clichés.

"Sure," he said, nestling the phone under his chin as he wrote the confirmation in his calendar.

"We would be interested in your views on the back-

ground of the so-called Japanese competitive threat,"
LaCoste said, his high-pitched voice squealing over the
wire. "And the Senator would also like to know how more
aggressive tax and depreciation allowances would help
your industry sector without depriving government of
needed revenues."

Art scribbled a few notes on the side of his calendar.
"Fine," he said. "I've already started to put my presentation together." He had to get access to some historical economic background on Japan before next week. He noted
that in capital letters. "May I ask the Senator's position on
this legislation?"

LaCoste paused. "We prefer not to prejudice the speak-
ers in any way, Mr. Garrett. It wouldn't be appropriate for
me to comment."

Bullshit, Art thought.

"Come on, LaCoste," he said. "Is the Senator prepared
to sponsor legislation in debate or not? If you can't tell me,
it won't be hard to find out."

Another pause. "Very well," he said. "I can tell you the
Senator wants no changes. He believes it would be detri-
mental to general revenues, and he thinks business already has the tax breaks it needs."

Art chuckled to himself. Christ, he thought, he ever
sounds like his boss.

"All right, Mr. LaCoste. Please inform the Senator that
I will be thoroughly prepared for my presentation next
week."

"Yank the cord, Barbara," Art said as he hung up. "No
more calls for the next hour."

She nodded, back to him now, as she continued her typing.

He began sorting rapidly through the remaining papers
in his pending file, putting back those he would have to
read more closely later.

As he spun back to his desk, he saw Roger Harris peering over the partition.

"Barbara said you had something urgent on McDonnell?"

"Yeah," Garrett said. "Come on in." He yanked open a

desk drawer and retrieved his notes from the previous day's meeting in St. Louis. "Martin's not happy with our performance on the opticals."

Harris sat down opposite Art's desk. "I know. I told you he chewed me out last week on the phone."

Garrett paused, looking at his notes.

"He says he's thinking of shifting some supply orders to other sources."

"Who, for example?" Harris said, smiling.

"Amdahl."

"What?" Roger's smile disappeared. "That's absurd."

"You're telling me? I tried to persuade Martin that his information was faulty, but his pals at Lockheed, who sit next door to Amdahl in Los Angeles, have apparently convinced him otherwise."

Harris scratched his head, looking across at Garrett with a frown. He shook his head.

"No way."

"I agree. But we've got to see what we can do to increase production, if we can. I don't want Martin even thinking about alternative sources of supply." Art leaned back in his chair. "You're going out to Sunnyvale next week?"

"Masters is expecting me Monday."

"When do you leave?"

"Sunday night, be there all day Monday. Flying the red-eye back Monday night."

"Good." Garrett glanced again at his notes. "Take a look at the automatic bonding machines," he said. "We just might be able to speed up the batching."

Harris shook his head again, more violently this time.

"You know the production speed for the 256K opticals has to be slower because of the more sensitive assembly process for the optical element. Volume is currently running about half the standard 256K run, which is all we can expect without serious deterioration in reliability."

"I know, but when you talk to Masters, see if there's some way we can improve those reliability numbers. At least, if we can't speed up production, we can try to give Martin a higher yield on existing batches."

Harris pulled a pen out of his pocket and made a note.

"I'll do my best." He looked up at Garrett. "Martin thinks he's serious about Amdahl?"

"Says they're talking letter of intent."

Roger thought for a minute, staring straight ahead. Then he shook his head again. "Impossible."

"Of course it's impossible. But do you tell one of your major customers you think he's crazy?"

"I guess not, not even if you're his only supplier for a key chip."

"Exactly. Hell, he even brought up the Magic Pantry case."

Harris laughed now. "The fucking *food* company?"

Art nodded, smiling. A thin smile.

"How'd you leave it with Martin?"

"I gave him my set piece on the dangers of Japanese domination in the 256K chip sector. Tried to scare him a bit."

"Any luck?"

"Maybe. He's given us at least through June to get output back to our fourth-quarter levels."

Harris stood up and stretched. "Anything else you need from me?"

"Oh, yeah. The market share component breakdown figures," he said, snapping his fingers.

"I'm bringing those at eleven for your meeting with Freddie Schmidt."

4

Promptly at eleven, Freddie Schmidt and Roger Harris popped their heads above the cloth partition, like kewpie dolls.

"We meeting here?" Schmidt asked.

Art glanced up, then looked at his watch. "Jesus, is it eleven already?"

Schmidt dropped into a chair next to Harris, across from Garrett's desk. In his late forties, he was a short man, and heavy. Thick-lensed glasses sat atop a broad nose, making his blue eyes look as round as a cat's. He retained only a whisper of dark hair around his temples. He wore a pair of light gray wool slacks and an open-collared flannel shirt, in green plaid. His sleeves were rolled up past the elbow, more like a laborer than an accountant.

Garrett's chief financial officer had had his fill of big companies after working as a partner with Arthur Anderson for nearly twenty years. When he heard that Art was starting up Micro Optix, he took the initiative in approaching the young entrepreneur. Art had been impressed with that. He had also been impressed with Schmidt's credentials and his desire to eliminate three wasted hours a day commuting.

Art stood up and reshuffled the colored file folders on his desk, like a casino dealer, pulling the orange file marked "Planning" from the middle of the stack. He dropped back down into his chair.

"LaCoste called about an hour ago. My testimony on industrial policy before the Senate Trade and Investment Committee is set for Thursday next week."

"The twenty-first?" Schmidt asked. He took out a Don Diego cigar and began moistening the outer leaf.

"Right. Which means I'd like to have everything in hand by Tuesday at the latest so I can go over it in detail before I leave."

"Where do you want to start?" It was Harris. He ran a hand through his coarse black hair and it sprang back instantly, like steel wool.

"I'm going to need a lot more background info on Japan. The Senator's apparently interested in the Japanese competition."

"Easy," Schmidt said, crossing his legs and setting his cigar aflame. Clouds of dark blue smoke temporarily covered his head like a thick veil. "We can give him MITI's figures on T&D." Tax and Depreciation. He flicked a dead match into Art's desktop ashtray.

Garrett shook his head. "He'll undoubtedly have those. We need to get behind the figures."

Schmidt shrugged his shoulders and exhaled. "For starters, you can give them two reasons almost unrelated to the Japs."

Art reached for his yellow pad, turned to a fresh page, and cranked out a sliver of lead in his automatic pencil.

"One," Schmidt began, "our own manufacturing companies are being run increasingly by financial types—lawyers, accountants, hotshots out of business school with no line experience—looking at everything in terms of the bottom line." He held up a finger for emphasis.

"Good point," Garrett said, writing as he spoke, "and true. More and more emphasis on short-term profitability, less commitment to the long haul."

"Second," Schmidt noted, holding up another finger, "we lack an international mentality. Outside the Fortune 500, how many American companies are motivated to sell overseas? Too few. They get lazy and think in terms of foreign markets being the same as ours: English as the only means of communication, and fat profit margins."

Garrett nodded as he continued to write. "That's a good place for some comparative figures on the Japanese." Turning to Roger, he said, "Do you think you could put your hands on some hard Japanese employment and capital investment numbers?"

"You mean, how they work their butts off over there—twelve-hour days, six-day weeks, no vacations?" Harris asked. "And their constant investment in new, state of the art technology—robots, automatic assembly equipment, computer-controlled machines?"

"Yeah, precisely that sort of thing. You know, how they consistently lower their production costs by investing in state of the art technology, how their productivity and quality control methods are so superior."

Now it was Harris's turn to nod. "I can talk to the Japan Productivity Center in Washington."

"Or go through the EIA."

"Or the EIA."

"Freddie, what about vertical sales?" Garrett looked up now from his yellow pad. "You have any numbers on the major Japanese electronics companies?"

Schmidt rolled the Don Diego between his lips, puffed and frowned.

"Like, how the bulk of their chip production either stays in the company itself and is used in components for other manufacturing divisions or goes to other group companies?"

"Yes. For example, Matsuzaka Electric selling to other Matsuzaka Group companies. Or Hitachi producing primarily for the Hitachi Group."

Schmidt made a note. "No problem. I should also have some numbers on how they get their unit costs down through higher volume production within their industrial groupings, as well. That's one of the factors that enables them to underprice us over here."

"Perfect. Roger, how did those market share figures come out?"

Harris uncrossed his legs and opened the sheaf of papers on his lap. "In the 64K sector, Matsuzaka is now the market leader. They've really put the pressure on Hitachi and NEC."

"Are you sure? Last I recall, Matsuzaka was like second or third tier."

"You're probably thinking of last year's figures, Art. This data is current through March 31 and is based on Japanese industry sources. MITI, primarily." He paused briefly, sifting through the sheets like a stamp collector looking for an uncanceled first-day-of-issue. "Matsuzaka alone now has over twenty percent of the global 64K market, twenty-two percent to be exact. Hitachi is number two with eighteen percent, and NEC and Fujitsu follow with fifteen percent and thirteen percent shares, respectively. The balance is held by a handful of smaller, less prominent companies."

Garrett raised his eyebrows in surprise, but jotted the figures down as Roger read them.

"Art, you'll need some hard data on our own T&D experience. Why don't I summarize our historical results for the past five years, as well as overall performance for the semiconductor industry as a whole?" Schmidt blew an oval smoke doughnut over his head.

"Fine, Freddie, but could you also restate those figures and do some pro-formas for the next five years based on estimates of new T&D formulas? Use a high-medium-low calculation, within the projected ranges." Garrett scrunched down in his chair, scratching his back.

"I'll feed the numbers into one of our microcomputers," Schmidt said, "and get you a clean printout."

"Are you going to give the Senator your thoughts on the virtues of small, entrepreneurial organizations?" Roger asked, a mischievous twinkle in his eye.

Garrett nodded. "The numbers speak for themselves. Lower overheads, no frills, no waste. No unions gumming up the works. Higher quality output, better product reliability, stronger frequency of repair records across the board. It's all demonstrable."

"Good. I hope you also hit him with your Sputnik theory."

"I intend to."

Schmidt coughed a mouthful of smoke across Garrett's desk. "Sputnik?" he said. "What's this all about, government subsidies for the 256K?" He tapped off a long, curling ash.

Art Garrett leaned back in his chair and twirled the letter opener in his hands. "Quite the opposite, Freddie. Something I've been discussing with Roger lately. You know how strongly I feel about the entrepreneurial spirit, how important it is that our American organizations try to recapture that competitive drive, that incentive and motivation to work harder."

Schmidt laughed. "Are you kidding? If I had a dime for every speech or article you've written in the past year on the topic, I could buy out your share of Micro Optix."

Garrett smiled. "Then you also know how pessimistic I feel about that happening. American business has grown fat and lazy, comfortable in their country-club offices, addicted to short-term profits, confined to a domestic market, no longer concerned about maintaining their long-term competitive edge through better product quality and innovation. So my theory is, unless some type of Sputnik-like event occurs, and soon, to shock this country back to reality, we'll all sit placidly by, eating our national junk food as the Japanese and the Germans continue to outpace us in practically every advanced industrial sector."

"But they've given us cheaper and better cars, and we've all benefited."

"Correct. But don't try to use that argument in Detroit. We know the Japanese already control eighty percent of the 64K market in chips, as Roger has just confirmed. American companies can't compete any more because they're overpriced, so they're trying to gear up to the 256K where they can be cost competitive." He drew closer to his desk. "But assume the Japanese come around and take eighty percent of the 256K market, Freddie. Our chip makers start to go out of business because they're losing too much money, and suddenly the Pentagon finds itself wholly dependent on one foreign country as the sole source of supply for the most vital components in our sophisticated electronic weaponry."

"Holy shit." Schmidt exhaled a slow cloud of smoke.

"Holy shit, is right. So my point is, to prevent this from happening, we need a shock, a cold shower, the emotional impact of another Sputnik. Look what happened after the Russians launched their man-made satellite in 1957: we turned around and mobilized the entire scientific resources of this country in response and ultimately dominated outer space as a result." Garrett tapped his desktop for emphasis.

"Christ, it would take another world war to unify this country like that again."

"Maybe. Or nationwide unemployment at depression-era levels. Which could happen if the Japanese corner the world market in the most advanced computer chips. That might just do it."

Schmidt was silent. He puffed a solitary stream of smoke.

"How soon do you want these performance figures?"

Art looked at his calendar. "What's today—Wednesday? By Friday, if you can. Then I can study them over the weekend."

"And I'll get the Japanese data for you by Tuesday," Roger said. "Depends on the Japan Productivity Center. Sometimes they're stingy with their data."

"Sometimes?" Garrett asked.

5

Barbara Tompkins craned her neck over the cloth-covered partition and found Art poring over a pile of papers at his desk. He looked up.

"It's nearly six o'clock. Don't forget you have a Japan Society meeting tonight."

"Ah, right, Barbara," he said, looking at his watch. "I'll run down and grab a quick sandwich." He walked over to her and took the file she held out to him. "Thanks."

"Anything else you need for tonight?"

He went back to his desk, surveyed the top. "Can't think of anything," he said. He checked the file to make sure the meeting outline was there. It was. Masao Kitagawa, MITI's New York representative, was speaking at the monthly seminar on Japan-U.S. trade friction.

"See you tomorrow?" she said, disappearing behind her side of the wall.

"Right. Breakfast meeting as I recall."

"Ted Quinn, seven o'clock, downstairs." Her voice rolled over the wall in a mellow, alto tone. "I'll put your daily schedule on your phone tomorrow morning, as usual. *Ciao.*"

With the Japan Society file in one hand, he headed for the cafeteria, where he picked up a ham and cheese sandwich and an iced tea, and sat down. He opened the file as he bit into the sandwich. His involvement with the Japan Society had not been his idea. Jane had been the one keen to stay involved in community affairs. But after . . . after it had happened, he decided to involve himself in a noncorporate function, both to reduce his addiction to his work and to force him to think about issues of a less technical nature.

130

He actually came to enjoy it, and eventually began serving on the Society's Public Affairs Committee.

He drained his iced tea glass, jammed the folder under his arm, and carried his dishes to the conveyor belt. He nodded to two software engineers on his way out.

"Guy's an absolute genius," one said to the other.

"How so?" His eyes followed Garrett out the cafeteria door.

"Listen, the way he's got this company positioned to compete with the Japanese? Brilliant. Only company in this country to automate fully the way the Japanese have."

More than an hour later, Art eased the maroon Rabbit quickly into a slot near First Avenue just as another car was vacating the space. That was the essence of parking in New York City, he thought, as he locked the door and leapfrogged a coil of fresh dogshit. Either you crawled into a parking space on someone else's tail, or you circled the block for two hours in vain.

Glancing at his watch, he stepped up his pace as he rounded First Avenue and headed up East Forty-seventh Street to Japan House. Traffic on the George Washington Bridge had delayed him, and the meeting was already in progress when he walked in. He tiptoed around to the side of the horseshoe-shaped table and nodded silently to Bill Wilson, the Society's Managing Director.

Kitagawa was summarizing his preliminary remarks as he sat down. ". . . which leads us to believe that the primary motivation of the U.S. government in the latest round of trade talks is purely political, resulting from the Administration's setback in the general elections last November."

In his early forties, Kitagawa had been sent to New York about a year earlier, principally to serve as a lightning rod for Washington's increasingly belligerent attacks on the Japanese government, prompted by the chronic bilateral trade deficits.

"I couldn't agree more."

The statement came from one of the few women participants, seated at Art's right. He squinted to make out the large, hand-printed letters on her nametag under the flickering fluroescent lights.

Sally Hendricks, it read. It belonged to a strikingly attractive woman with gleaming auburn hair and doll-like features.

Gesturing to the group, she said, "Mr. Kitagawa is absolutely right. The Japanese government is seriously worried about being made a scapegoat for problems that are essentially domestic American concerns."

"Like structural unemployment in the auto industry?" someone asked.

"Correct," she said. "Which led the UAW to force the issue of Japanese car imports with the International Trade Commission a few years back. And as everybody knows, the ITC decided overwhelmingly in favor of the Japanese."

An intelligent, knowledgeable, and attractive woman, Art thought as he raised a hand. Wilson acknowledged him.

"Miss Hendricks has made a valid point, I think," he said, looking in her direction and seeing her eyes focus on him. "But isn't there a danger of overgeneralization, Mr. Kitagawa? Don't forget, the Japanese are indefatigable strategists and will sacrifice just about anything at the altar of market share. Our government is simply trying to ensure an open market for American goods in Japan." Sally was nodding as she turned her attention back to Kitagawa.

"That's true, what you say, Garetto-san," the Japanese MITI official said. "I was merely trying to establish a motivation for the Administration's behavior, which I believe is primarily political." Kitagawa's manner was calm and self-assured. He sat comfotably in a gray, three-piece suit, white shirt and dark blue tie. His hair was black and smooth as a raven's feathers.

Bill Wilson broke in. Chairs squeaked as people rose and stretched, breaking into twos and threes as they walked to the coffee table. Art glanced around, looking for Sally Hendricks. It was the first time he had seen her at the Society's seminar, and he definitely wanted to say hello. He spotted her talking to Wilson.

As Wilson turned to fill his coffee cup, Art extended his right hand. "Hi," he said. "Art Garrett. You must be one of our new members. Welcome to the Greater East Asia Co-Prosperity Sphere." He smiled.

She laughed, shifting her coffee cup to her left hand. "Sally. Sally Hendricks," she said, taking his hand and gripping it firmly. "Thank you. This is my first meeting. I'm here as a guest observer."

He looked down at her as he sipped his coffee. Her eyes were dark chocolate, deep and expressive, and friendly. She had a ready smile that displayed a line of even, white teeth under her small, upturned nose. And she was tiny, barely five feet tall, but perfectly proportioned.

The comment you made earlier interested me," he said, swirling the coffee in his cup. "Of course, we compete head-on with the Japanese who, as you know, can be quite predatory."

Sally pursed her lips and blew softly on her coffee to cool it. "The ITC case was one I researched pretty thoroughly at the time. Our auto unions wanted to preserve their high wage rates any way they could."

"Are you a professional researcher?"

"I teach," she said. "History and economics, out of the East Asian Institute at Rutgers." She paused, eyeing Garrett thoughtfully. "And you?"

"I work at a small company called Micro Optix, in Basking Ridge."

"Work there? Hell, he runs the place."

It was Wilson. He extended a hand and Art shook it.

"Hello, Bill." He turned to introduce him to Sally. "Say hello to Sally Hendricks."

"We know each other," he said, setting his coffee cup down. "I asked Sally to join us tonight for Kitagawa-san's presentation. She had an interesting piece published in this month's *Foreign Policy* on Japan's competitive industrial strengths, and I thought she should meet some of our people."

They chatted together briefly. Wilson then excused himself to circulate among the others, smiling, shaking hands, playing the social diplomat.

"Run the place, huh?" Sally said as they walked back to their chairs. She glanced up at this chief executive in Levi's with a gleam of fascination in her eyes.

"Well, I started the company about five years ago with a few renegades from my former firm. We're small but growing like a weed."

They stopped beside her chair. Her smooth, autumnal hair danced lightly on her shoulders as she sat down. Art found it difficult to take his eyes off her bright, curious face.

"I'd like to hear more about your article," he said.

"I'd like to know more about your company," she said.

Art walked back to his chair. The word *ethereal* unaccountably popped into his mind. "Japan's competitive industrial strengths," he muttered inaudibly. He wrote her name down on his legal pad, and underlined it. Twice.

Kitagawa spent the next hour outlining several economic arguments to balance the political factors he had enumerated earlier, and the remaining discussion centered on Japanese import quotas, bureaucratic obfuscation, product certifications, testing standards, and government procurement policies. He rolled and unrolled his necktie as he spoke, in calm, matter-of-fact tones.

Art Garrett made only one comment during the final half of the meeting, when he disagreed with Kitagawa's assessment of the ability of American companies to compete in the domestic Japanese market.

"We don't have the infrastructure over there, we aren't willing to learn the language, and most importantly, we're too damn impatient," he said. "We haven't got the staying power necessary to compete over the longer term because we're too interested in quarterly profits."

That brought a barrage of negative retorts from representatives of other American firms who, individually and collectively, attempted to assure their Japanese counterparts that they were serious about exporting to the Japanese market and that they were keen to compete over the long haul. Their position was weak, Art thought, as he listened to the Japanese tear them apart, like piranha in a small pond.

He glanced across the table as Bill Wilson brought the meeting to a close and saw Sally pulling on a light blue windbreaker over her bright-yellow cashmere turtleneck. A green-and-yellow paisley scarf was stuffed into one pocket.

His stride lengthened as he moved to where she was standing. "Sally," he said, touching her lightly on the elbow.

She spun around. "Oh, Art. Excuse me, I mean, 'Mr. President.'" She smiled that easy smile again. Her dark brown eyes glowed softly under the fluorescent lights.

"Come on," he said. "Anybody calling me that at the office gets fired." He smiled back. "Give you a lift home? Can't offer you much in the way of comfort. An old Rabbit diesel is about my style, I'm afraid. But New Brunswick's right on the way."

"No Mercedes, no deal," she quipped. "Seriously, I've got a ride courtesy of Conrail." She held up a train ticket.

"Well, put it away for another rainy day. I'll throw in a nightcap at no extra charge. That's something our railway system can't offer." His tone was easy, but determined.

Sally thought for a moment, weighing the proposal in her mind. Then she glanced at her watch. "Seeing as how I've already missed the 10:10," she said, "I accept. But just one. I have a heavy teaching load tomorrow. Friday's my worst day."

"I'm scheduled for an early breakfast meeting that kicks off a busy day, as well."

They said their goodbyes and headed west on Forty-seventh Street, toward Third. Art suggested they stop in at P.J.'s, since it was close by, and Sally agreed on the condition that they sit rather than get jostled at the bar. She pulled on the paisley scarf as protection from the misty night air. Her light brown hair glistened with a soft sheen.

The bar was jammed, as always, with the late-night singles crowd, and the large mirror behind the bar made the narrow room seem even more packed as the reflected image psychologically doubled its size. But they pressed through, slowly and with apologies for flattened feet, and found a table for two in the back room.

"What are you having?" she asked.

"Glenlivet," he said. "If they have it, which is rare."

"That's the stuff like liquid peat moss, isn't it?"

He laughed. "But better."

"I'll try one," she said, smiling. "Straight up, lots of ice."

Art flagged down the waiter, a beefy white-haired Irishman whose face had as many wrinkles as the bar had bottles. He brought their drinks almost instantly, as if they had been waiting, all along, behind the bar.

"I can't imagine why, but somehow you remind me of my eleven-year-old," Sally said as they clinked their glasses together and sipped. "Maybe because you're very outgoing, and have a good sense of humor."

"My years in the theater as a kid," he said, teasingly. Frowning at the mention of children, he asked, "What does your husband do?"

"Former husband," she corrected. "He's a lawyer, a partner at one of those Wall Street firms with six names. And you?"

"My—I'm single, too," he said, taking another sip of Glenlivet and letting the rich, flavorful scotch slide smoothly down his throat.

"Divorced or just permanently single?" she asked, not pressing, but persistent.

His face turned down. He looked at his glass as he swirled the ice cubes, listening to them clink softly together. It was amazing that it was still so painful to say. "My wife committed suicide about five years ago." He looked back up.

"Jesus," she whispered, sinking back into her chair, her voice barely audible. "I'm very sorry."

He set his drink down, cleared his throat, jammed his hands deep into his pants pockets. "Mostly my fault," he said, shrugging his broad shoulders. "Pushing to get a new company up and running. Jerking her back here from California before she ever had a chance to sink any roots in. Postponing her decision to have a child until it was just too late." His voice trailed off.

And then it all came back again, in an instant, like it

had just happened. The clarity of that event would simply never leave his mind. It was permanently etched in his memory, like a nightmare in petrified wood. The call from Bea, her hysteria, the orange lights of the ambulance flashing, flashing . . .

". . . was traceable to an overdose of phenobarbitol, which she had been taking to help her sleep more easily." He picked up his glass and drained it. "I don't know why I'm telling you this. I didn't invite you out to get maudlin," he said. "Besides, that's enough about me. What brought you to Rutgers?"

Sally took a sip of scotch. "Moved there from New York. I was teaching at Columbia while my husband—my then-husband—commuted to Wall Street from the Upper West Side. An opportunity came up at the East Asian Institute, so I—"

"Uh-uh," he said suddenly. "Another woman?"

She shook her head, draining her glass. "No, not with him. A book. Complete and total involvement. The definitive work on mergers and acquisitions. He was totally, unilaterally, committed. Probably be a Supreme Court Justice someday. Jason—that's my eleven-year-old—and I simply ceased to exist. With his lack of attention, I got involved in a self-fulfillment group—metaphysical poetry, mostly—and we just . . . drifted apart. I found I loved my poetry more than I did him. But the divorce was all very amicable. A generous settlement, monthly stipends to supplement my income from Rutgers, educational expenses for Jason."

Sally swirled the ice cubes in her empty glass. Then she looked back up.

"It must be this pickled peat moss," she said. "I don't usually bare my soul after just one drink."

"Neither do I," Art replied. His eyes met hers. "Some Scots elf must have slipped a magic potion in the bottle."

"We can't risk another drink in that case," she said softly. Sally glanced at her watch. "Besides, it's getting late, and we've got at least an hour's drive ahead."

"You're right," he said, flagging down the burly Irish-

man for the check. He paid, and they moved out the rear
door rather than forcing their way back through the front.

"There," he said, taking her arm, "just ahead. The maroon Rabbit. The one covered with mud and the neon
bumper sticker on back that says, 'Support your local exporter.'" She smiled as he opened the passenger door.
"And watch the dogshit." Sally laughed now as she
stepped gingerly into the car.

The cool April mist continued to fall as they drove
through the city, like spray from a giant waterfall. Art
sped down Second Avenue through the East Village, and
then turned west to the Holland Tunnel. They were in
luck, there was little traffic in the tunnel.

"How did you come to specialize in things Japanese?" he
asked as they picked up speed on the turnpike ramp. The
Rabbit's tires hissed quietly on the damp pavement.

She frowned in the dim light. "Hard to say. Probably because I wanted to get away from home, and Fulbright
money was readily available at the time, so I took a crash
course in the language, did well, and got hooked."

Sally proceeded to tell him about her years in Japan, her
fondness for the language, her frustrations with the culture. She had completed her Ph.D. at Berkeley, where she
had met her husband, when he was in law school there. After Jason was born, they emigrated back East, and she had
decided early on to continue her career in teaching. Looking back now, at the age of thirty-nine, she believed she'd
made a wise decision.

The Rabbit sped ahead, its dark interior catching the
glow of the overhead turnpike lights as they winked by.
Art could see Sally's figure, delicate and graceful and soft,
out of the corners of his eyes.

Sally yawned, stretching her arms above her head and
pressing on the closed sunroof. "Your turn, Mr. Chief Executive," she said, smiling. "How did you get from there to
here?"

Art shifted his gaze back to the road now as he thought
about her question. He briefly summarized his youth in
Indiana, his summer in Japan, his engineering work at
MIT. "I started with IBM, actually, back in the mid-sixties

when they controlled the market for mainframes." He laughed. "Kept getting into trouble with them because I completed my sales quotas well under schedule. By the time I had been with them for five years—I was about thirty-two. I guess—I made my entire year's quota before the end of January that year."

"In less than a *month?*"

He nodded, watching the road. "That's when I first realized I would never be happy working for anybody else."

"So what did you do next?"

"Bought into a small, West Coast electronics firm called Semiconductor Arrays that specialized in sophisticated memory chips. All the tiny building blocks for the computer business." He pulled the Rabbit over as a large truck roared past, spraying them with a gray film.

"Sounds like what you're doing now at—sorry, what was it?"

"Micro Optix. Similar, but with two exceptions. I didn't control the company, and they were losing competitive advantage because the majority partners balked at investing heavily in new equipment that would automate the chip-making process. So I brought a colleague back with me—Roger Harris—and we cranked up Micro Optix. We'll be six years old next October."

By the time he had told her about the company's product specialization, its unique optical chips, and the Japanese competition, they had reached the New Brunswick exit ramp. Sally gave him directions and they soon pulled into a circular drive.

He killed the engine, then held her door open as she stepped out. The mist was still falling, but somehow it seemed softer, lighter. He walked her up to the front door, which was painted bright red.

"Thank you, Art," she said, extending a hand. Her grip was firm, her palm dry, her skin smooth to the touch, as he shook it. Her small hand practically disappeared in his.

Sally clicked her key into the latch and shot the bolt back with a flick of her wrist.

"Would you . . . ?"

He stopped as quickly as he had started.

She looked up at him, her eyes tired from the long trip into New York and back, the lids sagging, demanding a halt to the vertical state.

"Would I what?" Sally asked, raising her eyebrows. Her small chest rose and fell as she breathed.

He scratched his chin on the door frame. He suddenly felt very awkward. He didn't want to blow it with this bright, attractive woman by taking a heavy-handed approach. "I realize we've barely met," he said, "but this Japan thing has me concerned. They compete strongly with us in advanced electronics and employ some rather predatory selling techniques in carving out their market shares. They seem intent on domination, and it worries me."

Sally flicked on a small, indoor light. It illuminated her features with a soft glow.

"Calculation. Domination. Elimination. One, two, three," she said, leaning against the doorjamb. "Same thing they've done in other industries. Most people think they're harmless little midgets that bow and smile and suck in air, but they're very serious, very aggressive."

Art's mind suddenly clicked alive, despite the late hour. Maybe Sally could help him get a grip on the Japanese mentality, he thought, better understand the culture—what drove them, what made them tick.

"I've got to testify late next week in Washington," he said. "You know, technical stuff, tax and depreciation numbers, industrial policy, that sort of thing. Would you mind if I picked your brains on the Japs sometime soon? Could we have dinner on Saturday?"

She watched him as he pressed his moustache with a thumb and forefinger. "Interesting," she nodded. "I'd like to. As long as you don't call them Japs." She cocked her head at a slight angle. "Saturday should be all right. Call me late that morning." She pushed in the door and started to move inside.

He stepped back. "Wait," he said, "I don't have your number."

"In the book. S. Hendricks. With a 'cks," she said, over her shoulder. "518 Cold Soil Road." She yawned. "Thanks again for the ride, Mr. Wizard, but I'm done for. Call me

Saturday." She eased the door shut and snapped the bolt in place.

Art moved slowly back to the maroon Rabbit. The diesel engine clattered alive, and he headed out the drive toward the turnpike. Why didn't his fellow American competitors take the Japanese more seriously? He knew the Japanese were targeting the electronics industry for global domination. MITI had as much as admitted it in their white paper.

He snapped his fingers. What was it Sally had said? Competition? No, calculation. Yes, that was it.

Calculation. Domination. Elimination.

The words danced in his mind. He toyed with the concepts, juggled the words, and simultaneously tried to recall her soft, delicate features as he nosed the Rabbit home.

6

"Fire away, Ted," Art said, forking a wedge of French toast into his mouth. "I assume you have your usual laundry list of questions." His eyes burned; it had been later than he thought when he finally got home the previous night, and later yet when he managed to put Sally Hendricks out of his mind long enough to find the first stage of sleep.

Garrett was seated in the cafeteria with his corporate secretary, Ted Quinn, who headed a staff of five lawyers. He had been an antitrust lawyer at AT&T earlier in his career, and he, too, had hungered for the leaner life at a smaller company.

"Have you and Freddie given any thought to proposing a dividend increase this year?" Quinn asked, crunching on a crisp strip of bacon. "We're getting letters from stockholders complaining about your low dividend policy."

Garrett waved to a pair of young software engineers who had recently joined the company. "Can't see it, Ted," he said. "You know our earnings have taken a beating since we can't get a full price play on the chips. More importantly, we need every dollar we can get right back in the business. The shareholders should know that. We've always stressed capital appreciation through growth rather than steady income through dividends. They want quarterly checks, they should buy Ma Bell."

Quinn tugged at the neck of his blue turtleneck. At fifty-two, he was the oldest Micro Optix employee, and at five-four, the shortest. With a full head of coarse red hair, his looks belied his age. His face was rough, the skin toughened through years of exposure to wind and rain on the decks of his sailboats. Deep brown eyes squinted through small, wire-rimmed glasses, testimony to the nearsightedness developed through decades of poring over documents.

"Have you thought about how you're going to handle the hecklers at the annual meeting on the twenty-eighth, in that case?"

"God, is it that soon?"

"Two weeks from yesterday."

"Jesus." Art squeezed a lemon into his tea and stirred it, thinking. "We'll just have to be open, and give them the numbers. The marginal cost of borrowing, for example, in a double-digit environment. That's what they'd be forcing us to do in the absence of an aggressive retained earnings program."

"What about a treasury stock issue?" Quinn asked. He shifted his plates around, dug a fork into his sweet roll.

Art washed down the remainder of his French toast with a long swallow of tea. "How much treasury stock do we have on hand?"

"A few thousand shares, bought back at attractive prices in the open market during the past year."

"Not really enough to do much good, is it? We could do a one-for-ten, I suppose, but nobody would be fooled. Too meager. Besides, having a major stock split now would rob us of scrip we need for our annual staff bonuses."

Quinn nodded. "All good reasons, Art. I'm not pushing the idea, just playing devil's advocate." He sipped his coffee. "What about a section in the annual report on the Japanese threat? I know you're testifying on this next week in Washington, and it might make good copy."

"Won't we have timing problems? It's already at the printers for page proofs."

"We can get another five hundred words in. Send me a draft of your testimony when Barbara has it ready."

"Fine." The more he thought about it, the more he liked the idea. It would also reinforce the importance of their retained earnings policy and highlight the industrial policy issue.

"Urgent call for Art Garrett. Art, call for you on one."

A male voice crackled over the office intercom.

Art shot a glance at his wristwatch. "Who in hell could be calling at seven-thirty in the morning?" he asked, half to himself.

Quinn shrugged his shoulders. "Go ahead. I'll wait."

Garrett crumpled his paper napkin and stuffed it under a corner of his tray, then jogged out of the cafeteria and up the stairs, two at a time. He picked up the receiver at Barbara's desk and punched the flashing white button.

"Garrett."

"Art? Jim Masters. I've been trying to reach you since late yesterday."

"Meetings in New York last night. Didn't get home until nearly one." Sally flashed suddenly into his mind.

"That's when I gave up." His voice was raspy, and tired.

Garrett frowned. He recognized the nervousness in Masters' voice. "Jim, anything wrong?" he asked, his attention refocused.

"Afraid so," he said. "Our plant controller was matching payments to invoices this week. You know, like we always do near mid-month?"

"Yeah. And?" A list of possibilities raced through his mind. Defalcation? Computer crime? The ever-present fear of chip theft?

"Well, you're not going to like this, but you remember that shipment of 256K standard chips we made last month, the half-million dollar new order?"

"How could I forget? New customer, fifty percent down payment, two 10 net 30. Digital Systems, wasn't that the name?"

"Right. Well, we all thought the buyer was a local California company that makes digital readouts for the aerospace industry." Masters paused. "But their invoice was paid off with a check drawn on the Fuji Bank of California, and we know how tricky this Japanese situation is."

Garrett sighed. "That's not surprising. The Japanese banks in California are so aggressive, more than half of their local customers are American now."

"Yeah, but not this one. We did some checking, since we've become so sensitive to the Japanese thing."

"And?" Garrett's fingers squeezed the receiver more

tightly now. The long distance connection hissed in his ear.

"Digital Systems is controlled by Hitachi."

"What?"

Masters cleared his throat. His voice still scraped.

"That's right. Wholly-owned by a Netherlands Antilles company, of which Hitachi Limited owns seventy percent. The remaining thirty percent is held equally by Hitachi Seiki, the precision instruments company, and C. Itoh."

"The trading firm."

"Exactly."

"Shit."

"That's what I said."

Garrett sat down on a corner of his secretary's desk, stunned. Was this what it was coming down to, he wondered? An untraceable network of interlocking holding companies that disguised ultimate Japanese ownership?

"Art?"

"Yeah."

"You still there?"

"Yeah. I'm trying to think."

"I know your first question is going to be, how the hell did we make a shipment without checking out the customer thoroughly first."

"Close."

"Well, we did check them out. I signed off on it, in fact. What threw us off was the size of the cash payment. When a new customer pays half a sizable invoice amount up front, you don't worry so much about their creditworthiness for the balance. They have a Delaware holding company, which owns a hundred percent of Digital Systems, and the Delaware company is wholly owned by the Curacao firm."

"What's it called?"

"The Delaware paper company?"

"Yeah."

"Digital Holdings, Inc."

"And the Curacao company?"

"Digital International."

Barbara arrived at the top floor landing, and slowed her

pace when she saw the unfamiliar sight of Garrett perched on her desk. She stopped completely when she saw the serious look on his face, and silently set her handbag down on her chair.

"The check's already cleared, I suppose?"

"Yes. We confirmed that with Republic's San Francisco agency yesterday. Good funds credited to our account value Monday the eleventh."

Garrett was silent.

"Art, I know what you're thinking," Masters said, his words echoing over the line. "No way we can recall the chips. They're gone. Fifty of them, worth ten thousand bucks apiece."

"You're certain none of them were opticals?" Art asked, his eyes etching a random pattern on the distant wall as he thought.

"Positive. Checked and double-checked the batch number against the chip codes. All standards."

"Well, thank God for that."

"If there had been any opticals on the invoice, I would have caught them immediately. Those buggers are still costed out at $50,000 per, and we ship them to no one without a Pentagon clearance code."

Art turned as he heard Barbara drop her keys on her desk. "See if Roger's in," he said to her, cupping a hand over the phone. The connection buzzed and squeaked.

"Jim?"

"Still here. I heard it, too. Must be a satellite connection."

"What about the other new orders we've received in the past quarter? Any more surprises?"

"None that we've found so far. I've got the controller going back through the order book and we're checking all new names against the holding company index."

"Good."

"It'll take us most of the weekend, but we should have it completed by the time Roger gets here Sunday night."

Barbara returned with Roger Harris in tow. Art motioned for him to pick up in his office.

When Roger did, they explained the gist of what had happened.

"Shit," Roger said.

"That's three for three," said Masters. He was not trying to be funny.

Garrett's mouth was a tight line, his eyes narrow and probing. "Add this to your list for Sunnyvale, Roger. Jim said he'd have the checklist finished by the time you arrive, so we shouldn't have any more breakfast calls for a while," he said, stroking his moustache. "But don't let this distract you from the optical production problem."

"Right."

"Oh, and Jim?"

"Yes, Art."

"Better go over plant security with Roger and Herman on Monday, as well. A stitch in time, you never know." Herman Brewster was the Micro Optix security chief in Sunnyvale.

"Herman and I just did that at the end of March, like we do every month."

"I know. But it won't hurt to do it again while Roger's there."

"Fingerprint scanner, electronic door locks, ultrasonic motion detectors, the fence, the metal detector, the whole thing?"

"The whole thing."

"Art?"

Masters' voice was quieter now, and steady.

"Do you think any of those 256Ks have reached Tokyo yet?"

"What do you think?"

"I bet yes."

"You said it. Watch out, reverse engineering here we come."

When they rang off, Roger walked slowly out of Art's office.

"What do you think that'll do to our lead time?" he asked.

Art's face was grim. "Hard to say. Three months, maybe? We'll have a better feel for that when you get back." He folded his arms across his chest and turned to Barbara Tompkins. "Find Ted Quinn," he said. "He may still be in the cafeteria. Tell him I'll have to wait on the rest of his questions." She disappeared down the stairs.

To Roger, he said, "You know what I'm thinking?"

Harris nodded. "McDonnell Douglas?"

"Exactly. Amdahl's just a smoke screen. Martin must be talking to Digital Systems."

Roger smiled a half-smile. "And all legal."

"So far."

They stared at each other without blinking.

7

Saturday dawned with a brilliance rare for mid-April. Art propped a leg on the deck's redwood railing and watched the sun rise over the distant hillside, arch slowly higher in the menthol-blue sky, and then explode with fullness in the valley below. Through patches of ground fog that hugged the low areas like angel's hair on a Christmas tree he could see that the white cherry was beginning to bloom, and farther across the hill dogwood and apple and pear trees were budding. Another week and the valley would yield an artist's palette of pastels.

Shading his eyes from the bright sun, he sat down on the bench, picked up his orange planning folder, and turned to the pro-formas Fred Schmidt had cranked out. They showed a range of favorable cash flows based on the three T&D assumptions—high, medium, and low.

Art smiled. Even with a low value for both tax credits and depreciation, the potential impact was impressive. Micro Optix could generate enough cash to repay nearly a third of their outstanding bank debt, for example, or possibly consider a dividend, as Ted Quinn had recommended, to maintain shareholder loyalty.

The medium and high values showed even more impressive results. In both these cases, there was a multiplier effect: the company could generate enough cash to repay its long-term debt almost entirely and still strengthen its balance sheet through increased retained earnings.

Next, he flipped through Quinn's list of questions for the annual meeting, and for the first time in weeks, he felt a surge of confidence. The numbers were encouraging, and he believed the shareholders would come away impressed.

Now if Roger could make some headway with production output in Sunnyvale, they could gain valuable time with McDonnell Douglas.

Time. That's what this business was all about, he thought. Time. Sometimes six weeks wasn't even enough to prevent a giant like IBM or Texas Instruments from catching and then surpassing your own fragile lead. You could measure developments in this industry by heartbeats. So many creative people, with such fiery commitment, willing to work long hours, for big bucks. And occasionally with questionable methods, because the stakes were so large.

Questionable methods.

Digital Systems.

He stood and walked to the edge of the deck, stuffed his hands deep into his pockets, and felt that new-found confidence suddenly evaporate. He could see a cluster of Hitachi engineers in Tokyo poring over the Micro Optix 256Ks like ants in a sugar bowl. They would unplug, unwind, disassemble, and unbond the chips until they could compare their own circuitry and design with his.

Reverse engineering. Take an existing chip and back it down from finished product to individual components. Work backward. Step by step. The most feared process a competitor could use.

Garrett slumped back down on the redwood bench, shaking his head. Three months? he asked himself. Is that what Hitachi might have gained? And once Hitachi had a breakthrough for their own 256K, NEC, Fujitsu, Matsuzaka would all share the spoils: industrial cooperation existed in Japan the likes of which the country hadn't seen since the era of monopoly railroads and oil.

He leaned back and plugged the telephone extension into its outdoor socket, trying to think of brighter things. His index finger traced a vertical path down the far left column of names in the North Brunswick book. "Henderson, Hendley, Hendon," he mumbled to himself as he searched for Sally's number. "Here it is. Hendricks, S. 518 Cold Soil Road."

He dialed the number.

After a half-dozen rings, he glanced quickly at his watch and realized it was barely eight o'clock. He started to hang up when a tired voice answered.

"Hello?" It was Sally.

"Sally? Art Garrett. God, I'm sorry, I had no idea it was still so early."

"It's all right," she said with a stifled yawn. "I'm basically awake. I had to get up at dawn to get Jason off to a tennis camp."

"I'm afraid I lost track of time," he said. "I've been out on my deck since sunup going over a stack of papers. Days like today make all the snow and slush worthwhile."

"God," she said, "you would just love living in Japan."

"What makes you say that?" he asked.

"They're early-morning eager beavers, as well. Their limitless energy can drive you nuts."

He nodded now, thinking back to his summer in Kyoto.

"At the risk of ruining my chances by calling so early, are we still on for dinner tonight?"

Sally paused. "Tonight? I thought it was next Saturday."

Art's spirits took another nosedive. "Sally, less than forty-eight hours ago I asked if you were free tonight, and you said yes."

"And it was late, and I was tired, and I had my thoughts on Friday's teaching schedule. I honestly thought you meant next week. I have a poetry reading tonight."

Garrett stood and walked to the edge of the deck, facing the bright sun, trailing the telephone cord behind him.

"Picking your brains next Saturday won't do much good for my Washington testimony on Thursday," he said softly.

"God, that's right. Now I remember."

Neither of them spoke for a long, difficult moment.

"How often does your poetry group meet?" he asked.

"Twice a month. First and third Saturdays."

He thought quickly. "And there are five Saturdays in April this year."

Another pause.

"You're right. I'm just looking at my calendar. We have an extra session on the thirtieth."

"Bring some of your poems tonight," Art said. "I'd like to hear them."

Art was elated that he could hear not a hint of disappointment in her voice as she agreed to forgo the reading. He gave her directions, suggesting she come early, before seven, so they could have a drink on the deck and watch the sun set in the valley.

"Very poetic."

"Better than poetry," he responded.

He spent the day reading through his orange file, straightening the den, laying in food he would need that night, and running his 4.5 mile route down the hill through the valley, and back. He also spoke at length with Ted Quinn about the shareholders meeting, and talked to Roger before his departure for Sunnyvale the next day.

Just after six-thirty he heard the gravel crunch in the driveway. He walked out to the front as Sally was extracting herself from her little green Alfa.

"No wonder your poor Rabbit was splattered with mud," she said, stepping gingerly onto the gravel drive. "Don't you pay enough in taxes to get them to pave the access road?"

"Don't want them to," he replied. "More asphalt means more traffic. I like it quiet up here."

Sally wore a pair of gray corduroy trousers and a blue cotton workshirt. A red sweater was draped loosely over her shoulders. Her tiny feet disappeared into wooden clogs.

"Directions okay?" Art asked, taking her hand and leading her around the side, over the pebbled pathway, to the deck.

"No problem," she said. "I gave myself extra time, which is why I'm early." Her clogs knocked across the wooden deck as she glanced up at the rear of the house. "Lots of room for just you and the housekeeper," she said, her chocolate brown eyes sparkling in the late afternoon sunlight.

"Three of us, to be exact," Art said, and opened the sliding glass door to the den. Captain bounded out and rolled, stretching his long, golden frame across the redwood planks. Sally kneeled down and stroked his broad back. He flopped over and gurgled with a loud purr. "Say hello to Sally, Captain," he said.

"Captain," Sally said as the big cat rubbed its head against one of her clogs. "Interesting name. From your connections with the defense industry, no doubt?" she said, smiling up at him.

Art shook his head. "Strictly civilian background," he said. "He's a Captain of Industry."

She stood, laughing, and walked to the rear of the deck. "Nice," she said, looking out across the valley. "Especially with the ground fog moving in. I see what you mean about being better than poetry."

"Well, I better offer you a drink before our poetic view disappears," he said. "I have more peat moss, if you'd like. Or perhaps something a little less harsh."

"I'd love a beer," she said as Captain rubbed up against her legs.

Art reappeared quickly with two bottles of Furstenberg and a pair of glasses. "If he gets aggressive," he said, nodding toward the cat and pouring the beer, "bark at him. He must have some German blood in him, the way he responds to commands."

They raised their glasses in a toast and stood, silently watching the sun disappear beyond the soft, papier-mâché hills in the distance. The ground fog billowed as it moved in thick patches across the valley floor. Occasional lights blinked on in the town, mirroring the stars that began to appear above their heads.

Art turned his back to the valley. "Thank you for coming," he said softly. Her delicate auburn hair seemed to glow in the dwindling light.

Sally raised her eyes to meet his, then looked back into her glass. "I'm sorry," she said. "I should have been more alert on Thursday."

The disappearance of the sun brought a sudden drop in temperature, and they moved inside.

Sally walked across the darkwood floor and set her glass on the oval bar.

"This woodwork, it's unbelievable. You can't get carpentry like this any more. Who did it for you?" she asked, rubbing her hand along the polished pine of the bar. It was clean and smooth to the touch, like marble.

He sipped his Furstenberg. "I did," he said quietly.

"*You* did all this? How . . . ?" Her dark brown eyes widened in surprise.

He took her on a short tour of the house. "It was an old farmhouse, totally in ruins, when we found it six years ago," he said. He explained how he had learned his skills as a craftsman from his father. "Took me more than a year to get it done." He led her up the spiral staircase from the basement squash court.

He walked back to the bar and clicked on the small grill. "Am I the only one getting hungry?" he asked. She shook her head as he flipped a pair of steaks onto the fire and pulled a basket of leafy vegetables out of the minifridge to start a salad. The aroma of fresh meat broiling mingled with the scent of Sally's bath soap, a pungent pine. Art's nostrils flared as he sniffed the delicate, contrapuntal bouquets.

They ate informally, sitting at the bar, sharing a bottle of Fetzer. Slowly, carefully, they opened up more of their personal pasts to each other.

After a time, Art changed the subject. "I can't seem to put my finger on where the Japanese are coming from, what makes them tick."

Sally nodded and leaned forward on her elbows, pensively swirling the wine in her glass. The ring of ceiling lights overhead sparkled in the bloodred claret.

"You don't have to start with Shotoku Taishi and the introduction of Buddhism in the seventh century," she said, "but it's important to go back to the 1600s at least, to Tokugawa, to get a glimmer of what Japan is all about."

Art took a sip of wine. "You mean, Shogun?" he asked.

She smiled. "Not the only one, but certainly the most famous," she nodded. "Japan was a closed society at that time, shut off from the rest of the world. Japanese were not permitted to leave, foreigners could not get in. *Sakoku*, they called it, the closed country. This lasted for nearly three hundred years. What do you think would happen to any country from such a period of enforced isolation?"

Art frowned, swirling his wine. "Development of unique institutions? Strong, cultural pride, I guess."

"Exactly," she said. "This proud Asian country developed and refined its own religious and military philosophies, its art, its domestic commerce, education, diet, scientific research. Most important, the tiny island culture, this *shimaguni*, developed a strong hierarchical sense of values, based upon its own history and feudal structure. Jap was, of course, number one in the eyes of the Japanese. Their values developed in a vacuum, sealed off, if you will, in an impregnable cultural cocoon."

Sally paused, sipping her wine. "This all happened at a time when the West was coming out of its own period of feudalistic stagnation. First the renaissance, then the industrial revolution caught fire and spread like a new religion across Europe and later, America. The West was on its way to global domination. First England, then the United States. No one noticed, or cared, what was happening in Japan. When the Japanese came out of their self-enforced isolation in the 1860s, they noticed that they were not *perceived* by the West as being an advanced country. So they started borrowing from the West—parliamentary systems from the British, rail technology from the French, military organization from the Germans. All the while preserving their own unique social structure and system of devotion to the Emperor."

Art shrugged. "So? That's a very nice history lesson, Mrs. Hendricks, but how does it explain their persistence?" He refilled their wine glasses.

"Patience," she said. "The most significant aspect of this entire period of isolation was the development by the Japanese of an attitude toward performance, an almost perfectionist approach, to everything they did. That encompassed as well an embodiment of thoroughness in their approach to things technical."

She gestured with her wine glass. "It was almost as if their society had been in a state of suspended animation, chemically bonded in a process that would be permanently indelible."

"You mean, this bedrock of cultural values?"

"Precisely," she said. "At the same time, the Japanese adopted an attitude toward the West that was in keeping with their own feudalistic view of the world: respectful, adulatory, admiring. They played the role of apprentice and viewed the West as teacher; hence, it was easy for them to borrow and to learn from us. Unfortunately, we viewed the roles as permanent—we would always be master, the Asian the apprentice—but from the very beginning the Japanese saw these roles as only temporary. In due course, they believed, they would themselves become master."

"Which is what happened in Southeast Asia, didn't it, during their military buildup in the twenties and thirties?" Art stroked his moustache with thumb and forefinger.

Sally nodded. "The Greater East-Asia Co-Prosperity Sphere," she said. "Pyramidal, hierarchic. Japan at the top, all other nations strung out below. Japan the leader, the master, the guiding light. Southeast Asia the follower, the apprentice. The Japanese thought it was superb, a natural outgrowth of their own historical feelings of cultural superiority. The other countries had second thoughts once it was implemented; what was great for Japan wasn't so great for them."

"They couldn't accept the fact of Japanese superiority?"

"Oh, they could accept it, all right. They just couldn't swallow the blustery arrogance and high-handed snobbishness of the Japanese that went along with it. That started to erode the mortar between the blocks of stone in the cultural pyramid, so to speak."

Art nodded. "Just like IBM trying to dominate its smaller competitors," he said, half to himself.

"So think about these social and cultural systems the Japanese had firmly in place when we occupied their country after the war. Highly feudalistic, very rigidly structured, strongly xenophobic, with an Emperor at the apex of their social pyramid, revered by all. The industrial base was principally an oligopoly, dominated by a few massive firms.

"Mitsubishi, Sumitomo, Matsuzaka," he said quietly, names that evoked such a spirit of competitive drive today.

"Yes, and other great names. Mitsui. Yawata. Fuyo. Systems and forms uniquely Japanese. They had superimposed their own organizational structure around everything they had borrowed from the West in the late nineteenth century. A feudalistic society outfitted from a Sears Roebuck catalog, if you will. But a society that had grown incredibly strong during those three hundred years of isolation during Tokugawa. Like the bamboo that symbolizes so much of their great art, these social systems could bend and twist under tremendous outside pressure, but they would never collapse."

Sally took another long swallow of wine. She began to feel its warming, relaxing influence.

Art cleared the plates and set a platter of cheese on the countertop, carving off a few slices. Then he retreated a few paces to the darkened fireplace, set some logs in position, and started a small fire to take the chill from the room.

"Now look what happened after the war," Sally continued, munching on a piece of brie as Art rejoined her. "The Americans come in, demolish the industrial conglomerates, humanize the Emperor, and substitute their own institutions, right out of the conservative Midwest. We start *dominating* the Japanese. They accept us, of course, as their liberators, and they start in again on the apprentice kick."

"Only we view it as permanent, and they don't," Art said, picking up the thread now.

"Correct. We viewed the Japanese as grossly underdeveloped, by our own standards. But that didn't phase them," she said, looking across at the dancing flames in the fireplace. "They began to regroup into their more traditional structural forms almost as soon as the occupation came to an end. Then the Korean War reminded us that the Japanese would be pretty helpful political allies in a rather unstable area of the world. So we helped the Japanese government turn its attention to economic and industrial policies. They focused on protection of young Japanese industries in the domestic market, and determined where their strategic overseas markets should be. The feudal hierarchy, with the government at the top, was being rebuilt. And MITI was captain of their ship."

She edged off the bar stool and began pacing in front of the fireplace as she spoke. Her wooden clogs echoed sharply on the ebony parquet; she kicked them gently off to one side. The flickering light from the fire reflected in her dark eyes, created a halo effect about her head, accentuated the curved uplift of her small breasts.

Art swiveled around on his stool, watching her pace back and forth. He was fascinated by this delicate woman and by her impressive breadth of knowledge.

"The relevance here is in the highly systematic way in which the Japanese went about establishing themselves as a dominant force in the industries they chose as priorities," she continued, gesturing toward the far wall. "First, textiles and shipbuilding, labor-intensive industries that required relatively little in the way of advanced technology at the time. That was step one: Calculation.

"Step two?" she asked, turning to face him now. "Domination. Japan rose to the position of number one in the *world* in production of man-made fibers and shipping tonnage during the 1950s. Aggressive strategy, superior performance, all based on nothing more than their traditional cultural heritage: a need to succeed, a desire to dominate, a feeling of natural cultural superiority."

She took another sip of wine, felt it slide smoothly down her throat. "And then step three," she went on. "Elimination. Competitors were being destroyed right and left in this country and in Europe by aggressive Japanese pricing and marketing strategies, their incredible work ethic, and their decidedly lower costs. But the Japanese didn't stop there. They made concessions to our textile industry, of course, but they had already decided—through MITI, naturally—to move up the ladder of added value and to focus their national industrial policies on the automobile and television sectors: strong export industries, crucial to an island country hungry for valuable foreign exchange."

Art was nodding now. "And the same thing happened."

"Yes. Calculation. Domination. Elimination. More ministerial-level talks, more self-imposed restraints by the Japanese on exports of TVs and cars. While they geared up for the *next* level of attack."

"Electronics," Art whispered, his voice quiet, his eyes staring straight into the fire.

"Electronics," Sally repeated, turning to face him now. "Calculators, small computers, copy machines, numerically controlled machine tools, first-generation integrated circuits, now domination in the 64K chip market."

"And strategic positioning in the 256K," he said, meeting her glance. "Calculation. Hell, they've already destroyed American competition in the 64K market, and they're gearing up now for the 256K. Domination. Yes. Once they get on a roll, we'll have our backs to the wall again." He thought about Digital Systems and paused, nodding more slowly now.

"Elimination," he said, straightening. "Of course, it all fits."

It had jelled slowly, like water freezing in a small brook. But the natural conclusion clicked in his mind as Sally rattled off those examples in the electronics sector so familiar to him.

He walked over and stirred the logs. They cracked and popped as the flames leapt higher in the fireplace. He sat down on the couch.

Sally drained her wine glass and set it down on the end table, joining him on the couch, folding her legs beneath her. Her voice dropped to a whisper.

"You see," she said, leaning over and placing a hand on his knee, "I think we are beginning to witness a resurgence of the East as our own industrial and economic power in the West is on the decline. That fits the way the Japanese view the world. They believe they're on their way up, while we're on the way down. Period. Full stop."

Art gazed straight ahead, picked her hand off his knee, held it lightly in his. "I wonder," he said, half aloud. He turned to face her, told her about his Sputnik theory, his hopes for a resurgence, a revitalization, of American industrial competitiveness.

Sally squeezed his hand. "Even if we do experience another cultural Sputnik," she said, shaking her head, "it won't stop the Japanese. They're tough. They're relentless. They're . . . invincible."

"And that's why I'm going down to Washington."

The words had hardly escaped his mouth when her lips descended on his. Garrett drew back, unprepared. He felt warmed by the wine, by the fire, but he still withdrew. He wasn't sure why.

Sally pressed closer, reached behind his back, and pulled him to her. Slowly, gradually, he brought his lips to hers, and she responded eagerly.

He slipped his left hand around the small of her back, and with his right he lifted her chin up and kissed her, lightly, on the neck. He could feel her heart pounding against his chest as she held her lithe body firmly against his. He hungrily found her mouth again and their tongues resumed their darting, dueling dance.

How long had it been since it had meant something . . . the uninvited past flashed by, an unwelcome visitor. With trembling fingers Art reached under Sally's blouse and touched a small breast, its nipple hardening under the pressure of his touch. Sally shivered slightly, pulling herself closer.

He slowly unbuttoned her shirt and leaned down to suck softly on the erect nipple, circling it with his tongue. She shuddered in his arms and then quickly pulled off his sweater and unbuckled his jeans, sliding her hand down his body and curling it around his throbbing fullness.

As she took him in her hand and caressed him, he slipped her pants down her slim hips. His hand traced a path up the smooth insides of her firm thighs to caress her warm moistness.

She gently kissed his face, then brought her mouth down in a slow, circuitous path from neck to chest, her tongue toying playfully with his nipples. His head lay back as she then took him into her mouth and caressed him with rhythmical strokes of her tongue, swinging her body up onto the couch parallel with his.

Art buried his head between Sally's legs, moving her on top of him, tasting her sweetness and feeling her body quiver with joy. He slowly spun her around until their faces met again and her lips closed on his, their tongues searching, probing, as she moved her lower body to meet his erectness. When he felt her warmth envelop him, he penetrated her deeply.

Twisting and turning atop his body, she shook with uncontrollable pleasure as he exploded within her, their minds a million wordless miles away, unfocused, the two of them, united in a magical silence.

This fleeting feeling of physical and spiritual oneness, he thought. So rare, so special. He felt renewed in a way he had not experienced for such a long time.

They lay together then, enshrouded in a lazy halo of here, not here, Sally's head resting in the crest of Art's shoulder, an arm draped lifelessly across his chest. The glowing embers of the fire radiated a soothing warmth.

Art reached around her with his right arm, taking her small hand in his. Their fingers intertwined, flexing and unflexing. He could feel a feather-soft kiss against his shoulder, and then Sally arched up and kissed him on the mouth, tickling his moustache with her tongue.

He closed his eyes. Was he dreaming? Had it all been a figment of his imagination, that prison of fear and alienation after. . . . His thoughts were confused, feelings of intense pleasure crowded by remnants of pain, scar tissue not yet fully healed. In his mind's eye, he could still see that fateful flashing light, blinking, reminding. Would it ever disappear?

He looked down at her, holding her even more tightly. She brought a hand up to his face, held his head, caressed his neck.

"Death, divorce, disappointment, failure. Whatever the tragedy, the human psyche perseveres. Or so I tell myself," he said, his voice a hoarse whisper.

She lifted up briefly, nodding, her deep brown eyes following the contours of his face. She placed a finger on his lips. He kissed it, teased it with his tongue.

Shivering slightly, Sally reached down for his sweater and pulled it over her head. She lay her head back on Art's chest, listened to the palpitations of his strong heart. He kissed her hair, stroked her neck and shoulder with his hand.

Pulling on his jeans, he slipped quietly across the far corner of the room and sat down at the keyboard of his harpsichord and began flipping through his sheet music until he came to a melodic sonatina by the Czech composer, Czerny. He serenaded Sally with the clean, plucked tones of the piece. His fingers, soft-driving miniature pistons, played it flawlessly.

Sally walked slowly over to the delicate wooden instrument and sat down beside him. "Is there anything you can't do, Mr. Chief Executive?"

He smiled. "Lots. Relate to women, for one. Run a successful company, for another. Keep a step ahead of the Japanese, for a third." He leaned down and kissed her lightly on the nose.

Shivering again, she drew closer to him, snuggling against the warmth of his body. "How do you feel about your testimony now?" she asked, her voice quiet.

He sighed and wrapped his arms around her. "Simultaneously elated and depressed. Buoyed by your insights, but considerably less optimistic about my Sputnik theory."

"Listen," she said, twisting her head to look him in the eye. "Forget what I said about the resurgence of Asia. It's only a theory, too, and considerably harder to substantiate than yours."

He shook his head. "You struck a chord. What was it? Their . . . their *invincibility*. That's the scary part."

She kissed him on the cheek. "Hit them with it anyway," she said. "It's your poetic license." She flipped through the pages of the small notebook she held in her hand.

"That which is unspoken between us," she read, *"Returns to the bone,*

"Like a bell ringing,
"Past
"When it's rung."

She leaned her head on his shoulder.

"One of yours?" he asked.

She nodded, pressing her lips to his.

Was it possible? he asked himself as he held her in his arms. Can there again be sharing and lightness and laughter and love?

8

"I was afraid of that," Art said, as he sat in his office early Tuesday morning, listening to Roger Harris report on the Sunnyvale operations. "Those Teledyne machines are terrific. What we did to them after we bought them is better known than said."

"Turned a Chevrolet into a Cadillac," Roger said, his eyes red and streaked from the overnight flight back. "Even so, we've got them running on all eight cylinders now and we can't squeeze anything more out of them." He sipped hot coffee from a brown mug that said "We Will Win," glazed, in white capital letters, across one side.

Garrett nodded. He got up from his desk chair and stared out the window at the distant, mint-green hills. It was another one of those dark, overcast spring days, the skies full of heavy clouds that threatened rain, like an angry father about to scold his son. The wind tore across the landscape in strong gusts, whipping the trees with fury. Blows long enough, and hard enough, Art thought, they might escape the rain. He turned back to face his partner.

"The assembly and bonding stage is so delicate, as you know," Roger said, closing his eyes and rubbing them, as if that would lubricate lids that scratched like coarse sandpaper. "Sure, we could maybe try to squeeze through another ten percent in volume, but we risk a complete shutdown if we try."

"Yeah." Art looked at the Sunnyvale production figures for the 256K opticals. He pulled slowly at his moustache. "Which means I'll just have to put it to Martin as best I can. Somehow, his threat to secure an alternative source of supply just doesn't ring true."

164

"I agree. Certainly not with Amdahl."

"And certainly not since Gene Amdahl split with Fujitsu to go his own way, even if Fujitsu did retain the rights to the name. Gene always said he had to give away the store back in the early seventies when he was looking for money, and the Japanese were the only ones willing to take it." He frowned. "But Digital Systems is something else. The Hitachi connection sounds too real to be coincidental."

Harris nodded. "But the Pentagon would never certify them, even if they do develop the optical technology, because of the Japanese ownership." He took another sip of coffee.

"Yeah, but don't forget, Martin is banking on that Magic Pantry case."

"Art, will you stop being so paranoid? The Pentagon's got to see the difference between retort pouches and computer chips. Even if they do agree to buy freeze-dried cherries from the Canadians, they'll keep the electronics sector off-limits to foreigners."

"I hope so. It'll sure calm Martin down." Art sat back down in his chair, tapping his desktop with the letter opener. He laughed. "It'd serve us right, of course, if the Pentagon did as little checking on the old Amdahl company as we did on Digital Systems."

Harris closed his eyes again, in embarrassment this time. "No way we should've let that one slip through. But at least it was just a nose bleed and not a hemorrhage."

Art turned to Roger's written summary of the investigation in Sunnyvale. "You checked with Massachusetts, too, didn't you?" he asked, looking up.

"Talked to them yesterday," Roger said. "They're clean. This Hitachi case is the only one that slipped by Masters, and he's got the sales staff primed to prevent any repeats."

"God, let's hope so. Even with this one isolated case, Hitachi has got its hands on a potful of our 256Ks, which is almost like giving them the engineering plans."

"But even if it hadn't been us, it probably would've been somebody else. They could have ordered a minicomputer from Data General, for example, which uses our chips in their central processing units, taken the chips out of the machine, and then reverse engineered them."

Art laughed again. "That assumes Data General would've been as stupid as we were. Don't kid yourself. They're more paranoid than I am."

"With a fifty percent payment up front, Art? Nobody, believe me, nobody's gonna ask any questions when you get that much in advance. You worry about the buyer's solvency, not his nationality."

Garrett shook his head. "We pride ourselves on two things, Roger. Innovation and reliability. We've got to be as thorough in our own efforts as we know the Japanese are in theirs."

"Short of bending the rules, of course."

"Short of bending the rules," Art agreed, closing the report and handing back to Harris.

Roger tucked it under his arm. "Which leads to the question, which would you rather be, number one and cheating, or number two and playing by the rules?" His mouth stretched open into a gaping yawn, which he covered with the report.

"Number one, but playing by the rules," Garrett responded. "You and Masters go over that new Teledyne machine?"

Harris nodded. "Together with the design engineers," he said. "They agreed they could have another souped-up version ready by September, which would enable us to double our volume by year-end." He paused. "I added three months, which didn't make them happy, but is more accurate, given our experience with the initial machines. First calendar quarter next year is my guess."

Art did some quick mental calculations. "Which means a year from now, if everything goes well, we should be able to supply McDonnell Douglas with twice its present offtake of chips." He grabbed a small calculator off his desk and punched the buttons crisply. "Assuming no retrogression in quality."

"Fine. But that assumes renegotiation of the supply contract."

"So?"

"So maybe we ought to talk to Martin now, instead of waiting six months. Could take the steam out of his argument to push for a second supplier."

Garrett shook his head slowly. "If our present contract's not preventing him from thinking about alternative suppliers, I doubt a new one would. Gone are the days of iron-clad agreements in this industry." He smiled. "Still, you may be right. Could be worth a try."

Art's phone suddenly chirped. He froze, looked at Harris, then picked up the receiver.

"Mrs. Hendricks for you on line two." He sighed in relief, then jabbed the flashing light. "Sally?"

"Good morning," she said. "I know you're busy, but I have a counterproposal to make for Thursday."

"Shoot."

"When you get back from Washington, why don't you stop by here for dinner. My turn to reciprocate. Then you can tell me how your testimony went."

Art shot a glance at his calendar, raising a finger in the air to tell Roger not to go. "My flight's not due back into Newark until seven-thirty," he said. "By the time I get the car and get out of there, it'll be close to nine before I reach your place. That's too late."

"Nonsense," Sally said. "Can't possibly be any later than last week. Besides, it's on your way home, remember?"

He thought for a minute, studying his calendar and rubbing his moustache. Part of him wanted to see her, right now, but another part demanded time, distance, perspective.

"I've got a potful of appointments on Friday," he said, "starting with a squash match at six-thirty." He looked across at Harris, who nodded, scratching his head of wiry, black hair. "Couldn't we do it over the weekend?"

"I'm disappearing next weekend," she said. "Taking Jason off to Cape May for some birding. Thursday night, take it or leave it."

He paused. Tough negotiator, he thought. What was she doing in a classroom? "I'll take it," he said, watching Roger smile. "One condition: early to bed."

"Delighted," she said. "See you at nine."

She rang off before he could say that's not what he meant. He replaced the receiver, thoughts of another serious involvement crowded his mind. Could he successfully juggle it? Would he be up to it this time?

Roger stood up to leave. "I'm going to crash for an hour before I collapse," he said. "I'll be downstairs on the couch in my office."

"Before you go, give me a capsule summary of your findings on security with Herman."

"Oh, yeah." Roger flipped through the report, stopping at a back section. "Total systems reviewed. Negative. Closed-circuit hidden cameras on the peripheral fence checked out perfectly. Emergency power source, ditto. Ultrasonic motion detectors functioning without a flaw. Fingerprint scanner error-free." He paused. "It ought to be. It's our own goddam machine." He closed the report.

"What about the chip detectors?"

"You mean the metal detectors at points of entry and exit?"

Garrett nodded.

"Flawless. Only problem with them is that some of the technical staff is getting irritated at having to empty their pockets before they go home every day. And every time repairmen and cleaning staff go through, they set off the alarm with their keys and tool boxes, so we can only subject them to spot checks."

"Minor irritations, I can live with," Art said. "A major disappearance of our most sensitive integrated circuits is something else. The Russians would stop at nothing to get their hands on some of our chips." He smiled. "Thanks, Roger. Well done. Grab some sleep."

He walked over to his secretary's desk. "Barbara," he said, as Roger dragged himself slowly toward the stairs. She looked up from her typing.

"Get me Frank Martin at McDonnell Douglas."

9

Rehearse, that's what he had to do. Go over and over the points he would make in his testimony to Senator Mitchell's subcommittee until they burned a hole in his mind.

And he had to do it alone. Roger and Freddie had both offered to make their usual flash card system, of course, to pose as devil's advocates and hammer the points home.

But this time, Art felt he needed space. Space away from the office, away from people, where he could be alone with his thoughts, organize them, sort them, sift them, pump himself up with the adrenalin he knew he would need to withstand the pressure from the panel.

He slammed a fist down on the harpsichord's soundbox and heard the dissonant chords erupt. He had to get out, despite the rain. The music wasn't helping; it brought a too-pleasant distraction—memories of Saturday night.

Art walked to the corner closet and began pulling on his rain gear. He jerked the waterproof trousers on over his jeans and fastened the yellow slicker, tugging the hood tightly around his head. Fortunately, he thought, as he looked out the wide double doors at the downpour, there was very little wind. Tuesday's dark clouds had given birth to Wednesday's cold rain, making the night seem more like November than April.

Captain sat curled in front of the small fireplace, paws folded under his yolk-yellow chest, keeping warm, eyes blinking so slowly, incredulous at what his master was about to do.

Latching the doors behind him, Art walked out across the slick deck, its surface glistening in the house lights, a black mirror with a necklace of pearls. He slipped over the

169

railing at the far end, off the deck, onto the path he knew so well, the path to Hunter's Glen, his normal running route. It curved along a rocky ridge barely a mile from the house, and then shot down at a steep angle into the flat valley below. Out and back, four and a half miles.

Water cascaded down his yellow slicker in tiny streams, soaking his hands. He jammed them into his pockets and then shouldered his way through the trees. His feet told him he had reached the ridge. When his toes no longer jammed against the front of his boots, he knew the land had flattened out, so he slowed his gait as he curved to his right, boots slipping and sucking on the wet, rocky path. He stopped to take in the valley, looking out at the panorama below him.

It was magic there in the rain, somehow, alone in the darkness, stretching out his hand as if directing an orchestra of lights in the distance. The town sparkled in the wetness, quiet and serene, not even a dog's howl to mar the peace. Only the persistent patter of rainfall, softly striking the young leaves, sliding off the rocks at his feet, rushing in small waterfalls toward the valley floor in the depths below.

The rain started coming down harder, straight at him, as if some invisible force had twirled the cosmic tap wide open, and a river of water flowed around his feet, making it difficult to secure his footing on the stones.

It was fitting, in a way, that he had to fight against the rain. He had been fighting for the past five years, one way or another, fighting for the survival of his small company, fighting for the success of new products, fighting for himself.

Fighting Japan.

His teeth clenched as he drew himself slowly forward, focusing his mind on the trip he would have to make tomorrow. He began to categorize his arguments, starting first with the arithmetic tax and depreciation numbers Freddie had so thoroughly calculated. The T&D arguments would make a good beginning. They were hard numbers. Definable, defendable, dependable. They were the bricks.

But he needed mortar, and he began to summarize the

background that Sally had given him the previous weekend, trying to think of a mnemonic device, a key, that would enable him to lock these various points in his mind.

He had tossed out a half-dozen words by the time he reached the end of the rocky ridge and could stand, wetter and colder now, even with the treetops of the valley floor. He was growing tired of the sound of his own voice, punctuated only by the relentless, pulsating rain.

And then he had it.

A word that was as much a part of him as his hammer or his harpsichord. A concept that had been his life for the past twenty years.

CHIPS.

Of course. It suddenly became so simple.

C for cultural superiority, the attitude that the Japanese culture, their society, their system was superior to the West.

H for hierarchy, the unique, feudal structure which the Japanese imposed on the world, seeing themselves at the apex of the pyramid and all other countries falling beneath them in importance.

I for insularity. Cut off from the rest of the world in their island economy, insecure, vulnerable, resulting in a doubling of effort and renewed dedication to success.

P for perseverance, that winning-is-everything attitude that enables the Japanese to persist until the final battle is fought and the ultimate war, the economic struggle for control, is won.

S for—what was that word again? Sense—no, *sensei.* That was it. Teacher. Master. Master-apprentice. The inability of the Japanese to tolerate an apprenticeship to the West any longer. Their time had come.

He smiled inwardly as he complimented himself on his cleverness. The hell with five-by-seven cards, he would memorize the T&D numbers before he arrived in Washington the following morning, and use the mnemonic clue to recall the Japanese arguments.

There was another word combination, though, he thought to himself as he struggled slowly back along the ridge to the house, something that completed the conceptual circle, something Sally had mentioned in summarizing the Japanese attitude toward competition. It was a triad of words, he remembered now. A deadly triangle of concepts.

Calculation?

That was it.

Calculation. Domination. Elimination.

The concepts clicked into memory as the industrial examples Sally had cited flashed into his mind: textiles, shipbuilding, motorcycles, automobiles, cameras, consumer electronics. All representative of the same pattern. Repetitive. Thorough. Successful.

And frightening.

The very pattern that was repeating itself in the electronics industry, as well. The 16K was gone, and the Japanese now had control over the 64K market. How long before they had the 256K and controlled that?

And what would happen when they got the optical sensor?

A small pine branch slapped him in the face as he reached out to his left to steady himself. He had reached the path back up the hill, and as he looked down he could see a torrent of water pouring over his boots. The pressure would be on his heels as he headed up. He checked to make sure the cleats were free. Little good they would do, he thought. He would have to pull himself up through the trees in this mess.

His left hand slipped off the branch of a pear tree, tearing skin from the palm. He felt the rainwater sting the raw, exposed flesh, and cursed himself for trying to move too fast.

One. Step. At a time, he told himself, securing his position more firmly.

With each upward step, he reinforced his arguments.

The numbers.

The mnemonic device.

The deadly triangle: Calculation, Domination, Elimination.

Until he could focus so fully on his memory lesson that he shut the rain out of his mind. Until, at last, the crisp outline of his redwood deck reappeared and he pulled himself up, saturated with water, and disappeared inside to stand for what seemed like another night warming himself in front of the welcome fire.

And Captain never even lifted his head.

10

"What do you mean, a travesty?" Sally asked, refilling his coffee cup. She folded her napkin and set it on the table.

Art massaged his moustache with thumb and forefinger, staring intently at the trails of steam rising from his cup.

He looked up at her. "I mean, that subcommittee had about as much interest in considering new tax and depreciation ideas as I have in selling my company to the Japanese. Their concept of industrial policy is nothing more than outdated protectionism—they are more interested in bashing the Japanese than they are in learning from them."

His face was drawn and tired. He wore an adhesive patch, flesh-colored, on his left palm, where he had scraped it the night before. His eyes were hungry, hungry for sleep.

"He kept attacking me like I was a foreign spy, some beady-eyed Eastern European with a plan to balkanize the United States."

"Who?"

"That goddam Hobson Mitchell. He's an absolute egomaniac, him and his egghead lieutenant, LaCoste."

Art stopped and took a sip of hot coffee. It felt good, the warmth, the smoothness.

"Sounds like you might have provoked them," Sally said. She propped her elbows on the table, cupping her hands underneath her chin.

"Provoked them?" he said. He shot her an angry glance. "Bullshit. When I rattled off the T&D numbers, they countered by throwing their hands in the air and accusing me, and the Industry Association, of robbing the government of precious tax revenues."

She was silent, listening. She sipped her coffee, watching him over the rim of her cup.

He rubbed his eyes. "And when I summarized your cultural arguments concerning the Japanese, they were incredulous. 'Our staunchest allies in the Pacific,' they said. 'How can you possibly suggest that our Asian friends are motivated by a strategy of industrial domination when they have to trade as an island country to survive?' they asked." He waved his arms, mocking them. "They laughed."

"They laughed?" Sally asked. She frowned now, and set her cup down.

Art nodded. His voice was hoarse. "When I suggested that a strong American electronics industry was necessary to our own survival, Mitchell launched into his famous tirade about the United States being an unchallenged economic giant, the strongest military power in the world." He drained his coffee cup.

"More?" she asked.

He scowled, shaking his head.

"It still sounds like you may have antagonized them somehow," Sally said, leaning forward now. She picked at a mound of blue wax that had formed at the base of one of the navy candles.

He looked across the table at her. It was his turn to frown now. "How?" he asked. "I don't understand. I organize, practically memorize my testimony, and present them with a measured array of facts and numbers designed to support our case. Rational, dispassionate, objective." He paused, waiting for a response. There was none. He shrugged his shoulders, focused on the flame of one of the flickering candles. "I simply don't understand it."

In a quiet voice, Sally said, "My experience with politicians and government officials, who are usually blatant egotists, as you have accurately observed, is that you have to feed those egos. Make them feel that your ideas are their ideas. That *they* thought of these ideas, not you."

Art shook his head again, clenching and unclenching his fists, still feeling the pain in his left palm when he squeezed it. "That's a bit oversimplified, isn't it? I mean, these guys are supposed to be intelligent, hardworking, highly paid officials, and they acted like representatives of the John Birch Society today." He stared at the mound of melted wax she was playing with and suddenly saw his ideas, the hopes for his company, his industry, dead and dying under a pile of regulations and red tape.

Sally sighed. "All I'm saying, Art, is that in that kind of situation you should have been more cautious, more sensitive. Suggesting, rather than enumerating. Hinting, rather than memorizing. And proposing, in an indirect and casual manner, rather than overwhelming them with the brilliance of your mind." She raised a hand, palm upward. "You knew in advance from your telephone conversation with LaCoste that the Senator wasn't exactly going to welcome you with open arms. And yet you never asked me my thoughts about these people as people, only about ideas to stick in your arsenal of combative weapons. If I had known—"

He laughed a scornful laugh, interrupting her. "If you're so damn experienced with our legislators, why didn't you suggest going down to Washington instead of me?"

He pushed his chair back angrily from the table and stalked out of the dining room.

"Art?"

Sally blew out the candles and followed behind him.

"Hey," she said, grabbing his elbow. "I'm on your side, remember?"

"I'm sorry, Sally," he said, slumping into a nearby chair. "It's been a long week."

She sat opposite him, drawing her legs up under her chin and tucking her denim skirt under her feet. She rested her chin atop her knees.

"Did you tell them about your Sputnik theory?" She watched his crystal blue eyes, felt the desperation, saw the strain.

He nodded, unsmiling, his gaze fixed on some distant object across the room. "Mitchell said he hadn't heard such nonsense since he'd come to Washington. Asked who I thought I was, telling the U.S. government to consider a

National Industrial Policy to put our priorities in order."
He stretched his long legs out in front of him, crossing his
feet at the ankle and jamming his hands into his pockets.
He felt like a benched athlete, a basketball player who had
fouled out and lost interest in the game.

"Well, at least you made your point. Sometimes that's
all you can do. 'Play to win, be willing to lose.' That's what
you told me last week. You did the best you could." She
tilted her head at him but he couldn't, or wouldn't, meet
her glance.

Art simply nodded, staring ahead, as if in a trance. "The
funny thing is," he said philosophically now, half to himself, half to Sally, "my emphasis has always been on the
first half of that equation." He looked up at her.

She smiled. "Why don't I read you some poems?" she
asked softly.

"Poems?" he said, frowning. He shook his head. "I spend
the whole day trying to convince a collection of political
meatballs that our industrial policies are all wrong, and
you just want to read me a bunch of poems?" He stared at
her with a look of disbelief. "You must be kidding."

"I am most certainly not kidding," she said, irritated
now. "Your problem is that you grab onto something with
such tenacity you won't let go. Like a little terrier with a
rubber ball." Her eyes narrowed.

"And you think you can solve problems simply by
leaping into bed and reading metaphysical poetry as a distraction," he countered, his voice rising. "But that's all it
is—a distraction. The problems are still there."

"Please, not so loud," she said. "You'll wake Jason."

He was silent now, depressed by the turn of events in
Washington, still worried about his contract with McDonnell Douglas, concerned about Hitachi.

"Sally, I don't think you realize the seriousness of these
developments," he said, shaking his head. "And I don't
know what I can do to convince you."

He stood up, walked over to his briefcase and began
stuffing papers back inside it.

"That's the difference between us," she said to his back.
"You look at problems as things to be solved. But I know

they're always going to be there, in one form or another, and sometimes you need distractions from them to clear your mind."

He smiled, turning to face her. "I guess if you build up enough distractions you don't have to worry about problems any more, do you?" he asked. "Like husbands, for example."

She did not smile back. "That's enough," she said. "You're on very shaky ground, my friend, when you start throwing personal relationships into the fray." She stood and walked to the front door.

Opening it, she said, "You're so wrapped up in your own problems, Art, you haven't once asked me about *my* week, about *my* problems, what's happened in *my* life." She folded her arms across her chest, watching him stuff his briefcase. "You might be surprised how your relationships with people could improve if you didn't spend twenty-four hours a day on those damn chips."

"You mean, with women?" he asked quietly.

"And with people who don't share your own outlook on life." She looked down at her feet.

He stopped packing, left his briefcase open, and walked over to where she was standing. Reaching around her, he closed the door with a quiet click, mindful now of her sleeping son.

She raised her head. He looked down at her for a long, thoughtful minute. Then he kissed the top of her smooth, auburn hair, untying the ribbon that held it back.

"Read me a poem?" he asked.

11

"Fourteen-thirteen," Roger said, bouncing the black rubber ball and preparing to serve. He squeezed his racquet a bit tighter as he realized he had a good chance to win.

Art waited in the backhand court, twirling his racquet in his right hand, shifting his weight from foot to foot, trying to concentrate on the game, trying to recapture a lost week.

It was barely seven in the morning. They had been on the court less than a half hour, and already their shirts were soaked with sweat.

Harris glanced back at his opponent, wiped a wet wristband across his dripping forehead, bounced the ball again, and hammered a shot against the front wall that screamed directly back at Garrett.

Art sprang to his left, slicing downward with his racquet as his shoes squeaked across the wooden floor, propelling the ball forward with underspin. When it hit the forward wall, it bounced back hard and low. Roger fired it into the opposite corner.

Garrett spun quickly to his right, too late to catch the ball on its rearward path. He played it off the back wall. Harris anticipated the defensive shot and moved in to drop a soft floater into the front corner.

Art tore toward the front wall and dove for the ball. His body slid forward across the floor. The ball bounced just over his outstretched arm. Roger's game.

Pulling himself into a sitting position, Art flung his racquet against the side wall in disgust and desperation. Suddenly there was silence.

179

"Hey, fella," Harris said, breathing heavily. "It's just the first game." He mopped sweat from his dark eyebrows.

Art's face was red, half with the heat of battle, half with anger.

"Shit," he said, rising to his feet. "It's not just the game. It's everything."

Roger walked over and retrieved Art's racquet. He handed it to him without comment. He didn't know what to say.

Art moved wearily back to the receiver's box. Then he turned to face his partner.

"Don't you have that sinking feeling?" he asked. "Is there *one* thing that's going right for us?"

PART III

WATER

1

Rainclouds, bursting with moisture, hung low and heavy in the sky. The temperature was cool, the wind still, as Sakamoto Ryuji stepped off the bus near the port zone in Yokohama.

He had decided to walk the final distance to the docks, a sentimental journey carrying him circuitously through Sakuragicho, down along the central wharf and out onto Osambashi, where the small freighter waited to take him to America.

Sakamoto wore the crumpled, dirty trousers Fukuda had given him earlier in the week. He had not shaved for three days, and his long black hair was uncombed. He had removed his glasses and wore contact lenses instead. He blinked repeatedly in discomfort. A soiled T-shirt covered his upper torso; once white, it was now as gray as the sky overhead. His feet stuck out of a pair of short leather sandals which scuffed on the pavement as he walked.

He clutched his knapsack that contained his few personal articles—a change of shirt, a razor, a thin volume of English lessons. He touched his *haramaki* with a practiced gesture he would repeat often. The microimagizer, his identity cards, and the cash were all there, securely tucked inside the folds of his stomach band.

Suddenly, Sakamoto stopped. There it was, he thought, looking up and beyond the city. The Bluff. Symbol of foreign enclaves, foreign protection, foreign prestige. Extraterritoriality. *Kannai,* inside the barrier. Off limits to all Japanese, just a century ago, after Commodore Perry, backed by his powerful gunboats, forced the Shogun to accept unequal treaties with the foreigners.

He boiled with anger, and took a deep breath. He, his company, his country, were fighting the foreigners again now. But this time the battle was with exports, not with bullets.

His confidence rose, his chest swelling with eagerness, as he thought again of the job before him. He could not let Matsuzaka down! Matsuzaka would win this war with the foreigners. Japan would survive!

Sakamoto pushed on. He could no longer hear his leather sandals slap against the pier. Longshoremen shouted and whistled as products from the entire country funnelled onto the wharf. Neatly stacked cartons containing cameras and stereos, TV sets and tape recorders, sat dockside on wooden carts, or in giant sisal nets, being on-loaded into waiting vessels.

Sony. Mitsubishi. Matsuzaka. Panasonic. Sanyo.

His heart pounded with pride as he saw the countless crates of Matsuzaka products lining the long, concrete pier. There it was, the soft green pine tree, symbol of the company's impeccable quality. Symbol of unparalleled craftsmanship. Symbol of tradition.

Farther down the dock, Sakamoto could see endless lines of familiar Japanese automobiles snaking slowly into their floating berths, giant caterpillars of rolling steel. *Datsun. Toyota. Honda. Mazda.*

He stepped aside as a Kubota bulldozer soared above, suspended and silent in its overhead crane. The words of Kamakura plant manager Sumiyoshi rang in his ears as he watched.

Japan doesn't simply supply manufactured products. Japan creates dreams for the world.

Sakamoto searched for the tiny Vietnamese boat in the orchestrated chaos of Yokohama's busiest dock. *Taiheiyo-maru* was its name. Vessel of the Pacific. He wondered if he would ever find it among the huge freighters and tankers anchored snugly nearby. *Toyota-maru,* the car carrier. *Nisseki-maru,* an oil tanker. *Nippon-maru,* Sony's container ship.

Maru. Round, or complete. He smiled as he thought about the cleverness of his people in affixing these names to their ships. The suffix *-maru* gave the vessels a psychological advantage in helping them complete their voyages, make their round trips safely, ward off events or incidents that might create trouble on the choppy waters of the world's biggest oceans. *Maru.* Circle. Out and back. Safety.

Sakamoto Ryuji kept looking, squinting, trying to make out the names of the countless ships moored dockside. He passed by another shipload of Matsuzaka products being on-loaded for overseas markets. He stopped and bowed instinctively to the stack of cartons.

A voice suddenly cried out. "Sakamoto-san?" Uncertain, hesitating. Then more definite, louder. "Sakamoto-san!"

He spun around and frowned, looking hurriedly right and left.

"Domo, domo! Hisashiburi ne! Long time no see!"

"Takahashi-san!" he hissed, taking the man by the elbow and pulling him behind a Matsuzaka carton. They stood just beneath one of the solitary pines.

Sakamoto glared at his former colleague. *"Nan de!* What are you doing portside?" he asked, looking nervously again in both directions. The last thing he wanted was to be recognized.

"Me?" Takahashi said, laughing. "I work here! What are *you* doing here, especially dressed like a tramp?"

He fingered Sakamoto's soiled shirt, turning up his nose.

Sakamoto glanced down at his old clothes, felt the short stubble on his chin. Then he looked up. "I'm just . . . taking a leisurely Saturday morning walk, that's all," he said uncertainly. His eyes blinked in rapid succession and he tugged at his dirty trousers.

Takahashi shook his head. "On Yokohama's busiest pier? On a Saturday morning, when you should be in the office?" He stood back a step, eyeing Sakamoto closely.

Sakamoto tucked his knapsack under his left arm. He had to change the subject quickly. "What do you mean, you are working here?" he asked. "Last time I saw you, we were both in the Administrative Department. You were in charge of raw materials."

"Once we completed the Osaka assignment and I returned to Tokyo, they sent me on a short fill-in to Yokohama. Export supervision. Bottlenecks at the port, you know? Our exports were growing furiously." He still eyed his former colleague cautiously.

"How long now?" Sakamoto asked.

"Nearly nine months."

"But you live in Omiya! That's an hour north of Tokyo, over two hours from here!"

Takahashi shrugged his shoulders. "I'm a *kacho* now, Sakamoto-san, same as you. I am honored that my company has recognized even my limited abilities. Time is nothing when measured against our loyalty to Matsuzaka."

Sakamoto leaned against the tall stack of Matsuzaka crates. He popped the knuckles of his right hand.

"Congratulations," he said. "They must be very pleased with your work."

"My work counts for nothing without those who work with me. You know that." Takahashi folded his arms across his chest. His eyes narrowed. "But you look like a bum! That's an insult to your company." His voice was barely audible above the squeaks and groans of the heavy cranes moving overhead.

Sakamoto rubbed his chin, his eyes blinking. *Chikusho,* he thought. He had to get away.

"Maa," he said, tucking his dirty shirt deeper into his pants. "Informal style, Takahashi-san. I was granted a short holiday." He clutched his knapsack.

Takahashi looked at him, frowning.

"Leisure wear!" Sakamoto said, shrugging his shoulders and edging back toward the concrete walkway. He cocked his right arm and threw Takahashi a crisp wave. "See you," he said, and spun around into the throng.

As he exited from behind the packed cartons, he tripped over one of the large, python-like ropes securing a vessel to its berth. He stumbled into a stevedore, causing him to lose his grip on a guy-wire.

The mesh net full of Matsuzaka cartons sagged sharply.

Instead of clearing the hull of its intended carrier, it smacked into the side of the giant vessel with a crack.

Loudspeakers cracked. "What's going on down there?" Other workers came to the longshoreman's aid, shouting and cursing. The dockworker glared at Sakamoto. He spit on the kacho's pants and kicked at his shins.

"Gaijin!" he yelled. "Damn foreigner!"

Sakamoto picked himself up quickly as he saw Takahashi sprinting around the pillar of cartons. He limped away from the scene, skipping through the growing crowd, one hand clutching his knapsack, the other massaging his painful leg.

He stumbled again, this time into a packed crowd of other *gaijin.* Suddenly, he blended in. Then he saw the small boat. It reminded him of the ferry he used to take as a boy, from Shikoku to Hiroshima. Simple hull construction, berths underneath cut from a plain and uncluttered deck above. But the ferryboat had plied the calm waters of the Inland Sea. The *Taiheiyo-maru* would have to cross the wide ocean.

Sakamoto swallowed hard, tasting salt in his saliva. He shuffled slowly along with the group, imitating their silent, confused behavior. He said nothing, spoke to no one, looked only at his feet.

He looked up as a man dressed in a tattered captain's uniform appeared on deck. He leaned over the side of the tiny ship and began to issue instructions, in Vietnamese, to the crowd through a hand-held bullhorn, reading from what Sakamoto saw was a prepared script.

He swallowed again. He understood nothing, and feared he might be discovered as a stowaway. His stomach churned as he realized he would have to survive for a week on this small boat.

Behind him, a band of picketers waved and shouted, carrying large placards streaked with black *kanji.* They had their own bullhorns and exhorted the dockworkers not to service the Vietnamese ship.

"Boat People, Go Home," the signs said. "Back to Vietnam." "Japan for the Japanese."

Sakamoto read the *kanji* and cringed. The irony of his predicament struck him like a blow in the stomach.

An elderly Vietnamese man, standing next to him, addressed him with those unfamiliar words. Sakamoto looked down at the old man. Sweat and decay encrusted his clothes, like mildew. He simply shrugged his shoulders and nodded. He shuffled ahead.

He caught sight of a young Vietnamese girl as they were halfway up the gangplank. She looked across at him, feeling his eyes. He met her glance, his expression unchanged. When he did not look away, she did. Her eyes were as dark as the clouds above.

He could see the ship's captain more clearly now, and he could tell the man was not Vietnamese. *Gaijin,* he thought. Portuguese, perhaps, or Greek. Sakamoto watched him as he shuffled along the deck, wondering what kind of non-person would take charge of a boat like this.

He descended the steel steps into one of the cavernous freight holds below, which had been refitted with double-deck bunks, dormitory style. The sexes were not segregated. Family grouped with family, husbands with wives, brothers with sisters. He threw his gear down onto a lower bunk.

Suddenly he buried his mouth in his shoulder as the stale stench of defecation and vomit hit him. Tiny, make-shift windows, fist-sized, like a row of horizontal bubbles, had been punched into one outside wall to let in air. Sakamoto could see now the freighter was unfit for carrying people.

Part of the problem, he saw as he glanced around, was that there were only two toilets below. He guessed instantly that he would have to cut his intake of food. He cleared his mind. His zen training would fill the void, give him discipline, an internal gyroscope of control.

As the hapless refugees streamed into the passenger quarters, dazed and silent, Sakamoto noticed that only the outside of the ship had been repainted. Everything below deck was untouched. Rust clung to pipes like mould on old bread. Paint peeled from walls and doors. Spiderwebs arched upward from naked lightbulbs in thin, ghostly streaks.

Sakamoto shuddered. His resolve hardened further. He would survive. More than his zen training, his loyalty to Matsuzaka would see him through. He lay back on his hard, flat bunk and closed his eyes. The rotten stench pierced his lungs like poison gas.

He clinched his fists. He had a job to do.

For his Bucho. For his company. For his *country*.

2

"Cho nay da co ai ngoi chua?"

He heard the words, but he had no idea what they meant. Sakamoto froze, kept his eyes shut, pretended to sleep.

"Cho nay da co ai ngoi chua?" the voice persisted.

Sakamoto blinked once, twice, then opened his eyes. It was the young Vietnamese girl he had seen on the gangplank earlier. She was standing by the bunk next to his.

He turned slowly and glanced up at her. She wore a traditional silk *ao-dai,* a light blue dress, slit up both sides to the waist, over a pair of sleek white trousers. The sheer fabric was cut and torn, no longer the crisp, clean symbol of Vietnamese culture.

Her hair hung straight down her back, nearly to her waist, black and shiny and smooth as the silk of her *ao-dai.* Her face was bright and eager, like a child's. Her dark eyes reflected hope.

Sakamoto opened, then closed his mouth. "I . . . I think we should talk English," he stammered, groping for an escape. "We going to United States, need much practice." He smiled as he felt his palms moisten.

The girl eyed him cautiously. "I say, you don't mind, I take this place?" She gestured to the stained mattress on the neighboring bed. As she reached out with her left arm, the light blue top stretched across her small, firm breasts. Her nipples stood out like tiny buttons.

Sakamoto eyed her warily. How could this lovely girl possibly be threatening, he wondered? "No mind, no mind," he said, smiling more broadly now. He stood up to help her with her things.

190

"You Hanoi?" she asked as he lifted a large bundle, wrapped in newspaper and tied with hemp, onto her bed.

"Saigon," he grunted.

"Saigon?" she said, raising her eyebrows.

Sakamoto froze. Had Fukuda been wrong? Was this ship carrying only people from the north?

"You so short," she said. "Saigon people much taller." She raised her right hand over his head.

He smiled more easily now, rubbing the wiry stubble on his chin. He could not take his eyes off her firm, upturned breasts, felt his penis quicken in his crotch. He blinked the distraction away.

"Born in Hanoi, move to Saigon," he said. "After Amis leave." He used the military slang for Americans.

She nodded.

"You?" he asked.

"Cam Ranh," she said. "Port."

"Yes. Big base."

"Yes."

"Now? Still base?"

She brought her hands together, holding the palms just a few inches apart. "Not so big. No need."

"English very good," he said, moving back to his own bunk. "Where did you learn?"

She blushed. "Not good. Many years, no practice." She sat down on her bunk. "Americans have school in Cam Ranh. I study there."

Sakamoto stooped down to put his things under his bed. He tapped his *haramaki*. The key items were still in place. Satisfied, he sat down.

"You?" she asked now. "Also school?"

"No school," he said. He hesitated. "Studied in army to question enemy soldiers. Then no war, no job." He shrugged his shoulders.

"Tran," she said, thrusting a hand forward. "Tran Van Minh."

Sakamoto licked his lips, then swallowed. He stuck out his own hand. "Le," he said. "Le Duc Pho." They shook briefly.

The loudspeaker crackled, and they jumped. An announcement blared, the voice stark and gritty.

"Finally," she said, reaching out again with her hand. "We leave. Want to go up?"

He took her hand and they clanged back up the steel staircase to the main deck. Most of the refugees had gathered to watch the departure.

Sakamoto could make out the stacks of Matsuzaka products in the distance as the longshoremen untied the thick ropes holding the small ship to shore. Japanese customs and immigration officials signed the final documents that freed the vessel for its voyage. A small crowd of Japanese bureaucrats, dressed identically in charcoal gray, stood solemnly by to watch the departure.

One of them spoke into a small microphone. Sakamoto listened as he described the efforts of the Japanese government on behalf of the Vietnamese refugees. Refurbishing the ship. Preparing it for voyage. Renaming it the *Taiheiyo-maru.* Sakamoto smiled. He knew his government would never allow the refugees to stay in Japan. They were the wrong race.

He watched as reporters and photographers from the major Japanese press, the *Mainichi, Asahi, Yomiuri,* milled about, interviewing government officials and recording the event on film. The Foreign Ministry had not missed a trick, he thought. Tonight when the Japanese public sees the news commentary, they will be impressed with the efforts of their government to assist the homeless Vietnamese. He knew they would have no idea about the hell below deck.

Slowly, the tiny freighter eased from its berth, towed silently by a small tugboat that would pull it out into Tokyo Bay. Sakamoto felt the steel plates begin to vibrate beneath his feet as the diesel engines below rumbled alive. In the distance, he could see his friend Takahashi, busy with another load of Matsuzaka cartons. He suddenly wished they could exchange places.

Tran moved across to the opposite railing. Sakamoto stood alone and watched the giant ships of Yokohama become smaller and smaller, toy boats in the distance. The air was cool and fresh and void of the squalor below. He breathed deeply, reminding himself of the discipline he would need to get through the next week. It would be a long passage.

The dark April clouds began to part as the ship moved farther out. A few scattered drops of rain fell, splattering the bright blue, freshly painted deck. People milled about, chattering away in Vietnamese, watching the shoreline.

Sakamoto walked over to the far railing, catching sight of Tran as he pulled out the small book of English lessons from his *haramaki.* He knew his English was good. Very good, in fact. But the language book would give him protection.

He thought about the girl as he mechanically flipped through the pages. The wind whipped his hair as the ship rounded the last of the piers and began, under its own steam now, to head toward the mouth of the bay and beyond, to the great Pacific.

Closing the book and tucking it under his arm, he watched as the Bluff slowly disappeared from view. The ship's engines drummed in his ear as the crowd began to dissipate below deck.

His jaw tightened in his resolution to succeed.

Tran caught his eye and smiled. He smiled back, then moved slowly toward the hatch that would take him below. He realized he would have to keep his resolve firm, resisting every temptation. His eyes lingered on Tran's graceful form as he lowered himself into the hold.

He felt very much alone.

3

Taiheiyo. The Pacific. Ocean of Great Peace.

Five days out, so far so good, Sakamoto thought. His ploy with English had worked. He greeted Tran each morning as he arose, and in the evening when he went to bed, using basic English expressions and simply shrugging when she tried to get him to speak Vietnamese.

Slowly the word spread that Le Duc Pho was so intent on practicing his English that he refused to speak his native tongue. Some applauded his efforts. Many were cautious, doubtful, perhaps a little jealous. Most simply ignored him, since he made no attempt to be gregarious, and that suited him just fine.

On the afternoon of the sixth day, he stood topside, English book in hand, watching the ocean. It shone in the late sunlight like a giant mirror. Seagulls swarmed behind the boat in great crowds like giant flies, diving at the white wake to pick scraps of garbage tossed out the back.

Sakamoto sat down on the steel plates, temporarily distracted by hunger. He had lost several pounds in the past six days because of the meager provisions on board— mostly rice and sour vegetables mixed with a sweet Vietnamese soy paste. He had rejected the small quantities of fish and meat. Boiled rice was at least safe. Less protein, but lower risk of contamination.

The old and the sick, for the most part, had remained below, like diseased outcasts. Their families cared for them, brought them food, fed them water at regular intervals. Dysentery was their invisible enemy.

Sakamoto was determined not to spend another night in the stench and misery below. He slipped quietly down the

194

stairs, pulled his blanket off his bunk and took his knapsack as a pillow. His clothes, unchanged for nearly a week, smelled of dankness and decay. Seawater showers and unscented soap provided basic protection but little else.

Holding his breath against the putrid odors, Sakamoto bounded back up the narrow stairs and searched out a remote spot on the steel deck. Opposite one of the square hatches used for transferring cargo from hold to dock, he spread out his blanket and jammed his knapsack under his head.

As he lay back with his English book, he watched the sun, giant on the horizon, like the red ball in his national flag, the *Hi-no-Maru*. Slowly it sank out of sight. He pulled the blanket around his legs against the chill. His eyes drooped. Vibrations from the engine were so soothing . . .

"Duc Pho."

The soft voice whispered into his ear.

"Duc Pho!"

It was louder now. He was sure he wasn't dreaming. His eyes blinked open. Stars began to appear, floating on that undulating sea of black paste.

He glanced to his right and there, kneeling beside him was Tran, her blue and white *ao-dai* shimmering in the dull light.

"I no sleep either," she said. "Can we talk English?"

Sakamoto rubbed his temples, blinking rapidly to lubricate his lenses. "Of course," he said. He pulled himself erect and spread the blanket so Tran could sit next to him.

"What job you do after reach California?" she asked. Her soft, black hair trailed lazily behind her in the gentle breeze. The moist salt air glistened on her forehead. Her clear eyes disappeared in the darkness.

Sakamoto shrugged his shoulders. "No idea," he lied. "Try best, no skills, maybe work wine valleys."

She moved closer to him, shivering with a sudden chill.

He leaned back against the steel hatch. "You?" he asked.

She smiled. "San Francisco," she said. "All my life, dreaming of San Francisco. Some job, any job, no matter. Learn better English, teach Vietnamese."

He popped a knuckle. "American government give good help," he said.

"Yes. America land of dreams, no?"

No, he thought. "Yes," he said.

She placed her hand on his. Leaning over to him, she whispered something, in Vietnamese, into his ear.

He swallowed. His pulse quickened. He could not respond. He saw his disguise rapidly unraveling.

"English best," he said, his voice lower.

Tran reached over with her other hand and moved slowly, smoothly, along his upper thigh, as she whispered again into his ear.

He felt droplets of sweat forming on his forehead. His heart was hammering through his shirt as his penis pulsated against his pants leg.

When he saw her open her mouth again, he moved quickly, instantly, to close it with his. She pressed her body against his, taking his hand and pushing it against her breast. Her tongue leapt out and feathered his lips with a touch as light as rain.

Her hand crept upward until it found his hardening penis, her strokes circular, gentle, speaking a silent language.

Sakamoto's thumb and forefinger massaged Tran's erect nipple, twisting and turning it beneath the soft silk of her thin blouse. She pressed herself more tightly toward him, brushing her thighs agaist his, sighing softly, her voice a quiet, moaning purr.

Reaching down, she unbuttoned his fly and began to coax his hardness with her tongue.

Sakamoto leaned back, his head against the hatch lid, his knapsack crunched underneath his shoulders. His eyes were shut, his body weightless, suspended in time and space.

"Subarashii'n da," he moaned. "Incredible."

Tran lifted up at the sound of the strange language. Thinking the creaks and vibrations of the ship had caused the distraction, she returned her mouth to his miniature cannon, purple and pulsating in the darkness.

"Ahh!" Sakamoto shouted, his hand digging deeper between her thighs. *"Motto, motto,"* he cried. "More!"

Tran raised her head now. It was not the sounds of the ship. She had not been mistaken.

She frowned. "What?"

"Subarashii," Sakamoto said, coasting in a cosmic swing. Reason was temporarily overcome by desire, short-circuiting a basic Zen tenet.

Tran pushed back. "You not Vietnamese," she said, her face turning scornful.

Sakamoto's eyes flicked open as realized he had slipped into his native Japanese. He swallowed. His palms began to sweat again, and the wind froze droplets of perspiration on his forehead. They felt like tiny icicles.

As she backed farther away, mumbling to herself in Vietnamese, something told him he was no longer safe, something punctuated by the look of fear in her face.

Tran jumped and began to run. Sakamoto sprang after her, surprised at her nimbleness in the dark. She dodged a winch, grabbed a small pipe, turned and threw it at her pursuer.

Sakamoto saw the dark form hurtling toward him in the dim light, ducked and heard it thunk against the hatch cover. Blood rushed to his head, bringing him fully awake.

"Yoshi," he muttered under his breath, pulling himself into a *ninja* crouch as instinctive to him as his own language.

Tran headed, right, he bounded left. Spinning, he caught her left foot with a diving flick of his right hand. She tripped and rolled against the far railing.

He did a side somersault, rolled to his feet and sprang toward her with a quick push. He pinned her left wrist to the deck with his foot.

"Zannen da," he whispered to her in the darkness. "Too bad. My job is far too important to risk to fate, despite your beauty and your talents." He watched as her long, black hair whipped around her face in the wind.

She scrunched back against the railing, a cornered animal, but his foot pinched her wrist, cutting off all circulation. She screamed in pain.

His right hand came down quickly and slapped her hard across the face.

"I not tell," she whimpered, her eyes black pools of fear.

"Of course not," Sakamoto said. Keeping her wrist pinned to the deck, he kneeled down and grasped her narrow throat with the iron fingers of his right hand.

Thumb against Adam's apple, middle finger pressed against the thick, pulsating vein in the side of her neck, he squeezed.

Tran breathed in, but she never breathed out again. Her body convulsed in several upward jerks that almost pulled Sakamoto off his feet. When her body lay limp, he released his grip.

He quickly swept her up off the deck and held her light body out over the water, the wind weaving her black hair and white silk in a ghostly pattern.

Instantly she was gone, swallowed up by the black sea, disappearing into the foam that spun and churned under the boat as it cut through the deep water.

The stars overhead sparkled and winked. We know, we saw, they said. Your secret is safe with us.

Sakamoto returned to his blanket and knapsack, checked to make sure there were no further signs of her presence. Tran's hair clip had fallen out. He reached down and picked it up. It reflected the brightness of the stars, brown and bone-smooth and soft to the touch. He flicked it over the side.

Refolding his blanket and punching the knapsack to make it more comfortable, he lay back on the deck. Before he could find the North Star, exhaustion overcame him like a powerful drug and took him down, deep, to the storage locker of sleep.

4

He had done the right thing, of course. The captain was a stupid *gaijin*. How would he be smart enough to solve a murder? They would simply chalk it off as a person overboard.

Plus, Sakamoto reasoned, the captain wasn't even Vietnamese. Hadn't he *read* the announcements to the refugees each time? No doubt he was merely in it for the money, running a ferryboat across the largest river in the world. Dollars for bodies. Cash. In advance. Which meant stay away from trouble.

The iron steps creaked as Sakamoto made his way back down to the sleeping quarters, shortly before dawn. He heard the moans and the snores and the whines of sickness. No one would have noticed his absence, he thought, and no one did.

He tossed his blanket back on his bunk and clenched a fist. He would survive. He had a job to do.

He returned topside and leaning over the starboard rail, he heard a small group of young Vietnamese rush to the front of the ship, shouting, waving their arms, crying, kneeling, as if before a new god.

Sakamoto walked hurriedly in their direction, searching the horizon for a hint, any hint, of land. He saw nothing.

He blinked, his contact lenses like sandpaper on his eyes.

And then he saw it. Not land, but vertical rises. Two of them. Stanchions. A bridge.

The Golden Gate.

He smiled. They were getting nearer. They would be

docking soon. Which meant he could shortly begin his assignment for Fukuda.

For Matsuzaka.

For Japan.

Behind him, another commotion. Confusion, this time, more shouting. He spun around.

The captain and one of his mates had begun to undo the rigging on a lifeboat, ripping the canvas cover aside, fitting the oars into their couplings. A refugee flung himself at the captain, trying to push him away from the smaller boat. The captain kicked him aside, stepped back and pulled out a gun. He fired twice, into the air. The crowd was silenced. They understood authority.

Sakamoto watched as one of the lifeboats was lowered into the water and a string of Vietnamese filed slowly down the rope ladder. The ship would not be docking! They would have to row the rest of the way. He quickly returned below to get his things.

He stood with the second group, waiting and watching. The captain's face was expressionless as he stood above them, his gun still drawn. Sakamoto suspected he had negotiated a greater cash payment for dumping the refugees offshore instead of taking them in under an official registry.

Such were the motivations of westerners, Sakamoto thought. Greed. *Individual* enrichment. How petty! How inferior to our system of harmonious, collective goals!

The early morning sun bounced off the blue water, forcing Sakamoto to squint as he shuffled his way toward the edge of the ship. When he had safely lowered himself into the lifeboat, he tucked his knapsack under his seat, joining another refugee at the oars.

Hours later, when his muscles seemed stretched and torn and he could row no more, he saw they sat almost directly beneath the Golden Gate.

How many times had he flown over it on his way to America? How often had he seen it from above, its reddish-brown spires thrusting powerfully through the white clouds of fog? He looked up and saw the broad expanse of ironwork arching above their heads.

Their small boat caught in the current and swept swiftly forward into the bay, like a leaf on a spring stream. Sakamoto leaned against the side in relief. As they drifted past Alcatraz, a Coast Guard cutter intercepted them, its clean lines contrasting sharply with the chipped, leaking lifeboat.

The cutter hoisted a pair of refugees aboard. There was much shouting and waving as they tried to make themselves understood.

Then they were in tow, attached to the larger ship. Sakamoto collapsed against the wooden slats of the lifeboat, exhausted, and tossed the oar over the side. He could see the city as they churned silently through the Bay. The bright billows of fog toyed with the tall buildings, making them appear and then disappear from view. He knew none of the names of those famous buildings, but he didn't care. What counted was that he was getting closer to Silicon Valley.

"All my life, dreaming of San Francisco . . ."

Tran's words echoed faintly in his ears. It would be a long dream, he thought.

The next several hours were a confused blur.

The cutter docked at the Immigration and Naturalization wharf in Oakland. The refugees were guided into a holding area until transportation to a resettlement camp could be arranged. Food was hastily brought in. The Vietnamese consulate in San Francisco supplied interpreter and refugee identification services. The State Department was notified. Somebody called the press.

Sakamoto realized, as he munched quietly on a ham sandwich, that they were not in the resettlement area where they were supposed to be dropped. He reasoned that he might have a better chance of leaving before they were escorted to the camp under close guard.

He saw his chance.

"Bathroom?"

A young ensign in a beige uniform threw an angry thumb over his shoulder.

Sakamoto shuffled slowly across the gray room. Babies cried, children whined, adults slumped in tired pools of flesh on the dusty linoleum floor. An interpreter went from person to person with an immigration official who scribbled their names on a large clipboard.

Entering the restroom, he glanced under each toilet stall to make sure he was alone. Moving swiftly, he pulled a clean shirt from his knapsack and combed his stringy hair. Wetting his beard with hot water from the tap, he painfully hacked the whiskers from his face as best he could. He splashed clean water onto his face, flipped out the contact lenses and replaced them with his thick glasses.

He tossed the old shirt into a trash can, shouldering his knapsack. He cracked the door open, and watched. A pair of Coast Guard officers stood stiffly near the exit, mumbling to each other out of the corners of their mouths.

"Goddam gooks," said one.

"Oughta just send 'em right back," said the other.

Their looks told him they would rather be elsewhere. He walked purposefully back across the room, past the two guards, through the double glass doors. He was right. No one cared. He never looked back.

Outside, he kept walking. His tired legs carried him down a side street, away from the water, until he came to a broad avenue thick with traffic.

He hailed a cab.

"Bus station," he said with authority, climbing into the back. He slumped low against the seat, his knapsack tucked safely under his arm.

The driver nodded, punched the meter, and accelerated into the flow of traffic.

Sakamoto felt invisible, at last.

5

"San Jose. All out for San Jose."

The voice carried softly through the air, a faint echo. Sakamoto was on a boat, floating on water, drifting. A small boat, a narrow body of water. The boat spun, circled around itself, went nowhere.

The voice cried louder. Sakamoto squinted through the veil of fog that shrouded the shore. There was no one, only himself, cut off and alone, directionless. He had to get to shore, but how?

"Let's go, buddy. San Jose."

The voice seemed closer now, calling, beckoning. Who was that man, standing across the river? He wanted to reach out, but there was all that water. The man extended his hand.

"Hey, fella. Your ticket's good to San Jose and no farther." He reached across and shook Sakamoto's shoulders.

His hands suddenly felt free. He was getting closer, he could sense it. There was a purpose! There was direction!

Sakamoto could see the man through the parting mist now, a man in blue, very tall, very official. He bowed. He had a job to do. A job for the Bucho. For the company. For the country.

His hands whipped upward in an involuntary jerk. His eyes snapped open. He could see the man in blue now.

"Mister, I gotta get this bus moving. You gettin' off, or do I gotta throw you off?" His voice was quieter now, but firm.

Sakamoto nodded now, rubbing his eyes, still half asleep. He pulled himself erect and staggered down the row of seats, stepping slowly, unsurely, off the bus.

He blinked in the bright sunlight and stumbled forward, clutching his knapsack. A sign flashed "Food . . . 24 Hours." He realized dimly that he had not eaten since . . . since . . . His mind went blank. Visions of rice and mush and vinegary vegetables brought a rumble to his stomach.

He finished the San Jose Plate Special and ordered a third cup of coffee, opening a newspaper to the apartment listings. His finger traced a vertical path down the columns as the familiar community names leapt off the page.

Mountain View. Santa Clara. Los Altos. Cupertino. Sunnyvale.

His heart beat faster. He pulled out a pencil and circled some numbers. He got change for a dollar and clinked a dime into the corner pay phone, dialing the first number on his list.

It was a room in an apartment house in Sunnyvale, but it had been taken an hour before he had called.

The second number belonged to a gruff old man who asked too many questions when he heard Sakamoto's foreign accent. Sakamoto simply thanked him and hung up.

The third listing was called Sunrise Courts. A woman's voice answered when he dialed.

"Yes, we still have rooms available," she said. "Did you want furnished or unfurnished?"

Sakamoto frowned. He hated using a foreign language on the telephone. He couldn't see the other person's face, watch his eyes, read his expressions.

"Furnished means . . . ?" he asked, leaning against the black phone box.

"All furniture is included, but the rent's higher," the woman said. Her voice was high-pitched, droll.

"Yes, furnished," he said.

"Three weeks rent in advance," she said, speaking very rapidly. Sakamoto nodded, bowing curtly to the phone in response. "And no doubling up. If you rent single, you pay single. But if you're renting double for yourself and your girl friend—or your boy friend—we have to charge you double."

He asked her about the Santa Clara address, saying he was planning to work in Sunnyvale.

"No problem," she said. "Sunrise Courts is on El Camino Real. Sunnyvale is on a direct bus route."

He felt relieved. She agreed to hold a furnished room for him until five o'clock.

The cab almost missed it, the number was so small, but the driver saw the sign and angled his car into the curb. Sakamoto paid the fare and looked up as the taxi drove off. "Sunrise Courts," the large green-and-yellow sign read. "Where the Sun Never Sets."

He walked up the concrete sidewalk, counting his change. After all his trips to America, he still did not understand the concept of tipping. Individual greed, he thought again, shaking his head. Would Americans never understand that the group, working together in harmony, enabled society to function? The individual was *nothing* without his affiliation, his allegiance, his . . . his *obligation* to the group.

Sakamoto stuffed his change into a pocket, thankful that he had converted money back in Oakland. Another stroke of good fortune. He smiled. The Sumitomo Bank of California had been so helpful, especially when he spoke to the teller in his native Japanese. No formalities, no questions, just crisp American cash.

Entering the lobby, he saw a small formica sign that read, "Linda Kalinski, Manager." Two small, overstuffed chairs separated by a crooked table lamp sat against a bare wall.

The woman behind the desk in the management office was dressed in a green jogging suit and wore sunglasses. Her fingernails were painted purple. He walked up to the desk, filled out the registration cards and gave her the deposit for the room.

"Le Duc Pho," she said. She clicked a wad of chewing gum. "That's an unusual name. What do they call you?"

"Just Le," he said, avoiding her eyes. Dialogue was the last thing he wanted. He reached down for his knapsack.

"What kind of work do you do?" she asked, raising an eyebrow.

Sakamoto shrugged his shoulders. "Boat people," he

said. "Refugee." He took the receipt she gave him and put it in his pocket.

"Wow," she said, her jaws accelerating. "I do a little writing on the side. Free-lance, you know? I'd love to interview you for a magazine article."

Sakamoto smiled, looking down at his feet. "Not so interesting, miss," he said. "No job, no family, no hobbies."

"Oh, but that's just the point," she said, snapping her gum. "You're new in this country. I bet there are lots of people who would love to read about a real boat person." She looked up at him as she chewed.

He shook his head. "Please, no. Maybe if I find nice job and become success. Americans like big success."

"Damn," she said. She pushed her glasses up her nose. "Oh, I gotta see some ID. Boss'll ask when he comes back. You got a driver's license or something?"

Sakamoto reached into his knapsack and pulled out his white card. "This is all they give me," he said. He showed her the counterfeit immigration card.

Linda Kalinski took it from him and watched as he stood before her, his head down, hands clasped behind his back. She felt sorry for the man, no job, no family, no friends. She barely glanced at the card and handed it back.

"You know," she said, her voice quiet, "I bet my great-grandfather had to start like this."

"Your ancestors were immigrants?" he asked, pocketing the card.

"From Poland," she said, nodding. She pulled at the gum with her tongue. "Settled in New York, kept moving west, taking any job he could get. Wonderful man."

He nodded.

"We sure have it easy today," Linda Kalinski said. "I hate to think what life would be like if we had to work like they did." She shrugged her shoulders, jaws pumping.

Most of us still work that hard, Sakamoto thought. But we're not lazy Americans.

She handed him his room key. "23-A. Top floor, back side," she said, gesturing over her shoulder. "There's two keys, in case you lose one. Five-dollar replacement charge."

Sakamoto nodded again. He stuffed the keys into a front pocket, thanked her and started to leave.

"Oh," he said, turning back to face her, his hand on the doorknob. "Do you know bus schedule?"

"Where you going?"

"Job hunting, electronics companies. Control Data, big companies, you know?"

She smiled. "Easy. Walk two blocks west, to Lawrence. Then take any bus heading north. We're El Camino. The next stops are Reed, Kifer, Central, and Duane."

Central.

The name exploded in Sakamoto's brain like a cannonball.

Micro Optix. 185 Central Way. Sunnyvale, California. He had committed the address to memory long ago. His knuckles turned white as he gripped the doorknob.

"Thank you," he said. "Very helpful. Thank you." He executed a nervous bow.

Linda Kalinski giggled. "Good luck. Oh, and supermarkets, shops, stores, all easy walks from here. Three blocks the other direction," she said, pointing with her left hand as he left the office.

Sakamoto spent the rest of Saturday shopping. He followed Miss Kalinski's directions and walked the three blocks. He glanced at the traffic rushing by in a torrent of moving metal. No street cars, no subways, no overhead trains, every car almost empty with only the driver behind the wheel.

He felt a surge of pride as he thought about Japan's superior public transportation system that linked its cities and towns so efficiently, so cheaply, by rail. Of course, they had the population density to justify it. But then, so did California. As he glanced at the traffic he smiled. Practically every other car was Japanese.

The shopping center was jammed with small stores, like *mahjong* tiles, side to side. Sakamoto stopped and looked down the row of shops. Fast food. Pet supplies. Swimming pool service. Sporting goods. Bicycles, brassieres, baby clothing. He shook his head as he realized there was not a single bookstore in sight. How could America pretend to be

such a great power when it was *his* country, Japan, with
the world's highest literacy rate. Where bookshops out-
numbered even train stations.

In a local food market, he found what he needed. A box of
instant noodles, some tofu, soy sauce, a sixpack of Asahi
beer. A small variety store had a selection of watches, so
he bought an inexpensive Matsuzaka model and snapped
it onto his wrist. Next door, in a cheap men's shop, he
outfitted himself with a new pair of jeans and a Rain King.
Perfect, he thought. A waterproof jacket, light blue, zip-
pered, with countless pockets. Leisure wear. America's invisible uniform.

Sakamoto felt the tug of fatigue as he walked back to his
apartment, his new purchases tucked safely into his knapsack. The sign in front of his building was only half true,
he thought. Shading his eyes, he watched the sun sinking
in the distant sky, a ripe tomato hidden by a veil of smog.

An hour later, he was on his stomach under the bed,
screwdriver in hand, fastening a false outlet into the wall.
He had found a hardware store and bought a small conversion kit so he could change an ordinary electrical outlet
into a secret compartment. It was getting dark, and he
wanted to complete the conversion before dusk passed to
night.

Once he had the plate in place, he reset the circuit
breakers and threw the lights on. Satisfied that it fit
snugly, he put his remaining cash, his ID cards, and the
Matsuzaka microimagizer inside.

He glanced at his watch. By nine p.m. it would be noon
Sunday, Tokyo time. He could send Fukuda a short signal
confirming his arrival. The Bucho would appreciate that.
The Bucho would *expect* it.

But could he stay up that long? He stretched his tired
body and walked barefoot into the kitchen for a beer. He
put a pan of water on to boil, and ate a simple meal of instant noddles. He needed sleep now more than he needed
food.

Pulling the blinds in his room and switching off the
lights, he stretched out on the bed. He set the Matsuzaka
digital watch for 21:00 and closed his eyes. He smiled. The

room, the food, his new clothes, everything paid for in cash. It was all so simple, just like Fukuda had said. No forms. No questions. Money said it all.

Precisely at nine, the electronic beeper shot him awake. He pried the wall covering loose and retrieved the micro-imagizer. Walking back into the kitchen, he took a fork and tapped a brief message on the reverse side.

"Arrived today. Rented room. Micro Optix Monday."

As an afterthought, he tapped out the telephone number of Sunrise Courts.

Just in case.

6

"Line Inspectors. Chemical Compounder. Systems Analyst. Clerical."

Sakamoto stood in front of the Micro Optix building, its squat whitewashed adobe dazzlingly brilliant in the harsh California sun. What kind of practice is this, he thought, where a company advertises so blatantly the job positions it has open?

He squinted at the building, shading his eyes. Micro Optix employees returning to their Monday shifts passed him in large numbers, ignoring the solitary Asian standing by the help-wanted sign.

American workers must change into their uniforms once they are inside, Sakamoto thought. Surely they wouldn't work in their street clothes.

He followed the arrow around to a side entrance, where prospective applicants were directed, and entered a small reception office outfitted with several wooden chairs that had built-in writing tablets, like grade school desks.

He shuffled over to the young man seated behind a large desk marked "Personnel Inquiries." He stuffed his hands down into his front pockets, trying not to look nervous.

The young man glanced up. He wore a crisp blue button-down shirt tucked neatly into a pair of corduroy trousers, freshly pressed. His badge said simply, "Smith. #587. Micro Optix."

"I like to apply for job," Sakamoto said.

"Line or staff?" Smith asked with a helpful smile.

"Excuse me?"

"Line or staff? Managerial position or clerical job?"

"Clerical," Sakamoto said hesitantly. "Managerial, not qualified," he lied.

"What then?"

Sakamoto jingled the coins in his right front pocket, staring down at his feet. "Need job, any job," he said. "Janitor?"

Smith reached into a desk drawer and pulled out a multipage form. He handed it to Sakamoto with a pen.

"Staff," he said. "Fill out this form—you can sit over there—and I'll check with the supervisor." He scratched his head. "I'm not sure if we have any janitorial positions open. If we do, the supervisor will want to interview you."

"Interview?" Sakamoto asked nervously, taking the form and writing implement in his left hand.

"Required of all new applicants," Smith said, smiling. "Don't worry. Just a formality for the staff jobs. We would X-ray your past pretty thoroughly if you were applying for a line position."

Sakamoto nodded. So would we, he thought. But no foreigner would ever get through our doors.

He completed the long form, leaving the spaces blank that called for references, past addresses, previous experience, last salary.

The most important, he saved for last. He printed, very neatly, the nine digits of his bogus Social Security number in the proper space.

And he thought again how thorough Fukuda had been. But then, he was not really surprised. Matsuzaka training was excruciatingly thorough. The Japanese culture would tolerate no less.

Smith arranged for him to see the supervisor. The interview was brief and to the point. Micro Optix did have an opening on the janitorial staff. The salary was low, and it was a night shift job. He was glad to be able to offer the job to a recent refugee. Sakamoto was duly appreciative.

He could start, in fact, that same day, after receiving a tour of the factory. As he was guided through the various work stations, he noticed instantly that Micro Optix used processes fully as advanced as those at Matsuzaka's Kamakura plant.

After his application was processed, and his Micro Optix ID card was issued, he was shown the metal detector and instructed in the use of the fingerprint scanner. They went through a few drills to make sure he understood the optical machine. Le Duc Pho used the correct finger each time.

They gave him a locker, issued him a nylon gauze uniform which he was told to wear over his street clothes. He was shown how to cover his hair with a gauze cap, and how the paper slippers fit over his shoes.

When he asked about the concern for cleanliness, they explained in simple terms what their business was. Sakamoto nodded, pretending to understand. He smiled. He knew the business much better than they.

His shift would be four p.m. to midnight. Not as late as he had hoped, but still, he thought, he would be arriving when most of the others left. He should have sufficient time in the late night hours to reconnoiter.

He nodded repeatedly when they went down the list of duties. Smith stopped frequently and asked if he understood what he was being told.

"Are you sure now, Mr. Le?" Smith would ask.

"Yes, I think so," Sakamoto would answer.

His mind raced ahead as he thought of the successful completion of his assignment. He was surprised but relieved that the process had been so simple. He talked confidently to himself as he took the bus back to his room that afternoon, clutching his ID card and locker key.

Japan would easily overtake America, he thought. The Americans were too forgiving.

It took Sakamoto only two days to get a feel for the operations and flow of the Sunnyvale plant. He made mental notes as he pushed his broom, sprinkling the bright orange antiseptic cleanser ahead of him as he worked.

He had located the wafer fabrication area. That was relatively easy to do. Less easy was the assembly and bonding operation. The Americans did not use the same continuous flow equipment that Matsuzaka did, so the process had to be observed more closely.

The sizing system was also confusing. After the chips were probed, assembled, and bonded to their lead frames, they were packed and stored together to await shipment.

Sakamoto quickly realized he had to do two things. First, distinguish among the chip sizes. Micro Optix configurations differed from the Matsuzaka designs, so the bonding process led to a different sizing technique. He could not transmit circuit patterns of the 16K or 64K devices to Fukuda. Only the 256K optical would do.

Second, once he determined which were the 256K chips, he had to make sure that he transmitted the optical device, not the standards. That was key.

His role as a Vietnamese refugee kept him relatively isolated from the other night workers. As he expected, most of them were Mexican and spoke as little English as he pretended to speak. Two of them were black. They all avoided each other voluntarily, like victims of a vicious disease.

Sakamoto thought to himself often as he completed his nightly rounds, how lucky he was to be a Japanese! His society had no minority groups, no racial strife, no social unrest. Could a country as permissive as America really expect to survive as a major industrial power? With each passing day, his confidence in the success of his mission grew, his loyalty to his company and his love for his country swelled.

One night, a Spanish-speaking worker asked him to join them for a few drinks in a local tavern. Sakamoto thanked him in halting English, but begged off. He did not want to risk his position as a new worker by drinking, even after hours.

The Mexicans told him he was crazy. The blacks just laughed. They knew he was below them on the social pyramid. It was a feeling Sakamoto did not like, having to swallow his own cultural pride to play this demeaning role. They all snickered and pointed at his *haramaki* when he changed clothes in the locker room.

But he would persevere! He was nothing if not disciplined! They thought he was a stupid, illiterate Asian refugee. How he hated their looks of scorn and derision! Who did they think *they* were?

The next night, one of the blacks began nipping from a small bottle before leaving the plant. He walked out with Sakamoto as they finished their shift. Their key rings were picked up by the metal detector and activated the alarm. The guard merely glanced up at the two janitors and flicked off the bell.

"Hey, gook, why don't you come with us? We'll show you a good time." He winked at Sakamoto, jabbing him in the ribs.

"Very tired, no time," he said, shrugging his shoulders as he had learned to do so well. "Must work hard, make money to bring family." He flipped up the collar on his jacket to cover his neck. The nights were dry and cool.

"Shit, man, all you gooks do is work, work, work. That's no fuckin' fun, man." The black man glanced over at his friend. They both laughed now, clapping their hands, slapping their knees.

Sakamoto's glance never left the ground as they walked forward, he to the bus stop, they to their cars in the lot.

The black jabbed him again, taunting, teasing.

"Please stop," Sakamoto said. He held his right hand stiffly by his side, fingers together, flexed.

"Shit. Le Duc? That your name? What do they call you, just plain Pho? Little Duc? Quack, quack!" He laughed harder.

His friend intervened. "Hey, man. Leave him alone. He ain't hurtin' no one."

The first black stopped, his face bristling with anger. "Hurtin' no one, my ass. He's got a fuckin' job, ain't he? How many of your friends—our friends—lookin' for a job and can't get one. Count 'em."

His friend was silent. He knew he was right.

"All because these goddam gooks come sailin' into the country and our goddam government gives 'em free cards so they can get a goddam job. Well, fuck 'em, man."

With that, he jabbed an elbow, hard, into Sakamoto's midsection. Sakamoto heaved forward, gasping, his breath gone. His mouth moved noiselessly, without words, without air.

Out of the corner of one eye, he saw the black pull back his arm and start to come down on top of his neck. Straightening quickly, he spun on his left heel and brought up his right hand, fingers extended, jabbing it sharply, painfully, into the man's armpit.

"Shit! My arm! It's dead, I can't feel nothin'!" he shouted, holding it as his friend pulled him away.

"You goddam gook!" he shouted as he staggered backward. "I'll get your ass."

Sakamoto backed cautiously toward the street. He doubted it very much, he thought.

Unarmed, they could do him no harm. He could pulverize them with *aikido*. Empty hands. But strong as steel.

8

Wednesday, April twentieth. Sakamoto Ryuji had not communicated with Fukuda in four days. He would have to start transmitting circuit patterns of the 256K optical sensor.

He did his work more slowly that night, lagging so far behind the others that they had left by the time he returned his brooms and buckets to the closet.

He retraced his path to the storage area, where the chips were stacked awaiting shipment. The workers in the wafer fabrication area, which ran twenty-four hours a day, were isolated, and they concentrated so intently on their own work that his chances of being spotted were remote.

Sakamoto searched, he probed, he poked into all of the neatly stacked trays. *Chikusho,* he thought, as he went through the racks of circuits. They've not been done on a batch basis. They're all mixed together.

He pulled out an assortment of chips and arranged them on the formica counter, pushing aside the metal trays. He sorted through them quickly, saw there were two sizes, and judged from their relative widths that the smaller chips had to be either 16K or 64K configurations.

The larger, square devices were the ones he wanted. The 256Ks. He inspected them closely, pushing his glasses up on his head and holding the lead frames closer, squinting in the dim light.

Sakamoto went rapidly through six, then a dozen, then a second dozen, of the larger chips. *Chikusho,* he muttered to himself again. It was impossible to tell the optical sensors from the 256K standards. They were identical in size, and they were not specially coded.

He glanced over his shoulder to make sure he was still undetected.

The Americans were not as stupid as he had supposed. It would not be so simple, after all.

Sakamoto rubbed a hand through his coarse black hair, wiping beads of perspiration from his forehead. He glanced at his watch. He would have to get started. He was losing precious time.

He withdrew the microimagizer from his *haramaki*, selected a 256K chip from the assortment on the counter and placed it along the black plastic indentation on the reverse side. Using the key to his locker, he tapped quickly on the back side, activating its transmission power and hoping that Fukuda's printer circuit was plugged in on the other end.

It had to be. If Sakamoto was sending when he was scheduled to be, then Fukuda would be receiving. He chose the chips at random, calculating that half of them must be the optical sensor. Even odds.

He sent a dozen transmissions, judging that Fukuda would have enough circuit patterns on his readout to pick up the opticals. Sakamoto placed the microimagizer back in his woolen *haramaki* and returned the chips to their places in the racks. He snapped out the lights and shuffled back to his locker.

He glanced at his watch. It was nearly two a.m. He suddenly felt drained, a combination of physical tiredness and the emotional strain of being constantly on guard. Well, he thought, he didn't have to come back until four the next afternoon. Plenty of time to sleep.

Linda Kalinski was on the night shift herself when he returned to the apartment complex. "Mr. Le? Oh, Mr. Le! I'm so glad you're back. There's a telephone call for you. Strange language, lots of static. Pay phone out in the hall."

Suddenly he froze. Call? For him? No one knew he was there. No one, except . . . Strange language? Static? Can't be. Must be.

He walked out to the phone and picked up the receiver

which was dangling on its cord, swaying slowly against the wall.

"Le speaking," he said, raising the receiver to his ear.

"Moshi, moshi?" squeaked a distant voice. "Sakamoto-kun?"

He recognized the voice instantly. "Bucho-san? What are you doing?" He turned to face the wall, lowering his voice. "This is dangerous."

"Dangerous, but essential," Fukuda said, his familiar voice ringing over the wire. "The transmissions are clear, but they're all the same. You must transmit only the optical sensors."

Sakamoto's eyes narrowed. "I checked the quality control numbers before transmitting," he said. "There's no difference between the optical sensors and the standard chips. I sent a random sample, so you must have circuit patterns of some optical devices."

"Nevertheless, the circuit patterns are all the same!" Fukuda shouted. "They are useless to us."

Sakamoto was speechless. How could they be useless? There must be a difference.

"The microimagizer?" Sakamoto asked, turning to make sure no one was in the hall. It was so late, he doubted anyone but Miss Kalinski would be there. Since they spoke in Japanese, she wouldn't know the difference.

"All this time, this effort, must not go to waste," Fukuda screamed.

Sakamoto nodded. He knew it could not possibly be the fault of the Matsuzaka device. "What is your idea?" he asked.

Fukuda paused. "You must bring back an assortment of chips," he said. "It must be a representative sampling, from different batches, to make sure you include the optical sensor."

"But that will greatly increase the chances of detection," Sakamoto said, cracking a pair of knuckles against the wall. He was so tired now he could hardly stand.

More static on the line. The satellite connection with Tokyo was bad.

"I sent you because you are the most dependable. You have a job to do." Fukuda's voice was ice.

"I know," Sakamoto said quietly. "All right, a random sample, from several batches. That will require a large number of chips, perhaps a hundred or more."

"So?"

"So I better plan to disappear the same night. Which means tomorrow."

"Yoshi. Take the JAL flight back to Tokyo at noon on Friday. Check with the agent. He will have a ticket for you, in your own name."

Sakamoto suddenly sucked in air, the ritualistic hissing sound like steam escaping in the night.

"Nan desu ka?" Fukuda shouted through the static. "What's the matter?"

"No passport, remember?"

Fukuda was silent for a moment. "We'll take care of that. Check with the JAL agent. He will have a passport for you."

"But how?"

"Never mind, I have the authority. Just be there."

"But I have no other identification. What if the agent asks—"

"Nonsense! Just give your date and place of birth as comfirmation. He will not question your authenticity as a Matsuzaka man."

"Yoshi," Sakamoto said. "Friday then."

"And Sakamoto-kun."

"Hai."

"Persevere."

"Of course."

Fukuda clicked off, and the line squeaked dead. Sakamoto stood there, holding the receiver, staring into space. Failure was unforgivable, inconceivable, he told himself. But the risk. The risk!

He clenched his fist and smashed it against the black box.

Suddenly the collection of dimes and nickels came streaming out the rectangular mouth, clattering onto the floor in a waterfall of silver.

"Chikusho," Sakamoto muttered, holding his hand over the coin return slot in an attempt to stem the flow.

Linda Kalinski came running out of the office. "Hey, what's goin' on?" she yelled.

Sakamoto swept the coins toward the wall with his foot. "Box go crazy when I finish," he stammered. He forced a smile.

"Box, hell," she said. "You went crazy. You ought to know better, Mr. Le, trying to rip off the telephone company. You need a few bucks, just ask." She stood there, hands on hips.

"No my fault," he insisted. "Bring envelope. I give you all the coins."

She raised an eyebrow but did as he said. Sakamoto helped her scoop the coins into the large manila envelope.

He could smell her sweet, flowery perfume. She wore tight jeans and a deep V-neck sweater that revealed a generous bosom when she bent over to pick up the coins. He put the distraction out of his mind.

He had a job to do. He needed no further distractions.

"Sorry, Mr. Le," Linda Kalinski said, putting a hand on his shoulder. "I jumped to conclusions. Can I offer you some coffee?"

Sakamoto pressed his lips together. "Thank you," he said, shaking his head. "Very tired. Maybe tomorrow."

She smoothed her sweater, arching her shoulders and thrusting her chest forward.

"Sure?"

"Sure."

Her scent lingered in the air as she turned and walked back into her office. Sakamoto slumped against the wall, closing his eyes. Pulling himself up, he shuffled down the hall, up the stairs, and to bed.

He had a job to do.

9

The rain came down all day Thursday, sweeping across the great flat valley in horizontal sheets. Black, tumbling clouds squatted on the horizon, dense and low. Lightning ripped and cracked across the sky, exploding like flash-bulbs and drenching the ground below in waves of white light.

Sakamoto pushed his broom across the linoleum floor, glancing nervously at his watch. He had lots to do that night, and he was eager to get started. Perspiration dripped into his eyes. His palms were cold and wet.

He wore the light-blue windbreaker under his uniform, the one with all the pockets. He had wondered when he bought it why Americans put so many pockets in their coats. Front pockets, rear pockets, sleeve pockets, *neck* pockets. But he was glad for them now.

As he scrubbed, he went through the motions mentally. He visualized stuffing the spacious pockets with samples of the 256Ks like a child in a candy store shoplifting bubblegum balls. Quick. Deft. Undetected.

Because of the rain, there was more to do, more scum to clean. *Chikusho,* he muttered. Mud had hardened into dirt, scuffed into the cracks of the floor, splattered around the walls. His back pulsed with pain from the bending and stooping.

It was nearly one o'clock when he had finished his normal rounds, and he noticed that others were still there. The two blacks seemed to be working in slow motion.

Sakamoto eased around a corner, out of sight, into the chip storage area. There they are, he thought, sitting in their racks like dead roaches, their tiny aluminum leads sticking up like short legs. The dull fluorescent light covered the room in a gray-green glow.

Sakamoto closed the door behind him and pulled on his gloves. Taking a deep breath, he went from rack to rack, picking, testing, occasionally holding a circuit up to see if there was some way, any way, he could distinguish the optical chips from their standard counterparts.

He skipped the obvious 16K and 64K models, which were smaller and more rectangular, focusing on the larger 256Ks, the ones Fukuda needed. The ones for Matsuzaka. The ones for Japan.

He was certain that the circuits he pushed into his pockets—the square ones, with the black ceramic frames—were the right size. But he swore he could not tell the optical sensors from the standard chips. They simply were not coded separately.

Chikusho, he muttered under his breath, sifting, sorting, combing through the little ceramic-and-metal squares like an old woman at a mix-and-match table of costume jewelry.

When his coat pockets would hold no more, he began filling his front pants pockets, slipping the circuits through the vertical slits in his gauze uniform. Every two or three minutes, he would stop, swivel his neck and arch the small of his back in an attempt to stop the muscles from cramping. He cracked his knuckles at intervals to relax his fingers.

He blinked his eyes frequently, adjusting them to the dim light. Perspiration flowed down his face in tiny streams. Occasionally, he shot a glance over his shoulder to make sure he was still unobserved.

He worked swiftly. In fifteen minutes, he had his pockets filled with the tiny circuits. He stopped when he had over a hundred to take back.

"*Yoshi,*" he said. That should do. If there weren't at least twenty optical chips in that collection, he would . . . There *had* to be. He tried not to think of the consequences if he failed.

Nonsense! He would not fail. He could not fail. This was

the *meaning* of all the discipline, and the training, and the thoroughness, and . . . and the *loyalty!*

His mind clamped shut. He would not think of failure. He turned to flick out the light.

"Hey, man, what's this shit goin' on here?" The black with the big elbow stood by the door, blocking Sakamoto's way. "Whatcha got in them pockets, man? Gonna do a little number on the company?" He pointed at Sakamoto's bulging jacket.

Sakamoto jumped, his heart pounding. Licking his lips, he swallowed hard.

"Finish work, go home," he said, forcing a smile. He shrugged his shoulders.

"Bullshit, man. You gonna rip off the boss, sell them chips, get us *all* in trouble. Now, you put them things back or we gonna do a little business together."

The pale fluorescent light made the Negro's face look green. Sweat sparkled on his forehead. His wide shoulders jammed the doorway, huge hands thrust deep into his own pockets.

Straightening up, he reached into a hip pocket and whipped out a long, thin knife. He held the butt toward Sakamoto and pressed lightly with his thumb. The blade snapped out in a blur and clicked into place. It glittered in the soft, diffuse light, sharpened to a tapered edge on both sides.

Sakamoto stepped sideways, his hands free, his fingers flexed. His eyes burned holes in the black man's face.

Inconceivable, Sakamoto Ryuji thought, as he circled to his left. Inconceivable that a black man, a *colored* person, representative of the lowest social class in the world, could even think of stopping him. A Matsuzaka kacho against a . . . against a . . .

Sakamoto couldn't think of a word derogatory enough, unhuman enough, to describe the man who stood before him, a man who blocked his way back to Japan, a man who threatened the success of his assignment for his Bucho, threatened the Matsuzaka mission, threatened the survival of Japan.

"You cocksucking little gook! You think you can—"

Raising the blade, he slashed diagonally, forcing Sakamoto to jump back.

They circled to the right until Sakamoto felt the packing table bump against his hip, stopping his retreat. He reached back with one hand, touching the rack of tiny silicon chips. His fingers curled around a front leg, grasping the rack tightly.

With a frightening shriek, Sakamoto hurled the rack of ceramic leadframes directly at the black. The delicate devices sprayed out in a stream of plastic and metal, a swarm of electronic bees, temporarily blinding the man. Several hit the knife, bounced off his legs, scraped against his face.

As he raised his free hand in defense, Sakamoto kicked out instantly. His foot cracked the man's wrist and sent the blade clattering across the floor.

Sakamoto made his mind a blank wall, stretching out his sense perceptors, feeling with his nerve ends. His eyes were burning laser beams of intensity, every distraction was closed out. He felt as light as an autumn leaf. His legs told him, use us, we have the spring of the finest steel. His fingers flexed, his arms moved at the elbow, nimble and strong, like whips.

Spinning on his right foot, he kicked out with his left and caught the black man with a shot to the midsection. As his adversary's upper body collapsed, he whipped his right arm around, fully extended, fingers rigid, hard as stone.

The side of his hand cracked against the black man's neck, splitting the bone. His head sagged limply, silently, onto his chest as his body spilled heavily onto the floor.

Sakamoto felt the adrenalin speeding through his body now, like a supercharger. His hands began to shake, and his heart raced.

He stepped gingerly across the limp body, kicking the knife into a corner. He flicked out the light and made his way back to the locker room. He had to get out, and fast.

Others were changing as he walked through.

"Hey, gook, drinks tonight on us."

"Tomorrow's TGIF, man. Booze time tonight!"

His eyes were riveted on the far door, his pace lengthening as he tore off his gloves and gauze uniform and stuffed them into his locker. He never heard the voices as he pushed through, never even heard the alarm bell sound when the chips set off the metal detector. Without speaking, he slapped a finger onto the optical scanner, and when he heard the click, he swept out into the driving rain.

Sakamoto Ryuji was gone. In his mind, Sunnyvale and Micro Optix and the Sunrise Courts and Linda Kalinski with the clicking gum and the tempting breasts and the black man with the blue knife were all behind him now, forgotten, hazy distractions in a vague world, warped in time and space.

He sped up as he saw the bus approaching down the Lawrence Expressway, slowing now for its expected stop. He flipped up his jacket collar against the rain.

The bus was empty. He tossed two coins into the box and slumped into a back seat. The driver spared not even a cursory glance. Another two hours and *his* work would be done. What did he care about who got on and off his bus?

Sakamoto's thoughts raced ahead as he sat, bouncing, water dripping from his black hair, fogging his thick lenses.

Cab to San Jose. Bus to the airport in San Francisco. Disappear in the airport bar, a corner table, invisible in the anonymous nighttime crowd. Wait for morning, his passport, his ticket back to Tokyo.

He patted his pockets. Stuff the chips into small plastic bags, cram them into his knapsack, take nothing else onto the plane. He would even let the airport security guards search the knapsack, look at the chips, feel them, touch them.

"Samples," he would say.

What would they know?

After all, they were black too.

Sakamoto Ryuji smiled as the bus roared down the expressway, nearing his stop at El Camino Real. By the time Micro Optix began reconstructing the theft of their precious 256K chips, he would be nestled in a window seat on Japan Air Lines Flight 001, a Japanese businessman dressed casually, returning to Tokyo, chattering aimlessly with the obedient stewardesses, reading his *Nikkei,* drinking his beloved sake, eating *soba,* sleeping with the knapsack securely behind him as a pillow.

He listened to the rain pounding on top of the bus.

He sat alone, but he did not feel alone.

He felt at one with the rain.

He *was* the rain.

10

Fukuda Kenji's jaws clamped together tightly as he peered through the double-lens microscope. The muscles flexed as he ground his teeth.

He focused the lens, turning the knob back and forth, slowly now. More slowly. There.

"*Yoshi,*" he whispered. "Another one. Optical. No doubt about it." He turned to Sakamoto. "See the uniform area to the left? Responds to the light. Take a look."

He lit another cigarette as Sakamoto Ryuji looked down the long tubes. "*Naruhodo,*" he said, nodding slightly. "Impossible to tell without microscopic identification."

Fukuda placed the optical sensor to his right. He inserted another chip in the microscope and bent down to check it out.

"*Chikusho,*" he exploded. "Another standard chip." He pounded the table. The little chips bounced and jiggled.

Sakamoto flinched. He bent over to look through the tubes. He nodded. "How many optical sensors do we have now?" he asked.

"Twelve," Fukuda muttered as he tossed the standard circuit into a box at his left. "Twelve out of eighty. Maybe we'll get lucky on the final batch."

Sakamoto handed him the fifth and final pouch.

"You're sure your escape from the refugee group went unnoticed?" Fukuda asked, focusing on the microscopic image.

"Bucho-san, *ne.* There was so much confusion. Uncontrolled. It was *ideal,* I tell you." He smiled as he recounted the incident.

"You could have been followed."

"Unlikely. I caught a taxi immediately and disappeared into the crowd at the bus station."

Fukuda noted the chip type, and cursing again, removed it from the lens. He tossed it to his left. "Tell me again about this black man," he said. "Did you have to kill him?" He rotated the focusing knob, returning his eyes to the long black tubes.

"I *told* you, he was going to kill *me*. Plus it was my last night. You wouldn't be sitting here testing those chips if I hadn't." Sakamoto handed the Bucho another 256K lead frame. "Besides, you would have done the same."

"Yoshi," Fukuda said, under his breath. "Another optical chip." He spun around on his stool. *"Mochiron,"* he smiled, "black people count for nothing."

Sakamoto exhaled. He handed Fukuda another chip. Inserting it into the lens clip, he squinted into the eyepiece, smoke from his cigarette curling up into his face. He blinked the smoke away.

"I even cleaned up my room, left it neat and tidy," Sakamoto said, recounting his rainy retreat. "They're not expecting Le Duc Pho until Monday, anyway. He called in sick Friday."

Fukuda raised up from his microscope. "Good," he said, his hand resting on the focus knob. He flicked away a lengthening ash. "As long as you brought back the evidence I sent you over with."

"Of course," Sakamoto said. "I have the counterfeit cards in my desk downstairs, and the—"

He froze suddenly, his face pained, his eyes wide.

"And the what?" Fukuda asked, crushing out the remains and shaking his pack of Hi-Lites to dislodge another smoke.

"The microimagizer," Sakamoto whispered.

"Downstairs, too. Right?" Fukuda asked, striking a match and holding it quickly to his cigarette to catch the flaming sulphur.

Sakamoto swallowed. He wiped his brow. *"Chikusho!"* he shouted, slamming a fist on the countertop. He kicked the cabinet. Glass beakers and flasks vibrated off the top shelf and smashed to the floor.

Fukuda wheeled around on his stool. *"Nan daro?"*

Sakamoto's hands were shaking uncontrollably now. "I can't believe it!" he screamed. "I left the microimagizer in the wall compartment in my room!"

"You did *what?*" Fukuda shrieked.

Sakamoto buried his face in his hands. His body convulsed in waves. He had done stupid things before, childish things, forgetful things. But he had never embarrassed his company. Ever.

Fukuda leapt off the stool. He began pacing back and forth, flicking his cigarette in an agitated manner.

"Anyone see you install the wallplate?" he asked.

"Of course not," Sakamoto groaned. "How could I have been so *stupid!*" He slammed a fist onto the countertop again.

"Quiet!" Fukuda yelled. "This is no time for hysterics. Think!" He stopped, took a drag on his cigarette, then resumed pacing.

"The wall socket is like all the others?"

"Exactly."

"Inconvenient? I mean, less likely to be used?"

"Yes."

"Where is it?"

"Under the bed."

"Movable bed?"

"No, fixed. And heavy."

"Other sockets in the vicinity?"

"One across from the bed, another on the opposite wall."

Fukuda drew in a lungful of smoke, then exhaled. *"Yoshi,"* he said. "Not ideal, but not the end of the world, either." He thought for a moment.

"I have let you down, Bucho-san," Sakamoto whimpered. "I have failed you, I have failed my company. The assignment was not thorough. It was imperfect." He slumped into a corner, his glasses fogged with sweat.

The end of Fukuda's cigarette glowed a crisp red as he puffed and thought. He said nothing.

He stabbed out the cigarette. *"Chikusho,"* he muttered. "I want you to forget about the microimagizer. Put it out of your mind, do you understand?"

Sakamoto looked up at his Bucho, blinking. He shook his head. "I want to say yes, but—"

"Forget about it!" Fukuda yelled, slicing the air with his hand. "Put it behind you. It no longer exists! It's as dead as the black man."

"But—"

"I said, *ignore* it! We must put it out of our minds. The chances of discovery are small, and besides, by the time we have these optical chips installed it will make no difference anyway. So forget about it, is that clear?"

Sakamoto nodded now, his head low, unwilling, unable, to face his boss.

Fukuda walked over, put a hand on Sakamoto's shoulder. "It's like the parable of the Buddhist monks, Sakamoto-kun," he said, his voice quiet now. "You remember the *kotowaza* about the two monks who came across the young girl afraid to cross a stream?"

Sakamoto nodded, pushing himself to his feet. Of course he knew that story, he said to himself. Every schoolchild in Japan knows it.

"One of the monks helped the girl across the stream and set her down on the other side. Remember?"

"Yes, I remember."

"And what happened next?" Fukuda asked, a half-grin on his face now.

Sakamoto's eyes brightened. "They continued walking. The other monk said he was still worried about the girl."

"Exactly, Sakamoto-kun. And the monk—who had helped the girl—said what?"

Sakamoto cracked a pair of knuckles. "Wait. Yes, now I recall. The first monk said, 'Are you still carrying that girl with you? I set her down way back there.' "

Fukuda smiled. *"Yoshi.* So put it out of your mind. *Shikata ga nai.* There's nothing we can do about it now."

Sakamoto relaxed. He rubbed his fingers through his long, black hair. It can't be helped. *Shikata ga nai.*

"You brought back the optical chips, Sakamoto-kun. That was your assignment. You did not fail."

Sakamoto bowed deeply, his head almost touching his knees. *"Domo,* Bucho-san."

They returned to the microscope. Sakamoto kicked aside the glass shards. They finished quickly, identifying six more optical sensors from the final batch.

"I still can't figure out their numbering and identification system," Sakamoto said, closing the box with the standard chips and labeling it.

"Neither can I," Fukuda said. "Must be an internal code. The Micro Optix people are very smart. All these chips, the standard circuits as well as the optical sensors, have quality control numbers from an identical series. Very intelligent."

Fukuda picked up the optical sensors and placed them one-by-one into a small styrofoam box until he counted nineteen in all. He picked one up between thumb and forefinger.

"Send this to Sumiyoshi tomorrow under my name. He has orders to ask no questions. Tell him to have the design group perform the usual reverse engineering tests and analyze it. We've got to move ahead with our own prototype."

"Hai," Sakamoto snapped, clicking his heels together. He bowed and took the 256K optical sensor, dropping it into a small cardboard envelope marked for Matsuzaka's internal mail.

Fukuda clicked off the microscope. It went dark. He glanced at his watch. *"Yoshi,"* he said, with a stretch and a yawn. Let's go." It was after one in the morning.

They began closing down the lab. Sakamoto covered the microscope with a vinyl sheet and wheeled it into a corner. Above his head, a Matsuzaka poster hung from the bare wall, its dark green *kanji* stark and simple.

Genius is perseverance in disguise.

"Tell me again how you got your ticket and passport," Fukuda said, smiling.

Sakamoto laughed. He had clearly set the girl down behind him now.

"Absolutely no problem," he said with a smile. "Early Friday morning I got to the JAL agent, as soon as he had arrived. I told him my name was Sakamoto."

He paused. "Sakamoto of Matsuzaka."

"And?" Fukuda's eyes glowed.

"The agent looked at me like I was the Emperor's son. *'Matsuzaka no Sakamoto-sama?'* he asked. I nodded, and he disappeared into the manager's office. A moment later, the manager himself emerged with my ticket and the passport, bowing repeatedly as he handed them to me. The mere mention of the Matsuzaka name was enough."

"No questions?"

"None."

"No request for other identification, anything like that?"

"Absolutely not."

"Yoshi," Fukuda said. "Outstanding."

Fukuda recalled his late night meeting with the Foreign Ministry official who had arranged for the extra passport to be prepared by the Japanese Consulate in San Francisco. The official had not been pleased, but Fukuda's *oyabun* had nearly limitless power when he chose to intercede.

After the fake documents for Sakamoto's Vietnamese identity, Matsuzaka Electric was on the liability side of the Foreign Ministry official's favor ledger. Fukuda convinced the official that Matsuzaka's future depended on the new passport being issued.

That Japan's future depended on it.

And to wipe the obligation slate clean, to restore the *ongiri,* that delicate balance between favor and duty, duty and justice, Fukuda had thoughtfully brought along a small brown envelope containing a generous amount in unmarked yen bills.

Untraceable. No receipts.

More than enough to wipe the slate clean. More than enough to help the official understand the importance of Matsuzaka.

He had no trouble understanding the importance of his country. He especially had no trouble understanding the contents of the brown envelope.

Fukuda returned the various implements to the storage compartments. Magnifying glasses. Calipers. Dustcloth. Micrometer.

He pulled a sheaf of papers out of his coat pocket. "See these circuit patterns?" he asked.

Sakamoto walked over, took the computer printouts from his Bucho. *"Naruhodo,"* he said. "No wonder. They're all identical, just as you said. But you know, your call made me pretty nervous." He recounted the story of the malfunctioning telephone box.

Fukuda shoved the stool back under the counter. "I never had the slightest doubt about your chances of success." He paused. "Losing never enters my mind."

"I know," Sakamoto said, taking his jacket off the hook. His eyes were bloodshot, ringed by dark circles of exhaustion. He had come straight to the Matsuzaka central lab from the airport, and felt the full effects of jet lag now.

"A little sake?" Fukuda asked.

"Domo, Bucho-san. Another time." Sakamoto stood and stretched. "But you'll stay at my place tonight? It's so late."

Fukuda stood with his hand on the switchplate. *"Mochiron."*

He blanketed the room in darkness.

11

Major Nakamura Hideo sat cross-legged on the tatami, his body perched atop a soft, silken *zabuton*. Fukuda Kenji handed him one of the optical chips.

Nakamura held it up to the light, as if he could decipher the device with the naked eye.

Fukuda pulled his arm down. "Not so high, Nakamura-san," he said, looking quickly in both directions.

Nakamura dropped his hand to his lap, turning the tiny integrated circuit between thumb and forefinger.

"*Naruhodo*," he said, a thin smile cracking his face. "*Naruhodo!*"

Fukuda leaned back against the front of the seat behind him. He smiled. "I told you. Failure is impossible at Matsuzaka. Success is our only goal."

They sat together in Matsuzaka's center box on the opening day of the spring sumo tournament in Tokyo. The hot, white lights burned down on the packed arena as four long flags unfurled from the top of the square ceiling, facing each of the directions. North. South. East. West.

The banners proudly proclaimed another full house. The national coliseum exploded with a roar.

"*Higashi . . . Waka-no-Yama . . . Nishi . . . Ao-Zakura . . .*"

In a high-pitched whine, the *yobidashi* announced the next two wrestlers, one from the eastern stable, one from the west. As the official announcer, he wore a light blue, speckled *haori*, a formal cotton robe with half-apron fitting snugly at the waist. He read the wrestlers' names from a gold-leafed folding fan.

Waka-no-Yama. The Young Mountain. *Ao-Zakura.* The Blue Cherry Blossom.

Fukuda and Nakamura watched intently as the two rivals mounted the straw steps to the elevated mound of sand on which they would engage in traditional hand-to-hand combat. They were mammoth; each weighed over three hundred pounds.

In training since their early teens, they belonged to one of two stables, or teams, East and West. Their hierarchy was ranked according to skill, from *maegashira,* the junior level, to *yokozuna,* the grand champion, based on matches won in tournaments and tournaments won over the years. Atop the *dohyo* mound was a ring of straw some twenty feet in diameter. If any part of a wrestler's body touched the sand outside the straw, he lost.

Nakamura leaned in toward the Bucho. "Not a prototype, you say?" the Major asked, his eyebrows raised.

"Not a prototype," Fukuda repeated, taking the chip back in his hand. "The real thing."

"How many?"

"All together, nineteen."

"Yoshi," Nakamura murmured. "This is good. This is very good." He paused. "I would like to outfit the guidance systems as soon as possible."

Waka-no-Yama and Ao-Zakura ambled slowly to the center of the *dohyo,* tossing a handful of salt across its surface in the traditional rite of purification. They crouched at their positions, opposite each other, legs apart, fists clenched, fat bellies practically brushing the sand. They stretched their arms out from their bodies—a symbolic disclosure, no concealed weapons—and raised each leg in succession, high, to the side, crashing it down on the dirt surface. Out, out evil spirits.

A half-dozen *hatamoto,* the bannermen, circled the ring, vertical flags of their sponsors raised high, Roman-style, signifying the placement of bets.

Sony. Matsuzaka. Toyota. Sumitomo. Seiko.

The Major gazed down at the rust-colored ring. The bright overhead lights reflected off the top of his shaved

head, accentuating the deep shadows under the bony ridge
of his forehead.

He dabbed at his head with a handkerchief. "What? No
bets on Waka-no-Yama from Matsuzaka?" he asked.

Fukuda shook his head, recrossing his legs. "Waka-
no-Yama's not our man," he said. "We sponsor Fuku-
no-Hana. Flower of Happiness." He nodded toward the
vertical Matsuzaka *kanji* on the flag. "No doubt our chairman has put something personal on Ao-Zakura today."

Nakamura nodded silently, never taking his eyes from
the ring. He watched as the two wrestlers hunched in their
final crouches, getting set for the crucial lunge. The *gyoji*,
formal referee for this important opening match, stood between them, his gold and black brocade robe sparkling
with imperial grandeur under the lights. His feet were
clad in black silk *tabi*, and his toes curled into the sand as
he crouched low to signal the giant wrestlers to begin.

He lowered the lacquered wooden paddle with his right
hand, its shiny satin tassels resting gingerly in his left, until it sat in mid-air, floating, hovering, between the two
wrestlers, a centuries-old symbol. Symbol of survival.
Symbol of Japan.

The wooden paddle slapped back quietly against the referee's wrist, and the two *sekiwake* instinctively lunged at
each other, slapping, grappling, pushing, their carefully
combed topknots bobbing as each struggled to grasp the
other's black silk *mawashi*, a loin belt, thick as an inflated
innertube, circling the waist.

Waka-no-Yama shoved Ao-Zakura hard, on the shoulders, upsetting his balance. He deftly inserted a powerful
right arm around Ao-Zakura's left side, grabbing the
mawashi.

Waka-no-Yama brought his elephantine right leg up
now and pushed with his entire right side, accelerating
through his opponent.

Squeals of encouragement, shouts of classical Japanese
in a high-pitched tone, came from the referee as he enticed
the *sumotori* with his verbal commands. The crowd
shouted, clapping encouragement. Cries of "Waka-no-

Yama!" and "Ao-Zakura!" exploded like rifle shots in the arena.

Ao-Zakura's right arm swung up as he reacted to the thrust, leaving the right side of his *mawashi* unprotected. Waka-no-Yama grasped it with his left hand and, crouching slightly, lifted his opponent's entire frame up and out of the ring, over the circular straw barrier, grunting deeply.

Tsuri-dashi. Lift-out. Waka-no-Yama's first victory of the tournament.

Fukuda turned to the Major as the two *sumotori* bowed and left the ring. The *yobidashi* mounted the steps to sweep the sand and to announce the next two combatants.

"With the optical sensor now in hand, I see no reason why we cannot push ahead with a trial flight this coming weekend," he said. "Are the test rockets in place?"

Nakamura nodded. "Good idea." He smiled. "I'll alert the test site that we'll come on Saturday."

"The thirtieth." Fukuda paused. "Strictly routine, of course."

"Of course."

Short, squat vendors laden with tea, *arare* rice crackers, dried squid, and *mikan* oranges, climbed wearily through the box seats, their dark blue cotton *mompei* stained with sweat.

"Osake kudasai," Fukuda barked, raising two fingers.

The small man, perspiration streaming down his face, set his heavy bamboo basket down in the aisle. He handed across two small plastic vials of sake, followed by a pair of porcelain cups.

Fukuda poured.

The Major smiled. "You know, I've been thinking," he said. "The Russians and the Americans still think we're pawns in their global game of political superiority."

Fukuda nodded. He raised his thumbleful of sake to the Major and they toasted silently. *Kampai.* They sipped.

"When I think about the power we can now display," Nakamura said. "All the economic strength, all the diplomatic expertise, all the cultural harmony in the *world* is useless without military power to back it up."

"Exactly," Fukuda agreed.

Nakamura laughed as he downed his sake. "Russia is a joke. A *joke!* Papier-mâché society. They are *nothing!"*

Fukuda refilled their cups. "I'll never forget my first trip to Moscow," he said. "Soviet propaganda is superb, but their social structure, their economy, stinks like cow shit."

"Unbelievable," said the Major, nodding. "They have this immense arsenal of weapons and a culture built on shadows. The shallowness, the . . . *inferiority!* How can they *dare* to lead the world?"

Fukuda drained his sake cup. Nakamura refilled it now.

"It's like a magic show. Look, there's nothing in the hat. Now, watch!" Fukuda imitated the action of pulling a rabbit out of an imaginary hat. "The Russians tell the world their society represents the future, and they do it all with mirrors! There's nothing really there. *Nothing!"*

He laughed so hard he couldn't hear the announcement of the next two wrestlers. Tears cascaded from his eyes.

"Nothing but unmistakable military might," Nakamura hissed. "The largest, strongest, most powerful armory in the world. *That's* what people see. *That's* what people believe. Paper tiger? Nonsense. Iron bear."

They drained their cups. Fukuda raised his right hand to signal a refill. Then he loosened his tie. His face had started to redden as the warm rice wine flowed quickly through the small capillaries in his head. *Sakeyake.* A sake suntan.

"But the bear has no meat on his bones," Fukuda said, laughing. "The society is bankrupt, illiterate, poverty-stricken. Show me tradition, show me culture, show me death! Where is it?"

Nakamura laughed now, his voice disappearing into the noise of the crowd as it roared with the conclusion of the next sumo bout.

"It doesn't exist! It's a sham, invisible!" yelled the Major. "The peasants do what they are told, the glue of society nothing more than military control. What culture has ever strengthened its roots because it was forced to?"

"Yes!" Fukuda roared. "You plant weeds in rocky soil

and order them to grow? You get dead weeds!" He collected two fresh vials of sake from the vendor.

Nakamura pounded the tatami with his fist. "That's what we have to upset, Bucho-san. *We* have the society, *we* have the economic structure, *we* can supply the harmony that will unite the social systems of the world!"

"But we can't do it without power. And real power grows out of this little piece of silicon." Fukuda held the tiny chip in his fingers. It sparkled in the bright light.

They again drained their sake cups. The final pair of wrestlers was being announced.

"Look at this richness, the skill of this performance before you," Fukuda said, sweeping a hand out across his body. "Two thousand years of continuous culture and tradition. Two thousand years! Even China does not have the unbroken Imperial rule as we do!"

His voice dropped as the crowd grew silent, watching in anticipation. "We are meant to lead the world, Nakamura-san!" he hissed. "That's the message of the Sun Goddess. That's the purpose of our economic domination." He paused. "That's the meaning of the future!"

The Major nodded. "It's only a matter of time," he said. His nose glowed. "The Russians will grind themselves into powder. The human spirit will rebel and turn on their repressive system. It cannot last."

He drained his sake cup.

"And the Americans," he continued. "Ah, the Americans. Their story ended with Vietnam. Pax Americana. Equally bankrupt." His eyes were glued to the *dohyo*. "Their economy is rotting, a plastic culture dissolving in adulation of the god of leisure."

Fukuda nodded, swaying gently forward now under the effects of the warm sake. "Rotting," he murmured. "Yes, rotting. They can respond only to wars and catastrophes. With a deadlock in world power, they have no alternative but to match military might with the Russians and to follow the lure of their capitalistic greed."

The Major filled their sake cups for the last time. "Shallow! Inferior! Who do they think they are, my friend, telling us what to do? We are no longer the apprentice."

No longer the apprentice.

The words rang, sharp and clear, in Fukuda's mind. His eyes focused on the final pair of grappling wrestlers as their fat, pink bodies, glistening with sweat, struggled in the ring. They were locked in a four-hand *mawashi* grip, and the crowd roared with delight.

"No longer the apprentice," Fukuda whispered with a smile. "The master next time!" he yelled above the deafening tumult of the crowd. "The Americans will follow the path of greed and self-intoxication to their own destruction! They have no tradition to guide them! That role is left to us!"

The two men stood as the crowd rose to its feet in anticipation of victory. Their arms encircled their bodies as they raised their sake cups high, their red *sakeyake* faces shining.

"To victory!" they shouted.

The crowd roared, as if in response.

"To survival!"

The voice of the crowd was singular now, ear-splitting, as the two wrestlers teetered on the straw barrier at the edge of the ring.

Only one would win.

Only one would survive.

Only one would be master.

"To the master!" they shouted, the crowd screaming as the two wrestlers fell simultaneously to the sand, outside the straw ring, one twisting heavily onto the other at the last moment, in victory.

Oshi-dashi. A push-out.

"To the master!"

12

"I'm sorry about the last time," Fukuda Kenji said. He spread his legs as Kiku smoothed the oil-and-camphor mixture over his outstretched nude body. It shined in the softness of the corner lamp.

"I was very afraid, Bucho-san." Her hands glided across his skin. She nudged him gently at shoulder and hip. He turned onto his back.

His half-erect penis, curved and supple and pulsating with rhythm, lay at an angle across his scrotum. Fukuda reached back and clasped his hands behind his head. "There was no excuse," he said, his eyes closed, his lips pursed in a faint smile.

Her hands accidentally brushed the tip of his penis. It flicked up momentarily and then settled back in his crotch.

"Your project is going better, I hope?" Kiku asked. She wore the same blue halter top and matching shorts. Her knees were folded beneath her as she sat beside his body.

He smiled. "Oh, yes," he said. An image of the optical chip formed in his mind. "Ahead of schedule now. New source of supply."

She dug her hands into the muscles of his legs, kneading, pushing, squeezing. Her fine black hair dropped down over her forehead, partially covering one eye. She swept it back with an easy motion.

"It sounds very important, Bucho-san." She could see his eyes darting rapidly back and forth beneath his eyelids.

His smile broadened. "Oh, it is," he said. "It is! It is the most important project our country has had since the war." He paused. "No, since the Tokugawa period."

"Since Tokugawa?" Kiku asked, a puzzled look on her face.

"Since Tokugawa," he repeated. Suddenly, his smile vanished. Then it reappeared. "No, not since Tokugawa," he said softly. One hand whipped out from beneath his fuzzy, burr-cut head, index finger extended. "Since the Sun Goddess." He replaced the hand behind his head.

Her fingers stopped. She exhaled. "Since Amaterasu Omikami?" she whispered.

Slowly her fingers started up again, a frown etched into her face. What was this man talking about, she wondered? Who *was* this Bucho-san, this disarmingly appealing, supremely self-controlled man given to violence in the midst of sensual gratification?

A project so important it ranked in history with the creation of her country?

Kiku reached behind her and withdrew a ladle of warm oil. Slowly, carefully, she poured a thin stream over the upper half his torso. Her expert fingers began massaging his chest.

"Yes, I think we're ready now, to lead the world," he said, his face relaxed, his tone confident.

Kiku watched his face as she swept her hands down his stomach and massaged his abdomen. Her feathery touch rippled the muscles in his midsection.

His expression remained unchanged. Eyes closed, nostrils flared, that smile stretched across his face, like *daruma*. What was happening, she wondered? Was the pressure of his business beginning to warp his mind? Was he not visiting her often enough now to release that pressure, to ease the tautness of his emotional strings?

Her hands slipped around his testicles, slick and oily and glistening with the sheen of polished silver. She curled her fingers around his penis and began to pull and twist, slowly, caressing, soothing.

"What is this project, Bucho-san, that is so important it ranks with the Sun Goddess?" Kiku asked, unclasping the diagonal line of buttons across her blouse.

His face turned serious. "Oh, that I cannot say, Kiku-chan. But you will soon see. Everyone will soon see. We will all be proud again."

She shook her shoulders slightly and the halter top slid silently off her back, revealing her firm, young breasts. She pulled her shorts down over her hips and tossed them in a corner. With her silky hands, she rubbed her breasts briefly until the nipples popped erect. She closed her eyes in anticipation.

"Proud of what?" she asked quietly, kneeling again, her legs slightly spread, her damp crescent parted. She lowered her mouth to Fukuda Kenji's abdomen as her tongue began its ritual dance.

"Proud of Nippon, of course," he answered, freeing a hand and placing it between her legs.

She lifted up to say, "But we are all proud of our country. We have a wonderful society, harmonious and happy. Our economy, thanks to you and the corporate elite, is the finest in the world." She dipped her little finger into his anus. "And we are at peace.

He shivered with pleasure. "It is not enough," he said, a frown returning to his face. "It is not enough to be happy and content and at peace with the world."

Her lips formed an oval and slipped down over his awakening penis. Kiku could feel its pulse with her tongue as she moistened it with her saliva. She inched her knees farther apart.

His hand slid up her thigh now, gently stroking its soft, young skin. "No, it is not enough," he repeated. "It is not nearly enough."

She drew back briefly. "But that is what we have worked our entire lives for. That is the gift we will give our children, Bucho-san."

"No!" he said sternly. "That is no gift, to be powerless but free. Never before in our history have we been so weak, so low on the pyramid of world power. That is not Nippon. That can never be Nippon!"

Kiku stopped, started to say something, but covered his penis with her mouth instead. Her tongue leapt and spun, stroking his stiffness with an expert touch.

His hand rose slowly up her thigh until his fingers

glided into her waiting warmth. She shivered as she felt his touch. Her body shook with pleasure. She arched her legs wider.

Fukuda's toes curled inward as he felt the first wave of sensual pleasure pass over his body. He placed his other hand on the top of Kiku's head, forcing her mouth to make more penetrating motions.

"That's not what this country is all about," he continued, eyes closed, face relaxed. "Nippon was created for a purpose, to serve as an example for the rest of the world. To lead, not to follow. To be . . . *master!*"

He drove his fingers into Kiku's slippery smoothness, bringing a moan from her throat. Thumb and forefinger found the source of her joy.

She lifted up, her eyes closed, her body responding automatically. She guided her hips over his midsection until she was poised above him, her back to his face.

"To be master!" he cried, louder. "We will control the future. To be weak is not to survive, it is to die. We are done with dying."

He arched his lower back and found her silkiness, entering her slowly, his penis fully erect, hard and wide. He controlled his motion, slowly, ever slowly, to prolong the pinnacle of pleasure.

Kiku squatted on her hands and knees, rotating her lower body in harmony with Fukuda's upward thrusts.

"Because," he said, his voice a whisper now, "we alone have the secret of power. It's in our blood, purified for generations, sanctified for centuries!"

His motions became more pronounced, more vertical. Kiku's body began to quiver with ecstasy.

"It's emptiness become full," he said. "Darkness become light. Weakness become strength. It is our very essence."

His body lunged with a more powerful motion as he grasped her hips with his hands and pulled her down as he arched upward.

"It's . . . a . . . matter . . . of . . . *control,*" he said, thrusting, pushing, his penis penetrating and withdrawing, attacking and retreating. He kept his eyes closed, his face expressionless.

"Apprentice no more," he hissed. He could feel the second wave of joy spreading through his body.

"The master next time!"

He made a final lunge and his semen rocketed into her. Kiku's vaginal muscles closed quickly around his hot hardness. She held him tightly between her legs, shaking, her hands clutching his ankles.

She gasped. "Oh, *yes,* Bucho-san! To be *master!*" She exploded now, her body shimmering with sweat in the cool light, a glistening doll. She spun around, keeping him inside her, until she collapsed on his chest.

She kissed a nipple, toying at it with her tongue. "Master?" she asked. "Is that what you will be?" Her voice was as soft as the morning mist.

"Not me," he said, undulating quietly within her.

"Who then?" she whispered.

"You," he said.

"Me?"

"Yes, you."

"Why? How?"

He smiled. "Not you alone. You and me. All of us."

"All of us?" She licked his erect nipple.

"Yes. All of us."

"Nippon?"

"Yes, exactly."

The pungency of the camphor pierced his nostrils. He took a deep breath, and exhaled.

Kiku caressed his burr head. Why? How? she thought, again.

"All of us," he said, his lips barely moving. "Nippon." Their two bodies fused together as one.

"Kore kara sensei ni naru," he whispered. *"The master next time!"*

13

Kenshin's fingers glided with flawless grace across the shiny white keys of the Yamaha baby grand. Mozart's Concert in F Major. The harmonious rhythm and collected mellowness echoed softly in the tatami practice room.

His mother, Michiko, and his *sensei*, Kawakami Yasuo, sat, cross-legged across from him, on matching *zabuton*. A small lacquered table crouched between them, its squat, curved legs supporting a porcelain pot of *mugicha* and two cups.

"He's doing so well," she said, closing her eyes and letting the soft sounds of her son's music embrace her. "I am very grateful to you, *sensei.*"

Kawakami reached down for a teacup. "It's not my doing, really. It's Kenshin, Fukuda-san. His discipline, his motivation, his intense level of energy are the highest I have seen in a generation of piano teaching." His thin, bony fingers curled around the brown *mashiko* glaze and brought the cup to his lips. His cavernous eyes flashed brightly in appreciation of his best student.

"How is he doing on his exams?" the *sensei* asked.

Michiko lowered her head, focusing on the white silk handkerchief which she twisted nervously in her hands. "Not so well," she replied.

"I'm sorry."

"Doesn't matter. Can't be helped." *Shikata ga nai.*

"His performance on the piano is incredible for a seventeen-year-old."

Michiko bowed forward slightly in deference to the music master. *"Domo,"* she said. "Thank you very much."

He set his teacup down. "I mean, with the surreptitious

practice sessions we have organized, Ken-chan has not had access to a normal playing schedule. I am most impressed."

Michiko nodded. "He needs to enter the University, however. If he does not at least get in, his father . . . I do not know what his father would do."

Kawakami nodded. His long gray hair, combed straight back, tickled the collar of his blue *yukata* as he moved. He smiled, revealing a set of even teeth, yellowed with age and stained with brown streaks of tobacco from his bamboo *kiseru.*

"But he seems to do so well in his studies despite the difficulties with his practice schedule."

Michiko shook her head, sipping her tea. "No, *sensei.* I think he does so well *because* of the difficulties. It forces him to respond, to try even harder. It provides him with an obstacle to surmount."

"Naruhodo," the master nodded. He pressed a pinch of tobacco into the tiny mouth of his wooden pipe and ignited it.

The music of Mozart flooded the room, a *tsunami* of melodic sounds. Kenshin arched over the top of the piano, his hands a blur on the keys. His body denied the enforced rigidity of his black school uniform, bending and rising, like bamboo in the wind.

His head floated back and forth, left to right and back again, his eyes never leaving the keyboard. Although the sheet music sat propped in front of him, he never looked up. He had no need to.

Michiko tightened the folds of her maroon kimono, adjusting the wide, purple *obi* around her waist. Her fingers were nervous, the nails long ago having been chewed away. She pulled the bottom of her kimono snugly under her knees.

She closed her eyes. Engulfed by the music, she dared to think about Kenshin's personal fulfillment. Her son's happiness was her happiness. Her spirits soared inwardly because he was embarking on his life's goal.

Outwardly, she feared for the consequences of a forsaken academic career: the first of five generations of Fukudas not to qualify for admission to Tokyo University.

Kawakami watched his brilliant student closely, his head bobbing and nodding, inundated by a waterfall of sound.

Kenshin's hands sprang higher off the keys as the piece neared its end. The base notes thundered with vigor, partially absorbed by the natural acoustics of the soft tatami.

With a flurry and a flash of his fingers, he swept the concerto quickly to its conclusion. The clear, high-octave notes of the soprano keys fluttered lightly in the air, like autumn leaves. Finished, drained, Kenshin slumped on his bench, hands by his side, fingers flexing.

"Subarashii!" Kawakami exlcaimed, clapping loudly in response to his student's performance. "Outstanding, Ken-chan!"

His mother clasped her hands to her chest. Her eyes glowed with pride.

Kenshin rose from his bench and bowed, deeply, before his teacher.

Kawakami acknowledged the bow by lowering his head. "Kenshin," he whispered. "There is simply no more I can teach you." He drew in a lungful of smoke.

"You must," Ken-chan replied. "I have much yet to learn. Stay with me, *sensei.* It is your spirit I need. Only the mechanics are there."

The master nodded.

"But I need the infusion of your soul. My execution may be technically correct, but it needs the breath of life."

"Naruhodo."

"The breath of your life."

"I understand."

Kenshin paused, watching his teacher. "Then you will continue?"

"If you insist." Kawakami exhaled a stream of smoke above his head.

Kenshin kneeled on the tatami and bowed again, touching his head to the mat. His graceful hands stretched in front of his body, thumbs clasped. *"Domo. Taihen osewas-ama degozaimasu."*

He straightened up and glanced at his mother. Michiko sat stiffly now, erect with pride. She tried to contain her emotions, hide them, disguise them, as she had been taught to do through generations of discipline in her culture.

But she could no longer restrain herself. She raised her handkerchief to her eyes as she began sobbing with joy. The tears flooded down her cheeks.

"Ken-chan! Oh, Ken-chan!" she cried. "I am so proud of your achievements. Your future is so clear!"

He bowed to his mother as he had done to his master. A gesture deep in sentiment, delivered with love.

Michiko dried her tears, dabbed at her eyes. "Will you please try to do well on your exams?"

"Of course, Mother. You know that I do not wish to dishonor my family's name."

She nodded, hands clasped now, palms upward, in her lap.

"But I cannot promise. I hope you understand."

The look in her eyes told him she did.

"I will try to do my best," he said. "But you know better than anyone else that my spirit, my soul, my life, is controlled by my music."

Michiko closed her eyes. She knew. She understood.

"Dewa, sensei," Kenshin said, turning now to Kawakami. "Until Thursday."

The master bowed. "I shall be waiting."

Ken-chan smiled his thin, tight, toothless smile.

Majime-san.

Mr. Serious.

14

The pneumatic doors of the *Hikari* bullet train whispered open. Fukuda and Sakamoto stepped out onto the platform at Nagoya, sidestepping the mass of passengers waiting to board. The *Hikari,* sleek and white, sat silently on the rails. *Hikari.* Speed of light.

Kimono-clad women stood with umbrellas open, using the paper and bamboo *higasa* as protection against the hot late April sun. Most of them dabbed at their upper lips with a folded handkerchief to soak away droplets of dampness.

"Ekiben! Ekiben!"

A platform vendor hawked station lunchboxes in a high-pitched tenor voice, his wooden cart shrieking as its parched wheels rolled across the asphalt. *Bento.* The traditional assortment of fish, seaweed and vinegared pickles, layered atop boiled rice.

Most major railway stations in Japan had their own special *ekiben,* featuring a container that incorporated products of local fame, such as pottery or bamboo, as well as regional culinary delicacies.

The Nagoya *ekiben* was a small, kiln-fired, copper-colored clay bowl. *Kamameshi.* The kettle meal.

"Domo." Sakamoto ordered two, handed the vendor a note and pocketed the change.

"Ekiben! Ekiben!" The shouts faded as the two Matsuzaka men made their way down the crowded stairwell.

Fukuda took Sakamoto by the elbow as they walked along the dark concrete passageway underneath the rails. At track 14, he nudged his *kobun* to the right and up the stairs.

Sakamoto looked over his shoulder as they mounted the steps. "Destination: Ise and south," he saw on the multicolored *kanji* marker.

At the top of the stairs, another *kanji* banner spanned the platform. His eyes glanced up at the message, bloodred on the virgin canvas. He smiled.

In protecting your domestic market against foreign imports, your government is protecting you.

They headed for the orange-and-green train. The colors marked it as a JNR local. Six cars, all second class, all unreserved, towed by a small diesel locomotive.

"Chotto," Sakamoto said as they boarded the southbound train. "If we are going to Fukui, then we are on the wrong train." He looked across at his Bucho. "Fukui is north, not south."

"This is the right train, Sakamoto-kun."

"But . . ."

Fukuda Kenji settled himself in one of the soft, blue velvet seats, flipping his briefcase next to him as he sank onto the cushions.

Sakamoto glanced at the window to see where, how, why he might have missed something. He plopped his portfolio onto the overhead rack and sat down, facing Fukuda.

"Not to second guess you, Bucho-san . . ." he said, a frown etched into his forehead. He snapped his thumb joints.

Fukuda lit up a Hi-Lite, pressing a forefinger to his lips as he exhaled the first puff, signaling Sakamoto to silence. "Wait until we are underway," he said. "Then it will become clear."

"Mamonaku hassha itashimasu. Ise-yuki degozaimasu."
The conductor's crisp voice announced their imminent departure. Fukuda checked his watch. It was 11:14.

At exactly 11:15, a large electric bell mounted on a platform pillar sounded its shrill cry. When it stopped, the conductor blew his whistle and flagged the engineer. The doors clicked shut. Fukuda smiled. Teamwork. Precision. *Perfection.*

Sakamoto watched Nagoya begin to disappear as the train pulled away from the station. The city was endless, an infinity of concrete. In the distance, he could see the giant *kanban,* three characters in neon flashing proudly in red, pinpointing the worldwide headquarters of Toyota.

He swung around now to face his *oyabun.* "Well?" he asked, folding his arms across his chest.

Fukuda puffed on his cigarette, exhaling through his nose. "You have played a vital role in this important project, Sakamoto-kun. The truth is that this project, while very much involving the SDF, is not at Fukui."

Sakamoto pressed two fingers against his rib cage. The popping knuckles echoed in the nearly empty car. "Fukui is the only site the SDF has for its rocket and missile launchings," he said, his frown magnified by his thick lenses.

Fukuda remained silent. Smoke from his cigarette curled upward until it was swept out the half-open window.

Sakamoto uncrossed his arms and leaned forward on his seat. "Where *are* we going, Bucho-san? Tell me."

"Matsuzaka," Fukuda purred.

"Matsuzaka!" Sakamoto yelled.

"Not so loud."

Sakamoto looked around. None of the other passengers, few in number, even bothered to glance up. An old woman whittled slowly on a short *shakuhachi,* the traditional Japanese flute. Small wooden chips caught in the folds of her kimono or fell silenty to the floor as she carved.

"Matsuzaka?" Sakamoto said, his voice quieter now. "The home of our chairman?"

"The same."

"But why?"

"You will see."

Sakamoto shook his head. "I still don't understand."

"You will."

"An SDF project?"

"Yes."

"In Matsuzaka?"

"Yes."

"Using components supplied by Matsuzaka affiliates?"

"In part, yes."

"And this project relates to me?"

"In part, yes." A half-smile formed on one side of Fukuda's face.

"What kind of project?"

"You will see."

"It is confidential?"

"Oh, yes."

"Are we the only ones at Matsuzaka who know about it?"

"*Mochiron.*"

"Surely there must be others."

"Only one." Fukuda paused. "One who committed the enormous power of our company so that Japan would be able to assume its rightful position as leader."

"Our chairman?"

"Yes."

"What about the government?"

"In part, yes." Fukuda's smile etched itself across the full width of his face now. "Enough for now," he said softly. "We'll be there shortly, and all will be clear."

Fukuda reached across his seat and took one of the *kamameshi,* cradling it in his lap. He unwrapped the clay lid and snapped the wooden, chopsticks apart. Plucking a piece of fish from the top of the kiln-fired kettle, he placed it in his mouth.

Sakamoto opened his *ekiben* and they ate in silence.

The local train made brief, punctual stops at each station along the line. Kuwaha. Yokkaichi. Suzuka. Tsu. Hisai. Small towns scattered along the jagged coastline like corks in a fisherman's net.

Huge, bent pines jutted out from the coast at sharp angles, like a massive battery of anti-aircraft guns. In the distance, Sakamoto saw the famous wedded rocks, *Meoto-Iwa,* rough granite and sandstone boulders just off-shore, connected only by a thick straw rope, woven of tatami fibers. A small vermillion *torii* gate stood atop the larger rock, symbol of the stone's religious significance. Symbol of the creation of Japan.

"Meoto Iwa," Sakamoto said, half-aloud, half to himself.

Fukuda nodded.

"Mamonaku, Matsuzaka degozaimasu."

As they rose from their seats, Sakamoto looked at the Bucho for a signal, a hint, a clue. Fukuda's face was frozen behind a cold, glassy stare, expressionless and intense.

They exited the station quickly. Looking to his left, Fukuda saw the Matsuzaka driver waiting by his maroon Toyota.

"The usual, but by way of Ise first," he said, ducking as he lowered himself into the back seat. Sakamoto joined him, tossing his briefcase on the floor between his feet.

With a nod, the driver spun out of the station and onto the coast road. The Toyota's heavy tires hummed sonorously on the hard asphalt. They sped along the Ise Skyline Highway through rows of massive Japanese cypress and cedar, their long branches arching upward, protective. The soothing April sun, now at its noontime apogee, filtered softly down through the glowing leaves.

The driver pulled into an overlook and stopped.

Fukuda motioned for Sakamoto to get out of the car. They walked to the edge of the knee-high railing and stood, looking out across the green valley.

"There," Fukuda Kenji said, gesturing toward the buildings below.

Sakamoto stood and frowned. He removed his glasses and wiped them on his shirt.

"The Ise Shrine," he said, hands extended, palms up. "But I still don't understand."

Fukuda's eyes narrowed. He pulled a cigarette out of his pocket and lit it. The wind whipped the white smoke across his face like a veil as he exhaled.

"Ise," he said quietly. "Ise." Louder. *"Ise!"* His voice rose, his mouth became stern, the veins stood out on the sides of his neck. "The most sacred place in Japan. Dedicated to the Sun Goddess, Amaterasu-Omikami! The shrine, the symbol, of our most precious heritage: our history, our culture, our tradition!

"The Shrine of Ise, Sakamoto-kun." Fukuda's voice was mellow now, his words swept upward and away by the vortex of wind. "The holiest of holies. You, me, the entire nation of Nippon, symbolized by that sacred shrine."

Sakamoto nodded, entranced by the view below.

"Repository of the Sacred Mirror, the Yata-no-Kagami, one of our three Sacred Treasures."

The Mirror.

The Jewel.

The Sword.

"Three Sacred Treasures that constitute the regalia of the Japanese Imperial Throne."

Symbol of hierarchy.

Symbol of continuity.

Symbol of *superiority.*

Sakamoto Ryuji could see the pristine wood of the holy shrine below, its natural color contrasting with the light green leaves of the tall cypress and cedar above.

Beams crossed at the peak of the shrine's roof. The raw, unfinished walls stood straight and proud, testimony to over two thousand years of continous rebuilding in conformity with the original plans. The cypress fences, square and concentric, like sake measures, separated the sacred inner chambers from the crowds of visiting pilgrims outside.

Sakamoto held his breath. The shrine appeared to float, to hover, before his very eyes. It was there and it was not there.

The symbol of his creation.

The link to his past.

The road to his future.

"Perseverance," Fukuda whispered.

The Mirror.

"Victory." The words were pure velvet.

The Jewel.

"Survival!" The purpose of life.

The Sword.

You must achieve oneness with your sword!

The words of Kensei echoed softly in Fukuda's mind as he stood above the valley of glory. His fingers gripped the wooden railing in front of him until the knuckles turned white.

In his mind's eye, he spun and turned, his sword flashing in an arc above his head, light as air, invisible, deadly.

He lunged, he swung, his opponents vanished! He dropped to one knee and brought his sword upward, deflecting all blows.

He was invincible!

He was the culmination of a millennium!

He was Japan!

"Bucho-san! Bucho-san!" Sakamoto tugged at Fukuda's elbow.

Fukuda looked him in the eye. His eyes were as wide as Ise Bay now. *"Yoshi,"* he said, his voice a whisper.

Sakamoto swallowed. He could taste the pure, clear water that he had sipped so many times on his visits to this sacred place. He could smell the freshness of the cypress that was cut, new, every twenty years, to rebuild the shrine.

Staring down at the magic structure below, he moved his hands slowly along the wooden railing. He could feel its smoothness, the unblemished silkiness of the cypress used to construct the three concentric inner fences.

The purity!

The holiness!

The sacred home of his ancestors and of all his countrymen!

The outer fence.

Perseverance!

The central fence.

Victory!

The inner fence.

Survival!

Sakamoto swallowed again. His breathing became shorter as he stood, immobilized by the sacred scene below. His hands became one with the cypress.

He *was* the cypress.

15

Fukuda and Sakamoto returned to the car, and the driver eased back onto the ribbon of asphalt. The road curved steadily upward, rising ever higher above the magic valley of holiness below. The giant cypress and cedar grew even larger, their branches thicker, their leaves greener.

In moments, they arrived at the peak of the small mountain. A large, painted *kanji* sign at the end of the road gave a stern warning to all visitors: *Tachi Iri Kin Shi.*

TRESPASSERS WILL BE SHOT. SURVIVORS WILL BE SHOT AGAIN.

When the car came to a stop, Fukuda jumped out and motioned Sakamoto to follow. He led the way up a small path through the thick cypress; the trail was almost invisible among the massive trees. They heard no birds singing, could barely see sunlight through the dense leaf cover. The scent of fresh cedar sweetened the air, swept softly along by a light breeze.

Suddenly they entered a clearing. No trees, no brush, just a patch of skin on the earth, shaved of all hair.

Sakamoto perceived movement out of the corner of his eye. He turned his head and saw an armed figure, dressed in black, at the edge of the clearing. He grabbed Fukuda's arm.

Fukuda looked up, and then smiled. "One of many, Sakamoto-kun, who preserve this secret." He walked to his left. Uncovering a pair of electric buttons hidden inside the trunk of a towering cedar, he pressed, twice, with his thumb. The ground began to vibrate as the clearing parted into equal halves. The whine of electric generators poured out of the widening crack.

Moments later, they stood in a small wooden elevator, descending far into the ground. Fukuda put his hand on a side wall. He could feel the liquid-smooth cypress, soft to the touch, fresh as the air on a cold winter day.

He stared straight ahead. Sakamoto looked at him repeatedly during their descent. The Bucho remained motionless, transfixed.

When they stopped, Fukuda opened the single door and swung it wide. They stepped out onto a high platform and stood above a glittering display of stainless steel.

Sakamoto staggered forward, steadying himself on the railing.

It was the most awesome display of rocketry he had ever seen.

Before his eyes, so close he felt he could reach out and touch the smooth skin, two gigantic rockets stood, fully erect, as if at attention.

Sakamoto swallowed, wiping a sleeve across his mouth. Below to his left, a half-dozen workers, pure and clean in antiseptic white uniforms, busied themselves with a rocket engine under the chief technician's guidance. Master and apprentice. Behind them sat a pair of immense metallic spheres, painted white with a red circle atop the rounded surface.

Hi-no-Maru.

The Rising Sun.

Sakamoto's eyes moved to his right, his mouth open, his grip tight on the railing. He saw a group of smaller missiles, perhaps twelve feet in length, arranged against a far wall like vertical stakes in a giant picket fence.

Ahead, bannered across a far wall, the bright red *kanji* exploded into view:

Perseverance, and perseverance alone, will bring victory.

Footsteps slapped at the stairs of the viewing platform. Fukuda turned to greet them.

"Ah, Bucho-san. *Domo.* We wondered if something had happened." It was Major Nakamura, flanked by Katoh Shohei, of MITI.

"Domo. Sorry to keep you waiting." They exchanged bows.

Fukuda motioned to his *kobun* to join them. "My section chief, Sakamoto."

He stepped forward at the Bucho's signal. *"Matsuzaka no Sakamoto desu,"* he said, bowing deeply.

"Nakamura," said the Major, his bald head shiny and smooth.

"Katoh. *Domo."* The large, heavy-set MITI bureaucrat returned the bow. Beads of perspiration sparkled on his forehead.

"Let's proceed," Fukuda said, looking at the others. He led them down the polished cypress staircase that dropped below the viewing platform.

Sakamoto held onto the wooden railing as he descended the steps, in awe of the technology arrayed about him, more uncertain about the project's ideological implications than of his physical footing.

The three civilians were almost identically clad. Dark gray suits, white shirts, black shoes, charcoal neckties.

Major Nakamura was dressed in his military uniform. Medals of honor and merit danced on his chest, ribbons of red and blue and glistening green. His khakis, stiffly pressed, seemed to stand erect on their own. At his side, he wore his samurai sword, long and curved, proud possession of nine generations of Nakamuras. His shining head reflected pinpoints of light, a glowing buoy floating in a sea of black heads.

Fukuda escorted them into a small room outfitted with electronic tracking gear. Nakamura stood alongside various altimeter and high-velocity gauges, Katoh next to a radar screen. Its eery green sweephand traced a wide arc across a vast expanse of nothingness.

The Bucho positioned himself in front of a large television screen. He clicked it on.

The Major checked his watch as the screen flickered alive. "Two o'clock lift off, right?" he asked, winding the stem. He settled back in his chair.

"Sono tori," Fukuda answered, his eyes glued to the screen. "The test missile is ready for firing."

Eight eyes focused on the TV monitor. A small white

projectile sat on its launching pad, angled vertically upward toward the sky, its tail spewing trails of white gas.

Sakamoto's eyes widened. "Fukui?"

The Bucho nodded.

Sakamoto recognized the familiar surroundings of the Fukui Missile Test Center, the Cape Canaveral of Japan, site of official rocket launchings sponsored by JASA.

Fukui launched the first commercial communications satellite from Japan in the early 1970s.

Fukui launched the first long-distance space-tracker missile in the late 1970s.

Fukui launched Japan's first defense missile in the early 1980s, in cooperation with the U.S. Air Force and the SDF. The missile was an exact replica of the Hawk, manufactured by Raytheon but licensed under a special arrangement to Matsuzaka Heavy Industries. Matsuzaka Electric had supplied the guidance and electronic systems.

Sakamoto's eyes never left the screen. "This missile we are watching. A routine reconnaissance flight?"

Fukuda nodded. "Routine as far as JASA is concerned. After it is airborne, it is under our control."

"Our control?" Sakamoto rotated his head now, looking quizzically at the Bucho.

"The priceless optical chips you brought back from America."

"Yes?"

"One of those chips has been installed in this missile to alter its guidance system, which of course Matsuzaka Electric developed in the first place."

The Major picked up the thread. "Once the missile is airborne, it will proceed to a preset cruising altitude. It is a low-level reconnaissance missile, no offensive capability, powered by solid fuel, which limits its range."

Fukuda nodded. He pulled out a Hi-Lite and stuck it between his lips, unlighted.

"What will happen after the missile is launched?" Sakamoto asked.

"That is where the routine test ends," Fukuda said, the cigarette bobbing as he talked. "This particular test flight is scheduled for the Inland Sea."

Sakamoto fidgeted in his chair. "And once it gets there?"

"The Micro Optix chip has been preprogrammed with the geographical features of the Inland Sea." Fukuda reached into his pocket for a match. "It also contains the computerized coordinates and physical features of all coastal shipping expected to be on the water at exactly 2:10 p.m. today. This has been prearranged with the Ministry of Transportation," he added.

"So the missile will trace the area and transmit its electronic data back to this tracking station?" Sakamoto looked at the MITI man.

Katoh cleared his throat. "Essentially, yes. With one exception. Major?" He reached up to mop his forehead. Perspiration seeped from every pore now.

"Once the missile is over the Inland Sea, the optical sensor will assume control of its guidance system," Nakamura explained, rubbing a damp palm over his smooth head. "At that point, the microprocessor will keep the missile on a new course set by comparing the preprogrammed geographical features with the actual geography it sees during flight." The Major's medals clinked softly in the darkened room.

Sakamoto turned to face the Bucho. "But why the need for preprogramming if all it does is feed back what it sees?"

Fukuda rose from his chair. He could see the numbers countdown beginning now, seconds before lift-off.

"Because that's *our* test, Sakamoto-kun," he said, his eyes narrowing at the screen. "Once the terrain comparison mode takes over—called TerCom by the Americans—the optical sensor will steer the missile to a preprogrammed target. We have inserted the coordinates of a fishing vessel in the area which agreed to cooperate. The vessel will be steering an erratic course, at maximum speed."

Sakamoto's face brightened. It was becoming clear to him now. "And when the missile 'sees' the target—in this case, the fishing boat—it will lock in on the image and strike it?"

"Sono tori." Fukuda struck the match now and held it to his cigarette. His eyes, wide with expectation, reflected the flame. "But don't worry," he said. "The missile is not armed. It will merely hit the ship, causing minor damage. Operational errors will be cited, and the captain reimbursed for repairs." He took a deep puff on his cigarette and exhaled.

"Go . . . shi . . . san . . . ni . . . ichi!"

The crisp, tenor voice of the NHK announcer completed the countdown, and the small white missile was airborne. Specially mounted cameras carried the course of the flight nationwide.

For JASA, a routine reconnaissance flight.

For Fukuda, a test of his country's future. Of Japan's survival.

The thin pencil of white rose gracefully, partially hidden by the rose-colored cloud of exhaust in its wake. It slowly arched higher, until it reached its cruising altitude of just under two thousand feet.

Eight eyes in the darkened room watched as the airborne cameras took over.

2:03. An overshot of Nagoya. The Toyota tower, tall and red.

2:05. Osaka. Its historic castle clearly in view.

2:08. Kobe. The countless piers and shipping berths of Japan's largest seaport west of Yokohama.

Fukuda drew on his cigarette, fingers steady, breathing controlled. Oh, Musashi, he thought! If you could only be here now!

Major Nakamura held his breath.

Katoh clenched his white handkerchief in his right hand. Worry, doubt, concern, never left his face. Had they overcommitted?

Sakamoto swallowed. How fortunate he was, he thought, that Fukuda would include him in this historic event.

2:09. Takamatsu, Shikoku's principal city. Its central park, cool and green, shimmered under the Saturday sun.

2:09:30. A broad expanse of water. The Inland Sea.

2:09:45. A ferry boat. Heads upturned, hands waving.

2:09:53. A fishing boat, steering a zig-zag course.

2:09:55. *The* fishing boat.

2:10:00. Darkness. Squiggles on the screen, followed by a monochromatic NHK announcement: *Omachi kudasai.*

One moment please.

Fukuda and Nakamura leapt out of their chairs, shouting wildly, hugging each other, raising their hands high in the air.

"Banzai!" they shouted.

"Banzai!" they cried, in the traditional samurai victory cheer.

"Banzai!"

Katoh stood nervously to one side, his handkerchief twisted, his eyes afraid. He never thought it would actually happen, this science fiction tale of silicon chips and guided missiles.

But now he knew.

His stomach muscles cramped. A tight knot, a reminder.

Sakamoto bowed deeply to Fukuda. *"Domo,* Bucho-san," he said. "I am pleased and honored to have played even a small role in the success of this project."

The Major walked up to the TV screen and flicked off the sound.

They knew what they needed to know.

It worked.

The optical chip had functioned.

There was no turning back now.

16

Fukuda and the Major exchanged bows. Their faces were solemn, their eyes crystal clear.

"Yoshi," Fukuda said. "Let's coordinate the next schedule." They walked out of the viewing chamber back onto the cold concrete floor of the underground cave.

Sakamoto tugged at his Bucho's sleeve. "Fukuda-san, *ne,"* he said. "Surely the test flight is not the victory you are working toward. What about these massive rockets, the giant spheres with the Rising Sun configurations?" He gestured toward the gleaming white balls.

Fukuda stopped and turned around. "The test flight of the TerCom missile was successful," he said, his voice low. "That we now know. Of course, we were never really in doubt."

Sakamoto nodded.

The Bucho smiled that confident half-smile again. "Each of these rockets can carry twelve missiles like you just saw in the test flight. When they are high above the earth's surface in a randomly patterned orbit, they will be impossible to track. Preprogrammed by computer, they can be controlled by one of our most powerful microprocessors."

He rubbed a hand over his burr head. He was in full control now. His voice rose.

"These ridiculous missiles, in their pure reconnaissance phase, are harmless. A joke! They are nothing more than Nikon cameras flying at a thousand miles per hour. An insult to the real power of this nation!" Fukuda's voice pierced the subterranean stillness.

Sakamoto felt his palms grow cold with dampness. Butterflies fluttered now in his stomach. Was he ready for what was coming next?

"The age of innocence is over, Sakamoto-kun! Japan no longer has to be an apprentice! We can be the masters now!"

Fukuda was practically screaming. His words echoed off the cold stone walls.

"This missile, armed with a small nuclear warhead and outfitted with the optical sensor, is *unstoppable!* It is potentially more threatening than the American Cruise missile, more powerful than any armed bomb, more accurate than any ICBM!" His voice dropped. "This, my friend, is our ALARM."

Sakamoto blinked as a speck of sweat rolled into one eye. He rubbed it with the back of his hand.

"Air-Launched Attack and Reconnaissance Missile," the Major said, stepping forward. He raised his right fist high in the air. "With the emphasis on attack!"

"These rockets can be launched, propelling that satellite into space," he said, gesturing toward the Rising Sun spheres. "Twelve ALARM missiles, attack-ready, orbiting randomly. Each one preprogrammed to strike a different strategic target. With small-signal radar and low-level flight capability, the ALARM flies *under* electronic detection systems. It is impregnable!"

"What will be the twelve targets?" Sakamoto asked nervously, drawing nearer the platform.

"New York," said the Major, with a smile.

"Washington," said Katoh, his face now soaking wet. "Ottawa, Paris, London, Bonn, Rome."

"Moscow," Fukuda whispered, his eyes afire. "Leningrad, Peking, Shanghai."

"That's eleven," Sakamoto said, counting the world's political capitals on his fingertips.

"And Tokyo!" Fukuda murmured, a sigh so soft, so shocking, it was almost inaudible.

"Tokyo? That can't be true!" Sakamoto wiped damp palms on his trousers.

"Hai!" Fukuda shouted. "Even Tokyo!"

Katoh lumbered across the hard floor, mopping his moon-shaped face with a crumpled handkerchief.

"Wait," he said, his eyes darting, his fingers quivering like the tail of a carp. "You told us from the beginning that Tokyo would never be on the target list."

"It was a decision made at the highest levels." said the Major. "The coordinates have been set, and the geographical features of the city preprogrammed into the Micro Optix chip along with the others." He stood defiant, arms folded across his decorated chest.

Katoh swallowed. He tasted bile. "But that raised the risk of this operation unacceptably. If we fail . . ." He shut his eyes.

"Nonsense!" Fukuda roared. He jumped down and whipped the Major's sword from its sheath. Spinning, he turned and waved it above his head in a high arc, the silver blade sparkling in the bright lights. His eyes danced, alive and burning.

"There is no middle ground now, Katoh-kun. We win, or we lose. And we will win!" He slashed at an imaginary opponent.

Timing is strategy. There is timing in everything.

"But if we lose," Katoh interrupted. "The whole nation loses. We commit mass *harakiri* and exterminate our precious culture! Our samurai ancestors would—"

"Would *approve,* Katoh-kun! Musashi would be proud! Victory at all costs, no matter how long and hard the road, for without victory there is no survival!" Fukuda slashed out with his sword and watched the MITI man shrink back.

Perceive those things that cannot be seen.

"Imagine, my friend! A global strategy based on the ultimate power, and the willingness to use that power against oneself if it fails! It's the genius of self-denial! *Cultural suicide!"*

Fukuda Kenji whirled on his right foot and dropped to one knee. He brought the shining blade over his head in a vicious vertical slash, stopping it just inches from the floor. His face was dry and bone-smooth. His eyes stared ahead, piercing the past, leaping ahead to the future.

Timing of the void is born in timing of the cunning.

In an instant, he was erect again, his feet a blur, twisting, turning, spinning. The blade of his sword disappeared as he executed move after intricate move. He was Musashi. The Sword Saint. *Kensei.*

The ghostlike technicians, their white uniforms glowing softly, crept forward behind their chief until they formed a small circle around the whirling samurai.

Katoh's shoulders slumped, his head down, arms limp. Fear gnawed at his insides. He was afraid for his country.

The Major stood stiffly at attention, his eyes proud, his head erect. He watched Fukuda's artistry with a look of deep satisfaction.

Sakamoto drew up next to the Major, fascinated with the professional display by his Bucho.

Fukuda spun to his left now, and with a long, arching leap, sprang back to the staircase. He held the sword at his side, the blade curving upward, gleaming.

"These twelve missiles can be launched into orbit when we are ready," he said. His voice was soft. The words purred out in a quiet whisper. "By May 15, if necessary."

Katoh closed his eyes.

"Yoshi," said the Major. He smiled.

Sakamoto cleared his throat. "May 15," he said. "The negotiations with Moscow?"

Fukuda nodded. "And the date of our Security Treaty renewal with the United States. Two events that symbolize our past submission to the two fictitious world powers. Two events that can cause us to be humiliated again, unless we are prepared to act."

He swung the sword over his head, holding it high. "By May 15, if these negotiations are not moving in our favor, we can blast the *Hi-no-Maru* into orbit. Each missile can be armed with nuclear warheads. And they can be propelled by a radically new concept in propulsion!"

Fukuda brought the sword down in a diagonal slash, and climbed up a half-dozen stairs.

"We have eliminated the need for solid fuel," he said, tiny beads of perspiration forming on his burr head, covering it like dew. "Matsuzaka Electric has pioneered developments in nuclear *fusion.* This new fuel carries a hundred times more energy in each kilogram than chemical fuels."

He closed his eyes, the stillness of the deep underground chamber echoing in his ears. He clenched the sword in both hands now. His palms were dry, secure as sandpaper.

"Which is why we can make these missiles so *small!*" he roared. "We have packed ten times the energy in one-half the space at one-fourth the cost of conventional fuels! Each of these tiny missiles is powered by a miniature sun, hundreds of tiny nuclear blasts, controlled in succession by computer, propelling the projectile through space!"

Sakamoto stepped forward, looking up proudly at his Bucho. "Which means they can go into a higher orbit!" His face beamed.

"Exactly!" Fukuda stepped forward now, raising the sword high above his head. "Limitless fuel! Impregnable defense! Pinpoint targeting by the optical chip! Just the bargaining power we need to regain our islands from Russia and eliminate the humiliating Security Treaty with the United States."

Sakamoto bowed deeply. "We are the *masters!*" he cried.

"Yoshi!" Fukuda bellowed. "If the Americans or the Russians resist, we can proceed to fire our missiles at random. We will never suffer the humiliation of defeat again!"

"Banzai!"

The entire crowd of technicians raised its arms in the traditional victory salute.

"Japan will be the master!" Fukuda roared. *"Banzai!"*

"The world will be our apprentice!"

Nakamura and Sakamoto joined the workers in a salute to Fukuda Kenji, and the underground cavern thundered with their shouts.

Fukuda reached the concrete floor in a single, flowing leap. He stood before the Major, then bowed deeply.

The Major returned the bow. Fukuda handed him his sword.

Without looking down, the Major slid it deftly into its sheath, a talent centuries old, unpracticed, instinctive.

They bowed again.

Fukuda turned to Sakamoto.

They bowed. "I trust everything to your judgment," the kacho said.

Fukuda then faced Katoh.

The heavy-set MITI official bowed to the Matsuzaka Bucho. As he straightened up, tears flowed uncontrollably from his eyes in a waterfall of fear. He blinked, but his vision remained a blur.

"My God, what have we done?" he cried to himself.

Part IV

WIND

1

Roger Harris moved to the forehand court to serve the second game. As he raised his racquet, a red light connected to the telephone system began flashing above the court, indicating an incoming call upstairs.

"Serve it!" Art Garrett shouted. He bounced on the balls of his feet, his racquet ready, the flashing light visible out of the corner of his eye, a beacon of urgency. Nobody called that early in the morning, he thought.

Whether distracted by the harsh, blinking red light or by the accumulated failures of the long week, he blew the return. Harris had the first point.

"Shit," Garrett said, running forward to grab his jacket before he corkscrewed up the circular stairs to the phone. "I'll be right back. This match is not over yet."

After ten minutes had passed and Art still hadn't returned, Roger set his racquet down and went upstairs. As he surfaced through the wooden hatch, he saw Art sitting on the arm of a couch, one hand scribbling fast, the other gripping the receiver so hard his knuckles were white.

He poured himself a small glass of juice from the pitcher on the bar as he listened to Art's end of the conversation.

"We'll get right back to you, Jim. Stay close to the phone," was all he heard him say. Art cradled the receiver quietly and fell back onto the cushions, eyes closed.

"That's it," he said. "We're gone." His face was grim.

"What do you mean, we're gone?" Roger asked, half smiling. "Who was that?" He held the glass, undrunk, in his left hand.

"Masters," Art said, righting himself and walking over to the oval bar. "He said about five million bucks' worth of our 256Ks just disappeared last night, and one of our people was killed."

"He said *what?*" Harris asked, his mouth wide, his face pale with shock. "He must be joking." He set the glass down and leaned against the bar.

Garrett shook his head. "This is no joke. The early morning shift found about a hundred chips missing from packing and receiving. Figured it had to have happened during the night." He looked down at his notes, his lips drawn tight. "A janitor, an older man, was found dead, apparently from strangulation."

"Any idea how it happened?"

Garrett shook his head again. "Not yet. They're working on it with the Sunnyvale police."

"Standard chips?"

"Both."

"Both?"

Garrett nodded. "That's the kicker. Opticals, too."

Roger slammed a fist on the countertop. "That's impossible! We just went over security with a goddam—"

"I know," Art interrupted. "But they're gone, just the same. Masters checked the code numbers of the missing chips against the production batches. About twenty opticals in all. They're still working on the inventory count."

Harris shook his head in disbelief. He drew his sweatband across his mouth.

"Any signs of a break-in—what about the motion detectors?"

"Nothing. All the detection equipment is untouched, and working perfectly. They're double-checking the access points."

Turning to Roger, he said, "Book us on the breakfast flight tomorrow morning out of Newark. Something this big you and I both have to check out."

2

United's flight 35 out of Newark had left on time, and the absence of normally heavy headwinds put its arrival in San Francisco ahead of schedule.

Art Garrett and Roger Harris clicked their seatbelts shut when the steward announced the final approach. Both men were dressed casually, as usual—Garrett in Levi's and an open-necked, short-sleeved knit shirt, striped horizontally in red and green, Harris in wide-wale maroon cords with a plaid workshirt. Their hand luggage rested snugly under their seats.

"You've been strangely silent the whole trip," Harris said, flipping up his tray table and securing it.

Garrett glanced at his colleague. "Sorry, Roger," he said, forcing a half-smile. "Trying to put together a list of options, you know, running the alternatives back and forth through my mind." He pressed his moustache with thumb and forefinger.

The wheels of the giant jet screeched onto the runway. Small puffs of blue smoke swept past the windows. Heavy gray clouds clung close to the small hills like a thick blanket, promising rain.

As the aircraft taxied to the gate, Roger asked, "Anything you want to share? You're always several steps ahead."

Garrett unbuckled his belt and stood to join the throng of disembarking passengers. It had been a full flight.

"Nothing, really," he said somberly. "One thought—well, I'll mention it to you in the car."

The line at the Avis counter was six-deep all across. Garrett's patience was near the breaking point as one customer in line, a younger man elegantly dressed, argued with the harrassed clerk about a nonexistent luxury model he had reserved.

"I've told you," the attractive brunette repeated, her eyes narrowing in frustration at the uncooperative client, "the Mercedes is gone. Somebody else rented it out. We'll *give* you another car."

"And I've told *you*, Miss," he replied, his voice harsh and uncompromising, "I don't *want* another car. I want the Benz."

Art glanced up at the ceiling for the fifth time, rolling his eyeballs in agony. He muttered unprintable criticisms about efficiency in the rental car business and handed Harris his bag.

"Here, you hack through the red tape. I'm going to phone Masters to tell him we'll be there in an hour."

He glanced at his watch. He also wanted to give Sally a call. News of the theft had driven everything else from his mind, and he hadn't called her on Friday to thank her for listening. He walked over to the bank of pay phones and slumped down onto the hard stool.

He clinked in a dime and had started to dial when a voice carried out across the rotating baggage carousel.

"Hey, Art! Art Garrett!"

Art swung around on his seat, his eyes scanning the sea of faces at the baggage claim. Small children played on the carpeted surface just inside the turnstile while their parents struggled with the family luggage. A stewardess tried to put her bag onto her small metal roller, but the case was too heavy and split the frail steel frame. A couple argued with the skycap by the exit, claiming that the airline had given them the wrong claim stubs.

Art's eyes lit up as he recognized Charlie Wosniak, president of Signal Systems, a nearby competitor in Sunnyvale. He stood up to great his old friend.

"Charlie, how are you? God, how long has it been?"

"Good to see you, Art. How's the industry's chief whipping boy?" Wosniak extended his hand and Art shook it warmly.

"Whipping boy? Where'd you get that term of endearment? We're the quiet ones on the block."

"You're kidding. Haven't you seen the papers this morning?" He pulled a newspaper from under his arm and unfolded it. "Full of pictures of you and Senator Mitchell in full tilt Thursday. Quite a show!"

Art frowned. He had been so absorbed by the chip problem that he had ignored the papers.

"Let's see," he said, taking the newspaper from Wosniak's outstretched hand. His eyes scanned the article and accompanying pictures on the first business page of the Washington Post. He winced as he recognized himself gesturing dramatically in mid-speech. "Could have been a lot worse, Charlie," he said, handing the paper back. "I let my impatience get the worst of me."

Wosniak laughed. "Still the tough competitor, aren't you? My only problem was, I had to follow your act yesterday."

Garrett managed a smile. "Christ, the guillotine of His Majesty resharpened for another slice? How did you fare?" He stuffed his hands into his pockets, his face serious.

"No better than you did. The Senator was still bristling from your testimony and was in no mood to listen to any more arguments about the need for a national industrial policy." He took the newspaper and folded it.

"Not surprising," Art said, looking down at his friend. "Do me a favor, Charlie—spare me the gory details. I've got to go lick my own wounds."

Wosniak put a hand on Art's shoulder. Once rivals at IBM, they had both left the computer giant to start their own firms. Signal Systems specialized in airborne electronic communications equipment. Voice-activated, two-way miniature radios. Missile tracking gear. It was smaller than Micro Optix but used much of the advanced chip technology Garrett had developed. And despite their competitive rivalry, the two men remained close. Especially where policy and security issues were concerned.

"Don't take it so seriously. The Senator's bullet holes don't even show."

Art pressed his drooping moustache, exhaustion showed

in his eyes. "It's not the Washington thing, Charlie," he said, lowering his voice. "We've just lost a shitload of chips. Disappeared, stolen, gonzo."

Wosniak's smile evaporated. "Jesus, I'm sorry. Any idea how it happened, who did it?"

Garrett shook his head. "That's what we're here to find out." He glanced over Wosniak's head as he saw Roger approaching. "Here he is." He signaled for Roger to join them.

"Car all set?"

"Yeah, after that asshole settled for a Cadillac." He turned to Wosniak. "Hi, I'm Roger Harris. R&D, Micro Optix."

"Charlie Wosniak."

They shook hands.

"Sorry, Roger. Charlie and I used to be at IBM together. He runs Signal Systems now."

"Right, now I remember," he said. "You testified yesterday afternoon, after the Lone Ranger here shot up the conference room on Thursday."

Wosniak nodded.

"How the hell did you know that?" Art asked.

"Read it in the papers on the flight out this morning. You were so lost in thought, I decided not to bother you with it."

"Art, I'm stunned to hear about your chip theft," Wosniak interrupted. "Do you know what they took, exactly?" He was frowning now.

"Yeah," he said. "Potful of 256Ks."

Wosniak let out a long, low whistle.

"Holy shit."

"You said it."

"Opticals?"

"In part," Roger said, drawing in close and lowering his voice. The passenger traffic around them was dense enough, and loud enough, to protect them from being overheard. "We haven't had a chance yet to get an exact count from inventory controls."

"When'd it happen?"

"Either very late Thursday night or very early yesterday morning," Art said.

Wosniak shook his head, silent for a minute, sympathetic. "Any idea of the total value?"

"About five million bucks," Roger said, "give or take a dime."

"Five million dollars!" Wosniak's eyes widened.

"Not so loud, Charlie," Art said, placing a hand on his shoulder and looking around. When he was certain no one was paying attention, he turned back to him and said, "Over a hundred chips disappeared in all, maybe twenty, twenty-five opticals. That's all we know."

"Five million bucks, though. Jesus, that's gotta be some kind of record for a single theft."

"Yeah, well, keep it to yourself because this isn't going to hit the papers."

"I will, I will." Wosniak paused. "You know, when we got hit last year, we lost about a million worth of our voice-activating devices that use your 64Ks."

Art snapped his fingers. "That's right. I had forgotten about that. Ever find out who did it?"

"Sure. It was our own security chief who masterminded the job."

Art froze as his eyes met Roger's. Masters had said that there were no signs of forced entry in their own case. An inside job? Herman Brewster? *Herman?* Art put the thought immediately out of his mind. He'd known Brewster for more than ten years. He was unimpeachable.

"We had the devices stored in a locked room, protected by a heavy layer of steel mesh, you know?" Wosniak went on. "Closed circuit TV, motion alarms, ultrasonic detection equipment, the whole thing. Turned out the security guy helped several others cart away the circuits, took his cut and just disappeared." He stroked his dark-brown beard as he talked. "Same thing happened to Monolithic Memories a few months later. They lost about $3 million worth of 64Ks."

"Ever get him?" Art asked.

"Who?"

"The security guard."

Wosniak shook his head. "Nope, just diappeared." He paused. "Surprising thing is this doesn't happen more often, considering the stakes."

Roger nodded. "We're all covered by insurance, but that's the least of our worries. The value of these sophisticated devices . . . in the wrong hands . . ." His voice trailed off.

"When I was at Semiconductor Arrays," Art said, looking down at Wosniak, "I had a hell of a time convincing my seniors on the need for better controls over the chip batches. If they had a production batch of a hundred chips and more than half of them were defective for one reason or another, they'd just toss the whole batch out, good chips and all."

Wosniak nodded, shrugging his shoulders. "Cheaper to chuck 'em than to check 'em, I know. Gotta keep an eye on that bottom line," he said, with a hint of sarcasm he knew Art would appreciate.

Roger picked up the thread. "And when those batches got chucked, they wound up at the local garbage dump, of course. The company also junked perfectly good chips that were simply outdated and no longer on the product list. Then the specialists moved in, bribed the dump supervisor to let them poke around, and hauled off entire batches, bad chips and all. They did the sorting, put counterfeit logos and bogus serial numbers on the good chips, and sold them to parts dealers as TI or Intel products. End users never knew the difference."

"It all boils down to the same bottom line," Wosniak said. "Greed. Hell, some of those parts distributors sell bogus chips through Singapore to Russia and Eastern Europe. Big bucks."

"God, don't get me started on the Russians," Art said. He shivered. "I'm paranoid enough as it is." He managed a half-smile.

Wosniak looked at his watch. "I better get moving. Anything we can do to help, give me a call," he said, reaching down for his bag. "You know we're all concerned about security."

"Thanks, Charlie. I appreciate that. We'll let you know."

They shook hands again and parted. Garrett and Harris exited to board the Avis bus, Wosniak headed for the parking lot. When they got to the Avis lot, Art called the plant to let Jim Masters know they were on their way.

3

Out on the road, they headed south on 280, deciding to take the longer but faster scenic route through Palo Alto and Los Altos, rather than the shorter but more congested 101, which curved around the Bay.

Roger drove while Art sat next to him, yellow legal pad open, making notes. A fine mist had started to fall. Harris clicked the wipers to "intermittent" so they would scrape the windshield at automatic intervals. He opened the airvents and flooded the small green Escort with a cool breeze.

Art thought about their conversation with Charlie Johnson as he wrote. Chip theft was the industry's dread disease. You walked in constant fear of it, like cancer, knowing it could strike at any time but never really certain when, or where, or even if.

Last year, the industry had lost over $50 million worth of advanced electronic devices. Bribed security guards. Parts dealers sifting through mountains of trash. Inside deals, with security staff bribing stewardesses on Singapore Airlines to get the chips out of the country, using them as runners. Customs agents never even checked the crew's luggage, of course, and you could stick an awful lot of tiny chips in bras and pants.

Or a large end-user, Art thought, like Lockheed, would put in an emergency call for specific parts, knowing they can't wait for normal delivery because they have a crash deadline to meet or they'll lose a Pentagon contract. So the parts dealers enter, with their bogus chips, and jack the price up. Way up. Or some of the smaller companies start shoddy testing procedures to save time. Get the chips out faster, sell them all, is their motto. But sell them untested. Lockheed will never know, retesting is not their responsibility. And the Pentagon will never know until the radar malfunctions one day and the jet crashes.

But it all boiled down, like Charlie said, to money. Bottom line, pure and simple.

Art glanced at the list of items on his yellow pad, avenues he wanted to explore with his Sunnyvale staff:

1. Security. Full internal report.
2. Inside job.
   a. Motive
   b. Access
   c. Night shift staff check
3. Outside job.
   a. Point of entry?
   b. Perimeter controls
   c. Motive
   d. Means
4. Joint job?
   a. Contacts
   b. Check visitor list past 3 months
   c. Vehicle check, yard security
5. Industrial espionage?
   a. Competition
   b. Motive
   c. Foreign?
6. Violence
   a. Job dissatisfaction—revenge?
   b. Racial factors—cause
   c. Interview janitorial staff
   d. Method and motive

"Did you and Wosniak ever work in the same department at IBM?" Roger asked, his eyes ahead on the slick road.

Garrett remained silent, his attention focused on the growing list. He penciled a big question mark next to number five, and then underlined it.

"I said, did you and Charlie compete against each other at IBM?" he repeated, looking over at Garrett now. The

Saturday traffic was thin and he was bored. He wanted to be in Sunnyvale *now,* working on the problem.

"Sorry, Roger, did we what?" Art asked, clipping the pencil to his shirt pocket.

"You and Wosniak. You know, really get on each other's nerves?"

He laughed. "Now what makes you ask a question like that? We were bitter rivals."

"I thought so. Two people who are friendly competitors now probably had one thing in common, splitting off from a giant prison like IBM as you both did."

"What's that?"

"A David and Goliath mentality."

Garrett nodded as Harris pulled over to let a faster, more powerful Mazda pass them on their left. "Mind if I try to find us a little music?" he asked, reaching down and snapping on the radio. Art located a distant FM station that was playing Mozart, so he locked it in, static and all.

They drove a while in silence, the baroque piano mixings with the sound of the tires hissing on the wet pavement. The small Escort hugged the curves well, unusual for an American car, as they sped along the California coast. Mozart created a soft, lulling effect.

"You mentioned when we landed you would share some thoughts in the car," Roger said, checking the rearview mirror.

Art smoothed his moustache, pressing it with his fingers.

"Yeah," he said. "One of the alternatives intrigues me."

"Which one?"

Art paused. "Industrial espionage."

Harris was silent. The sounds of Mozart filled the car.

"Espionage?" he repeated.

Garrett nodded.

Harris stared straight out the windshield.

"The Russians?" He remembered Art's parting comment at the airport, about paranoia.

Garrett shifted in his seat to adjust his large frame to the tight interior. "Not just the Russians. Technology as sensitive as the 256K is a sitting duck for anybody."

Roger clicked the wipers on full as the mist turned into a steady light rain.

"Like the Germans, for example?"

"Not directly, as end-users. But as intermediaries, certainly. Remember the von Schimpfen case?"

Roger frowned. "No, not off hand."

"It was unbelievable. Von Schimpfen, operating out of Hamburg, sets up an office in the U.S. and one in Canada. He orders the integrated circuits from Advanced Micro-Devices—in which Siemens has a minority share, don't forget—and they're shipped to his American office in Chicago. No questions asked. A U.S. buyer for a U.S. product. Chicago sends them to his office in Toronto. Very clean. No export license required for Canadian shipments. And Toronto ships them off to Hamburg. Lots of movements, lots of paper, impossible to trace."

He paused. Mozart receded into soft static. The quiet hissing of the tires was the only background music now.

"How'd they get the chips out of Germany?"

"Easy," Art said, spinning the radio dial. "Bribe a customs agent and send them by surface mail. Or take them over themselves. Lots of Germans vacation in eastern Europe, visiting relatives, taking advantage of cheap currencies." The radio crackled and squawked. He gave up.

Harris pulled over to pass a slow-moving truck. Impossible to track, he thought. When Art mentioned the Siemens ownership of Advanced Micro Devices, he remembered another case, year before last, in which a Russian agent had bribed a purchasing agent at the giant German electronics company to accept delivery of bogus Intel chips from a parts distributor in Cupertino. Siemens manufactured so many components for NATO weapons that they automatically got an export license from the Department of Commerce. No questions asked. When the chips arrived in Munich, the Russian was notified and picked them up at Siemens in exchange for substantial sums of cash.

"Big bucks," Roger said, echoing Wosniak.

"You said it. Our shareholders would be delighted with those kinds of profit margins." Art tapped the yellow legal pad against his knee. "Of course, the end-user's not always a communist country. From Hamburg, they can send the stuff to banana republics in Africa and Latin America." He looked across at his colleague. "It's so hard to crack, I almost want to cross it off my list."

"The chips have to get out, first. And we know in our case they weren't ordered by some fictitious trading company. They were stolen."

"Still doesn't preclude the possibility of Russian involvement. They're the prime suspects as far as I'm concerned. Bought over a billion dollars' worth of electronics equipment through Germany last year, which is just where our chips may turn up. At least, they've got an authentic Micro Optix logo stamped on them, and they're serialized."

Harris frowned. "There's one possibility you've omitted. Maybe on purpose."

"What's that?"

"The Japanese. Your own arguments in Washington would seem to make them a serious candidate. And now that Hitachi has some of our 256K standards, maybe one of their big brothers decided to go whole hog."

Art winced. That was the first thing he had thought when Masters broke the news, but he had almost as quickly discarded it. "Thin, Roger. Very thin. In the first place, we know the Japanese are already so close that it's just a matter of months before they have their own 256K prototypes in production." He glanced briefly out the car window, watched the passing hills, lush and green in the spring rain. "In the second place, the Japanese are so smart, so really bright, they would simply triple the number of specialists and create a crash team approach if they wanted to accelerate their 256K program. You know how they work. They're fanatics."

He turned his head back, looking at his colleague now. "Besides," he said his voice softer but no less serious, "the Japanese wouldn't resort to outright crime. They're too intelligent to try that. They know they don't have to."

He began twisting the radio dial again and flicked through a half-dozen stations. He was about to punch it off when he heard his name mentioned in a newscast.

". . . following heated testimony Thursday in Washington by Mr. Arthur Garrett, president of tiny Micro Optix, Inc., Senator Mitchell's committee spent over six hours in session with the semiconductor specialist hearing his views on industrial policy reforms necessary to save the U.S. electronics industry from, as Garrett put it, 'annihilation by its Japanese competitors.' "

The announcer's voice was cold and unemotional. Roger pulled over onto the shoulder and stopped, so they could hear out the story. Garrett turned up the volume.

". . . asking the Senator about Garrett's allegations. He had this reply.

" 'Let me just say, for the benefit of the American people, that this myth of Japanese industrial domination must be put to rest once and for all. The United States, as the world's strongest and most stable industrial power, faces no threat whatsoever, in my opinion, from anyone, to its position of economic and political leadership.' "

Garrett and Harris eyed each other, like two parents overhearing their child tell a lie.

"Shit." Art snapped off the radio in anger. "That goddam egotist. Be just his style to sic the SEC on us and start some infantile investigation of our stock price movement as a little friendly harassment." He stared out the window, angry at the system, angry with himself.

Harris was reflective. He shifted into gear, accelerated slowly, and eased the small car back out onto the highway.

"He even referred to Micro Optix as tiny, did you hear that? Fortune 500 we're not, but we're no corner drugstore, either," Roger said.

Art looked out across a rich green valley dotted with empty farmhouses. Raindrops streamed down the side window of the car like tears, solitary and isolated.

He felt empty. His shoulders slumped down further in the seat. "Let's just get there, Roger. I'm sure there'll be more bad news waiting for us when we do."

4

There was only one police car parked in the lot when Art and Roger arrived at the Micro Optix plant early Saturday afternoon. The big, red plastic bubble on top was dark.

They dodged around puddles of water as they ran through the rain into the flat masonry building. Once inside, they cleared themselves through the fingerprint scanner, signed in with the security guard, and walked directly to the office of Jim Masters, plant manager.

Masters sat behind his wooden desk, running a hand through his red hair. Across from him, on a long sofa against the wall, sat two men: one uniformed, the other casually dressed.

Masters was a double-E transplant, an electrical engineer who had moved from the East Coast to California and now swore he'd never return. His origins still showed in his conservative attire—blue shirt, neatly knotted maroon tie, gray trousers, tasseled loafers. Garrett himself had hired Masters and respected his ability to manage people.

Masters leaped up when he saw Art and Roger.

"Art! Thank God you're here. Roger?"

They exchanged greetings and shook hands.

Art turned to the large man who had been in charge of plant security since the company was founded. He knew the man was solid, dependable as bedrock, and put any thoughts of complicity out of his mind.

"Hello, Herman."

"Afternoon, Art, Roger."

Brewster extended a large paw, simultaneously tipping the bill of his undersized baseball cap. The letters "MO" in white stood out on the red peak. He wore a pair of loose-fitting khaki trousers and a knit shirt, open at the neck. A small caliber pistol hugged his right hip. His eyes were streaked with red.

He turned to the uniformed policeman standing by his side. "This is Sergeant Tanaka, Sunnyvale Police." They shook hands.

"No offense, Sergeant," Art said, gesturing to the large signs on the office walls. Two color posters hung behind the couch. Their red-and-white messages left nothing to the imagination.

One of them, hanging vertically, showed a large fist powering toward the viewer with the overlay, "Team Up to Win!"

The other contained a background of popular Japanese names, in gray—Sony, Mitsubishi, Nissan, Fujitsu, Matsuzaka, Kawasaki, NEC—and the warning, in bright red letters: "Watch Out for the Japanese!"

The policeman smiled. "No problem, Mr. Garrett. I saw the papers this morning. You have to do what you have to do. I don't take it as a cultural insult."

"Thank you. It's not intended as such."

Art and Roger settled into straight-backed, wooden chairs next to Masters' desk.

"What've you got, Jim?" Art asked, opening his yellow pad and twisting his automatic pencil to draw out the lead.

Masters looked down at a file folder full of papers on his desk. "Not very much, I'm afraid. Herman, you want to brief Art on the sketchy details?"

Brewster sat back on the couch and closed his eyes. With photographic accuracy, he reproduced the condition of the shipping room as he had found it early Friday morning, the disarray of the racks, the random chips gone, the janitor dead.

"What about the dead man? Could he have been involved somehow?" Art looked at the policeman.

Tanaka shook his head. "Highly unlikely. My hunch is he just got in the way. Minimal violence, maximum punishment." He fiddled with the badge on his dark blue shirt as he buttoned his pocket flap.

"How did he die?"

"Crisp chop to the neck. Instant death.

"Strangulation?"

"Nope. Probably a board or blunt object. Could have been the side of someone's hand, if the guy knew karate. But it was quick."

"The dead man Mexican?"

"Black. Older man. Fine worker," Masters said.

Garrett made a few notes on his pad.

"Did he have any family, Jim?"

"A sister seems to be the only next of kin."

"Okay. Make sure we pick up the tab for the funeral—whatever she wants. And lean on our insurance company to pay the death benefits as soon as possible. I'm afraid that's about all we can do for the poor guy."

"You have a list of the missing chips?"

Masters pulled printout from his file and handed it across the desk.

Art's eyes raced down the list. "No pattern. Interesting. Some opticals, most standard, but all 256Ks."

"Precisely. QC had the same reaction."

"Did Quality Control think the guy knew what he was doing?" Roger asked, looking across Art's lap at the list.

"To pass over the 16Ks and the 64Ks and pick out only the most advanced chips? Definitely." Masters leaned back in his chair. "Fortunately, whoever it was didn't know our coding system, so he couldn't distinguish the optical sensors from the standard chips. He—or she—took a large number, over a hundred in all."

"Herman, what do you think he—they—were after?" Art asked, turning to the security expert. "Just the opticals?"

Brewster scratched the stubble on his chin. "No idea at this point. Too early to tell. Could be either."

Garrett nodded. He checked off the optical chips on the list. Nineteen. He circled the number.

"You'll have a full report for me later? Complete write-up, perimeter checks, access points, visitor control lists, delivery calls, pick-ups?"

"Absolutely. You'll get a complete file from me early next week."

"Fine, Herman. I've never had less from you." Turning

now to the policeman, he said, "Any leads at this point, Sergeant?"

Tanaka pulled a spiral notebook from his shirt pocket, shifted his gun butt so it no longer jabbed him in the ribs, and turned to a page of handwritten notes.

"Nothing very substantial," he said, shaking his head. "Been discussing it with Brewster here. We've interviewed most of the night shift—called them early yesterday to talk to us. Still missing a few people who obviously took off for the weekend. Won't be able to catch them until Monday."

Garrett wrote, nodding as he listened.

"Who haven't you talked to yet?"

Tanaka checked his list. "Couple of people in, what do you call it? Assembly and bonding. One in front-end inspection, and—let's see—three guys in probe." He looked up at Masters. "I think those are the right departments."

Brewster glanced over his shoulder. "You forgot the gook."

Art glanced up. "Herman. I've asked you not to use that term."

"Sorry. Knee-jerk reaction."

"So there's an Asian suspect?" Garrett asked, looking at Brewster. His thoughts went back to the car, to the hissing tires on the slick, wet highway, to the discussion of Japanese spies. He told himself not to jump to conclusions.

Masters ran his hands through his hair again, exhaled at the ceiling. "Vietnamese," he said. "Recent hire. Refugee, came off one of those boatloads that's always landing in the Bay. He was on duty Thursday night, but no answer when we tried his apartment. He called in sick yesterday morning."

Garrett doodled on his pad. "Since when did we start hiring boat people to make computer chips? Are we that hard up?"

Masters shook his head, smiling. "Not technical staff, Art. Janitorial."

"Cleaning staff?" Roger asked. "Is the attrition rate still so high?"

"Afraid so," Masters said, nodding. "That's the problem. Over fifty percent turnover ratio. Christ, we've got every imaginable type working here, Asian, Mexican, American, a veritable United Nations. Still, they leave as soon as they find something better. Can't blame 'em."

"We'll be contacting these people repeatedly over the weekend, Mr. Garrett," Sergeant Tanaka said, pocketing his notebook. "But it may be Monday before we can see them."

"And nothing from the people you have talked to?"

Brewster shrugged his shoulders. "Nobody was in the area when it happened. Packing and shipping's dead that time of night, as you know. The Sergeant checked for fingerprints and found none. We've talked to the other cleaning staff who were here that night, but they didn't see or hear anything."

"Well, shall we all go take a look?" Masters asked.

Art nodded, pocketing his pencil. As they stood to leave, he glanced at his watch. "Jim, I'll join you all in a minute. I'd like to make a quick call."

Masters turned the phone around and punched a button for a direct outside line. He led the others from the room.

Sitting on the edge of the wooden desk, Garrett dialed Sally's number again. It rang distantly in his ear, repeating, echoing.

He had given a lot of thought to what she had said Thurdsay night, things that made him uncomfortable, things that were true, things that got shuffled to the side again when Jim Masters shattered him with that early Friday call.

But he wanted to hear her voice again, wanted to ask her about her own Friday, which she had said was the worst day of her week, wanted more than anything to tell her she was right, to thank her for jolting him out of his own selfish stupor.

On the eighth ring, he remembered.

Sally and Jason were heading for Cape May this weekend to go birding. Of course. How stupid of him to forget. It would be Sunday evening before she returned, before he could try again to reach her. Rising, he glanced out at the rain. It would be a long, wet weekend.

They were poking around the packing room when he caught up with them, Brewster showing Harris the vacant slips on the storage racks, Masters and Tanaka inspecting the chalked circle that outlined the dead man's final position.

The five men talked for the remainder of the afternoon, questioning, analyzing, probing. Garrett ran down his list of notes with Brewster and Tanaka. They looked at several possibilities, questioned motives, hypothesized alternative points of entry, asked about outside contacts, conceivable revenge by former employees.

They discounted them all.

Brewster hoisted himself up on a countertop. "Gotta be an inside job," he said, holding up his right hand and ticking off the points on his fingertips.

"One, no sign of break and entry. We checked all the access points. Two, knowledge of the area. He—or she—knew where to go and what to take. Three, no external visitors after four o'clock Thursday afternoon. The list is clear on that point. Four, must've walked right through the optical scanner since the chamber didn't seal itself off, which implies an optically coded thumbprint from somebody around here." He paused, four fingers in the air. "And five, disappeared the same way. Scanner and motion detectors undisturbed."

He held up his thick palm, five fingers outstretched, then made a fist and folded his arms.

Tanaka nodded. "Only problem is the dead black. Doubt if anyone on your staff is so knowledgeable about killing, Mr. Garrett." He stuffed his hands in his rear pockets.

Garrett nodded, ironing his moustache with a fingertip. "Still, I'd like to focus on the assembly and cleaning staff that you haven't talked to yet. And subject them to the same body searches as everybody else from here on out."

He closed his eyes. Five million dollars' worth of the most sophisticated, technologically advanced computer chips in the industry. Gone. Aside from the national security risk—assuming foreign espionage was even remotely involved—the competitive dangers commercially were appalling.

Micro Optix could now lose its lead on the experience curve. Which would mean a fall-off in sales. Lower margins. Reduced earnings. And more pressure from shareholders already threatening the company's dividend payout policy.

Art had long feared the possibility of someone from his software staff—those computer geniuses with the unmeasurable IQs and the Micro Optix program language in their heads—leaving the company and joining another firm, taking all that proprietary knowledge with them. He just never thought a hardware theft would hit him as it had so many others.

"Right." It was Masters, bringing his attention back to the matters at hand. "We'll keep trying their homes, including those who we think may be away until Monday."

"You know where you can reach me, Mr. Masters," said the Sergeant. He started for the door to the hallway, back to Masters' office. "Let me know if you're able to contact anyone and I'll come right over to handle the questioning with Herman."

"Thanks, Sergeant," Art said, as they moved back down the hall. He glanced at his watch, saw that it was nearly five o'clock, past dinnertime in New York. The jet lag made his stomach rumble.

"We got anything to eat around here?" he asked when they had reassembled in Masters' office, absent the Sergeant. "That plastic airline food's for shit."

Masters started making a list of sandwiches as they indicated their preferences. He buzzed for his secretary and handed her the list. Turning to Art, he said, "I don't think it's really necessary for you to spend the whole weekend out here. I thought we'd have more for you than we did."

Art dropped his large frame onto the couch against the wall. "I don't know, Jim. I'd at least like to see the results of those remaining interviews before I head back."

"Some of the people may not get back until late Sunday night, which means we won't get to see them until Monday, most likely." He gestured in Harris' direction. "Roger and I can handle them."

Art thought about the upcoming annual meeting and

the speech he had yet to draft, as he stretched out his long legs. "Maybe you're right," he said. "Still—"

The phone rang. Masters picked it up. He looked at Art. "For you."

Art frowned as he took the phone from his plant manager.

"Garrett."

"Art?" The voice was unmistakable.

"Sally!" His spirits suddenly soared. "How's Cape May? I tried calling you earlier, but—"

She cut him off. "Not now," she said, her tone strained and nervous, as if she were tired. Or afraid. "We never made it to the Cape. Jason had a bad accident early this morning."

Art froze. His hand gripped the receiver. "What happened? How is he?" He heard commotion in the background, footsteps, a door slam.

"He's in the hospital. I'm with him now. His condition is stable, but he's been badly hurt."

He sat down limply on a corner of Masters' desk. "How did it happen?"

"Delivery truck. Blind-side hit. He was on his bicycle, not far from home. Both legs broken, ribs crushed on the right side. Miraculously, no head injuries." Her voice shook as she spoke.

"Where are you now?"

"Highland Park Memorial."

He paused and took a deep breath. "Are you all right?" he asked, staring at the rain-splattered window.

"I'm . . . all right," she said. "Exhausted but otherwise okay." She stopped, letting the long-distance static fill in the gap. "Art, is there any way . . . ?"

As her voice trailed off into silence, he thought instantly of her former husband. He was the boy's father, he was legally responsible, he was the one who ought to be there. But he blinked it away. Sally was calling him, not Jeff.

"Absolutely," he said. "I'll be there as soon as I can." He spun around at the sound of Masters' secretary entering the room with a tray of sandwiches. "And Sally?"

He heard her sobbing punctuate the stillness. "Yes?"

"Try not to worry. Don't make it worse than it is." He couldn't tell her about his latest setback. Not now.

Her reply was almost inaudible. "Thank you," she said softly. "I'll be here."

He hung up when he heard the connection click off.

"Bad?" Roger asked.

"Bad." He explained cryptically what had happened. "I'll take the car to San Jose and catch the red-eye back to New York. You stay here with Jim and Herman and push on with the investigation. Anything you learn, let me know. *Any*thing, okay?"

"Right," he said, nodding. He picked up a sandwich from the tray on Masters' desk and tossed it to him. "Here, you'll need this."

Art stuffed it in his briefcase as he pulled it out from under the chair. He turned to Brewster.

"Herman, one small favor."

"You name it," the big man said. He reached across the desk and plucked a pencil out of a ceramic cup that read, "We Will Win."

"I think you and I ought to have a little talk about industrial spies."

Brewster scratched his head with the eraser tip. "Yeah, well, you know me, Art. James Bond and Charlie Chan are a bit out of my league. My strength's hardware."

Art shook his head. "Yeah, but you're sitting in the middle of things here and I need to pick your brains. Talk to your buddies around the valley—your pals. See what you can find out."

"Russians?"

"And Germans and Japanese." He paused. "Even other valley boys."

The security chief jotted himself a reminder.

Garrett turned back to Harris as he snapped his case shut. "Call me."

5

He sprang up the steps to the hospital two at a time, still wearing the same clothes he'd put on twenty-four hours earlier. A fuzzy blond halo enshrouded his face, making his moustache appear smaller. Ten hours in a cramped sitting position at 35,000 feet had put horizontal creases in his jeans.

Garrett stopped at Reception to identify himself, glancing at the crowd massed around him in the lobby so early on a Sunday morning.

An elderly couple sat in one corner, holding hands, waiting, hoping, her head resting lightly on his shoulder. Opposite them, on a beige couch leopard-spotted with coffee stains, a pregnant mother breast-fed her infant, holding it with one hand while she tried to control a young, hyperactive daughter with the other. Two youngsters chased each other around a distant vending machine as their parents sat gazing absently into space, uninterested, uninvolved. Their faces were blank, empty of feeling, void of hope.

Art slowly pushed himself up the stairs. The fatigue from his overnight flight began to hit him, and made his feet feel like stones. It had been a long night, and the hospital scene just made it seem longer. But the long days were just beginning, he felt. The production problem for McDonnell Douglas was at least manageable. How was he going to make any headway against the disappearance of those chips, which were probably halfway around the world by now? And the industrial policy measures? Well, they could just kiss their retained earnings goodbye; what the government didn't get, the shareholders would.

Sally was asleep in a corner chair when he cracked open the door to Jason's room and tiptoed in. He saw her son lying stiffly in bed, both legs bound in stiff plaster casts, angled upward like miniature cannons, and counter-balanced by heavy weight at the ends of steel cables. His chest was wrapped in a thick polyvinyl vest, making his midsection look like a small barrel, his arms like small twigs jutting from the trunk of an old tree.

As he walked slowly toward the bed, he could feel the boy's forced sleep; the frown on his forehead radiated pain and discomfort. He touched the plaster casts, felt their stiffness, their rigidity. He smoothed the fine auburn hair, so like his mother's, that lay matted against his scalp. Pearls of perspiration stood out on the child's forehead and traced tiny paths down his temples, softening the white pillowcase underneath his head.

Art turned and walked to where Sally sat, asleep. Her face was drawn, her green dress crumpled and stained. Her eyelids were dark and heavy.

She held a small book open in one hand, its pages yellowed and torn, her thumb marking the place where she stopped when she had dropped off to sleep. Art reached down and gently pried the book from her hand. It was a collection of Sally's unpublished poetry.

He leaned down and softly kissed the top of her head. She stirred as she felt his touch, slowly opened her eyes, and reached up to him. He gently pulled her from the chair and wrapped his long arms around her small frame.

"He's going to be all right," she whispered quietly in his ear as he held her. She felt heavy as she collapsed, exhausted, in his arms. "Dr. Rosen wants to X-ray again tomorrow, to double-check the bone set." She reached around him with one arm and pulled him closer.

"Any further complications?"

"Not yet," Sally said, drawing his hand to her mouth and kissing it. "We'll know more tomorrow, but they said he'll be here for at least three weeks."

He looked down at her. "When was the last report?"

"Late last night, around eleven."

He glanced at his watch. "Would it do any good to call the doctor now?" It was nearly ten in the morning.

Sally shook her head. "He said he'd come by this evening for a look. There's really nothing more he can do until he X-rays again tomorrow." She looked up at him.

He nodded. "I could provoke him," he said, a half-smile cracking the corners of his mouth.

She threw her arms around his shoulders, hugging him tightly, her head buried in his chest. "Thank you for coming," she said simply, her voice muffled by the folds of his shirt.

He lifted her chin up to look into her eyes. "You have only yourself to thank for that," he said quietly. He kissed her forehead. "I just feel so helpless, like there's something I should do."

She shook her head again. "We've got more doctors and nurses than we can use," she said. "It's just important to me that you're here. That you care."

He put his hand behind her head and pressed it to his chest. They stood together, silently, two as one, their worlds converging.

Resting his head on hers, he explained the reason for his unscheduled trip to Sunnyvale, the disappearance of the optical chips, the rough possibilities, the value.

"My God," she whispered, her eyes wide with concern for him now. "If I had known—"

"Put it out of your mind," he said softly.

She watched him for a long minute. "What are you going to do?"

"Everything possible," he said, shrugging his shoulders. "If it is a case of industrial espionage, we may be in real trouble." He mentioned the Russian involvement, the German connection, the national security implications. And he told her about the optical chip's significance in TerCom.

Turning her back to the window now, she reached up and held his face with both hands. "Too bad we can't just get away," she said, her eyes brimming with tears. "The two of us, alone, together." She pressed his moustache with her fingers.

He stared past her, out the window, his eyes darting

from tree to tree. His mind leapt from Senator Mitchell to McDonnell Douglas to five million dollars' worth of stolen chips. Ten percent of his annual sales. He was silent.

His silence was not an answer, he told himself. He was tempted. After all, it was only a weekend, and he could leave a number for people to call. And yes, he could probably use a change of pace. But how would it look to the others?

He shook his head, looking down at her now. "Sally, you know we can't do that. Not now. Not with all that's going on."

Echoing his own thoughts, she said, "I can't leave Jason and you can't leave Micro Optix, even though we both really need the time away."

"I know," he said, nodding slowly as he watched a single tear curl down her cheek.

She lay her head on his chest again, eyes closed. She knew it wasn't possible. But she also knew how delicate that relationship was between work and overwork, between commitment and addiction.

"Promise me," she said, raising her head and looking at him with brimming eyes.

"Promise you what?" he asked quietly, touching away the tear.

"Promise me a weekend—any weekend—once things ease up for us."

Assuming they ever do, he thought. He couldn't see it. But then, if he couldn't, someone had to. He realized that now.

6

On Monday, the office was chaotic.

Barbara handed Art a sheaf of telephone messages as he walked into his office to find a mountain of accumulated mail, internal memos, and project reports. At that moment, Ted Quinn arrived with a long list of further questions to review for the stockholder's meeting on Thursday.

Art began setting priorities. He agreed to meet with Ted in the afternoon, then turned to his first concern.

"Barbara get Roger for me as soon as California opens. Try him around eleven, our time."

He shuffled through the wad of notes. "I'll never get all these calls returned. The Times. Newsweek. The Industry Association. Even the Morristown Journal-Ledger. Give them to Quinn. He can say I'm unavailable for comment."

"They all want to talk about your testimony last week in Washington. Nobody knows about the 256K theft yet."

"I suspected as much. Roger and I heard part of it on the radio Saturday morning as we drove to Sunnyvale. Don't remind me." He wound the stem of his wristwatch. "And don't say a word about the chip disappearance yet."

"Of course not." She pushed her outsized glasses up the bridge of her nose with her pencil tip. "And if they insist on talking to you about your testimony?"

"Tell them I'm simply unavailable. Tell them I'm out of town. Tell them I'm out of the *country.*"

She nodded.

He snapped his fingers. "No, tell them I've gone to Japan to sell my company to Hitachi for an undisclosed amount of cash and a lifetime management contract." On the surface, his eyes sparkled. "My golden parachute."

"Great idea, we'll tell them just that."

Art flipped through the remaining telephone messages. "Nothing from Frank Martin?" he asked. He needed to talk to McDonnell Douglas to see what they thought of his proposal to add another Teledyne machine so he could increase delivery of opticals by year-end.

"Spoke to his office late Friday," she said. "His secretary told me he was with Pentagon brass all day. Left word you wanted him to call." She looked at her calendar.

"If he hasn't called us by the time I'm through with Roger, let's call him again."

"Right." She turned to her desk.

He knew he couldn't tell Martin about the disappearance of the chips. Not yet, anyway. Not until they had a chance to assess the impact the nineteen missing opticals would have on deliveries to McDonnell Douglas.

Standing at his desk, he began sorting through the pile of reading material, sifting, delegating, deciding. The brief period of total absorption in the day-to-day problems of Micro Optix was refreshing after the defeats of the past week.

Fred Schmidt's lengthy memo recommending new and higher levels of capital investment for the next year was there, as well as a production report from Sunnyvale citing better yield ratios from their new wafer slicing techniques. The Sales Department confirmed implementation of new customer investigation procedures designed to prevent another Hitachi case from surfacing. And field reports from customers using Micro Optix chips reaffirmed their confidence in the quality of the company's products.

Some good news for a change, he thought to himself, immersed in his paper world. It was a welcome distraction.

"Line two for you Art." Barbara's voice carried over the short wall, interrupting his concentration.

He punched the flashing button. "Garrett."

"Art, good morning."

"Roger, good to hear your voice," he said, his tone hopeful, expectant. "Any news?"

"Not a whole lot to report," he said. "We talked to all the remaining night staff over the weekend, assembly as well as janitorial, but didn't turn up anything. Nobody saw anything unusual that night. Lotta dry holes."

Art slumped back in his chair. "Police still cooperating?"

"Oh, yeah, that guy Tanaka is terrific. Bundle of energy. Thorough, persistent, very bright."

Thorough. Persistent. Very bright. Where had he heard those words before? His mind searched for the connection.

"But no leads."

"No, no leads."

"Any reaction from the local competition?" Garrett asked, flipping his yellow pad to a clean page. He knew word would get around in Sunnyvale. It was a small community.

"Very supportive. The biggies have called to express their concern—Motorola, National Semiconductor, TI. The small fry, like us, are calling in to ask if they can help, offering security people, suggesting motives, reporting strange occurrences of their own."

Art nodded, making notes on his pad. "That's reassuring at least. Amazing how one incident like this brings everybody together."

"Well, they're all concerned about plant security, as you know. Bob DeVito at Intel told me about a recent case involving one of their security guards. Soviet agents here in California tried to buy the guy off with an unbelievable cash offer if he'd smuggle out some of their advanced memory devices."

There was the Russian connection again. "How much?"

Roger told him.

"Shit."

"Yeah. And Fairchild said they caught a phony repairman walking out of their 64K plant loaded to the gills with random access memory chips. Guy broke down and confessed that the Soviets had gotten to him, too."

"More money?"

"Exactly. Turned out the man had no real choice. They confronted him with pictures of his wife and kids, and—well, you know how it is. He had a lot of overdue medical bills to pay with three young children and a sick mother."

"They get him with the metal detectors?"

"In part. Funny thing was, Fairchild scheduled a spot search on everyone leaving the plant the very afternoon he was there. Found his lunchbox full of chips, and when they discovered those, he broke down and showed them the rest, hoping they might be more lenient with him."

"Don't tell me. Taped to the inside of his hard hat."

"Nope. Hollowed-out shoe soles and in a false bottom to his tool kit. Ingenious. Half a million bucks' worth right there. Fairchild was damn lucky, and they know it."

"I assume you looked over our own visitors' list again, just to be sure," Garrett said, frowning.

Roger coughed into the connection. "Yeah. Herman and I both did. Only guys in here for repairs lately were the Teledyne team. So we talked to the company. They were real cooperative."

"And?"

"Clean. Spoke to the fellows myself. One of them was out here last Monday while I was here with Jim. Nothing doing."

Art spun around in his chair, faced the window, watched the sun play on the distant hills. "Anything come of the interviews with the janitorial staff on duty Thurdsay night?"

"Not really. Long talk with one of the blacks, friend of the guy who died. Took it pretty hard. Said they had had some words a few nights earlier with one of the other mop-pushers, but nothing that amounted to anything."

Art squeezed his jaw with his thumb and forefinger. "What about that Vietnamese guy, the fellow off the boat?"

"Oh, yeah. Meant to tell you. Haven't seen him yet."

Art sat up straight. "What do you mean, you haven't seen him yet?"

"Not back from the weekend."

"What? Wasn't he on duty last night?"

"Nope. Had Saturday and Sunday nights off. Called in sick Friday morning, remember?"

"Oh." Art did some mental calculations. "Then he ought

to be back tonight. Maybe he's gone off to the seaside, or into San Francisco to visit friends."

"Maybe. We're still waiting. He's the only one we haven't talked to yet, but I gotta say, what do we really expect to learn from an immigrant who's still got salt water on his skin?"

Art clenched his teeth. He knew Roger was probably right, but he didn't want to admit it. "Look, Roger. I know it sounds ludicrous, but for all we know this Le Duc Pho character may be some North Vietnamese pro recruited by the Russians for the very purpose of lifting these chips. We can't discount anything. Push the guy when you find him, hound the hell out of him. We haven't got much more to go on at this stage."

"Right. I'll call as soon as we contact the guy. With Tanaka helping, maybe we can turn up something."

Tanaka, Tanaka.

Thorough. Persistent. Very bright. It was coming back.

A week, two weeks ago, Art thought, the words burning in the back of his mind. Dialogue. Description. Pleasure. Sally. Japan.

Japan! That was it. Those were the very words she had used to describe the Japanese. No wonder Roger had been so impressed by the Sergeant.

"Well, keep me posted. And thanks."

"No problem," Harris said. He paused. The line squeaked as an electronic pulse throbbed in transmission. "Art, how's Sally's boy?"

Garrett sighed. "All right, we think. Still under light sedation, so he can't talk yet. Looks pretty beat up."

"I'm sorry. Doctor's report optimistic?"

"They X-ray again today. They're hopeful."

"Tell her, when you can, I'll write a new Adventure program for the kid's computer when I get back."

"Sally'd like that," he said, turning back to his desk. "She says Jason's pretty much got the dwarf psyched out in his other game."

"Tell her not to worry. Mine is much tougher."

"Thanks, Roger. Call as soon as you have anything."

Art glanced at his watch as he replaced the receiver.

Time for a quick sandwich before he and Ted Quinn sat down to start their long review.

A note from Barbara caught his eye. She had tried Frank Martin again but he was in a meeting and would call back. He stuck his head over the squat partition and, seeing that she had nothing in her typewriter, took her by the elbow down to the cafeteria a flight below.

7

Le Duc Pho never returned, of course, but there was no way his employer could know that. Or his landlord.

When he didn't show Monday for the night shift, Brewster told Roger and the two of them thought about that for a while. Maybe the guy *was* sick, Herman had said. Away from his native fish paste so long, turned his stomach now that he was exposed to American fast food and bland cooking.

Or he got tied up in weekend traffic, always a problem in the Bay area. Or into a fight with his friends in San Francisco, if that's indeed where he went. Maybe they were jealous of his job security as a new refugee.

Or none of the above, Brewster thought. He didn't believe it for a second. He knew it was an inside job, and the delayed return of a member of the night crew was the first glimmer of anything they had had to go on.

So he persuaded Roger to call the Sergeant, and the two of them flipped a coin to see who would go with Tanaka to the Viet's apartment. Roger won the toss. Tanaka was on duty at the station until ten, but agreed to pick Roger up at 10:15.

Linda Kalinski was there when they arrived.

"Last I saw Mr. Le was Thursday night, I think," she said, fingering the Sergeant's indentification. Her jaws rotated mechanically as she chewed her gum. She shrugged her shoulders. "Why? He done anything wrong?" Her jaw suddenly stopped.

Tanaka pocketed his badge and pulled out his small spiral notebook.

"Just a few questions we want to ask him, Miss Kalinski. That's all."

"As far as you know, he hasn't been back to his room since Thursday?" Roger asked. He scratched the black stubble on his chin.

"I'm usually not here weekends," she said, snapping her gum at him, "so I can't say for sure. But I didn't see him Friday night, that's for sure. What about you," she said, nodding her head at Harris, "you got some ID?"

Roger showed her his Micro Optix card. "We've lost some valuable electronic equipment," he said. "We're interviewing all the staff, and we just need to ask Mr. Le a few questions."

Linda Kalinski picked up his plastic scanner card. She laughed. "Some ID," she said. "Fingerprint and name. Big deal. You could be anybody. How do I know you're you?"

He took his card back and slipped it into his shirt pocket, rolling his eyes at the ceiling.

"He's for real, Miss. Number two in the company," the Sergeant broke in. "Mind if we wander up and see if he's in?"

"Help yourself," she said, popping the gum with her tongue. Her thin pullover stretched across her large breasts as she gestured toward the staircase. "23-A."

"Thanks," Roger said, his eyes riveted on her cleavage.

They mounted the outside stairs. The weather was still cool and damp. Puddles of water formed on the uneven asphalt walkway, reflecting the harsh yellow bug lights that hugged the perimeter of the red brick building.

When there was no answer to the Sergeant's knock, he tried the door. It was locked.

Harris then banged his fist on the door, hard, and shouted the man's name. There was no response.

They peered in the window, but the drapes were drawn. They looked at each other.

"Nothing," said Tanaka.

"Nothing," Roger Harris repeated.

They walked back downstairs.

"Miss Kalinski," the Sergeant said as they returned to the reception area. "Sorry to bother you again. You got a spare key to the room by any chance? Mr. Le's apparently decided not to come back." Tanaka held out his hand.

"Hey, wait a minute," she said, her jaw motionless again. "First you want to talk to this guy, now you want to search his room? Uh-uh." She folded her short arms across her wide bosom.

Tanaka and Harris looked at each other again.

"Look, I don't want to cite you for obstruction, but you realize you are refusing to cooperate with a police officer?" Tanaka's voice was soft, pliant.

Linda Kalinski shook her head, sweeping long, blond curls across her face. "You want in his room, you get a search warrant. I watch TV."

Now Tanaka's eyes rolled to the ceiling. He had hoped that wouldn't be necessary. "Phone?" he asked.

She pointed to the hallway.

In less than an hour, one of the county court night clerks brought in the required document.

Tanaka drained his third cup of coffee, broke the seal, and handed the onionskin to the girl.

Her jaw stopped again. "Gee, a real search warrant," she said. "They really do exist." She reached under the counter and handed the Sergeant a shiny key with a plastic number tag attached.

They walked slowly back up the stairs.

Tanaka fitted the key into the doorknob. He withdrew his Smith & Wesson .38, holding it ready.

Turning the knob, he kicked the door open. It banged against the wall.

Nothing.

They waited at each side of the doorway, backs to the wall.

Still nothing.

The Sergeant reached in and flipped on the hall light, legs crouched, pistol ready. They moved cautiously through the door, Tanaka in front.

The apartment was empty. Not just vacant. Empty.

Tanaka made a quick check of the bedroom and bath. "Gone," he said, rejoining Roger in the living room. "Scattered clothes in the bedroom, like he left in a hurry."

Harris sat down in a chair, shaking his head. "This is weird. I mean, it's like the apartment hasn't even been rented. Nothing's been disturbed. Are you sure we're in the right flat?"

Tanaka went to the front door and pulled out the key. "23-A," he said, reading the numbers off the plastic tag. "Matches the door, fits the lock."

Roger drummed his fingers on the arm of the chair. "It's so antiseptic."

"What do you expect, a janitor with a Brooks Brothers wardrobe? The guy's a refugee, for chrissake." Tanaka glanced around the room. "Still, it is strange. Hardly been lived in."

They spent the next few minutes poking around the apartment, opening drawers, checking closets, going through the place room by room. And finding nothing.

"Check the kitchen," Roger said. "I'll do another search of the bath."

He found a toothbrush and shaving articles, nothing out of the ordinary. A plastic cup sat on the washstand, its lip white with dried toothpaste.

As he made his way back to the kitchen, he glanced around the bedroom a second time. The bed was half-made, a brown-and-cream bedspread flung up across the mattress in a standard, two-second toss. A soiled T-shirt and an old pair of jeans hung on a wall hook.

Harris wandered back into the kitchen, scratching his head. "Nothing," he said. "Absolutely nothing."

Sergeant Tanaka was sitting at the tiny kitchen table, frowning and sipping a beer.

Harris stopped. "What's this?" he asked. "Miller time?"

The Sergeant took a long pull and set the bottle down on the table.

"It ain't Vietnamese," he said.

"So?" Roger asked. He stood and looked down at Tanaka, hands on hips. "Since when did the Vietnamese have their own beer?"

Tanaka shook his head. "That's not what I meant. This is Japanese beer."

Harris froze. "What did you say?"

"I said, it's Japanese. Asahi. Rising sun and all. Here, take a look." He handed Harris the bottle.

Roger's eyes fixed on the red rising sun emblem under the black *kanji.*

"So maybe our friend has expensive tastes," he said, handing the bottle back. He didn't know what to think. Imported beer on a janitor's salary?

Bill Tanaka shook his head again. "Uh-uh. You don't understand, Roger. The southeast Asians hate the Japanese, after what they went through during the war. They would never choose a Japanese product like this."

Harris stared at the Sergeant, then at the half-empty bottle. "So what's your hunch?"

Tanaka shrugged his shoulders. "My hunch is that Mr. Le Duc Pho is not Vietnamese."

"Shit," Roger said, turning toward the door. "Where was that telephone?"

8

He sat atop the wings of the great bird, soaring high above the shore, his knees pressed against its smooth, shiny back. It dropped into a dive and he began to feel that dizzying, euphoric sensation of free fall.

The shoreline came slowly into focus. Moonlight bounced off the smooth, shining water. The beach glowed, as if on fire.

When the bird swooped down, he grasped it firmly around the neck. It gathered speed, and he closed his eyes. It dove down, deeper and deeper. He felt himself becoming weightless, lifting from the bird's back but at the same time fused with its body.

He felt at one with the bird. He *was* the bird.

He opened his eyes and looked, felt the wind pressing against his face, distorting his features. He saw a face in the moonlight, silhouetted against the shore.

The bird flattened out its dive now and hovered, quiet and still, over the shoreline.

That face. He knew that face.

It couldn't be.

It was.

Sally.

"Sally . . . !"

He stretched to take her in his arms, but his reach was short.

Then the great bird began its ascent, pulling away from the shore, away from Sally. Suddenly he felt the weight of gravity tug at his body, holding him tightly against the massive expanse of the bird's great back. They soared higher, and faster, into the sky, heading straight for the moon, lifting, accelerating, completely framed by the soft light.

And the quick ascent brought a ringing to his ears.

God, the ringing, the pain. Stop!

Art Garrett's eyes suddenly snapped open.

He shook himself free from the lure of his dream.

The ringing persisted. He flicked on a light, snapping his eyes shut again from the brightness.

Squinting, he reached for the receiver. His chest was wet. Perspiration dripped from his moustache.

"Garrett," he mumbled.

"Art? Roger. Sorry to wake you. God, you must have really been out. Rang seventeen times before you picked up. I think that's a new record for you."

"Shit. What time is it?"

"After midnight here. Three your time. Like I say, sorry."

Art struggled to a sitting position, propping the damp pillow behind his back. He looked at his watch. 3:05 a.m. He rubbed his eyes and yawned.

"What've you got? Must be something."

"Potentially, anyway. Not sure what we can do with it yet, but it's at least a lead."

"Shoot." Garrett was wide awake now, listening.

"Remember that Vietnamese guy who joined the cleaning staff recently?"

"Fellow just off the boat. Of course. You were going after him on the shift tonight. Last night." He looked at his watch again. "Whenever."

"Exactly. Well, he never showed up."

Art remained silent, listening, thinking.

"So the Sergeant and I went to his apartment. I'll spare you the punctuation."

"Thanks. What happened?" Art's voice grew clearer as his mind accelerated.

"Got to the guy's place, searched it, found nothing of substance beyond a pair of skivvies."

"So?" His eyes narrowed as he frowned at the phone.

"So Tanaka digs a six-pack of Asahi beer out of the guy's refrigerator."

"So?" He still didn't make the connection. "So the guy likes beer."

"Art, it's Japanese beer. Southeast Asians don't go out of their way to express a fondness for Japan."

"So maybe Duc Pho is different. If he's a Russian agent, as we think, he may be trying to implicate the Japanese."

"That's what I thought," Roger said. "But the Sergeant is pretty adamant about one thing."

"What's that?"

"Le Duc Pho's definitely not Vietnamese."

Art thought for a minute. He was already getting ahead of himself.

"What's Tanaka doing now?"

"Making out a report, simply stating what we found. No conjecture, just fact."

"Look, stay there for a couple more days. This Duc Pho character could still appear. We might be wrong."

"Fat chance, but I'm not planning to come back just yet."

"Then ask Herman to call me in the morning. If we are, somehow, onto a case of industrial espionage, I need to talk to him."

"Will do. Any thoughts?"

"About what?"

"About what this might mean?"

He shuddered. He knew all too well what it might mean.

"Not yet. It's easy to jump to conclusions. Let me sleep on it, and you do the same. We'll talk again in the morning."

"Fine."

"Oh, and Roger? One more thing."

"Yes?"

"Don't get the FBI in on this yet. Keep it between yourself and Tanaka at this stage."

"Right."

"And tell the Sergeant I said thanks."

He hung up and tried to go back to sleep, but his mind wouldn't let him.

Japanese?

Shit, he thought. Preposterous.

Japanese.

Not so preposterous?

The competition? he wondered. A put-up case, a planted clue? He turned on his other side and tried to doze off.

A purely commercial theft? But why? The Japanese were so close with their own technology. Couldn't be. Besides, the Japanese were too smart to have to steal. Had to be the Russians, everything pointed in that direction.

Brewster. He had to talk to Herman.

He finally dropped off to sleep, his brow furrowed, his mind churning.

Shit, he thought. Preposterous.

Japanese.

Not so preposterous?

The competition, he wondered? A put-up case, a planted clue? He turned on his other side and tried to doze off.

A purely commercial theft? But why? The Japanese were so close with their own technology. Couldn't be. Besides, the Japanese were too smart to have to steal. Had to be the Russians, everything pointed in that direction.

Brewster. He had to talk to Herman.

He finally dropped off to sleep, his brow furrowed, his mind churning.

9

Art Garrett paced his office. He had still not heard from Herman Brewster.

He picked up the phone and called Sunnyvale. Masters told him that both Roger and Herman were out with the Sergeant. Checking out something in San Francisco, was all he knew.

"Well, get a hold of him somehow and tell him to call."

Art hung up, moved to the window and threw it open. As the April coolness came surging in, he took a couple of breaths. Step by step, he kept reminding himself.

He grabbed the phone again and put a call to the hospital. A nurse answered and told him that Jason Hendricks was still under sedation but doing fine. She said that if he wanted the X-ray results he would have to speak to Mrs. Hendricks directly.

He then called Freddie Schmidt, and the two of them went downstairs for a late lunch and spent an hour reviewing the final figures for presentation to the shareholders on Thursday. Results for the past year had been good, very good, but it was inevitable that the no-dividend policy would come under heavy pressure. Now that Micro Optix was five years old, it was no longer a venture capital gamble, and more and more shareholders wanted a part of the profits.

The other serious problem was the Sunnyvale theft. Art's instinct was to disclose it because it was a material event, but Freddie dissuaded him. Its impact on earnings was still uncertain, he argued, and if it were disclosed at the meeting, the press would have to be notified. Art decided to wait.

Garrett walked back up the carpeted staircase to his office. Why the hell hadn't Herman called? And where was Frank Martin? Closeted in meetings all day?

Barbara flagged him as he neared her desk.

"Herman Brewster finally called, while you and Freddie were at lunch. Want me to get him for you?"

"Right away," he said, raising his eyebrows. "And keep trying Frank Martin."

When he picked up the telephone, he heard the soft rumble of Herman's deep, confident voice. Just listening to it made his own confidence grow.

"Roger told me what he and the Sergeant found last night. Maybe puts a new light on things."

"Maybe," Art said. He picked up a pencil. "Where the hell you guys been?"

"Checkin' things out, Art," he said. "We've looked into that white card the Vietnamese fellow—or whatever he is—used to get a job here. Talked to somebody in Washington, in Immigration."

Art sat down at his desk and flipped open his pad.

"They ran down the number and found it belonged to a series of cards stolen about six months ago. They canceled the series, of course, and sent standard notices out to all employers of more than twenty-five people. But, hell, no company reads those government notices that closely."

Garrett nodded. "Like those wanted posters, at the post office."

"That's it. At least, we now know the guy's card was bogus."

"Thanks. What else?" Art asked. He scribbled down a notation about the white card.

"Well, we went into San Francisco," Brewster said. "Tried to find out which refugee ships had put in recently. Talked to the local INS office. They said a Vietnamese boat dumped a load just before our boy showed up here."

"Excellent, Herman," Art said, straightening. "That may be something."

"That's what we thought, too. Unfortunately, we couldn't go any further. The ship never docked. Captain dropped the refugees in lifeboats outside the Bay and took off again. No reports, no controls, no numbers, but of course more money."

"Of course." Garrett sighed and slumped back in his chair. One step at a time, he thought. But every time they managed to take one, they hit a dead end. "So there's no way of knowing how many they originally started with compared with how many actually landed."

"Right. This has been standard practice for the past year, according to Immigration. Washington has bitched about it in the UN and sent official complaints through diplomatic channels to Hanoi, but Christ, you know how bureaucrats work."

Garrett nodded, fully aware of the multitude of government regulations his own company had to follow. Thoughts of his testimony the previous week in Washington also flashed through his mind, but he blinked them away.

"An interesting thing, though. Based on when the ship actually made its drop, the INS figures it left Hanoi around the end of March. If it's the same one, it stopped in Yokohama en route."

"So maybe the Japanese government has some numbers, you think?" Garrett asked, scribbling. "They keep statistics on everything."

"Hey, Art, do me a favor? Stop leap-frogging ahead."

"Sorry. You mean, you checked that out, too?"

"Yeah. At the Japanese consulate in San Francisco. They passed us around to different people before one finally knew what he was talking about. He admitted, off the record, that the Japanese government wanted nothing to do with the Vietnamese. That their only role was to get those boats out of Japan—reconditioned, if necessary—as soon as they came in."

Garrett fingered his moustache. "So nothing there."

"Nope. Sorry."

Both men paused, thinking, wondering what to say next. The line clicked and squeaked with static.

"Well, Herman, no more second guesses from me. But I want to push this espionage link."

"Don't blame you. Give me a couple of hours to call my buddies at Monolithic Memories and Semiconductor Arrays. I want to compare notes before we go any further down that line."

"Herman, we've got to talk today."

"I'll get back to you this afternoon."

"Guaranteed?"

"Guaranteed."

"All right." Garrett tossed the pencil onto his desk. "Roger around?"

"Harris? Yeah, hang on."

Art heard the hold button click as Herman passed the phone. With another click, Roger was on.

"Hi. Sorry we don't have more for you."

"Herman seems to have things pretty well in hand. Listen, why don't you come back on the red-eye tonight. I could sure use you for the annual meeting Thursday."

"Doesn't Ted have that all wrapped up?"

"Basically, yes. But you know the kinds of sticky questions that come up, and it's good to have more than one lightning rod in place. Need be, you can fly back out later in the week."

"Fine. I'll leave my notes with Brewster. If I'm not on the red-eye tonight, I'll be in by the close of business tomorrow."

"Good. Oh, and one more thing."

"Not another speech?"

"No, better than that. Squash."

"You're on. But not if I'm on the night flight."

"Fair enough. See you when you get in."

10

Art hung up and looked at his watch. It was getting late. His top priority was to complete preparations for the annual meeting.

He began by jotting down his estimates of overall domestic U.S. market growth—in excess of twenty percent per year for the next five years. Then, based on Freddie's numbers, he calculated that the semiconductor sector alone— just the advanced integrated circuits, 64K and up—would in five years double to over ten percent of the total market for electronics products. A submarket sector in and of itself worth over $100 billion.

Garrett estimated, based on EIA statistics, that the 256K, in its nonoptical, standard state, would gradually increase to become the highest dollar-volume product in the history of the semiconductor industry, growing to a peak annual level of more than $15 billion within the five-year period.

And he noted that this specific market sector had been targeted for penetration by the major Japanese electronics companies—NEC, Hitachi, Matsuzaka, Fujitsu—with pricing strategies already showing an aggressive trend, and volume commitment strong.

He singled out the unique Japanese pricing strategy for emphasis: their philosophy of forgoing near-term profits to achieve dominant market shares and keep their unit costs down on the experience curve. He summarized the Japanese government's policy of granting aggressive subsidies for joint research and development, heavy front-end depreciation for new capital investment, sponsorship of long-term, low-cost financing. Factors that would enhance the ability of Japanese companies to increase global market shares by executing strategies designed in partnership with their own government. Perfect teamwork, he thought. No wonder they executed their industrial policy with such skill: consensus was anathema to Washington politicians.

At the conclusion of his remarks on the seriousness of the Japanese challenge to domination in the electronics industry, he made an appeal to the Micro Optix shareholders for continuation of their original policy to retain fully all earnings in the company's business. Not simply to rely less on borrowed money. Not simply to benefit from higher levels of new capital investment. But to keep pace with the competitiveness of the Japanese on the all-important experience curve.

Art sat back now, massaging his moustache, reading over his notes. He penciled in reminders to keep his comments brief and objective in tone. To let the facts speak for themselves. Satisfied that his basic approach was sound, he then made a short list of recent Micro Optix achievements to remind the shareholders of the company's own innovations in current technology:

(1) Electron beam direct slice writing to replace optical techniques for channel sizes below one micron. A new breakthrough in the industry.

(2) The 256K microprocessor, with four times the computing capability and operating at twice the speed with only half the power of its 64K predecessor. Micro Optix was clearly the leader in this dramatic new sector.

(3) Its counterpart, the 256K optical chip, invented by Micro Optix, its development spurred by the R&D policies set by Roger Harris. He included a list of the optical chip's military, industrial, and technical applications, including TerCom. An industry "first" for Micro Optix.

(4) A new speech synthesis product, the AutoReminder, which would soon replace alarms and buzzers in the dashboards of most automobiles. These voice synthesizers would remind drivers to "Check Engine Oil," and "Fasten Seat Belts," without the annoyance of loud buzzers and flashing lights.

(5) New programmable components for the electronics
industry: logic arrays, microcomputers, speech synthesizers for foreign language study, and a range of smaller,
more powerful ROMs and EPROMs: Read-Only Memory
chips and Erasable, Programmable, Read-Only Memories.

At the very end of his speech outline, he wrote in
"Sunnyvale?" and circled it. He was still not sure whether
he wanted to disclose the fact of the chip disappearance
yet. In any event, he knew he was not ready to face a press
conference without more hard evidence and *some* indica-
tion of motive or rationale. He left it circled, with a question mark. He'd sleep on it.

Absorbed in his notes, he never noticed the phone ring.
After a few shrill reminders, it stopped.

A face appeared over the partition. "Mr. Garrett? Call
for you." A cleaning woman, head wrapped in a faded blue
scarf, held the receiver over her head.

"Thank you," he said, glancing at his watch. It was
nearly seven o'clock. He punched the blinking button.

"Garrett."

"Art? Herman. Got through to my boys. Want to talk?"

"Absolutely." He sat up straighter now, reaching for his
yellow pad. He pulled the Sunnyvale file toward him and
opened it.

"I'm still bothered about the possible Japanese involvement in this case. The bogus white card, the beer, the Vietnamese ship stopping off in Yokohama en route—"

"Nothin' we've come up with so far takes the heat off the
Russians," Brewster said, interrupting.

"I know, Herman. But on the one hand, the Japanese
could sure use the technology we've got. On the other,
they're so close to developing it themselves, I don't see
what they would have to gain by stealing ours." He tapped
his pencil on the yellow pad.

"Know what Monolithic said?"

"What?"

"On the Japanese, they ain't the thievin' kind. Beg, borrow, and cheat, yeah. But they don't steal. They're too
fucking smart to do that."

"That's the common wisdom. We keep coming back to that."

"Ever hear of a guy named Faroush?"

"Faroush? Not offhand. Sounds Middle Eastern. Why?"

"My old Monolithic buddy reminded me of his exploits. Points the finger pretty convincingly at the Russians. He's Iranian, with a West German passport and an American wife. Lives in Moscow but shacks up in New York, to keep a U.S. address."

"And?"

"The guy is fucking unbelievable. Single-handedly responsible for getting the Soviets more hi-tech hardware illegally than any of the greasy trading companies you hear about."

"Like von Schimpfen?"

"Yeah, them. Russians like Faroush so much they put him up like a goddam prince. Big house in Moscow, like I say, black Mercedes, driver, vacation pad on the Baltic, elite schools for the kids. The works."

Art wrote his name down, circling it. "Obviously, he doesn't work on his own. Who's in with him?"

"Ex-CIA types, mostly."

"What?" He wasn't sure he heard correctly. "Did you say, CIA?"

"Yeah. These guys operate like vultures. Contacts up the kazoo, in and out of Washington. They know who wants the hardware—Faroush, for example—and they know where to go to get it. Security clearance gets them plant entry and export licenses, no questions asked."

"But their clearances must expire when they leave the service, Herman. That's so easy to check."

"Bullshit. A driver's license you have to renew every two or three years. A security clearance—once you get it— hell, it's good forever. Assuming you don't get busted. I oughta know. And I've never been busted."

Garrett swung around in his chair. Dusk was settling in, and he could barely make out the distant hills against the darkening sky. "So Faroush uses these guys as his agents, you mean."

"Sorta, yeah. He contacts them, gives 'em a shopping

list. They order stuff, or steal it, from American manufacturers, have it sent to New York, where they either run it to Germany themselves—if it's small, like chips—or ship it over in big cartons marked "Commercial Washing Machines" or "Industrial Ovens." Nobody checks the stuff. Customs couldn't care less, or gets bought off."

"Chips, mostly? Advanced memory devices?"

Brewster shuffled through his notes. "Hell, chips, lasers, radar devices, orbiting particle beam weapons—whatever they are, satellite detectors, heat sensors, the works."

"Same basic chip technology that goes into video games," Art muttered.

"Don't know about that, but there's a big demand for all of it. Russians pay top dollar for this stuff. That's why Faroush is so rich, and these CIA guys have bank accounts in Switzerland and a lot of cash across the border."

Garrett paused, nodding. So far he had kept the chip theft between Micro Optix and the local police, except for a few close friends in the industry. The more he learned about how the Russians—and now the CIA—operated in the gray market, the more troubled he became. At some point, he would simply have to turn things over to the FBI, he thought. There was a limit to what Tanaka could do.

"Everything conveniently points to the Russians, Herman, but nobody seems to know how to catch the bastards."

"We're dealing with a very well-organized group of people as serious about their business as you are about yours, Art. Semiconductor Arrays told me about this former Soviet agent—Arkov's his name—who claimed diplomatic immunity here not long ago. Testified in Washington, confessed outright the Russians are bent on stealing U.S. technology. One, to pass us in sophisticated weapons and two, to copy our chips. Reverse engineering, boss. That's the name of the game."

Reverse engineering.

Art froze when he heard the words. His mind snapped back to the Hitachi case, and the sale of his 256K standard chips to Signal Systems. The Japanese again. He doodled on his yellow pad, drawing a circle around the words.

"Which brings us back to Tokyo, Herman. The Japanese are geniuses at reverse engineering. Did your chums think of *any* plausible reason they might have wanted our chips?"

The line hissed softly as Brewster sorted through his notes. "None. Monolithic said the potential flap from Washington would just be too great. They said, look at all the hell the Japs are catching just in the trade war. Said they don't have to pull any crap like that. It's just not their style."

Not their style.

Somebody else had said that, in almost exactly the same words. Art thought back to his conversation with Roger in the car on their way to Sunnyvale last Saturday. Brewster was right. The Japanese didn't have to resort to outright theft to accomplish their ends. The Signals Systems case proved that.

"So where does that leave us, Herman, based on all this stuff?"

"Hard to say. Could still be a plant. Could also be a possible imitation of the job two years ago at Monolithic: bribe a janitor, sell to the local competition, and then skip off with the dough."

"That the best we can do? Fake the thing to put the monkey on the Japanese? Pretty elaborate, don't you think, pretending to be Vietnamese and all?"

"Christ, Art, from my experience out here, you can drag a sawbuck through Chinatown on the end of a string and come out with a dozen eager-beavers licking their lips. Know how many Asians live here in California, especially around San Francisco?"

Garrett closed his eyes. Another dead end.

"Oh hell," Brewster went on, "some Russian agent got to this gook—sorry—paid him, gave him blow-ups of the stuff they wanted, and told him what to do. You said yourself he just took random handfuls. Since he's a refugee—or pretending to be—the Soviets would have no trouble killing him afterward and then dumping the body. They're so

fucking efficient they make the Germans look like Po-
lacks."

Hopeless. That's what Art thought. That's what he felt.
He sighed. "Well, thanks, Herman. If you turn up anything further, let me know." He twirled the pencil in his
fingers as his mind visualized a dead body floating under
the Golden Gate Bridge.

"Oh, Herman?" He had one final thought.

"Yeah?"

"Just assume, for a second, that it *was* the Japanese. If
you wanted to follow that hunch, who would you turn to?"
He kept circling the words "Reverse Engineering" on his
pad, like a school boy marking a misspelled word.

"Art, like I say, it's not their style." Brewster shouted
into the phone now, impatient, disbelieving.

"I realize that. We all do, I think." His voice showed just
the slightest irritation. "But just *assume,* Herman. That's
all."

"You mean, hypothetical-like?" he asked, in quieter
tones.

"Yeah, hypothetical-like."

"Hell, I guess I'd go straight to the FBI."

"The FBI?" It was Garrett's turn to be impatient. "Your
average third-grader could figure that out! But they're
strictly domestic. You know they don't get involved in international affairs—"

"Easy, Art. Easy," Brewster broke in. "Let me think."
Another pause. "You must know somebody pretty high up
in the Pentagon who could keep this thing quiet."

"The Pentagon?" His voice was calm.

"Yeah. D.O.D. Because of the national security implications."

Garrett snapped his fingers. Department of Defense.
Roger had a contact down there, somebody responsible for
annual technical briefings. He made a note.

"We'll check it out." Art sighed into the phone. He
wasn't very optimistic. All he could see in front of him
were dead ends. "Thanks, Herman. Keep in touch, huh?"

"Hey, Art."

"Yeah."

"Just an assumption, OK?"

He paused. "Yeah, I know. Just an assumption."

They rang off. As Garrett cradled the receiver, he shook his head, forcing a half-smile. Wouldn't he be the laughing stock of the industry if he went to the Pentagon on the basis of a six-pack of Japanese beer found in the deserted apartment of a presumed Vietnamese refugee who had worked for Micro Optix for all of two weeks?

He slammed the desk so hard his fist stung.

It had been a long week. Thursday night brought a piece of good news, a small victory, temporarily halting the hemorrhage of defeats.

Sally called to report that Jason's X-rays were favorable, and his condition was no longer critical. He was off sedation and sitting up. He really had only one serious problem.

What was that? Art had asked.

"Boredom," she said.

"Leave that to me," he said.

When they met on the hospital steps on Friday afternoon, Art was carrying a canvas bag. Sally couldn't hide her curiosity.

"What's in the bag?"

"You'll see."

They found Jason in good spirits. His legs were no longer in traction, the color had returned in his face, and he did not appear to be in pain. He expressed both the hopeful anticipation of a young boy and the boredom of restricted movement.

Sally kept staring at Art's bag. Finally, he arranged a vertical screen around the bed, with Sally and Jason on one side and himself and the hospital's TV set on the other.

He then unloaded the canvas bag, setting out a spider's web of wires, connectors, leads, integrated circuits, a cassette unit, a videx plug board, screws, wing nut, solder, and a small assortment of tools.

He wheeled the TV chassis around, unscrewed the back panel, and went to work.

Ten minutes later, the cassette unit rested on top of the

reassembled TV, and Art was holding a vertical lever behind his back.

When he pushed the screen aside, neither mother nor son could guess what he had done. They saw the wires trailing behind him, but it wasn't until he whipped the vertical lever out from behind his back that Jason recognized instantly what it was. A joy stick. His eyes widened with pleasure.

Art had rewired the hospital TV; it was now a video game player.

Jason took the lever in his hands as Art reached into his coat pocket and fished out a handful of cassette tapes: Sabotage, Missile Command, Space Invaders, Galaxy, Yar's Revenge. He set them down on the bedside table.

Pain forgotten, confinement ignored, Jason plugged in Space Invaders first and played a round with Art, then one with Sally. He won both handily.

As they left the room, Sally saw excitement and intense joy in Jason's eyes. He was totally absorbed in a happy and more familiar world.

"How did you . . . ?" she had started to ask when they reached the parking lot.

"Never mind," he said. "Let's just drop your car off and I'll explain it all over dinner."

12

His opponent swept the white terrycloth wristband across a wet forehead, soaking off the sweat.

"Twelve all. You ready?"

Art Garrett nodded, breathing hard and jumping lightly on the balls of his feet, racquet poised, body angled toward the side wall for the next serve.

It arched high, a soft lob off the front wall which he attacked aggressively, sending a backhand straight down the line. The response came floating back, weakly. Art pursued it immediately and sliced a drop shot to his right, out of reach.

"Thirteen-twelve," Art puffed, his white T-shirt dripping wet. Beneath the red Micro Optix logo on the front of the shirt were the words, "Smaller Is Better." On the back, also stenciled in bright red, was the caption, "Less Is More."

Shifting to the backhand serving box, Art whipped a hard, flat serve straight at his adversary's body, forcing a pushed floater toward the front wall. Garrett's sneakers squeaked across the hardwood floor as he aced toward the ball. When he pivoted in center court, his left foot slipped on a trail of sweat and his legs shot out from under him, as if he had stepped on oil. He flicked the ball with a snap of his wrist and watched it carom off the side wall, floating forward. His opponent scrambled hurriedly but missed the return, then knelt down to help him up. "You OK?"

Garrett nodded, flexing both ankles and doing knee-bends to make sure no tendons were strained. "You almost lucked out," he said, walking over to the telltale where he retrieved his towel and mopped up the small pool of perspiration that had caused his fall.

" 'Play to win, be willing to lose.' Seems to me I've heard those words somewhere before."

"Come on, let's finish it off." He licked drops of sweat from the ends of his moustache. Serving with a two-point edge, he won the next point for game and match.

The two athletes, breathing hard, their bodies still slick with sweat, slumped onto the floor at the front of the court and collapsed against the cool metal telltale.

Art draped his towel over his head and exhaled. The towel billowed out. "Long time since you've played, my ass," he said.

"It's true." Sally dragged a wet wristband across her forehead, still sparkling with pearls of sweat. "I told you tennis is my game. I just anticipate well." Her small chest rose and fell rapidly as she recovered her breath. "Sounded like you were starting to get a little crotchety in that last game."

Garrett pulled the small white towel off his head, down his face, dragging his matted hair into his eyes. He brushed it back with a flick of his hand, exhaling audibly. "I'm sorry. Last week, I guess I was paranoid about the Japanese. This week, I see Russians everywhere I look."

"Well, the squash was your idea, remember. You were so pumped up, you couldn't wait to get back from the hospital to play." She took a towel now and dried her arms, then wiped her legs. "I can't remember ever losing so many points by getting hit by the ball!"

Art laughed. His body felt more relaxed now, his breathing back to normal. "Only way I had a chance of winning was to aim at your body." He winked a drop of sweat out of one eye.

Sally fanned herself with the towel. "If I could charge you a buck for each bruise, I could live like a princess on my sabbatical next year."

"Is that definite now?" he asked. He stretched his long legs out on the smooth oak floor, and crossed his arms behind his head, looking down at her.

"Not yet," she said, wriggling lower on the telltale, then turning away from him. "Scratch my back?"

He reached under her white cotton shirt and massaged

her lower spine. He could feel the solid muscle in her back, evidence of her lean tennis condition.

"But it's on request," she continued. "I should know in another week or two."

"Know yet what you want to do?" He used the base of his hand now in tight, circular strokes.

"That's fine, thanks," she said, leaning back against the wall. She drew her knees up and circled them with her arms. "Not really. I've thought about combining my interests in poetry and Japan and maybe doing something in Japanese literature for a change."

"Would that mean you'd be there for the whole year?" Art buried his face in his towel to hide the disappointment he felt.

"Depends on Jason, really," Sally said. "How well he's recovered, how he feels. I wouldn't want to turn his school year into a revolving door." She reached over and pulled Art's towel from his face. "That was very thoughtful of you, what you did for him today."

He shrugged his shoulders modestly, looking back down at her. "I did it for you, Sally," he said.

She ran a hand through her tangled hair. "Nonsense," she said. "I saw the look in your eyes when you gave Jason the joystick." She paused, taking one of his hands in hers. "You really can do anything with these, can't you?"

He smiled. "That stuff's simple. You should see what the high school kids are doing with computers now. Make me look like an auto mechanic."

Sally settled back, closing her eyes. A moment later she popped forward and grabbed Art's arm. "Hey, you didn't tell me about the annual meeting. So much has been happening, I forgot to ask."

He draped his towel over her head. "I'm just as glad you didn't ask," he said. "I pushed the Japan thing too hard, and almost got sandbagged."

She swung around on the floor and sat cross-legged, facing him.

"I thought you were going to soft-peddle the Japanese issue."

"I was, I was."

"Don't tell me you got carried away again."

He smiled a half-smile. "A little, I suppose. You know me."

Sally cupped her hands under her chin, resting her elbows on her knees. "What happened?"

Art jammed his sneakers under him and pushed his butt up off the floor, keeping his shoulders pressed against the wall, flexing his lower vertebrae.

"There was a shareholder from San Francisco, I forget his name now, a banker, representing a ten percent block of shares. He had a fistful of statistics about how important Japanese imports are to the California economy, how many jobs would be lost if we tried to keep their products out of our market. Very effective. What is it, something like a third of California's entire GNP is derived, in whole or in part, from Japan?"

"Forty percent," she said. "Big numbers."

"Yeah. So he put me in my place, I guess. Reminded me that companies like ours are several steps ahead of the general public in its perception of the Japanese threat."

Sally nodded. "They're still having love affairs with their Hondas."

"Still, I feel I had to make the point, at least for our industry. You know, the calculation-domination-elimination theme."

"I know." She saw the frustration in his eyes. "What did this man do with his ten percent block on the dividend vote?"

Art smiled. "Oh, he voted against paying a dividend."

"So you lost the battle, but won the war."

"Yeah, barely." He scratched his head. "We got fifty-eight percent of the votes."

"But you won. That's what you wanted, wasn't it?"

"Yeah." His lack of enthusiasm belied his response. "We were hoping for a much larger percentage, Sally. An overwhelming vote of confidence, I guess." He looked down at the floor.

"But you *won.* Jesus, whether you win a squash match by ten points or in a tiebreaker, you still win. Give yourself a little credit for a change." She reached out and touched him on the knee.

His eyes met hers. "Maybe you're right," he sighed. "I'm just so used to defeat these days, I can't recognize victory for what it is." He put his hand on top of hers.

"I know you're worried about the chip theft," Sally said. "And how important that industrial policy legislation is for you, and for the industry. But you've got to use these little victories as springboards, or stepping stones, one at a time. Just like with Jason this afternoon."

Art remembered the look of ecstasy on the boy's face when he saw the video game hookup. Despite the pain. Despite the defeat. Despite the restricted confinement of his stiff plaster casts and the colorless hospital room.

He nodded. "You're right, you know? That kid was beside himself with those games." He squeezed her hand. "And we've got a full year before the dividend vote comes up again. Lots can happen." He sprang to his feet.

"One more game?"

"Wait," Sally said, pushing herself up. "What time is it?"

Art plucked his wristwatch out of his jacket pocket, in a corner on the floor.

"Just after seven. Why?"

"Because today's the Emperor's birthday," she said, collecting her gear. "He's eighty-four today. There may be something on the news. It's always a big event in Japan."

"Who's eighty-four today?" he asked, squeezing the stiff ball.

"Hirohito. The Emperor of Japan. He became Emperor sixty years ago, which makes this the sixtieth year of the Showa period."

Garrett zipped himself into his jacket, then tightened the racquet press around his strings. "The what?"

"Showa Jidai," Sally said. "The era of peace and harmony. Come on, let's watch it together." She extended a hand.

"You go ahead," he said. "TV's in the den. I'll close up the court and find us a bottle of wine for dinner."

Sally gave him a quick kiss, then ducked out the undersized door at the far end of the squash court and disappeared up the spiral staircase.

Art clicked the door shut behind him and turned off the bright court lights. Stuffing his squash gear under one arm, he turned down the darkened hallway toward his basement collection of wines, reflecting on what Sally had said.

Maybe the shareholder's vote was a small victory, but that seemed to be the only one. His telephone conversations with the EIA in Washington had convinced him that passage of any industrial policy legislation was unlikely. And Masters had called just before the annual meeting to say that the Vietnamese had never returned. A new tenant was moving into the apartment, so they'd gone through it again, thoroughly, and had found nothing more. Otherwise, no new developments from Sunnyvale.

He snapped on a light in the cool, dark corner he used for storing his wines, and after yanking a half-dozen bottles from their horizontal pigeonholes, he finally decided on the same Fetzer he and Sally had had two weeks before. That had been a little victory, too, he thought, and he wasn't above being superstitious.

As he flicked out the light, he made a mental note to follow up on Herman's suggestion to take the chip theft to the Pentagon. He would call Roger right after dinner and ask him to pursue it with the D.O.D. on Monday. He could also tell Roger that Frank Martin at McDonnell Douglas had still not abandoned the idea of approaching an alternative supplier for the optical chips, like a believer clinging to the virgin birth. Maybe, just maybe, he thought, the right people at the Pentagon could be helpful in persuading Martin not to pursue the idea if it meant a possible Japanese supplier. In the name of national interest.

Yeah. Little victories as stepping stones, he thought, tucking the bottle of wine under his other arm. Not a bad analogy.

13

He was halfway up the circular stairs when he heard Sally's voice explode through the hatch cover above his head.

"Art! Come up here, quick!"

Not knowing what to expect, he sped up the remaining stairs two at a time.

"What—?"

"Shh!" she said, pulling him toward the TV. "Just sit down and watch. It's incredible."

He lowered himself slowly onto the edge of the couch as he heard the familiar voice of a network newscaster and watched scenes of apparent violence and destruction unfold on the screen.

". . . with the worst political riots in the history of postwar Japan," the announcer said, methodically and matter-of-factly. "Hundreds of thousands of students marched through Tokyo today on the Emperor's birthday protesting the Japanese government's proposed stand on forthcoming treaty negotiations with the U.S. and the U.S.S.R. . . ."

Art set the wine on the floor and dropped his squash gear behind him on the couch, his eyes never leaving the screen. Sally stood to his left as they watched videotaped footage of helmeted students marching, ten abreast, through the streets of downtown Tokyo.

They wore red kerchiefs across their noses and mouths, protection against the water and tear gas the riot police sprayed at them. They danced, they chanted, they brandished staves and threw cobblestones at the police. Windows shattered, glass flew, shopkeepers darted about like scared cats to escape the throng.

". . . primary factions of the Zengakuren, the national student's association, united today in opposition to the government's decision to renew the Security Treaty in Washington on May 15 and to concede ownership of the northernmost Kurile Islands to the Soviet Union in exchange for mineral rights in Siberia . . ."

Five students wearing gray trousers, black knee-length raincoats, and white plastic helmets emblazoned with the letter "Z" used a telephone pole as a battering ram on the main gate to the Imperial Palace.

Sally stood, motionless. "Those characters on their helmets," she whispered, "on the sides?"

Art nodded, wincing as they crashed through the gate. *"Sakakuka,"* she said. "The radical wing of the Zengakuren. Their most violent faction."

The picture shifted to Shinjuku, a major commercial section of Tokyo. Thousands of students, arms linked, legs synchronized in a military step, snaked through the streets shouting. *"Han-tai! Han-tai! Han-tai!"*

"What are they shouting?"

"Opposition! Opposition!" Sally shook her head. "Unbelievable."

They watched a wedge of students running behind makeshift shields, throwing stones at a massive cream brick building.

"My God!" Sally said, covering her mouth. "That's Tokyo University, symbol of the elite."

Streams of water from high-pressure hoses knocked the students down, spun the helmets from their heads, doubled them over in pain. But they were not deterred. Wave after wave of black, fist-sized stones hurled over the wall as wisps of white tear gas hung in the air.

The film cut to the central government quarter in Kasumigaseki.

"Foreign Ministry," Sally said, pointing as the camera panned the front of a modern, squat building, the *kanji* characters "Gaimusho" reflecting the bright television lights.

Windows on the first two floors had been completely smashed. Shards of glass lay on the concrete perimeter, and a cordon of blue-uniformed policemen now guarded the building. Cherry trees, which normally lined the broad avenue fronting the building, had been viciously hacked down.

"Jesus," Sally said, averting her eyes as two students were carried into a waiting ambulance, their faces smeared with blood. "Kasumigaseki is normally the quietest section in Tokyo."

"These Asian students demonstrate all the time, don't they?" he asked. "They're just fanatics."

The camera panned across the front of the stark, limestone National Parliament building, then down to street level to record the arrival of a fleet of limousines. Dark-suited politicians, somber-faced and angry, emerged and marched quickly up the flat stone steps, their maroon velvet chysanthemum lapel pins glowing softly.

Sally shook her head. "Local demonstrations by students from time to time is expected behavior. Happened three or four times while I was there—opposition to nuclear war, protesting U.S. involvement in Vietnam. Chanting, marching, sure, but non-violent."

Art sat forward now as the TV picture switched from Tokyo to Washington.

". . . Foreign Minister Hotta Tetsuya, seventy-three, leader of the central faction of the LDP, is in Washington this week for preliminary talks with the State Department, preparatory to the May 15 signing . . ."

He was shown leaving the dungeon-like State Department earlier in the day. His eyes were dark and heavy, deep lines creased his face, and his soft, white hair floated almost weightlessly on his head. He walked with the aid of a small bamboo cane.

". . . our Washington correspondent, Tom Jenkins, caught the Japanese official as he was returning to his Embassy. Tom?"

Garrett frowned, pressing his moustache with thumb and forefinger.

"Mr. Foreign Minister, many observers predict the Japanese government will now be forced to change its position on the forthcoming Security Treaty renewal. Is that true?"

Hotta looked at the microphone, not into the cameras, as he listened to the question. He conferred with an aide standing nearby, then said, in correct but halting English, "We . . . the Japanese government's position on this issue has been well-established. There is . . . we see no cause to reverse course at this time."

"Does this mean that your government will ignore the significance of these riots on the Emperor's birthday?"

At the mention of the Emperor, the Foreign Minister stopped and stiffened, turning to face the newsman.

"My government is committed to a policy of international cooperation and interdependence," Hotta said, his fine white locks ruffled now by a gentle wind. "We will not be pressured into changing course by an undisciplined group of young, immature radicals whose views do not represent the majority of the Japanese people."

With that, he angrily waved off further questions and crawled into the back seat of his waiting car.

Sally emitted a low whistle. "Wow, did you hear that?" she asked. She sat down on the arm of the couch, placing a hand on Art's shoulder.

"Hear what?"

"The emphasis, the emotion. Highly unusual for any Japanese, let alone a high government official."

"What do you mean?" he asked, putting his hand on hers.

"The forcefulness of his remarks," she whispered. "They wouldn't have been so emphatic unless there was a real factional struggle taking place right now in the LDP."

"Cabinet shuffle, you think?"

"Maybe more significant than that. Could be one of the right-wing factions has the votes to force a show of no-confidence."

"Which would necessitate new elections."

"Exactly."

They watched as the words "News Commentary" flashed across the screen. The network's chief political analyst began to comment on the implications of the day's dramatic events.

"What, exactly, this portends, nobody knows," he intoned in the deep voice that belonged to everyone in broadcasting and to no one in real life. "But what is certain to happen tomorrow, if not early next week, is a major cabinet shuffle among the heads of government by Prime Minister Tanaka."

Art raised an eeybrow. "Same Tanaka that was kicked out years ago in the Lockheed scandal?"

Sally nodded as the announcer turned to a new page of text. His eyes flicked up at the camera.

"Despite the avowal of Foreign Minister Hotta to renew the Security Treaty on May 15 and to sign the commercial accord with Russia, local observers here suspect that both negotiating sessions will be characterized by hard bargaining from the Japanese side, now that these violent demonstrations have occurred."

"Understatement," Sally murmured.

"Can the Japanese government reverse course?" the voice continued. "An independent Japan, rearmed, militarily strong and no longer dependent upon the United States for its principal means of defense, could pose a serious problem for regional political stability in Asia.

"And the commercial agreement with the Soviet Union, while giving Japan vital access to needed raw materials in Siberia, could spark even more serious political opposition at home if the Kuriles are officially ceded back to the Russians."

"Christ," Art said. "All we need is more political unrest."

"Quiet," Sally whispered.

"Policy makers in Washington seemed convinced that the riots today will force the Japanese government to reassess its basic strategy. While renewal of the Security Treaty does not appear in danger, they nonetheless agree the negotiating sessions will be long and arduous.

"Hardliners in the Soviet section at the State Department believe the commercial accord with the Russians *could* weaken a new Security Treaty by making the Japanese less dependent upon the U.S.

"This is ABC News. Good night."

Art leaned forward and snapped off the set.

Sally eased onto the couch and sat facing Art, her legs folded beneath her. Captain wandered over from a distant corner and jumped up between them, competing for space. Sally stroked his broad back.

"Some birthday party," he said.

She was silent, her eyes fixed on Captain as she smoothed his yellow fur.

"I think there's more to these student riots than meets the eye," she said, glancing up at Art.

"What do you mean? You said yourself you saw three or four of them while you were in Japan." He reached down and rubbed the tomcat's big ears.

Sally shook her head. "Not like these. Passive demonstrations, yes. But destructive, violent riots are uncharacteristic of Japan. The whole culture is dedicated to harmony, to preserving tradition."

"That may hold for the society as a whole," he said. "But students everywhere are a distinct subculture. They can't reflect the broad spectrum of values, because they're only one part of the whole."

"True. But we're not talking about the whole society here—just one segment of it. An established faction. With its hierarchical behavior." She shook her head. "When they demonstrate, they get paid. Pocket money, to be sure, but student allegiances are fuzzy. They gravitate to whoever has the cash—political parties, mostly, but sometimes corporations."

Art frowned. "Somebody must have put big bucks behind the birthday party today," he said.

"That's what I'm thinking," Sally said. "You know, Japan has its ultra-conservatives just as we do. I wonder . . ."

Her voice trailed off momentarily.

"Xenophobia," she whispered. "Hatred of foreigners. Of course! A thread that runs through all of Japanese history. You heard the news analysis—the Security Treaty renewal and the commercial accord with Russia. Suppose the right wing of the LDP has financed these student riots to bring pressure on the mainstream faction. Suppose they've joined forces with some high-ranking military types who share their desire to see a rearmed Japan. Then they really *could* force a vote of no-confidence and bring on new elections."

Art grabbed a handful of fur as Captain jumped down and wandered off again. He thought for a minute. Then he shook his head.

"Pretty thin, Sally. You're talking about a possible coup in one of the most stable political democracies in the world. This isn't the time of Tojo any more." He stood and stretched, picking at his damp shirt.

Sally leaned back and folded her arms behind her head. "Did you ever see a movie, made years ago, called *Japan's Longest Day?*"

Art nodded as he reached up to touch the ceiling. "I think so. Dealt with subversion in the military government in the 1930s, attempts by young military officers to push it more to the right?"

"That's the one. And you think, after watching these riots tonight," she said, pointing to the blank screen, "something like that couldn't happen?"

He reached down for the wine, walked over and set it on top of the oval bar. "Japan has everything to lose, and nothing to gain, by doing something like that," he said. "At least, in the thirties they had the Greater Southeast Asia Co-Prosperity Sphere and a defacto military government. But you heard the Foreign Minister. The Japanese are vulnerable. They're committed to international interdependence."

"The present government is, that's right," Sally said, rising from the couch and leaning down for her shoes. "But Hotta could be out of power this weekend." She pulled her fingers through the wet tangle of hair at the base of her neck. "I'm going to shower. But somehow I have a gut feeling that the right wing faction has an ace in the hole, something really big they're backing their position with."

Art uncorked the wine as she disappeared up the staircase. He frowned as he pondered her last comment. What could the right wing have up their sleeve? The military? He laughed and decanted the wine. Japan is limited to defensive weapons. How could they possibly expect to rearm?

Even if they wanted to, the Pentagon would be looking over their shoulder.

Pentagon. Roger! He snapped his fingers. Glancing at his watch, he grabbed the phone.

It rang a dozen times before Art heard the familiar voice.

"Roger? Art. Got a minute?"

"Sure. Sorry I was so long getting to the phone. Pam was arriving as you called."

"Want me to call back later?" He pulled the phone to the bar and set his tired body on one of the stools.

"No, I have a hunch now is better than later."

Art told him about his conversation with Brewster. "Forgot to mention it to you yesterday because we were so preoccupied with the annual meeting. Plus it seemed we weren't getting anywhere in Sunnyvale."

"I know."

"But Herman may have a point. It might not hurt to talk to the Pentagon and pick their brains. Didn't you know someone down there who coordinated briefings every year by the big electronics companies?" Art reached behind the bar and turned down the gas burner.

"Sure. Ed Hightower."

"Sounds familiar."

"Advanced Electronic Warfare. Invites the guys down to Washington once a year to demonstrate the latest weapons applications so the brass can drool over their potential new toys."

"Yeah. That's the guy."

Roger paused. "Well, I can call him on Monday if you want, but what's he going to tell us that we don't already know?"

"I'm not sure. Maybe he'll have a new thought or two." He spun around as he detected a fresh, soapy scent. Sally stood beside him, wearing a pair of dark brown corduroy culottes and a yellow plaid shirt. She was barefoot.

Art made a tipping motion with his free arm, bending it at the elbow.

"Beer?" she asked softly.

Nodding, he turned back to the phone.

"I guess he could at least confirm whether we're on the right track," Roger said. "So far, all roads lead to Moscow."

"Plus," Art said, taking a glass of Furstenberg from Sally and sipping it, "there may be something else Hightower can help us with." He mentioned the nagging McDonnell Douglas problem and his idea to get the Pentagon to put a little fear into Frank Martin.

"Not bad, not bad. In fact, the more I think about it, the more I like it. I'll start with that, and then work up to the chip theft."

Sally sat down opposite him, hitched up her culottes and raised her glass in a silent toast. Art took a long swallow of beer with her, closing his eyes as he tasted the cold liquid, felt it bring relief to his thirsty body.

"You know the guy, so use your own judgment. But tell Hightower to keep this to himself for the time being."

"Absolutely. Bottom-line, he's solid. No problem."

As he hung up, he drained his beer glass. Sally refilled it.

"Did I hear you mention the name Hightower?" she asked.

"Yeah." He frowned.

"Ed Hightower?"

"Yeah. Why?"

Sally took a sip of beer. "I got to know him a couple of years ago when I was researching a piece on Japanese security issues." She paused, swirling the beer in her glass. "He's a pro, Art. Not your ordinary government bureaucrat."

"So?"

"So he also happens to be one of the few Pentagon specialists trained in a non-European language. Good linguist, as I recall. Studied at the Defense Language School in Monterey."

"Studied what?"

"Japanese. He worked on East Asia defense problems for a while, which is why I went to see him. For all I know, maybe he still does."

Art relaxed his frown. "Maybe Herman's not so crazy after all. Start the meat for us while I shower?"

Ten minutes later, the phone began to ring as he walked back into the den, tucking an old workshirt into his jeans.

"I'll get it," he said as Sally stood behind the bar, tending the grill. "Probably Roger with an afterthought. I'll mention what you said about Hightower." He picked up the receiver.

"Garrett."

The line hissed with static. Art guessed instantly it was long-distance.

"Art? Jim Masters. Sorry if you're in the middle of dinner, but we've come across something weird out here we think you ought to know about."

Sally walked out from behind the bar when she saw Art stiffen slightly.

"What is it, Jim?"

She understood now it was not Roger, and leaned in to listen. He angled the phone so she could hear. "Masters," he whispered. She nodded.

"You remember I told you our Vietnamese friend never came back."

"Yeah. But we never expected him to."

The line crackled with static.

"And you recall they rented out the guy's apartment to someone else?"

"Yeah, I remember." Art's frown returned. "What's the point?"

"I'm getting to that," Masters said. "Just hang on." He coughed into the connection. "Well, this new tenant's been in the apartment a week now, I guess, and complained to the desk today that she could never get one of the electrical outlets in her bedroom to work."

"Hey, Jim," Art interrupted. "Is this another one of your kinky stories?" He looked at Sally, who was frowning now.

"No way. Listen. So the new tenant told the desk, and that Linda . . . Linda . . . ."

"Kalinski?" He recalled the name from Roger's reports.

"Yeah, Kalinski. Well, she called an electrician and the

guy came out late yesterday to fix the plate. Apparently, our Vietnamese friend installed a phony switchplate as a hiding place, and the electrician found a piece of fancy metal in the box. He took it out, you know, replacing the wires. It works fine now."

"Great," Art said, shaking his head. "So what's the big deal?"

Sally looked up at him, shrugging her shoulders.

"Well, the big deal is he was going to toss the thing out, but he noticed some funny writing on it and gave it to Kalinski. She couldn't make anything out of it either—looked Greek to her, she said—so she called the Sergeant for lack of anything better to do."

"Tanaka?"

"Yeah. Our boy. He went out to take a look at it right away and called me as soon as he saw what was on it."

"What was it, a Vietnamese coin?"

"You ready?"

"Come on, Jim. What the hell was it?"

Masters paused. He cleared his throat. "Japanese," he said. *"Kanji* characters clear as day. Hill of Pine."

"What?" Art shouted. "What are you talking about?"

Sally backed away, her eyes wide.

She knew.

"Hill of Pine," Masters repeated. "No idea what the gadget is, but that's what it says in Japanese."

"Matsuzaka," Sally whispered.

The static exploded in his ear.

PART V

FIRE

1

Roger Harris spent most of Saturday afternoon hunched over the lab bench. He was using a jeweler's magnifying lens to examine the contents of the express mail delivery from Sunnyvale.

"Get a pencil," he said.

Art Garrett reached into his shirt pocket, unclipped his automatic pencil, and twisted out a sliver of lead.

"Shoot." He pulled a yellow pad closer to him.

"K3 dash 000173. No, wait a minute." Harris squinted as he arched the gooseneck lamp closer to the small brass object. "Goddam figures are hard to read. Make that KB. KB dash 000173."

Art jotted down the numbers. "Anything else?"

"Zip. Want to take a look?" He spun around on his stool and handed Garrett the eyepiece.

Art took the device in his hands and rubbed his fingers along the sides. Less than two inches square, it resembled a flat pill box. He pressed his thumb on the oblong plastic strip that covered about a square inch on the back side. It flexed firmly in response, like a piece of film in a metallic clip.

He screwed the magnifying lens into his right eye and bent down, holding the microimagizer between a thumb and forefinger. He focused on the distinctive *kanji* characters. They jumped off the surface, bright and gleaming. Unmistakable.

Matsuzaka.

Hill of Pine.

"KB dash 000173?"

Harris glanced down at the figures on Art's pad. "Right."

"What do you think—quality control?"

"Either that or a batch code of some sort."

Art tapped the backside with a small screwdriver.

Nothing happened.

He shook it.

Also nothing.

Flicking the edge with a fingernail, he detected a small seal, like a sausage casing, that bonded front and back together. "Hand me one of those microblades," he said.

Roger reached across the bench and pulled a miniature hacksaw off the wall. Viewed from a distance of more than six inches, it appeared to have no blade.

Garrett screwed the microimagizer into a small vice and checked the tautness of the thread-thin blade. He then cut through the seal, one edge at a time, until he could separate the two sides.

"Needlenose."

Roger handed him the pliers.

Unscrewing the vice with one hand, he pinched the brass object together with the pliers and held it directly under the lamp. Carefully, he pried the two sides apart.

"Holy shit," he whispered. He twisted the magnifying lens to refocus it.

Roger peered over his shoulder, squinting through his glasses. "Holy shit is right," he said. "Take a look at that 64K." The familiar shape of a standard microprocessor chip was unmistakable. "What do you think?"

Art shook his head. "No idea. Pretty powerful, whatever it is." He tapped the 64K chip with his pliers, then held it closer. The same distinctive *kanji* appeared on a corner of the integrated circuit.

"Check for power?"

Garrett nodded. Roger handed him the twin leads of a voltameter and clicked it on.

Art touched one of the leads to the microprocessor, the other to the handle of the vice nearby. "Christ, look at that," he muttered. They both watched as the needles whipped wildly on the voltage scale. "My guess is it's some kind of transmitter. Give me one of those videx connectors."

Harris plugged the lead from a small videx board into a nearby line printer and handed Art the spaghetti-like connector. When Garrett held the connector to the dark plastic backside of the microimagizer, the daisywheel in the printer clicked and spun.

"Gobbledegook," Roger said, walking over to the paper roll.

"Figures." Art removed the videx connector, then snapped off the voltage meter. He swiveled around on his stool.

"A high-powered transmitter of some sort. It uses a 64K microprocessor for transmission, miniature cadmium battery for power. But it might as well have come from outer space." Art set the cylindrical lens down on the lab counter.

"I've never seen anything like it, that's for sure," Roger said. He fitted the two pieces back together and sealed them with a strip of electrical tape. "But it puts the spotlight right on the Japs now."

"Maybe." Garrett clicked off the lamp as he sat on the wooden countertop. He stared at the windowless wall across the room. "Don't discount the possibility of a plant."

"We've got to figure out what this gadget *is* before we can discount anything," Roger said, dropping it into a stiff cardboard envelope. He sat back down on one of the waist-high stools.

"Why would a Matsuzaka product turn up in the Sunnyvale apartment of a Vietnamese refugee?"

"A product nobody even knows Matsuzaka makes."

"Or has."

Roger tapped the envelope. "If it was a plant, to put the finger on the Japanese," Roger said, "somebody had to have access to a Matsuzaka factory in Japan. But why would they bring it all the way over here just to do that? There are lots of easier ways."

Art frowned as he seemed to search for an answer in the tangle of equipment on the pegboard across the room. "Didn't you say Hightower knows about hardware?" He looked back at Roger.

Harris nodded. "Advanced Electronic Warfare."

"Well, I think you better take that thing with you when you see him in Washington. Show it to him. Maybe he can tell us what it is." He paused. "In fact, rather than waiting, why don't you go down tomorrow night and camp on his doorstep first thing Monday morning?"

"No problem," Roger said as he stuffed the envelope into his briefcase and snapped it shut.

Art tossed the tiny pliers back into a box and hung the microblade back on the wall. "I wonder if there's any connection."

"Between what and what?"

"Between this thing and the student riots in Japan yesterday. Sally thought they were precedent-setting. If the Japanese are responsible for this theft, there's another brand new precedent."

"But, the Japs are our allies. Why would they engineer something like this for political purposes?"

"I don't think they would. Their interests are strictly commercial, I think, if they're involved at all," Art said, reaching for his jacket. "And don't call them Japs. Sally's trying to break me of the habit."

As they moved toward the door, a trio of young software engineers entered the lab. They had just come in from the outside and their coats were slick.

"Good afternoon," Art said, looking at their damp clothing. "Still raining?"

A pair of heads nodded. "New project, Mr. Garrett?" asked the third, a woman in her late twenties dressed in coveralls. Her raven hair glistened with moisture. "Haven't seen you in the lab on Saturdays in quite a while." She smiled.

"Pentagon business," Art said with a wink.

"Oh," she said. Her smile vanished.

Garrett moved to the door. "Just be sure to shut everything down when you leave. Electricity's not getting any cheaper."

They walked down the first-floor hallway toward the fingerprint scanner and the exit.

"Call me as soon as you learn anything on Monday."

"Right," Roger said.

They pressed their thumbs on the scanner. When they heard the latch click, they pushed through. "Where are you off to now?"

"Sally and I are going to see how Jason is doing," Art said, zipping his jacket. "X-rays were encouraging, but the leg bones apparently aren't setting right."

Roger stopped in the lobby and opened his briefcase. He pulled out a cassette and handed it to Art. "I almost forgot."

"What's this?"

"A new Adventure program for the kid," he said. "With a dwarf that's guaranteed to keep him guessing."

As they flashed their IDs at the security guard on duty, Roger caught a glimpse of the book he was reading and nudged Art.

Garrett smiled when he saw the title.

Japan as Number One.

2

The sound of the *takeboki* clawing through the small rocks echoed in the early morning stillness. The hump-backed old woman scraped a bamboo broom across the pebbles and then turned to lift a handful of litter into the bamboo basket she dragged along behind her. Her face was expressionless. The gnarled lines of age stretched to infinity.

Fukuda Kenji inhaled deeply on his Hi-Lite as he waited. He exhaled and the smoke dissipated slowly into the warm, humid air. Squinting in the near-darkness, he saw a form pass under the massive gate just ahead.

Sakurada-mon. The huge gate soared to a dozen meters overhead. The largest of its kind in the country, it guarded the entrance to Yasukuni Shrine, founded in 1870, the second year of the Meiji Restoration. Yasukuni housed the divine spirits of those who gave their lives in defense of the Japanese empire.

Yasukuni.

Peaceful country.

Many had died so that the Empire could enjoy peace and tranquility. Nearly three million souls enshrined, souls who suffered so others might live, souls revered by the people of Japan.

Fukuda drew on his cigarette and exhaled again as he walked toward the approaching form. Despite the heaviness of the air early that first morning in May, his skin was as cool and dry as talcum.

A flashing sign through the tall trees to his left caught his eye. Giant red *kanji* blinked their modern message from atop a brick building in the distance.

Matsu.

Zaka.

Two simple characters expressed centuries of tradition.

His gaze returned to the familiar form ahead and a half-smile softened his features.

The Major's step was bold and confident. He held himself proudly, chest expanded, shoulders square. Colorful ribbons bounced on his uniform jacket as he walked, a rainbow streak through a khaki sky.

They bowed deeply.

"Ohayo," said the Bucho, a single trail of white smoke rising lazily from the cigarette at his side.

"Good morning."

"Where's Katoh-kun?"

"Should be here."

They looked around, but saw nothing. The only sounds came from the bamboo basket of the old woman as it scraped along the pebbles behind them.

They crunched slowly ahead, leaving the stone *torii* behind and nearing the gate that guarded the temple's inner precinct. Its mammoth pillars stretched thirty feet above them to support a huge bronze crosspiece, oxidized to a soft, luminescent green. Rows of stone lanterns, tall as the trees that flanked the walkway, stood guard like silent sentries.

As they neared the bronze *torii,* they heard a car door slap shut and hurried footsteps. Pebbles sprayed as the MITI bureaucrat sprinted toward his waiting colleagues.

"Sorry!" Katoh said, breathing heavily and bowing deeply. "Sorry to be late."

"Yoshi," said Fukuda. "Never mind." He gestured toward the inner shrine.

Katoh pulled out his handkerchief and wiped the perspiration from his face. Like Fukuda, he wore a slate gray suit, white shirt, black shoes. The invisible uniform. Under his left arm, he clutched a small folding umbrella.

Approaching the central *dojo,* they kneeled on the ancient wooden steps, clasping their hands in prayer across their chests. The Major's bald head reflected the light of a single white candle flickering nearby.

Fukuda Kenji, in the center, kneeled with eyes closed, face calm, breathing controlled. Katoh glanced nervously at his colleagues, first to Fukuda, then to the Major. His chubby face glistened with moisture.

Fukuda clapped his hands three times and then reached into his pocket for a handful of coins. He threw them into the wooden box to his right and listened as they clattered to the bottom. Major Nakamura followed suit.

Katoh jerked a few coins from his trousers, spilling some on the wooden steps. When he tossed them skittishly into the box, half missed and bounced noisily off the floor.

"Nani?" Fukuda asked, watching Katoh's trembling hands as he retrieved the coins.

"Daijobu, daijobu," he said, his head bobbing in deference. "It's all right, don't worry."

The fact was, he *was* worried. Very worried.

The student riots on Friday had badly disturbed him. Fukuda had promised no violence. He was upset, and fearful. He needed reassurance.

Fukuda inhaled the sweet smell of incense. Black joss sticks burned in a small bronze bowl. They stuck vertically in the sand like miniature trees, shorn of leaves. White trails of perfumed smoke hung heavily in the air.

A smile cracked Fukuda's emotionless face. "We're right on schedule," he said. "In all my years of political activity, I don't think I've ever seen a more effective series of demonstrations. *Ne,* Nakamura-san?"

The Major nodded. "Brilliant. Simply brilliant, Buchosan." He shifted himself on his knees, rubbing a palm over his smooth pate. "I was afraid we would have to resort to financial pressure on some of the key politicians, but the demonstrations were so dramatic, so well-orchestrated, so . . . so *professional.*" His chest swelled as he voiced the word. "And the timing. That was a nice touch, arranging it on the Emperor's birthday."

Timing is strategy. There is timing in everything.

The words of Musashi rang in Fukuda's ears. His scalp tingled. He gazed at the shiny bronze statue of Buddha squatting on the tatami inside the hall. It gazed back at him, its hands clasped, lotus-style, across its abdomen.

"But it wasn't cheap, my friend," Fukuda chortled. "It's not as simple to bribe the students today as it was when we were young."

Katoh stiffened when he heard the word.

"Chotto, Bucho-san," Katoh said, his hands shaking as he held them in the vertical prayer position. "Was it absolutely necessary to resort to bribery for those *demos?"*

"Baka!" Fukuda hissed, glancing down at the MITI official now. "The payments were made in cash, distributed through the Zengakuren. No receipts, no traces." He paused. "And we used *all* of the factions, Katoh-kun. Not just the radicals."

Katoh nodded nervously. He dabbed at his face again with the handkerchief. "But the ensuing cabinet shuffle was so dramatic, so forceful," he said.

Fukuda and the Major glanced at each other, smiling.

"Wasn't that what we wanted?" Nakamura asked.

Katoh fidgeted with his necktie. "To remove Hotta as Foreign Minister, yes," he said. "But the Prime Minister didn't stop there. He replaced the cabinet posts in Finance, Welfare—"

"And MITI, of course," Fukuda broke in. "The new MITI minister should be most responsive to our plan." He smiled. "That was an unexpected bonus."

Katoh shook his head, spraying Fukuda with droplets of perspiration. "It's dangerous," he said. "I mean, for me to have a new minister at a time like this! At least his predecessor was totally naive."

Fukuda nodded. "Perhaps. But the Prime Minister showed great resolve in executing this sweeping move. It proved he is no longer beholden to the centrists, those cowards who continually capitulate to the demands of the inferior American and Russian governments."

The Major leaned over in Katoh's direction now. "Think, Katoh-kun. It took Tanaka-san more than a decade to resume power as Prime Minister and head of the LDP. Now he is in position to fulfill his promise to rebuild the Japanese archipelago. Not just to bolster his domestic political leadership, but to put Japan in a position of *global* power!"

Retto Kaizo. The words echoed in Katoh's ears. He had been a middle-level kacho at MITI in 1972 when Tanaka first promulgated his comprehensive plan to rebuild the Japanese islands. He twisted the handkerchief in his hands.

Fukuda rose and stood before the bronze icon. He bowed in silence.

Buddha gazed back as if to say, "Be tranquil. Peace is power."

The three clapped their hands in a final tribute, then turned and stepped back onto the loose stones.

Fukuda walked over to a small vending machine. With its tiny, thatched roof, it resembled a miniature temple. He dropped in a coin and extracted a bag of birdseed.

As they walked along the footpath in the shadow of the giant *torii,* Fukuda tossed a few grains to the clucking pigeons. He watched them peck at the seed, powerless creatures of habit.

"With Hotta out, and Kobayashi in as Foreign Minister, the treaty negotiations should go much more in our favor," he said.

The Major nodded. "And if he suspects, during the final phase, that our hands are still tied, we will be ready to go." He stopped and pulled down on the sides of his military jacket. It conformed to the contours of his lean body.

"Naruhodo," Fukuda said. As they neared the wooden doors under the Sakurada-mon, he scattered the remainder of the birdseed across the pebbles with a flick of his hand. The pigeons swooped down in a mass of flapping wings.

Fukuda glanced up at the chrysanthemum crests emblazoned on the heavy timber doors as they stood at the base of the giant gate. "Symbol of our past, guiding light for our future, Katoh-kun," he said, pointing to the golden crests.

The MITI man stared at the smooth, curved emblems in silence. He swallowed, felt his Adam's apple stick in his throat.

"Now is not the time to doubt the wisdom of our plan, my friend," Fukuda said, his voice rising. His eyes grew wide. "Who else in the world has the depth of cultural harmony, the breadth of understanding, the height of economic achievement?"

Katoh nodded, blinking.

"Nippon," Fukuda hissed. "The future is ours."

A temple gardener pushed his wooden wheelbarrow across the loose stone path. They waited until the old man scraped to the other side, then proceeded on their way.

"What if the Americans suspect something when Kobayashi takes a tougher stand?" Katoh asked, shaking his head. "What if Kobayashi's team stonewalls them in Washington? What if—"

Fukuda Kenji lashed out with his right hand and slapped Katoh hard, across the face. Beads of perspiration sprayed into the air. The folding umbrella dropped from under Katoh's arm, crunching onto the pebbles below.

The Major stooped down to pick it up.

"You ignorant fool!" Fukuda shouted. His eyes burned holes in the MITI man's glistening face. "Where is the nerve, the fortitide, we cultivated together so many years ago?"

Fukuda clenched his fists by his side.

"Listen, and listen well," he said. "There is to be no turning back. We are committed, and we will see it through. We will *persevere.* Is that clear?"

Katoh nodded nervously, clutching the umbrella with both hands. His eyes darted from the Bucho to the Major, who stood, cool and passionless, at Fukuda's side.

"Is that clear?" Fukuda roared.

"Hai," he stuttered, his voice squeaking. He looked down at the ground.

They crunched their way forward. The soft gray light of morning covered them like a veil.

Fukuda held out his hand and looked up as it started to rain. *Kirisame,* he thought. Weightless drops.

"The technicians have their instructions?" Major Nakamura asked. He stared straight ahead.

Fukuda pulled a cigarette from his pocket and stopped briefly to light it. The flame from the match illuminated the intensity in his dark eyes.

"Of course," he said, tossing the match aside. "The mis-

siles are ready. We will be watching the progress of
Kobayashi-san's talks." He exhaled twin streams of smoke
from his nose. A small dragon.

Katoh jammed his hands into his pockets. They felt
damp. His eyes twitched.

"*Dewa,*" Fukuda Kenji whispered, looking up at the
massive wooden gate. "Until we meet again at Yasukuni."

Those magic words, spoken by untold millions on their
annual pilgrimage to this holy shrine, hung softly in the
warm damp air.

Ken-chan sat cross-legged in front of his mother. He
stared at the tatami, fingering the silken tassels on his
tabi. His head was bowed.

His piano master, Kawakami, sat off to one side, silently
smoking a *kiseru,* his eyes focused on the black piano. Its
silence dominated the room.

Michiko dabbed at a tear in one eye, trying hard to retain her self-control as she had been taught to do by her
parents. She sat stiffly erect in a formal, white-and-gold kimono, kneeling, with her legs folded beneath her.

"I simply don't believe it, Ken-chan," she said. "You
studied so hard. You had the best tutors." Her lower lip
quivered.

Kenshin shook his head, not raising his eyes. "I also do
not understand," he said. "It is a mystery to me. There is
no excuse." His head dropped lower.

"*Maa,*" the master interrupted between puffs on his
pipe. "Not entering Tokyo University is not the end of this
boy's world, Fukuda-san. His is another path, a new tradition."

Michiko rotated her head slowly until she faced the
elderly music master. She noticed his eyes remained fixed
on the gleaming piano.

"One thing I must ask you to understand, *sensei,*" she
said, her voice a hoarse whisper, "is the horror Ken-chan
will go through when his father learns of this."

Kawakami shrugged his shoulders. "We must not lose
sight of the ultimate goal, Fukuda-san. Kenshin is a bril-

liant artist. His star will shine if he never even starts
Todai." He tapped the ashes from the bamboo pipe.

"That is the problem," Michiko said, her knuckles whit-
ening as she twisted her handkerchief. "You underesti-
mate my husband."

Kawakami reached behind him and removed a yellowed
book from the small shelf near the floor. The pages cracked
as he turned them.

"Let us not forget the teaching of Kembo," he said,
clearing his throat. "One of the Buddha's most enlightened disciples."

> *Spring has come!*
> *The doors hang plumb*
> *again; there is no*
> *challenge like no challenge.*
> *No thing so blank*
> *as plain sufficiency: the mist*
> *each day unfolding into sun,*
> *the clarity you wanted*
> *and you want undone.*

Kenshin looked up at his teacher now. Perhaps there is
hope, he told himself. Even outside my family, beyond tradition. He looked down at his feet when his mother glanced
again in his direction.

"When shall we tell your father?" she asked. "He will
almost certainly insist that you spend another year preparing for the entrance exams again."

Kenshin frowned. His hope was real, but then so was his
mother's concern. "We should tell him as soon as possible," he said. "He should learn it from us, not from the
school officials."

Michiko turned her head, looking now at Kawakami.
"That was a very profound teaching from Kembo," she
said. "But you must understand my husband's tenacity."

Kawakami nodded sadly. "We do not want to lose
Kenshin. The world will be the worse without his music."
He pushed a lock of deep-black hair back from his bony
face.

"Let us choose the time carefully, my son," Michiko said. "We must not wait long to tell him."

Kenshin picked at a loose strand of tatami. "I have brought great dishonor on my family," he said. "Even if I study for another year and pass, I can never erase the shame my failure has caused."

Michiko shook her head. "The dishonor can be erased when you pass next year. Notice I say *when*, and not if," she said. "Don't worry. You will discharge the obligation."

His mother's resolve gave him confidence. "I hope so," he said, half to her, half to himself.

Kawakami refilled his pipe and lit it. The gray smoke hovered, like a cloud, above his head. "We will embark upon a new program, Kenshin. To focus on the spiritual side of your playing, while keeping your technical skills sharp."

Kenshin nodded humbly, his head down. "It will be harder now, concealing my practice from my father. We must be very careful." Then he looked up at his mother.

She inhaled, drawing herself erect.

"Yoshi," she said. "Let's try."

3

Art kept telling himself there was no connection. Violent political demonstrations in Tokyo and a strange Japanese electronic device sitting in the wallplate of a Sunnyvale apartment. It just didn't make sense.

He sat at his harpsichord and tried to pick his way through a Bach concerto as his mind ran through a half-dozen possibilities and rejected each one in turn, like a debugger that spotted programming errors.

Commercially motivated, by Matsuzaka? Almost as quickly as he thought it, he discounted it. Why would they resort to such tactics when they were so close with their own chips? The answer was, they wouldn't.

It was so . . . so *imprecise*. So uncharacteristic of the Japanese thoroughness he had come to respect—and fear. He tossed out that possibility as well. Matsuzaka was not in a position to have to resort to outright thievery, and even if they did, they wouldn't be so stupid as to leave behind one of their own products. The IBM of Japan? Inconceivable.

But there were other Japanese companies that wanted to become IBMs in their own right, like Fujitsu and Hitachi, for example. They could have engineered the chip theft and planted the microimagizer to implicate Matsuzaka. Which, on the surface, was not all that implausible, Art thought, from a purely western point of view. The operative word was teamwork, however, not competition. MITI played offensive coordinator to make sure the team had an aggressive assortment of plays.

Fair enough. There were plenty of competitors, American and Japanese, willing to give their eye teeth for a way to steal market share from IBM. And willing to engage in a little creative skullduggery to do it, even breaking the law. God knew there were enough "consulting firms" around that specialized in selling "proprietary information" to IBM's competitors, and you never asked whether that information was obtained legally or not, you just bought it. That was what hamstrung Hitachi and Mitsubishi Electric back in 1982, Art recalled, so it was doubly doubtful that the Japanese would risk more industry criticism by pulling off a stunt like this.

But what about IBM's American competitors? Burroughs or Control Data, for example, or the aggressive boys at Digital Equipment? Pinch the Micro Optix technology and point the finger at the Japanese. An easy out, an easier alibi.

But would it fly? How would they get through the elaborate Matsuzaka security systems to steal the device in the first place? The answer was, they wouldn't. There were simpler ways of getting at superior domestic technology, as the Russians had proved, without having to play James Bond.

So commercial reasons may be suspect, but political motivation was laughable. For the Japanese, anyway. Senator Mitchell had been right about that. Politically, the Japanese were America's strongest allies in the Pacific, a bulwark of defense against the expansionist aims of Russia, a cultural and economic Great Wall in support of capitalism and freedom.

Russia. Had to be. Despite the Matsuzaka connection, he felt the roads still led to Moscow. His weekend with Sally was plagued by this distraction as he picked and probed. And came up empty.

He slammed his fingers down hard on the keyboard.

"So that's where I come out, Sally" he said, as they sat on his redwood deck in the welcome warmth of a Sunday afternoon sun. May's first day brought promise of relief from the wetness of April.

"I think you're afraid to make a leap of faith," Sally said. She folded the front section of the Sunday *Times* and tossed it on the bench between their chairs. "You keep on giving the Japanese the benefit of the doubt. But there *is* a connection, Art. I can't tell you why the Japanese needed your chips, but too many things point to Japanese involvement, and the riots in Tokyo are part of it." Her head disappeared from view as she hid behind the second section.

Art reached over and yanked the weekly news summary from underneath Captain, who lay preening himself in the warm sun. As the section slipped out from under him, he gave it a casual slap with his paw, claws sheathed, as if swatting a pesky fly.

Garrett scanned through the week's events and stopped when he found a synopsis of the political events in Tokyo. It was combined with an article on the Cabinet shuffle which had been announced the previous day, as Sally had predicted.

"Listen to this," he said, folding the section in half and tickling Sally on the soles of her bare feet until he had her attention. She collapsed the section she was reading and listened.

" 'Dateline Tokyo, April 30. The Chairman of Matsuzaka Electric Industries confessed today to the theft of sophisticated electronic devices valued at several million dollars from the tiny American firm, Micro Optix,' " he read, his eyes twinkling.

"What? Let me see that!" She grabbed for the paper but Art jerked it back.

"Wait," he said. "There's more. Hell, we can head straight for Cape May right now. 'It was the only way we could begin to stem the Russian threat,' the Chairman said to a packed news conference. "The Americans wouldn't license their advanced chip technology to us, so we had to take matters into our own hands.' "

"Come on," Sally said, and snatched the paper from his hands. She found the article, saw its analytical content relating to the riots and the Cabinet changes, and laughed. "Nice try."

"You see how nonsensical that sounds?" he said. "Hell, I'm the first to admit the Japanese are our toughest commercial competitors, but your asking me to make a *political* leap of faith. You know damn well Matsuzaka has about as much to do with political demonstrations as Micro Optix does with organized religion."

"Not true," Sally muttered. "They could have paid the demonstrators."

Sally suddenly sat upright as she scanned the section. "Wait," she said. "You missed something."

Art got up and refilled his beer glass. "Did you hear anything I said?"

"Listen." Sally concentrated on the same page Art was reading moments earlier. "JASA—that's the Japan Aeronautical and Space Agency—had a test run yesterday of a reconnaissance missile, near Fukui. Strictly routine—low overflight, normal ground tracking—until it veered off course."

Sally looked up, her face serious.

"Art, tell me again how your optical chip is used in guided missiles."

He frowned. "Features of the terrain target are preprogrammed into a microprocessor. When the preprogrammed target area matches what the optical chip sees, the missile locks on, and bang." He imitated an explosion with his hands.

"Okay, okay. Now listen to the rest of this. The missile's original flight path was across the Inland Sea to Kyushu, where it was preprogrammed to drop harmlessly into the water near a waiting Navy vessel," Sally said as she skimmed the rest of the article. "But halfway out, it changed course abruptly and rammed a moving fishing boat, despite the fact that the ship captain was apparently steering an erratic course to avoid debris in the water. The Japanese government has agreed to compensate the fisherman for damages."

"Are you—? Let me see that." Reaching out with a long arm, he snatched the page from Sally's hand.

"Lower right side," she said. She was not laughing.

Art's eyes narrowed as he scanned the article. "Says the government refused to let the ship captain be interviewed." He looked up at her, his own expression serious now. "And that's all. You weren't joking." He thought immediately of TerCom.

Sally nodded. "JASA doesn't have attack missile capability. They're limited to simple defense and photo-recon missiles under the Constitution."

"I know." Art paused as he thought. TerCom? Impossible. "The Pentagon would never allow the Japanese a license to manufacture the guidance system for their own use," he said, shaking his head. "It's still classified."

Sally folded her arms. "So how does a passive recon missile suddenly develop such pinpoint accuracy?"

"There's only one way that missile could have rammed the fishing boat the way it did. It had to have one of my optical chips," Art said, staring past her now into the distant valley. With the wind down, the trees were still, as if at attention. Everything was quiet.

"Look," Sally said. "You saw the extent of the Cabinet shuffle. They even replaced the MITI minister with a man more loyal to Tanaka."

Art nodded. "Yeah. I saw."

"So the Japanese may be trying to prove a point, flex their political and military muscles prior to the Security Treaty renewal," she said. "If the Japanese have the optical chip technology for a system like—what did you call it? TerCom?—they don't *need* the United States anymore for defense purposes. And once they arm the missiles, it's goodbye Uncle Sam. Don't you see? It fits right into their master-apprentice mentality."

Suddenly for Art the picture became more complicated, the road signs to Russia faded and blurred, the commercial motivation for the chip theft almost laughable.

"I'm no computer expert, you know that," Sally said as Art stared past her into the distant valley. Her voice was hushed. "And maybe this fishing boat incident has nothing to do with anything. But I'll bet you one thing: that Matsuzaka device in Sunnyvale was no plant." She got up from her chair and walked over to where he was sitting.

"No more Mr. Nice Guy," he said, sitting up and taking her hand in his. "Remind me next time not to take myself so seriously." He stood up and walked toward the door. "Don't go away. I'm going to call Roger to make sure he tells Hightower about this errant missile thing."

Moments later, when he reappeared, Sally was sitting on the redwood railing. Captain had joined her, balancing himself on the top rail. Sally stroked his back as he folded his striped paws beneath him.

"Any luck?" she asked.

He nodded. "Nothing confirmed yet, of course. Roger's trying to see him tomorrow."

She paused. "Well, when he gets back, thank him again for me, will you?"

"For what?"

"For programming the Adventure game for Jason. I think it's going to keep him interested for quite a while." She reached up and clasped her hands behind his neck, pulling him to her.

"Part of the man's genius," he said. He held her chin in his hand and watched the sunlight melt her chocolate eyes. Then he shook his head. "This missile thing. It's crazy."

Sally looked up at him. When she spoke, her voice was a hoarse whisper.

"What are you going to do when this is all over? Assuming it ends, of course." She wrapped her legs around his, anchoring herself on the railing.

He shrugged his shoulders. "Haven't given it that much thought," he said. "The megachip, I guess. We've got plans for the next generation of microprocessors. A million bits of data on one computer chip—four times the capacity of our 256K." He reached up and stroked her auburn hair.

She pressed his moustache with her forefinger. "Is that all you want out of life?" she asked softly. "Chips and more chips?"

His mouth opened, and then closed. He remembered being asked the same question, years earlier, by another woman he loved.

"I don't know the answer to that any better than you do," he said. He leaned down and kissed her forehead. "What about you?"

She drew him to her, held him tightly, whispered in his ear. "Listen," she said.

"I am sick of the song
of the self,
that old melody
for one voice
running up and down
and up the scale
like a mouse maddened
by its own elusive
tail. I have heard that voice
shatter glass.

"Nor do I ask
for martial music,
trumpets or drums
or the thoroughbass
of marching feet.
I long, instead, for bells
or for a simple trio: one bird
in the sycamore singing,
two birds in the oak
singing back."

Art remained silent, thinking. "One of yours?"
Sally nodded. "Want to climb an oak tree sometime?"
He could feel her heart beating through his shirt.
"Not a bad idea at all," he answered.

4

Fukuda Kenji sprang up the subway steps two at a time.

Momentum was on his side now, and he felt it in the lightness of his step. He shouldered his way through the throng of early Monday commuters pouring out of Tokyo station.

A new government banner flapped in the light breeze against the red brick facade of the Tokyo station tower. Fukuda glanced over his shoulder, saw the message and smiled.

Make the foreigners obey, but do not let them understand.

Rain began to fall as he cut across the broad plaza fronting the station, but he paid no attention. His mind was focused on the negotiations in Washington and Moscow. He swam through a sea of black umbrellas as he turned into Nakadori.

Sakamoto was waiting for him.

"Bucho-san, *ne,*" he said, brandishing a copy of the morning paper. "Did you see the Nikkei article on the abortive test flight Saturday?" Sakamoto shoved his thick glasses up his nose.

Fukuda stepped to one side, out of the pressing crowd. He stiffened noticeably when he heard the word "abortive."

"Nani?" he asked. "What are you talking about?" He continued toward the Matsuzaka building, pulled a cigarette out of his pocket and lit it.

Sakamoto drew nearer. "The test flight. Saturday. You know." His voice was low as he looked over both shoulders to make sure no one could hear them. He decided they were safe in the rush hour crowd.

Fukuda exhaled a whisper of white smoke. "Let me see," he said.

Sakamoto handed him the article. On an inside page, hidden among other domestic news stories, was a short article about the fishing boat incident, a picture of the damaged vessel sandwiched between lines of vertical *kanji* text.

"Maa," Fukuda said, his heart quickening as he skimmed the story. "It's nothing. Just a human interest feature about the poor fisherman, that's all." He handed the paper back to his *kobun.* He pushed ahead again, his cigarette trailing smoke behind him.

Sakamoto stayed by his side, step for step. "But what if NEC or Hitachi sees this article and talks to MITI?"

"About what?" Fukuda stopped to let a messenger pass by on his bicycle.

Sakamoto cracked a pair of knuckles. "About a usually reliable surveillance flight ending with a direct hit on a *moving* fishing boat, for example." He paused to think, dodging an open umbrella. "Or, even worse. Our competitors know we don't have a sophisticated optical guidance system in development yet. What if they go to MITI and ask why a small photo-recon missile turns out to be an attack missile?"

Fukuda turned and blew a stream of smoke in his kacho's face. "Sakamoto-kun," he said sternly. "This was an accident. It was reported as such. Besides, the story is buried on an inside page, and nobody will notice it."

Sakamoto squeezed his index fingers under his thumbs, snapping them loudly. "The industry knows that Matsuzaka Heavy Industries builds those missiles," he persisted, his voice louder now. "And that Matsuzaka Electric supplies the internal guidance systems. *They* know we don't make mistakes. *They* know our quality is the best. *They* know our reliability—"

"That's enough!" Fukuda tore the folded newspaper out of Sakamoto's hands and ripped it in half, tossing it aside. "There is no way that freak accident will be misread. Now forget about it!"

The crowd pressed around them as they stood near the

entrance of the Matsuzaka building. Sakamoto took a step backward. He saw the intensity in the Bucho's eyes, felt his persistence, his cool self-confidence.

He bowed obediently and followed him inside.

It rained all day that day in Tokyo, a precursor to the midyear *tsuyu*, the monsoons that hit the Japanese islands regularly by early June. No lightning, no thunder, just day after day of slow, gray rain.

Fukuda Kenji returned home late that night, as usual. He kicked off his wet shoes in the *genkan* and padded across the tatami in his socks. He could feel the dampness in the straw mats.

"Tadaima," he grunted at the base of the stairs.

"Okaenasai." Michiko's voice cascaded down the wooden staircase. "Is that you?"

"It's me," he said. He stretched, flipped on a ceiling light, and stopped to look through the day's mail. Bills, which Michiko would tend to, flyers from local merchants, the evening edition of the Asahi News.

He tossed it all back on the squat table and turned out the light.

He entered the bedroom and began disrobing. His wife was already half-asleep on her *futon.*

"Any word from the University?" he asked.

Michiko did not move.

He tossed his coat and trousers onto the tatami and climbed into his own *futon* in his underwear.

He nudged his wife. *"Ano ne,"* he said, jostling her with an elbow.

She stirred. *"Nani?"* she asked quietly, without turning to face him.

"Kenshin's results on the entrance exams. Any word yet?"

Michiko's eyes snapped open. She closed them quickly. "Nothing yet," she lied. "Should be sometime this week."

"I better give them a call."

"Let me do it," she said. "You're so busy these days."

"Yoshi," Fukuda agreed. "But do it tomorrow."

Reaching behind him, he clicked the switch on the long

cord that stretched into the study. They lay on their *futon* in the darkness, back to back, husband and wife, untouching. Their bodies were separated by inches, their minds by millions of miles.

As he drifted off to sleep, his computer printer chattered alive in the next room. *"Nani?"* he thought to himself.

It continued its clacking. Michiko stirred on her *futon*.

Fukuda Kenji opened both eyes. Switching on the light, he threw back his quilt and stumbled into the adjoining room.

The facsimile printer clattered lines of *kanji* across the green-and-white striped sheet. Fukuda tore off a section and held it to the light.

"Kuzumono," he muttered. "Garbage." He scratched his burr head. "Who would be sending me this nonsense?"

Then he froze.

He remembered the microimagizer Sakamoto had left behind in California.

His eyes were as wide as *go*-stones as they flickered with the first tinge of fear.

5

Roger Harris looked at his watch for the fifteenth time that night as the shuttle circled Newark Airport.

He glanced out the window again and cursed. Still nothing but cement gray clouds. The wind sheared across the wings as the pilot banked into a turn, and another half-dozen drinks tipped off their trays.

Art was like a caged animal, pacing his office, when he finally walked in.

"Fucking shuttle," Roger said. "But I've got a shitload of stuff. Looks like we're right in the middle of it." He tossed his briefcase in a chair and sat down on Art's desk, fishing the Matsuzaka device out of his coat pocket. He lifted it carefully out of its stiff protective envelope.

"It's called a microimagizer," Roger said, handing it across to Garrett. "Hightower said he's never actually seen one, but he had some reports on it from his boys in Tokyo."

Art sat back down in his chair. "What does it do?" He turned it over again in his fingers, saw the familiar Matsuzaka *kanji* on the back. The two sides were still taped together.

"It transmits a high-frequency electronic signal through the 64K microprocessor," Roger said.

Art slowly unwound the tap. "So it is a transmitter."

"Well, yes and no. When you place it on a small object, like a memory chip, for example, so that it straddles the oblong black square on the bottom"—he reached over and touched it with the eraser end of a pencil—"the microprocessor inside automatically translates and sends circuit patterns of the object to a preprogrammed receiver. It's activated by simply tapping the top with a piece of metal, such as a nail or a safety pin."

Art frowned. "What for? Why would you need a gadget like this?"

"Military use. You remember the numbers we found on the back?"

Art nodded. "Yeah. Batch code?"

"No, nothing to do with either batch flow or quality control. The KB designate stands for *Koku Bo,* which means National Defense in Japanese. Matsuzaka Electric makes these things for Japan's Self-Defense Forces. The SDF."

SDF. The Japanese equivalent of the Pentagon. Sally's reference to military subversion in the 1930s flashed through his mind. *Japan's Longest Day . . .*

"Matsuzaka is apparently the only Japanese electronics firm that makes these things, so they're the SDF's sole supplier. Hightower's guess was that they use it for military espionage purposes. It's less risky than microfilm, and ten times as accurate."

Garrett nodded. "Reverse engineering. Of course. Hell, once they get the design coordinates for a small weapon or a piece of precision machinery, they can easily construct it."

"Or the circuit patterns of a computer chip," Roger said, looking Art in the eye. He pulled a sheaf of papers out of his briefcase now and set them down on Art's desk. "They can use this thing practically anywhere."

"Transoceanic transmission?"

"Assuming you have a feeder satellite in the right position, sure." Harris picked up his yellow pad. "Hightower said Motorola and TI had applied for permission to make the microimagizer here for the D.O.D., under license from Matsuzaka."

"But MITI stonewalled them, I suppose." Art placed the small device in front of him and just stared at it.

"It's still under negotiation, but so far they've been able to stall successfully," Roger said, nodding. He leafed through his notes. "Any coffee around here?"

Art pushed a thermos across his desk. "So how does all this hang together? Here's a massive Japanese electronics company that supplies advanced detection devices to the SDF. Five million bucks' worth of our 256Ks disappear, and a Matsuzaka microimagizer materializes on the scene."

"It's a complicated story," Roger said, uncorking the thermos and pouring himself a cup. "Apparently, defense spending in Japan has been limited since the war to an arbitrary figure of one percent of GNP. That suited Washington fine, until the sixties when the Japanese economy exploded. Then the one percent level dropped, of course, in relative terms, but it had become such a sacred cow, no politician would touch it."

Art frowned. "So they looked at alternatives."

"And found two," Roger said. He took a sip of coffee. "One was an attempt to displace civilian control over the SDF. The other was miniaturization. Electronic weaponry. More bang for the buck."

"Smart bombs, laser guns, that sort of thing?"

Roger picked up the Matsuzaka device. "Yes, along with microimagizers and computer chips. The Japanese also felt pressured to downsize and computerize their weaponry because their constitution prohibits them from having nuclear weapons. Hightower said that former Prime Minister Fukuda stirred up a hornet's nest a decade ago when he said that Japan could possess any type of weapon, nuclear included, as long as it was only for defense."

"And that encouraged the militarists?"

Roger nodded again. "Something called the Mitsuya Incident. Twenty-six young turks in the SDF tried to overthrow the civilian bureaucracy. Encouraged by guess who?"

Art shook his head.

"Kobayashi. The same man who just took over as Foreign Minister. He was the civilian Director General of the SDF at the time."

"This is beginning to sound more and more like *Seven Days in May,*" Art said, shaking his head. "What ideas did Hightower have about the chip theft?"

Roger paused. "Three. The Russians—nothing new—the

Germans, and the Japanese." He took another sip of coffee. "He said you can forget about the Germans."

"And the Russians," Art said. "Did he see the article on the errant missile yesterday?"

"Yes."

"I think we've got to start looking in Tokyo."

Roger smiled. "Hightower agrees."

"Excellent," Art said, clapping his hands together. "Now we're getting somewhere. Is he going to help us track the chips down?"

"He can't."

"What do you mean, he can't?" Art tossed his pencil on the desk and watched it skitter across the top. "What does he think we are, international crime detectors?"

Roger held up a hand. "Wait, not so fast. That's what makes it complicated. Washington and Tokyo have a number of sensitive issues under discussion right now, bilaterally. First, there's the Security Treaty, which we know about, plus a new bilateral aviation agreement. JAL and Pan Am both want expanded landing rights in the other country."

"So?"

"So there's also the on-going trade war between MITI and Commerce. The bilateral deficit for the fiscal year ending last March 31 was over $30 billion in Japan's favor, and the Democrats are howling at the Japanese, accusing them of causing our structural unemployment problems." Roger paused, sipped his coffee. "Hightower's hands are tied. He'd like to help, but these other issues are just too tense. If he started an investigation, no matter how covertly, into supposed Japanese complicity in the theft of our advanced 256Ks, he'd catch all sorts of hell from the White House. Any one of the other programs could be endangered."

"Hightower said that?"

Roger nodded.

Art scowled. "So we just twiddle our thumbs and wait? Come on, Roger, you can do better than that." He stuffed his hands into his jeans pockets and stood facing the window. The stars blinked overhead in the dark sky, like ceiling lights above a dance floor. "Hell, the missile incident and that piece of Dick Tracy hardware should give us enough leverage to start asking questions in high places. If the Japs do have our optical chips, we can sure stop worrying about Moscow and the banana republics."

Roger drained his coffee cup. "Hightower agreed. Said as much himself, in effect. But he can't lift a finger." He glanced down at his notes. "Offered the services of his man in Tokyo, guy named Charlie Eisenstadt. Good man, supposedly. But that's as far as he can go."

Garrett whirled around and slammed a fist on his desk, hard. "Goddam politics," he growled. "We bust our asses making the best fucking chips in the business, and when some of them disappear, our government is hamstrung to help." His eyes were wide with anger, and the veins on the sides of his neck pulsated visibly. Lowering his voice, he asked, "Did you tell Hightower about our situation with McDonnell Douglas? Can he at least help us with that?"

"No problem," Roger said. "Hightower said he'd call Martin this week. I told him we'd be in position by year-end with additional production capacity, that we just needed to buy time."

"Well, thank God for that."

"Hightower agreed completely with your assessment of the national security angle. Last thing he wants is for a Pentagon contractor to start developing foreign sources of supply."

"Possible foreign sources."

"Even so."

Art paced back and forth behind his desk now, rubbing his eyes. "I feel like a goddam orphan," he said. He looked his colleague straight in the eye. "Well, if they won't come to us, we'll just have to go to them."

"What do you mean?"

Garrett yanked the red push-pin out of Silicon Valley on the world map behind his desk and jabbed it, across the ocean, in the heart of Tokyo. "That," he said, "is what I mean."

Roger rubbed his own eyes now, trying to push the tiredness out of them. He looked at his watch. It was nearly midnight.

Art sat on a corner of his desk, arms folded. "What do you think?" he asked.

"Go over there ourselves?" Roger shook his head. "I think we ought to dump this in the FBI's lap, if the Pentagon can't take it. They're the ones with authority to investigate."

"If it were strictly a domestic case, I'd agree. But the FBI has no clout overseas."

"They handled the Hitachi and Mitsubishi cases back in 1982, remember?"

"Those were domestic cases."

"With two Japanese companies?"

"California subsidiaries. Strictly domestic."

Roger rubbed his eyes again. "You're right. I remember now. Local guys, out of control." He reached for the coffee thermos and peered inside. It was empty.

"Besides, if Sally's right and this chip theft has something to do with the Security Treaty renewal, we don't have all that much time. To pull in the bureaucracy at this stage would drag the whole thing out."

"May 15, wasn't it?" Roger pulled out a pocket calendar. "Less than two weeks."

"Exactly. So I think we have to hit two nails with the same hammer. In Tokyo."

"Matsuzaka?"

Art nodded. "And MITI."

"Why MITI? Why not the SDF?"

"Because of MITI's power and control. Also because they're still the one Japanese government agency committed to international cooperation. I'm going to call Kitagawa in New York first thing tomorrow morning."

Roger rose from his chair and stretched. He bent over and tried to touch his toes. "And you know what Kitagawa's going to say?" He held an imaginary telephone in his right hand. " 'Velly solly, Mistah Gallett. Must be mistake. Matsuzaka fine company. Everybody blame Japanese for everything these days.' "

Garrett smiled. "Maybe. But you know what he'll do?

He'll fire off a telex to Tokyo instructing his colleagues to get the facts. I've seen him work. He's thorough as hell."

He edged off his desk and walked over to the window. He was so tired himself he thought he saw the stars start to blink out. He picked up his own calendar and flipped through the pages.

"Give Hightower a few days to contact Martin, then call him and ask him what our customer's reaction was. If you need to call Martin yourself, go ahead, but soft-pedal it."

"You're serious about this, aren't you?" Roger reached down to tie a loose shoelace.

"The final proofs of our annual report should be ready by the end of this week. You and Ted Quinn can go over it together." Art tossed the calendar back on his desk. "That's the main stuff. You can handle the bits and pieces with one hand."

"What about the industrial policy legislation? Anything to be done on that?"

Art shook his head. "The EIA is putting together some new numbers for us. Nothing to do, unless they call you."

Roger began stuffing his briefcase. "Thank God for Barbara Tompkins," he said. "But you still haven't explained how you plan to maneuver your way around Tokyo. If you feel like an orphan now, wait 'till you get to Japan."

"Sally's going to help me," Art said, as he snapped his own briefcase shut.

"Sally?" Roger asked.

Art nodded. "But she doesn't know it yet."

6

"I am very grateful for your kind understanding."

Fukuda Kenji, dressed in dark blue, formal *hakama*, sat with his legs folded beneath him on the tatami of the University official's small office. As he bowed deeply, he pushed a small brown envelope across the squat table.

The elderly scholar tucked the packet into the deep sleeve of his own kimono, and bowed to Fukuda in return.

"Would you care for more tea?" he asked. He reached for the ceramic teapot by his side.

"Thank you very much," Fukuda said, holding his porcelain teacup aloft and averting the man's dark eyes.

They sipped in silence.

Fukuda shifted his position slightly on the padded *zabuton*, staring down at the small wooden table. Except for their two teacups, resting on lacquered coasters, it was totally bare.

His hands were clasped tightly at his abdomen, in a pose of rigid formality. His burr head was neatly trimmed, his face cleanly shaven. He craved a cigarette, but he dared not smoke.

He stared into his teacup now. "I am greatly humbled by your decision, *sensei*," he said. "My son will do well. You will see. He is a Fukuda."

The old scholar gazed into his own teacup.

"It is unthinkable of the University not to educate the fifth generation of Fukudas," he said, his voice a whisper. "It is our obligation to do so."

"No, it is we who are obligated, *sensei*," Fukuda said softly.

They drank from their teacups, sipping quietly.

Fukuda breathed in deeply. "New tatami? The fragrance is unmistakable." He felt the fresh mats with his hands and smelled the scent of new straw.

"Last winter," the official nodded, looking down at the cream-colored matting. "I like the scent, don't you? It is so fresh, so clean, so . . . so . . ."

"So *pure?*" Fukuda asked, tilting his head up slightly, still averting his eyes.

The scholar nodded. "So *pure,*" he whispered. A wisp of graying hair fell across his smooth forehead.

They sipped again in silence.

Daylight filtered thinly through the paper-clad *shoji* in the solitary window at the scholar's back. Tiny particles of dust hung in the still air.

Both side walls in the tiny cubicle were lined with books. A small writing desk, for use on the tatami, rested on rails, containing sharpened pencils, calligraphic painting brushes, and a thimble-sized bottle of *sumi* ink.

Fukuda straightened the folds of his dark *hakama*. As he bowed again to the official, he said, "The Fukuda clan is forever grateful. We trust this matter to your complete discretion."

The two men rose, and bowed again. Fukuda's hands remained stiffly at his side, his burr head nearly touching his knees.

Straightening, the elderly scholar said, "We will send your son official notification at the end of this week, citing unpardonable errors on the part of the exam graders. The restated test scores will be enclosed." His words settled softly into the cracks of the tatami.

"With my profound respect," Fukuda Kenji said, staring at his white silk *tabi*. With a final bow, ever mindful that his head remain lower than the *sensei*'s, he rose, turned, and slipped quietly from the room.

He hurried home to change clothes.

He had an early evening meeting with Sakamoto in the Ginza, at one of his favorite pubs.

Outside the house, he flagged a taxi, giving the driver directions. "Step on it," he said gruffly.

Gazing out the window of the cab, he was unmoved by the warm weather of early May. The late afternoon sun shone brightly in a clear and cloudless sky. He hardly saw the trees lining the narrow streets as the cab sped through Shinjuku, their small forms shading the sidewalks like green umbrellas. His dark eyes narrowed as he thought of the crucial days ahead.

He pulled out a Hi-Lite and puffed it alive.

The driver scanned him in his rearview mirror. "Do you mind not smoking?" he asked, bobbing his head slightly and tipping his cloth cap in the mirror.

Fukuda caught his eyes in the reflection and gave him a scornful glance, exhaling a lungful of smoke at the back of his head. *The customer is god,* he thought. You do what *I* say.

The driver stopped at the *sakaba* with a jerk, refused the fare and sped angrily off, whining in first gear, closing the automatic door only after he had accelerated back into traffic.

Fukuda flicked his cigarette aside, then pushed through the blue *noren* hanging limply in the doorway, the *kanji* emblazoned vertically in white. *Takebashi.* The Bamboo Bridge.

Inside, he glanced down the long, narrow bar running across the back. The same *kanji* was burned into its polished pine front. Sakamoto was not yet there.

He took a table away from the bar. As he waited, he downed a bottle of sake and shouted immediately for a refill.

"*Dozo,*" said the waiter, replacing the *tokkuri* and bowing.

"*Domo,*" Fukuda glanced at his watch. Sakamoto was not really late, he thought. He was just early. He had a lot on his mind.

Fidgeting nervously with a match, he tapped another cigarette on the raw, wooden tabletop. He pushed it into his mouth and lit it. At the table next to him sat a fish wholesaler, his black rubber boots glistening the full length of his legs. A blue and white *hachimaki,* twisted diagonally, was tied around his head. He caught Fukuda's eye and raised his sake cup in salute, smiling a toothless smile. Fukuda scowled back at him.

That feeling gnawed at his guts. It wouldn't let go.

Fear, that's what it was. Fear, pure and simple. It bothered him. It was so . . . so *unfamiliar.*

He poured himself another thimbleful of sake. Drawing on his cigarette, he exhaled at the ceiling.

Bothered him because he was so cool, so unflappable. There wasn't a *kendo* master in the country with his degree of confidence, his emotional detachment. He *knew* the ways of his opponent. He did *nothing* that was of no use. He *perceived* those things that could not be seen.

And yet, that feeling persisted. He had to confront Sakamoto with it, push it out of his mind, eliminate it.

"Chikusho," he muttered. Where *was* Sakamoto?

But what was he really worried about? he asked himself. He took a deep breath, felt his palms, touched his cheeks. Dry. Bone dry.

Everything was set according to plan. Victory was practically theirs. The touchstone of victory. Of perseverance. Of survival.

Except for those erratic pips on his facsimile printer. Something must have happened. The Americans have it, they're dissecting it, they've put it all together, the goddam *foreigners.* He spit the word out in disgust. How much better things will be when Japan is finally in control!

Nonsense, he reasoned now. They're nowhere near. They can't be. Not after all his careful planning. Not after all his thorough strategy.

Impossible.

He saw Sakamoto's familiar form come hurtling through the blue and white *noren,* and waved.

"Sorry, Bucho-san," he said, settling himself onto one of the small wooden stools.

Fukuda glared gruffly at his colleague as he poured him a cup of sake. "The microimagizer," he said in a low voice. "They've found it." He sucked a final puff from his cigarette and stabbed out the remains.

Sakamoto's eyes exploded. "What do you mean? That's impossible." He downed his cupful of sake.

Fukuda explained the random signals he had received on his hi-speed printer. "Not just once," he said. "Several times during the night!"

Sakamoto poured himself another cup. "Impossible," he said, looking his Bucho in the eye. He thought again, then shook his head. "Absolutely impossible."

"Then explain the transmissions."

Sakamoto shrugged his shoulders, cracking his index knuckles. "Easy. Could be anything. You said yourself the signals were random."

The Bucho pressed. "For example?"

"Earthquake. The whole area around San Francisco is like Japan. They get tremors all the time."

Fukuda shook his head. "I thought of that. *Kishokyoku* says no ground disturbances of any kind in California the past ten days."

Sakamoto was unperturbed. He had learned that from his boss. "Rats, maybe, in the hollow wall. Any movement at all may activate the printer if it's during transmission hours, you know that."

"*Baka!*" Fukuda shouted. "Utter nonsense."

Sakamoto swallowed another mouthful of sake. His face was beginning to redden with the effects of the alcohol. He snapped his thumb joints. "Well, supposing someone did find it," he said, more boldly now. "Suppose the new tenant found that the switchplate didn't work, so he took it out himself. Place like that, not the sharpest minds. Probably threw it away."

He laughed softly.

"It's probably bouncing around in some garbage truck somewhere on its way to a dump. That's why you're getting garbage on the printer!" Sakamoto roared with laughter, feeling more confident the more he drank.

"This is no joke!" Fukuda yelled back, slapping the table. "This is our future!" He slammed a fist down, hard. Heads turned, eyes stared.

The kacho quieted down. "What else can they do but look at it, tap it, scratch their heads and toss it out?"

"*Baka!* They'll call in the police. Remember, Le Duc Pho

just disappeared with several million dollars' worth of the world's most sophisticated computer chips."

"Call in the police? For a piece of meaningless metal that looks like a woman's compact? I know the girl at the desk, a dumb foreigner. She'll throw it out."

"They'll be curious."

"They'll toss it."

"They'll want to ask questions."

"They'll toss it."

"They'll read the Matsuzaka logo."

"Meaningless. They'll toss it."

Bucho and kacho sat face to face, *oyabun* and *kobun*, *sensei* and *deshi*, trading blow for blow.

"They'll dissect it and figure out what it is."

"Baka!" Now it was Sakamoto's turn. "Sorry, but that's supremely ridiculous. You, the big Bucho for Matsuzaka, worried about that stupid gadget. It's your job to be thorough, but now you're worrying like a woman."

Fukuda winced at the cruel words. "They'll take it apart and find out what it is," he said, his voice softer. "They'll send it to the CIA."

"Well, suppose they do," Sakamoto said. He cocked his head, leaning closer to his Bucho. "Suppose they do send it to the Pentagon and they pick it apart. And they read the Matsuzaka logo and inform Micro Optix. And Micro Optix complains through normal channels."

Fukuda's face suddenly relaxed. He downed his sake.

Sakamoto continued the thread. "Micro Optix goes through their Commerce Department, or maybe the Department of State, and the American government does what?" he asked, his voice a quiet purr.

He refilled his Bucho's cup and raised the empty *tokkuri* to order a replacement. It came immediately.

"They go to MITI," Fukuda said, his voice calmer now, more self-assured. His eyes stared at the *kanji* on the *noren* across the room.

"Which means who, specifically?"

"Katoh," Fukuda whispered, barely moving his lips. "Head of Special Industries. *Naruhodo!*" He rubbed a hand across his burr head.

"Which means obfuscation. Nobody better at it than Katoh-san," Sakamoto said, raising his cup to his lips. "You know how bureaucracies work. What can they possibly learn?" He snapped the remainder of his finger joints in triumph.

"Yoshi," Fukuda whispered, nodding. He smiled. Sakamoto's words echoed, like a temple bell, in his mind.

You know how bureaucracies work.

7

The Pan Am 747SP lumbered down the runway like a pregnant elephant to taxi into takeoff position. Rain swept across the airfield in sheets, whipped by the wind into a great white spray.

Art glanced out the window and watched the rain pelt down. He suddenly felt very exposed, sitting in a plane bound for Tokyo with nothing more than a hunch and a vague plan. He was so accustomed to negotiating from strength, to being thoroughly briefed and armed with the facts, driven by his own innate aggressiveness.

Well, he thought, he was being aggressive, all right. If not downright foolish.

As the giant jet veered around, its massive turbofan engines roared alive. Within minutes, they were bouncing through the black clouds into softer airspace above, whining as they climbed.

Sally nudged Art with her elbow as they unbuckled their seatbelts. "Don't worry," she said. "I'll extract my pound of flesh when we return."

He looked down at her and smiled. "I know," he said. "But I couldn't have done it alone." He took her hand in his. "I need you every bit as much now as you needed me when Jason was hurt."

She squeezed his hand. "I brought some poetry along," she said. "It's a fourteen-hour flight."

Later, after a nap and their first meal, as they cleared Alaskan airspace and headed out across the Pacific, Sally caught Art's eye. He followed her glance to a group of Japanese businessmen, five abreast, sitting in the same row, across the aisle.

Their hair was neatly trimmed, identical white shirts were buttoned at the neck, ties were in place. Each focused intently on his work, impervious to distractions around him.

Two of them held electronic calculators, running through columns of numbers and making notations on tabular sheets. One pored through a stack of Japanese documents fully three inches thick, penciling comments in the margin as he read. The other two, sitting in adjacent seats, argued with each other in Japanese over what appeared to be industrial blueprints they held between their chairs.

Sally looked up at Art. "Calculation . . . Domination . . ."

". . . Elimination," he said softly, completing the triad. He continued to stare until the Japanese closest to him looked up and met his gaze. Art did not immediately look away. He waited until the man in the invisible uniform turned back to his work.

"That'll be their downfall in the long run," Art whispered into her ear as he settled back in his seat. "They'll push so hard they'll run themselves into the ground."

"Or they'll achieve total control," Sally said, shaking her head. She shifted her tiny frame, crossing her legs under her denim skirt. "They want to get to the top of the pyramid first, but sometimes they forget their own philosophy."

She reached into her pocket and pulled out a small volume of verse by Mo Ti. "Listen," she said.

By letting go, it all gets done;
The world is won by those who let it go!
But when you try and try,
The world is beyond the winning.

"Read me some more," Art said. He unlatched their tray tables and poured them each a Glenlivet from his pocket flask. He signaled for ice.

Thirty spokes will converge

In the hub of a wheel;
But the use of the cart
Will depend on the part
Of the hub that is void.
Advantage is had
From whatever is there;
But usefulness rises
From whatever is not.

When Sally nudged him a second time, he was hovering thinly in stage-one sleep. She pointed toward the window.

He watched through scratchy eyes as the large jet dropped across the narrow, craggy coastline of Honshu, the main island of Japan. Soft, undulating hills came into view, dotted with pockets of ricefields.

As the big aircraft neared its approach path, Art began to make out the forms of rice farmers below, tilling their paddies, wading knee-deep in the muddy water. Small Hondas waited to take them back to the brown, thatch-roofed huts in the distant village. Except for the motorized bikes, he thought, the rice culture was unchanged from its origins centuries before.

The huts disappeared as the jet dropped toward the runway. "I remember Japan being all urban landscape, gray concrete and smokestacks," Art said, settling back in his seat for the landing.

"That's the *Tokaido,* between Tokyo and Osaka," Sally said. "We're east of Tokyo now." She tugged on her seatbelt. "This is Narita, all farmland. Big scandal back in the early seventies when former Prime Minister Satoh arranged to buy up all this land in parcels so they could build the new international airport. The farmers banded together and revolted violently when they heard what Satoh wanted to do. It was years before the mess could be cleared up."

"I thought you said violent demonstrations were exceptional." Art snapped his briefcase shut and tucked it under his seat.

"Exception that proves the rule. The Japanese will protest when one particular subgroup in the culture is taken advantage of. Like the Narita farmers, for example, or the people in Kyushu who suffered from the terrible Minamata disease. But when something affects everyone the same, whether interest rates or inflation, they accept it stoically. Harmony prevails."

Flight 813 landed effortlessly on the broad expanse of asphalt and taxied up to the gate. The seatbelt sign flashed off.

Art and Sally made their way quickly through the immigration formalities, and in moments their bags appeared on the luggage carousel in the modern, cavernous lobby.

"Never fails," Sally said, lifting her suitcase onto a nearby cart and following Art to fetch his.

"What?" he asked over his shoulder.

"Japanese efficiency. Particularly where any contact with the outside world is concerned. Fast, polite, performance-oriented. Just look at all these technicians."

Art glanced to his right as two bespectacled, official-looking young Japanese stood among the crowd with clipboards and stopwatches in hand, timing the baggage process. One clicked and punched the watch, shouting out the minutes and seconds, as the other made notations on his sheet for that flight.

To his left, dispatchers directed disembarking passengers to the customs counters with the shortest lines. They ran, they did not walk, between carousels.

"High premium on performance," Sally said. She pushed her cart toward a flashing sign that said "Non-Resident," in *kanji.* Art followed close behind.

They elbowed their way through the mass of well-wishers who choked the exit area. Sally bought two tickets for the terminal bus from a smartly dressed young woman wearing the bright orange uniform of the Tokyo Air Terminal Service. Their baggage was tagged immediately and hustled to a waiting bus outside.

"We're in luck" she said, tugging on Art's shirt and handing him a ticket. "The next bus is just boarding."

He turned slowly around, fascinated now with the military precision of the airport scene. Crowds under control.

Announcements in crisp, articulated tones. And technicians, everywhere, running around like wind-up toys.

Art settled into a narrow, cramped front-row seat built for shorter and smaller people. After the bus had filled, he stretched his long legs diagonally across the aisle.

The bus driver laughed when he boarded, tipping his hat to the passengers. He pointed to Art's legs as he lowered himself into his seat, commenting with a smile in Japanese.

"He said only *gaijin* could have legs that long," Sally whispered. "Foreigners." She poked him in the ribs.

"Shall I show him what I can do with them?"

Later, as they neared the industrial outskirts of the capital city, Sally shook him gently. He struggled to open his eyes, the lids seemed glued together.

They were stuck in late afternoon traffic, moving in short spurts. As the cloud cover overhead dissipated, a light rain began to fall, further slowing their progress.

Art noticed the cramped apartment buildings alongside the highway, tucked tightly next to each other like dominoes stacked side by side on a tabletop. Their dull gray forms seemed doubly depressing to him on such a miserable day.

Then came the tiny factories, unzoned, uncontrolled, growing like weeds in a small garden. Steel processors. Junkyards. Lumber mills. Scrap dealers. Used car lots. A miracle mile without the miracle, he thought.

He shook his head silently as he looked at the squalor around them.

"*Sushizumi,*" Sally said, following his glance. "Packed like sardines. Half the population of the United States crammed into the state of California."

They crept, they crawled, they measured their progress in car lengths until, two and a half hours later, they pulled into the Tokyo air terminal. It was nearly six in the evening.

Sally commandeered a taxi as they transferred their luggage and started on the last leg to the hotel. Art took in the bland, lifeless character of the buildings along the way. Japanese *kanji* hung outside the smaller shops and businesses on drab cloth *noren* or flickering neon signs.

"I had forgotten what it was like when I was here as a student," he said, glancing at the *kanji* with tired eyes. "It's like being a child in an adult's world. Everything is simply unintelligible to the foreigner who can't read or speak the language."

Sally broke off from her animated conversation with the driver. "Takes the Japanese almost twice as long to become fluent in their language as an American or European in his," she said. She pointed out various landmarks as they neared the hotel.

"Nihonbashi Bridge," she said. "The starting point of the old Tokaido Road from Tokyo to Kyoto." It was now almost invisible under crisscrossing ribbons of expressway. "That's where official distances from Tokyo were measured from, during Tokugawa."

"What's that huge banner say, suspended above the bridge?" Art asked, noticing the wide, white canvas with its red *kanji* glistening in the rain.

Sally scanned the vertical columns. "Nippon," she said. "That's Japan." Then she paused. "One family. One country. One race." She smiled. "It's an old Tokugawa slogan."

The driver slowed as they passed Tokyo Station. Its distinctive Meiji architecture and red brick facade contrasted strongly with the drab, concrete buildings nearby. He accelerated around the next corner, through a traffic light, and into the driveway of the Palace Hotel.

After they had registered, Art got his second wind, and Sally led the way through the financial district of Marunouchi to stretch their legs. They ventured into a small *sushiya* called Edobashi and sampled some raw fish. When they came out, the somber buildings were shrouded in a light mist and soft haloes glowed around the streetlamps.

Sally tugged on Art's arm after they had wandered for a block or two in silence.

"What?" he asked, rubbing his chin now and feeling badly in need of a shave. He was reminded again of the time differential and exhaustion sagged in his bones.

"Up there," she said, pointing to a tall, concrete-and-glass building with its brightly backlighted *kanban* shining in shades of green.

"So?" Art said. "Another slogan, or another monument to drabness?"

"You wish. That's the headquarters of Matsuzaka Electric."

Art suddenly felt a surge of adrenalin and anger. His physical tiredness lifted momentarily as he looked up at the large *kanji* sign. Then he recognized the two distinctive characters.

The green light threw an eerie shadow over the street, turning their skin a pale yellow. Art walked backward, neck arched, watching the *kanji* recede. Sally looped her arm through his, just before he stepped off the curb.

They headed back to the hotel, arm in arm, neither saying a word.

"I know what you're thinking," she said as they moved quietly through the narrow streets. The headquarters buildings of Japan's elite were dark and empty. Other than the occasional whine of a taxi accelerating in low gear, the streets yawned a hushed silence.

Art stopped under a streetlight and looked down at Sally now, holding her chin in his hand. He was frowning. "You do?"

"Yes," she said, smiling into his eyes and rubbing her fingers across his stubbled cheeks. "And I don't think we should be accusatory when we see these people tomorrow."

"Not accusatory," he repeated, stroking the back of her head. Her auburn hair glowed in the soft wash of the streetlamp. He would have preferred to be anywhere else but Tokyo right now.

"Remember, we're here to learn," she said. "That's the plan. To make sure the Japanese aren't unfairly implicated in this thing."

"Of course," he said. He leaned down and kissed her softly on the mouth.

"You're not listening."

"Of course I am. You said we should be up front with these guys tomorrow and tell them right from the start we know what they're up to."

Sally laughed, tugging at his arm.

"That's what I was afraid of," she said. "Let's get some sleep."

The sounds of their solitary footsteps echoed faintly in the deserted streets.

8

"Moshi, moshi."

Katoh's voice was unmistakable. Fukuda flicked an ash off the end of his cigarette and turned in his chair, swinging away from the other desks.

"It's worse than I thought," Katoh said, his voice squeaking. "They've found it."

"Found what? What are you talking about?" Fukuda drew in a lungful of smoke and exhaled.

"The microimagizer. I *told* you it was too risky. The whole plan is crumbling. It should be called off."

Fukuda's fingers tightened around the receiver when he heard the word. He had been right. His fear was real.

"How do you know?" he barked. He stood now and walked to the window, staring at the thick clouds that blanketed the city.

Katoh cleared his throat. "Kitagawa. Our man in New York. Just sent a telex, said Micro Optix has the device and has translated the Matsuzaka logo. They strongly suspect Japanese involvement in the theft of their computer chips. Kitagawa also said Micro Optix representatives are prepared to come to Tokyo and have requested MITI's assistance."

"To Tokyo?"

"Hai."

How stupid, he thought. Exhaling audibly, he crushed out the remains of his cigarette in a metal ashtray nearby.

"How did he handle it?"

"Something about surprise and shock, wait a minute."

Fukuda heard the paper rattle as Katoh scanned the cable.

"Here it is. 'Told Garretto-san there must be mistake. No Japanese company would resort to such technique. Expressed shock and outrage that he would blame Japanese. Suggested sources unfriendly to Japan had stolen the device and planted it to implicate Matsuzaka.' "

Smart, Fukuda thought. Very smart. Even though Kitagawa was unaware of the plan, his defense was sound. Teamwork. One country, one race.

"How much does Micro Optix know about the microimagizer?"

"Apparently not much. All Kitagawa says is that they discovered the 'device.' They described it to him, but even he didn't know what it was."

Of course not, thought Fukuda. How could he? His mind leapt back to his discussion with Sakamoto the previous night.

You know how bureaucracies work.

It was just as he had said. They were just going through channels. Micro Optix to MITI to Katoh. Perfect.

He calmly pulled out another cigarette. "Is that all?"

"Is that *all?* Isn't that enough? I told you this was starting to get out of hand, and now—"

"Quiet!" Fukuda shouted into the mouthpiece. He looked around now to be sure he was not overheard. Then he lowered his voice. "You've got to bring yourself under control, Katoh-kun. You're behaving like an old woman." Sakamoto's own criticism of him the night before still burned in his ears.

"But what should I say? What should I do?"

"Baka! So Micro Optix has the gadget, so what? They merely *suspect* Japanese involvement, they can't prove it yet. So we will push them off track."

"How? If they are coming to Tokyo, then they'll demand to come here and to see someone at Matsuzaka, as well. It's too dangerous, Bucho-san. We should abandon—"

"Nonsense!" Fukuda interrupted. "Do you think we would have gotten this far if we had responded to every irrational fear you've had along the way? Pull yourself together and strengthen your resolve!"

The line went silent at Fukuda's outburst. Cradling the receiver under his chin, he sucked in a lungful of smoke and blew it at the ceiling.

Katoh exhaled into the connection. Finally, he said, "What do you suggest? I will do whatever you say."

"Yoshi. That's better. Kitagawa has given us the opening we need. Telex him back, tell him you've spoken to officials at Matsuzaka and that they are as shocked as he that the Japanese should be suspected of stealing Micro Optix computer chips. Tell him—"

"Wait. I'm making notes."

Fukuda stopped. He flicked an ash onto the floor and kicked it with his shoe.

"All right."

"Tell him to tell Micro Optix it is out of the question for Japanese to resort to such tactics when we have twice the number of electrical engineers as the Americans and spend five times the amount they do on research and development." Fukuda turned to the window and watched heavy raindrops begin to splatter the pane.

"Got it."

"Tell him," Fukuda said, his voice calm as his eyes scanned the crowds thirteen floors below, "tell him Matsuzaka is outraged at their accusation, that we suspect the American government of stealing our device and planting it in Sunnyvale in order to bring pressure on the Japanese side in the current trade war." He drew on his cigarette and smiled at his reflection in the window.

Katoh did not respond immediately. When he did, his voice began to shake again. "We can't accuse the American government, Bucho-san," he said in whispered tones. "They'll never believe it. Besides, for me as a representative of His Majesty's government to make such an accusation—"

"Why not?" Fukuda interrupted. "Don't you remember what happened in 1982?"

Katoh paused. "You mean the Hitachi-IBM case?"

"Exactly. Do you think for a minute our Hitachi colleagues would purposely steal illegal information? *Never!* The American government coerced IBM into passing its secret computer manuals to a consulting company in California controlled by the FBI. The FBI trapped Hitachi and arrested them but nobody else, even though this kind of shabby practice is common in their market. We're still convinced Hitachi was singled out by the Americans so they could generate more pressure on Abe-san in the trade talks with Tokyo."

"Naruhodo," Katoh said in a hushed voice, embarrassed at having forgotten the precedent that case set.

"So you'll send that to Kitagawa?" Fukuda asked.

"Hai."

Fukuda took a final drag on his cigarette and flicked the remains out a crack in the window. "Let me know his response."

"Chotto," Katoh said. "Just a minute."

Fukuda listened as another voice broke in. "I'll call him back," he heard Katoh say.

"It's Eisenstadt," Katoh said nervously.

"Eisenstadt, of the American Embassy?"

"My assistant says he's calling to arrange an appointment for Garretto-san, of Micro Optix."

"Already?" Fukuda frowned.

"Apparently he's on his way to Tokyo now. You see, Bucho-san?" Katoh's voice was calm now, and self-assured. "I told you. Even if we telex Kitagawa, it won't do any good."

"Send the telex anyway," Fukuda said. "Kitagawa will know who to contact in Garretto-san's absence."

"But what about Garretto-san? He wants to see me."

"So see him," Fukuda said, watching the rain come down more heavily now as the clouds darkened overhead. "American impatience, Katoh-kun." He smiled. "The man is obviously reacting impulsively."

Katoh paused. "But what do I tell him when he comes? How do I behave?"

"Tell him nothing," Fukuda said calmly. "Stick by our story."

"And?"

"And leave him to me."

9

"Come on, let's go," Sally said, shaking Art by the shoulders. He stirred briefly, then turned on his left side and pulled a pillow over his head. "I've already spoken with Eisenstadt."

She sat down on the bed and snatched his pillow away. He covered his eyes with his arm, turning back to face her. "God, what time is it?" he asked. "Feels like everything's in slow motion."

"It's almost nine," she said, propping the pillow under his head. Except for her shoes, she was fully dressed. "We've got time for breakfast, but we're expected at MITI at eleven."

MITI. The crispness of the four-letter word suddenly snapped his eyes open.

"Who are we seeing?"

"His name's Katoh. Head of Special Industries, a *kyo-kucho*. Bureau chief. Top dog." Sally got up and walked to the windows. She threw the curtains open with a quick pull and sunlight screamed into the room.

Art rolled over again, groaning and covering his eyes. "Torture. That's what it is, torture," he mumbled into the sheets. "In China, they use water or rip out your fingernails. In Japan, they wake you in the middle of the night and turn on the sun."

Smiling, Sally walked back to the bed, reached down and poked him in the ribs. He whipped his arms down in self-defense, moaning as the sun attacked his eyelids.

"I was raring to go about four o'clock," he said, squinting at her with one eye and pushing himself into a sitting position. "Then I couldn't get back to sleep

again. Where do you get all that energy?" He blinked
and glanced at his watch. "It's still Wednesday night
back home."

"Fluids," Sally said, grabbing an arm and tugging him
out of the bed. He blinked his eyes, adjusting them to the
bright sunlight. "Eight ounces every hour in flight, no alcohol, long hot shower when you arrive. Saturates the
cells." She gave him a playful push. "Cures jet lag like a
wonder drug. Now move!"

"Seeing is believing," he said, walking slowly toward
the bathroom. "I think I've had my last scotch in the air."

When he emerged shaved and showered, Sally was
standing at the window. She reached up and kissed him on
the chin as he joined her.

"I requested a room on the front side, so you could see
the Imperial Palace," she said, pointing to the flat,
bronze-roofed buildings nestled among the cryptomeria
trees in the distance. The sunlight struck her auburn
hair and gave it a soft sheen, like cashmere. He stroked
it at the base of her neck, felt its smoothness. She put a
hand on his.

"Two thousand years," Art said quietly. "Makes you
stop and think." He looked down at the graceful structures
below.

"A pity the capital's no longer in Kyoto," Sally said.
"The Tokyo buildings are nice, but nowhere near the elo-
quence and grandeur of the Kyoto Palace." She pointed to
the moat surrounding the Palace grounds. "That's where
the Tokugawa Castle was until the 1860s. *Edojo*. The
Shogun's residence."

Art watched the mid-morning traffic snake slowly
around the perimeter of the moat, across from the hotel.
"It's never-ending, isn't it?" he said. "Like another moat,
a perimeter of chrome and steel." The sun glinted off the
unbroken line of windshields below, flashing back in their
eyes.

Sally glanced at her watch. "We better get going."

"Wait," Art said, pulling her back. "What in the world
are those?" He pointed at a row of colorful flags flapping in
the wind.

"Koi-nobori," Sally said. "Today's Boy's Day. They're carp streamers, flown every year from tall bamboo poles on the fifth of May. *Tango-no-Sekku,* the Japanese call it, a festival started during Tokugawa to celebrate the health of young boys and to encourage them in the traditional virtues of courage and strength."

"Carp?" Art asked. He watched the bright fish streamers snapping in the wind, mouths open, tails billowing, brilliant rainbow colors of red, orange, yellow, and midnight blue.

Sally laughed. "Of course. Carp have long been associated with courage. They're as vigorous as salmon, swim upstream with ease, very hardy. Confucius started the tradition, and the Japanese improved on it, as they have with so many things."

"Like computer chips, for example," he said, shading his eyes now and gazing down into hers.

She smiled up at him. "For example," she nodded. "But the carp are just one part of the festival. Indoors, every family with a male child will erect a small samurai doll, representing famous warriors known for their fighting skills. They impress upon young boys the importance of discipline, self-control, and the samurai spirit."

Later, through the open taxi window on their way to Katoh's office, they could hear the canvas *koi* snapping above their heads. Sally tugged at Art's arm as they passed the Foreign Ministry.

"Look at the *sakura,"* she said, pointing at the cherry trees paralleling the street. "They've been replaced since a week ago."

Art saw the rioting students again, heard the rocks crashing through glass, winced as he thought of the bloodied bodies. "Saplings?" he asked.

"Must be. The other trees were older, and much larger. Until the Zengakuren hacked them down."

Minutes later, they stood in the colorless interior of the main MITI building. Its drab walls contrasted vividly with the bright streamers outside.

"It's like Henry Ford," Art said, glancing around the

lobby. "You can have any color you want, as long as it's dull gray."

Sally approached the lobby guard. *"Ano, Tokubetsu Sangyo no Katoh Kyokucho onegai itashimasu."*

He bowed stiffly in his crisp gray uniform, checked an internal directory, and dialed a number. After a brief exchange on the phone, he showed them to an elevator, waited, then punched the third floor button, bowing again as the doors whispered shut. His face was expressionless.

"Katoh's expecting us," Sally said as she watched the floor lights above the door. Listed in cursive *kanji* were the bureaus and sections on each floor. "Third floor is right," Sally said, pointing to the characters for Special Industries.

Art shook his head as they got off and walked down the darkened gray hallway. "I haven't seen one goddam word in English on any sign since I got here," he said.

"Except 'entrance' and 'exit,' of course," Sally said, a twinkle in her eye. "It's a closed society, remember? You're a *gaijin*, an outside person. These signs are not for you anyway." She stopped in front of a glass door, checked the number, also in *kanji*, and the bureau designation. "This is us."

A young official, dressed in a dark gray suit and scuffed black shoes, bowed as they entered Katoh's office. Sally gave him their names, and he bowed again in silence. He showed them to a nearby conference room, flicked on the lights, inserted a small plastic sign on the door which read, "In Use," in *kanji*, and bowed again as he shut the door.

"See?" Sally said. She pointed to a small warrior doll on the wooden conference table as they sat down on a short, antimacassared couch against one wall. "Miyamoto Musashi, I'll bet. Perhaps the most famous samurai in Japanese history."

There was a short, double knock on the door. Art and Sally stood as Katoh entered.

"Garretto-san desu ka?" the portly bureaucrat said, wiping his forehead with a handkerchief. "I am Katoh."

"Arthur Garrett, Micro Optix."

They shook hands. "This is Sally Hendricks, a specialist in the Pentagon's Department of Advanced Electronics."

She greeted Katoh in flawless Japanese, and bowed.

Katoh raised an eyebrow as he gestured for them to sit. "You speak very good Japanese, Miss . . . Hendricks. Where did you learn it?"

"Defense Language School," she lied. "But it's just passable, I'm afraid."

"Very impressive," Katoh said, shaking his head. "May I offer you tea?" He pressed a button, and the same young Japanese face appeared. *"Ocha kureru? Mitsu."*

He asked them about their flight over, their impressions of Tokyo, the weather—pleasantries that always preceded a serious discussion.

"Sate," he said, signaling the end of the preliminaries and turning to face Art. "Kitagawa of our New York office cabled that you might be coming. He mentioned your . . . problem, but unfortunately you left the country before receiving our reply. We could have saved you an unnecessary trip." He twisted the handkerchief around the fingers of his left hand.

"So Mr. Kitagawa explained the situation to you," Art said, watching the perspiration form in a line across the top of Katoh's forehead. "What was your response? We'd obviously appreciate any assistance you can give us."

Katoh shrugged his shoulders and dabbed at the trickle of perspiration. "I wish there was some way we could be of help," he said. "But there must be some misunderstanding. This is not a case for the Japanese authorities."

"We just want to be sure the Japanese are not unfairly accused," Sally said, mentioning the discovery of the microimagizer in the Sunnyvale apartment.

There was another short tap at the door. An elderly woman dressed in a faded brown smock entered, carrying a lacquered tray with a gray ceramic teapot and three matching cups on small wooden coasters. She set the teacups on the table, nestled each one in its wooden saddle, and slowly, methodically, filled them, swirling the teapot each time. As she left, bowing, the young official reentered the room and sat in the empty chair next to Katoh. Propping a small pad on his knees, he waited, eyes down, silent.

"Dozo," Katoh said, gesturing to the teacups.

Art sipped the green tea. "Our first suspicion, quite frankly, was the Soviet Union," he said, wincing slightly at the bitter taste. "Because of their keen interest in obtaining advanced electronic devices by illicit means."

Katoh nodded. "We would agree that the Russians may be suspect in this case, too," he said, steadying his teacup on the arm of his chair. "But this microimagizer, as you call it, is such a sensitive device in our own government that they would never have access to it." When he sipped his tea, his hand shook, dripping the liquid on his tie. He dabbed at it with the handkerchief.

Sakeyake? Sally wondered. Was his red face due to a sake hangover? Not at eleven in the morning. Had to be nerves.

She eyed the MITI bureaucrat over the rim of her teacup. "Someone left it behind, Mr. Katoh," she said, "either accidentally or with the full intent of implicating the Japanese."

"It's the breach of secrecy we're concerned about," Art said. "Some of the advanced devices they took were highly sophisticated optical chips, the only ones of their kind in the world."

Katoh swallowed hard. His throat suddenly felt dry, despite the tea. "Did you say optical chips?" he said hoarsely.

"Yes." Sally edged forward on the couch. "We know the Japanese are close—very close—to developing their own 256K. But Micro Optix is the only company in the world with optical chip technology, and the Pentagon is very concerned about those devices falling into the wrong hands." She watched the young assistant scribble her comments, in vertical *kanji,* as she spoke.

Katoh uncrossed his legs and nervously poured himself another cup of tea. "Your insinuation," he said, replacing the teapot and looking at Art, "is very hard for me to understand. As a computer expert, you must know that the number and quality of our young electrical engineers far exceeds yours. MITI subsidizes nearly half a billion dollars in R&D costs for the Japanese semiconductor industry each year, and our industrial policy measures are perhaps the most aggressive in the world." He paused, weaving the damp handkerchief around his fingers, and leaned forward. "We will shortly have our own 256Ks, Garretto-san, as Miss Hendricks just said, and not long thereafter, the megabit chip. The fifth generation. We don't need your chips. We don't *want* your chips. We can make our own without having to steal from you or from anybody else. That's not the way we do business!"

Art let the MITI man have his say, then leaned forward and faced him eye to eye. "I don't care about the standard chips, Mr. Katoh," he said, jamming a finger in his chest. "It's the opticals we're worried about. They're classified top secret by my government." He glanced at Sally. "But we've got to get the opticals back. Do you think Matsuzaka will be able to develop their own by May 15?"

He wasn't sure why he asked the question. The words just tumbled out of his mouth, like dice onto a gaming table.

Katoh backed away from Art's probing jab, and suddenly felt like he was mired in quicksand. "We are veering off the track, Garretto-san," he said, twisting the handkerchief tensely. "In our response to Kitagawa, we strongly suggested that elements unfriendly to Japan should be the principal suspect." Anger flared in his eyes. Or was it fear?

Sally shook her head. "We told you we suspected the Russians, Mr. Katoh, but you rejected them out of hand."

Katoh's voice dropped to a hoarse whisper. "Not the Russians, Miss Hendricks. The Americans." He referred to the Hitachi/IBM case, the attempt by the American government to pressure the Japanese in one area—trade deficits—with leverage in another—the theft of corporate secrets. "It wouldn't be the first time, you see?" A drop of perspiration ran into one eye. He flicked it away with a finger.

Garrett was speechless. What could he say? For a senior Japanese bureaucrat to implicate the U.S. government was simply too far-fetched. But then, the IBM case was still unresolved, and he knew the Japanese had strong opinions about the way in which Hitachi had been singled out for blame. He decided to parry, rather than to press.

"So you're saying MITI is powerless to help in this case?"

A smile of relief appeared on Katoh's face as he smoothed back his damp black hair. "Not powerless, Garretto-san," he said. "We believe our help would be inappropriate. As you said at the beginning, it would not be right to falsely accuse a loyal ally of the United States, now, would it?" Perspiration trickled down his temples, collecting at the base of his chin.

"We still plan to see Matsuzaka," Art said, "to hear their side of the story." His eyes bored right through the MITI man.

"Who are you planning to see there?"

"Takahashi," Sally said. "Public Affairs, I believe."

Katoh nodded, looking to his left as his assistant rose, bowed, and left the room. "You might also ask to talk to Fukuda Kenji, head of their Planning Department." He paused. "He'll set you straight if Takahashi can't."

"Thank you," Art said coldly. He gestured to Sally and they rose from the couch.

They started to leave when Sally hesitated, pointing at the samurai doll on the small table. "Musashi?" she asked.

Katoh's eyes relaxed, pupils dilating, lids snapping briefly shut. "How did you know?"

"Just a guess." Sally moved toward the door. "He was always shown holding his sword above his head, in both hands," she said. "In the attack position."

"Hung over?" Sally asked as they surfaced from the subway near the Sengakuji temple on their way to Matsuzaka Electric. "I think it was nerves. Did you see how he practically choked when you mentioned May 15?"

Art wearily trudged up the final steps, feeling the full impact of jet lag—small stones seemed to be tied to his eyelids. "I think he knows more than he was willing to tell," he said. "The guy was sweating like he was on a witness stand. Very defensive."

"I agree." She stopped to catch her breath. "But I think we were right not to push him."

"I don't know. Maybe we could have forced the issue."

Sally shook her head. "Then he would have just clammed up, excused himself on the pretext of other business, and left us with Charlie McCarthy."

Art took deep breaths to restore his circulation as Sally led him down a winding alleyway, away from the masses of people. The street noise receded as they inched, single-file, through the sidewalk clutter of the shops and stalls that were sandwiched between tiny office buildings.

"That's it," Sally said as they pushed into a clearing and glanced up at the small, graceful pagoda that rose, umbrella-like, above the black-tiled rooftops. "Sengaku-ji. Site of one of the most famous samurai tales in Japanese history. *Chushingura.*"

They mounted smooth slate steps that shone like small reflecting pools in midday sun. "The forty-seven *ronin,* masterless samurai, who were ordered to commit mass suicide after they had avenged the death of their former master." She flipped a small coin into the wooden prayer box, its edges rounded with age.

"A classic story of honor through death. Lord Ako had been killed for committing the crime of drawing his sword in the Shogun's palace when insulted by another *daimyo,* Lord Kira. His vassals decided to get even."

Art stepped back to look up at the five-storied pagoda and almost trampled several small school children. The children scurried away from the tall, blond foreigner.

"Gaijin!" they shouted, giggling as they ran.

"There's that word again," he said.

"Outside person," Sally murmured. "We who don't be-long."

"So what happened to these guys? Their boss got knocked off so they decided to commit suicide?"

"Not exactly. They attacked the residence of Lord Kira and beheaded him. Then they took his head and offered it to the tomb of their master, avowing eternal allegiance. When they reported their deed, en masse, the authorities decided the penalty should be death by their own hands. This they did together one snowy night, near this temple, in 1701."

Art shivered slightly. "Creepy," he said.

"Yes," Sally said, looking up at him. "But you know, this story is as important to the Japanese as General Custer and Little Big Horn is to us. It's the choice between living as a coward or dying with honor. The difference is, in Japan, it's etched indelibly into the national conscious-ness."

They slowly made their way back through the crowded streets to the subway entrance. Art towered above the shorter Japanese, and many stopped and stared as he pushed through.

At the bottom of the stairs, Sally punched a button on the computerized ticket dispenser and withdrew two tick-ets for Hibiya.

They started for the turnstile when something caught Art's eye. He stopped, looked back, and grabbed Sally's arm. "There it is again," he said, pointing to the distinc-tive characters and the unforgettable logo. It slapped him in the face.

"Matsuzaka," Sally said, nodding.

The same logo appeared on the manufacturer's plaque in the gleaming stainless steel car. Sally pointed it out to him as they were swept aboard by the pressing throng. "Matsuzaka Heavy Industries," she said. "Another core company in the group."

The doors sighed shut, and the train sped into a tight curve, its wheels shrieking. The Japanese covered their ears to block out the sound. Art reached for a plastic handring to keep from falling. As he did so, he glanced up at the row of multicolored advertising posters that snaked horizontally along the top of the car, and saw one with a likeness of the samurai doll in Katoh's office.

"Isn't that what's-his-name?" he asked, jabbing Sally with his elbow.

She looked up and smiled. "Musashi. The same."

"What's it say?"

"It's a Boy's Day message," she said, scanning the script. "From the spirit of the seventeenth century to the young men of Japan today." Art watched as her eyes ran down the vertical rows of *kanji.* "It says, 'Beware the foreigner! He is a dagger pointed at the heart of Japan.' "

The train crept to a halt, and they pushed out the narrow doors onto the Hibiya platform.

"That's a little jingoistic, isn't it?" he asked as they shouldered their way up the packed stairs.

"The Japanese would call it inspirational," she said. "A reminder that life is not frivolous, that you have to fight for what you get."

Sally took his arm as they squeezed down another narrow side street jammed with local shops. "Let's grab a quick bite," she said. "I know a little *soba* stand where they serve a spicy assortment of noodles."

The mention of food forced a rumble in Art's stomach. "Just in time," he said. "We can talk about how we want to handle Matsuzaka."

They hooked arms as they walked. "So tell me how you recognized that warrior doll in Katoh's office," Art said as a spicy aroma laced with garlic assaulted his nostrils. "He seemed impressed that you knew who it was."

Sally ducked to her left, brushing aside a pair of black *noren,* stitched, in bright orange, with the traditional characters for *soba.*

"Musashi is Japan's most famous samurai warrior," she said, leading them to two small wooden stools at the counter. "Part myth, part mystery, he was nonetheless a masterful swordsman who cultivated strict self-control and inner personal strength through his austere, Zen-like discipline."

"A Japanese Robin Hood?"

"More than that," Sally said. "He alone influenced three centuries of swordfighting in Tokugawa Japan, gave the samurai a moral code to fight by, burned with such intensity that he practically became a deity. In fact, his fighting name was Kensei—the Sword Master."

Art picked up a menu, saw the *kanji*, handed it to Sally. "We probably ought to be talking to him. I have a feeling Takahashi's not going to be much help."

10

"Wareware no shorai, wareware no bunka, wareware no keizaitekina gyoseki . . ."

Fukuda Kenji's voice rose in harsh, strident tones as he completed his speech before the packed auditorium.

"Our future, our culture, our very economic achievements," he said, "depend upon a stronger Japan, a militarily independent Japan."

He paused for a sip of water.

The silence was awesome. No one coughed. Not a chair squeaked.

"As the most successful economic power in the world, we can no longer afford to remain silent on issues that affect us directly. We can no longer permit our politicians to accept provisions in international agreements that weaken our status in the global hierarchy of nations!"

The hall exploded with applause. Occasional shouts of *"Banzai!"* echoed in the roar.

Fukuda tugged at the coattails of his black suit and adjusted his white silk tie. His burr head glistened faintly in the heat of the spotlights, but in his face burned with intensity. He raised both hands to quiet the crowd.

"Long enough have we suffered the frustration of being second-class citizens in this world!" he shouted, his eyes flashing with fire. "Long enough have we swallowed the insults of others far less experienced and cultured than we!"

The crowd erupted with a piercing roar. Everyone stood now to hear the Bucho's final words.

"Long enough have we played the role of *deshi* in the world, apprentice to the so-called superior nations! Those

413

days are over!" He lifted his hands, palms up, and the crowd roared. The noise tingled his scalp, brought tears to his eyes.

"In the words of Musashi, *'Deshi no kawari ni, sensei ni naru!'* No more the apprentice. The master next time!"

"*Banzai! Banzai! Banzai!*"

The crowd roared as with one voice, punctuating Fukuda's every sentence. The sound was deafening.

Above his upraised hands, on either side of the platform, hung two flags, both symbolic, both inspirational.

Hi-no-Maru. The Rising Sun. The national flag of Japan.

Matsuzaka. Hill of Pine. The mint-green crest symbolizing a century of economic achievement and tradition.

An enormous blood-red banner unfurled below his feet, at the base of the platform. The brilliant *kanji*, white as snow and fully a meter high, proclaimed another proud name.

Keizai Dantai Rengokai.

Kei. Dan. Ren.

Keidanren.

The Federation of Economic Organizations, the most powerful commercial and industrial group in Japan. More than a National Association of Manufacturers, Keidanren represented the leadership of Japan's Fortune 500.

The Influential. The Powerful. The Elite.

Fukuda held himself stiffly erect following his final bows, scanning the audience of white-haired, elderly men, chairmen and presidents of Japan's largest and strongest firms. He felt overwhelmed. As a Bucho, he would not normally be granted the privilege of speaking before such a group.

But Matsuzaka Yukio, Chairman of the Matsuzaka Group and current Chairman of the Keidanren, was in Brussels, meeting with the EEC to defuse European market share disputes. He had selected Fukuda as his personal representative to deliver the annual Boy's Day message.

Fukuda had written the speech himself. Matsuzaka Yukio had read and approved every word.

Even now, as Fukuda collected his papers from the podium, bathed in the blanket of applause, he could see the Chairman's seal, in red *kanji*, affixed to the first page. His heart burned with respect and adulation for his *oyabun.* A pity he could not be here tonight to hear the praise himself.

The crowd began to disperse. Several corporate leaders marched quickly up to the front to congratulate him on his speech.

"Domo, Fukuda-san. Nakai, of Sumitomo Trading. A superb effort. I only hope our political leaders were listening." He bowed his appreciation.

Fukuda bowed in return. "This was Mr. Matsuzaka's speech, Nakai-san. I will relay your comments to him. As you know, global harmony through Japan's enlightened leadership is one of his priorities."

Another chief executive approached, and another.

"Watanabe, of Mitsubishi Bank. Please convey my warmest wishes to your chairman."

The two men bowed deeply, their heads almost touching, their bodies see-sawing in a ritual as old as Japan.

Fukuda Kenji walked toward the rear of the massive hall, wiping his closely cropped hair with a handkerchief, listening with head bowed as the President of Ishikawajima-Harima Heavy Industries commented in agitated tones.

". . . in the memory of Amaterasu Omikami, Bucho-san. Perseverance and sacrifice are sacred to us. Please tell your Chairman we are dedicated to seeing that Japan is no longer a defenseless island in Asia!" He bowed, deeply, in silence.

Outside, in the warm night, Fukuda bowed his final goodbyes, waiting for the Matsuzaka limousine. He glanced up and smiled as he saw the Keidanren's banner emblazoned with blood-red *kanji* against the backlighted marquis.

Genius is perseverance in disguise.

Fukuda stepped forward as the polished black sedan slid silently to the curb. Small, mint-green flags with the Matsuzaka pine fluttered from each front fender. With a final wave, he climbed in the back and shut the door.

As he pulled away, another body crawled in from the other side, and slammed the door shut.

"Nani!" Fukuda growled. When he flicked on the reading lamp, his intake of breath was swift. "Katoh-kun!" he hissed. "What do you think you're doing?"

The MITI man smeared his perspiring face with a damp handkerchief. He looked quickly out the side and rear windows to make sure no one saw him get in.

"I realize this is most impolite," he said. "But I wouldn't have risked it without a reason."

Fukuda glanced out the back window as the shiny sedan sped through the Ohtemachi district. "What are you talking about?" he asked, snapping off the tiny beam of light, satisfied that they were unobserved.

"Garretto-san," Katoh said. "He called on me this morning, but he was not alone."

Fukuda pulled a cigarette from his coat pocket and lit it with a steady hand. It glowed deep red in the dark interior of the car. "What do you mean, he was not alone?"

Katoh wiped his wet forehead. "Someone else was with him, a young woman, from the Pentagon."

"The Pentagon?" Fukuda exhaled a stream of smoke. The efficient Toyota ventilation system sucked it immediately forward.

"Yes. Said they were concerned that the Micro Optix chips not fall into the wrong hands."

Fukuda frowned. Did they know more than they were letting on?

"So? I assume you told them about your response to Kitagawa, as we discussed?"

"Yes, yes." Katoh clasped his hands together now to keep them from shaking. "But they must know what their optical chips are going to be used for now!"

"Baka!" Fukuda yelled. "How can you jump to such nonsense conclusions? They are merely going through channels! Like we said!"

Katoh shook his head. "But Garretto-san even mentioned May 15 specifically. I tell you, they *know!"*

Fukuda cracked the car window and flicked out his cigarette butt. Sparks danced like fireflies when it hit the street.

May 15? he thought. The date of the Security Treaty renewal was of course public knowledge. But not the disappearance of Garrett's optical chips. Had they somehow linked the two?

"Maybe you're right, Katoh-kun," he said at last, watching out the window as the car slowed for a turn near the Imperial Palace. "Or maybe we just need to deal a bit more firmly with our friends."

"I don't know," Katoh said, twisting his handkerchief now. "Maybe we need more time to rethink our plan."

Fukuda abruptly grabbed Katoh by his lapels and shook him, hard. "Pull yourself together! *Gambare!*" He shoved him back against the side of the car.

The driver stopped to pay a toll and accelerated up the freeway ramp. As they picked up speed and headed west, Fukuda watched the outline of Tokyo Tower sparkling with its necklace of white lights, an imitation Eifel against the dark-tiled rooftops. Behind them, the flickering neon of Ginza and Roppongi faded from view. Ahead and to the left, an electronic billboard flashed the magic Matsuzaka message in brilliant shades of green.

Matsu.

Zaka.

Yume.

Utsutsu.

Matsuzaka.

The Dream.

And the Reality.

Katoh straightened his necktie, trying to regain his composure. He dabbed at the perspiration on his face and neck and pulled his sodden shirt away from his skin.

"We began with a commitment to a common goal, Bucho-san," he said softly. "We have fought to put our country where it rightfully belongs, atop the hierarchy of nations."

Fukuda glared at him across the car. "What are you trying to say, Katoh-kun? That we have lost that commitment? That we should panic because we find a temporary

obstacle in our path? Nonsense! Panic is for the Western
barbarians. We must think only of victory."

"Of course. And survival." He blinked as the street-
lights reflected off Fukuda's lapel pin, making the solitary
Matsuzaka pine glow briefly in the dark. "But if our efforts now are only for the elite—for the *zaibatsu,* for the
politicians—then our commitment has become warped. We
are moving backward to an age of feudalism, not forward
to enlightened world leadership."

Fukuda reached across and grabbed the MITI man's lapels again. Katoh cringed. Another tirade?

"We are so close, Katoh-kun!" he whispered. "So close, I
tell you!"

Katoh straightened his crumpled jacket, relieved. They
may be close, he thought, but they still seemed so far
away. So very far away.

"Nothing can stop us now," Fukuda murmured as the
shiny sedan decelerated off the highway onto the curved
exit ramp. "Nothing!"

In minutes, they neared Fukuda's house. Flashing yellow lights pierced the car's interior.

"Ambulance," Katoh muttered, his doubts temporarily
forgotten. He could see his reflection in the side window,
his face pale and drawn in the yellow glare.

"No concern of mine," Fukuda said, his eyes cold and
distant. "Wait here. Let me call Nakamura. I think we
could all benefit from a quiet stroll."

Fukuda slammed the door and walked around the ambulance, ignoring the crumpled form inside. A body was
draped in a blood-stained, cream-colored sheet. A jar of
clear plasma hung from the ceiling, its rubber-throated
end jammed into the body's right wrist. Two technicians
worked hurriedly with an oxygen mask.

When he reached the *genkan,* he noticed the lights blazing brightly indoors. Kicking off his shoes, he took two
steps onto the tatami and saw Michiko sobbing in the arms
of a hospital aide.

"Nani?" he shouted as he approached the paramedic.
"What's going on here?" He stopped as the technician,
comforting his hysterical wife, handed him a bloodied

note. He retreated slowly to the squat table covering the
kotatsu and kneeled down to read.

> *Otosama, okaasama,*
> *Makoto ni fumeiyona koto degozaimasu ga . . .*
> I have brought shame and dishonor to the Fukuda
> family name. There is no excuse for my behavior.
> To be the first generation of Fukudas denied admis-
> sion to Tokyo University was, in itself, sufficient to
> bring my father, and my family, into disgrace.
> And to have my examination results altered, by whom
> I can only surmise, was to compound this dishonor which
> I, and I alone, have caused.
> But the ultimate humiliation, I see now, was my deci-
> sion to pursue an artistic career, failing to heed the ad-
> vice of my father.
> This tarnish on the family name can be removed in
> only one way, and assuring you both of my eternal re-
> spect, I await the day when we might be reunited again
> in the tranquility and harmony of Buddha's ultimate
> world.
>
> Your son,
>
> Kenshin
>
> *Tango-no-Sekku*
> In the 60th year of
> the Era of Peace and Harmony
> *Go-gatsu itsuka*

Out of the corner of a tear-filled eye, Michiko saw her
husband crumple the note. Lurching out of the aide's
arms, she ran to where he was kneeling and threw herself
at him, thumping him with her fists.

"Jisatsu da!" she screamed in a voice that ripped
through the paper-thin house. "Our only son! And because
you had no tolerance for—"

In a flash, his left hand swept across the front of his body
in a wide arc, the back of his fingers snapping into
Michiko's face with such force that her head rocked back.

The crack of flesh against flesh brought silence to the room.

Michiko crumpled to the tatami, her chest heaving, her body limp. She clenched her fists under her shoulders.

"Chotto," Fukuda said, motioning to the paramedic.

Fukuda whipped a notepad from his suit pocket and scribbled hurriedly. He tore off the top sheet and handed it to the attendant.

"This is the telephone number of my mother," he said, his dark eyes focused on Michiko's huddled, quivering body. "Call it. Have her come here immediately."

He turned to glance at the young man who stood, expressionless, by his side.

"Stay here until she comes. Is that clear?" He rose, pocketing the pad and pencil.

"Hai," he said, bowing obediently. He looked around for the telephone.

"In the kitchen," Fukuda said, his wife forgotten, his son a pale memory. "But I have a more important call to make first."

The young paramedic followed Fukuda and watched, impassively, as he picked up the black receiver. He looked at his watch as if he were waiting for a public phone.

The clicks and squeaks seemed distant and faint in Fukuda's ear.

"Moshi, moshi," a voice finally answered.

"Boku da," Fukuda said in a hushed tone. "It's me. The Americans are here. In Tokyo. Katoh's equivocating again."

He remained silent for a moment. Then he nodded. His eyes narrowed.

"Yoshi," he said. "I think so, too. Meet you at Tsukiji in thirty minutes."

He handed the receiver to the young man without turning around.

The peak of honor comes from fighting to the death.

Fukuda walked slowly back to the car; Musashi's words had a special sweetness for him at that moment.

"Tsukiji," he said in a crisp, even tone.

The driver nodded and eased the black Toyota out of the narrow passageway.

Fukuda turned to Katoh and said, "Sorry to keep you waiting. The Major will meet us in thirty minutes." The flashing yellow lights of the ambulance grew dimmer until they finally winked out of view.

The two rode for a while in silence, insulated from the outside by the Toyota's superior soundlock system.

"I told Garretto-san that he should see you," Katoh said finally. "Said you'd set him straight."

"Oh, I will, Katoh-kun. I will." He lit another cigarette and watched as smoke streamed out the window crack.

"Then you're not displeased?"

Fukuda blew a cloud of smoke in the MITI man's face. "Remember what Musashi said? *Pay attention even to trifles.*" His voice was as quiet as a spring breeze.

Katoh frowned. "What do you mean?"

"I think Garretto-san and his friend will meet with a little accident tonight," he said, smiling softly in the dark. "It won't be necessary for me to see them."

The black sedan slid noiselessly into the flow of traffic toward downtown Tokyo, accelerating briefly, then easing into a far lane.

Fukuda leaned back against the contours of the dark velour cushion, still smiling.

They had plenty of time now.

11

"Obfuscation is right," Art said, linking his arm in Sally's and letting them be carried forward, like flotsam, with the flow of the crowd. "That meeting with Takahashi was totally senseless."

"I told you not to expect much."

"I didn't. And I was still unimpressed."

The Ginza was paved with people that night. The Ginza was packed every night, but this was Boy's Day.

A shower of neon lights sprayed the black heads of the people with brilliant colors. Window-shoppers, revelers, families, and foreigners merged in a whirlpool of quiet hysteria.

Art leaned to one side as a Japanese woman, knock-kneed in a tight kimono, sliced through them, using her hand as a forward rudder.

"I feel like we're caught between two extremes," he said. "At one end, we have Katoh at MITI who knows more than he is willing to say. At the other is this guy at Matsuzaka who talks a lot but knows nothing."

"He fulfilled his role by arranging for us to see Fukuda tomorrow morning," Sally said. "That was his only obligation, really."

She stopped and pointed up at the long banner draped over Mitsukoshi's stone facade.

"Another Boy's Day message?" Art asked.

Sally nodded. "This one says, 'The samurai is the guardian of justice and the model of our moral conduct.' Not inappropriate for the Ginza. After all, this area was just swampland three hundred years ago when the Shogun's samurai set up the first silver mint here. It wasn't until

Meiji that the swamps were drained, streets paved, and a commercial center established."

A young couple, laden with packages but still managing to cling to each other, stumbled into Art. A package fell. He leaned down to pick it up.

Embarrassed, the young girl took the box back, never looking up. *"Sumimasen,"* she said, bowing repeatedly. "I'm sorry—"

"Gaijin," her boyfriend muttered. She looked up and giggled. He hustled her away.

Art turned back to Sally. "Did you hear Takahashi sucking all that air? Christ, he must have balloons for lungs."

Sally smiled. "Nervousness, that's all."

"Nervousness or not, the guy was very evasive. Like a sponge, like a fucking sponge. You can hit it forever to no effect."

"Fukuda may or may not be more helpful," Sally said, wincing as a coil of firecrackers exploded nearby. "At least, he has line responsibility. If we don't get anything out of him, we still have an alternative."

"You bet we do. We go right back to Katoh."

Sally nodded. "Possibly with Eisenstadt. Definitely with the intent of threatening an official investigation. I doubt the Japanese would welcome that any more than the Americans."

At the next corner, Sally tugged at Art's jacket. Art looked up. The red-and-blue electronic NEC sign bubbled with computerized graphics, pulsating concentric circles that expanded with each beat, denoting the company's annual growth in market share.

Art stood and watched the characters ignite, repeatedly, in endless succession, overwhelmed by the power of the ideographs which tumbled down, like illuminated dominoes, one character after another.

He suddenly felt miniscule among the masses of people, despite his size, despite his height. Afloat in a sea of anonymity, showered by a rainfall of unintelligible *kanji,* he grabbed Sally's hand. "Let's get out of this mob," he said.

They edged across the intersection, abandoning the Ginza for a side street that would take them toward

Hibiya, over the moat surrounding the Imperial Palace, and back to the hotel.

As they crept around a corner, Sally's eye caught the distinctive Matsuzaka *kanji* in the headline of the *Asahi News*. The black characters leapt off the page.

"Wait a minute," she said, unhooking her arm and shouldering through to the kiosk. She picked up a copy of the paper and unfolded it, scanning the banner headline.

"Come on, Sally. Let's go."

"You're not going to believe this," she said, handing the old woman behind the newsstand a coin. The elderly vendor made change out of a canvas bag stained with newsprint, bowing her thanks from underneath a white wooden plaque. It bore the blood-red, Rising Sun emblem of the Asahi newspaper chain.

Sally opened the page to the Matsuzaka article. "Hey, this is the guy we're supposed to see tomorrow morning," she said. "He's speaking tonight at the Keidanren."

"What?" Art moved in back of her, looking down at the unintelligible script. He felt a surge of adrenalin when he saw Fukuda's picture for the first time, posed in front of the company's familiar corporate logo.

"Strange haircut for a nation of conformists, isn't it?"

Sally ignored his comment. She was concentrating on the text, reading as rapidly as she could, pressing against the side of the newsstand to avoid the crowd.

"Our friend Fukuda is delivering the traditional Boy's Day speech tonight in place of Matsuzaka's chairman. He is expected to put emphasis on Japan's military weakness and to call for its political leaders to assert themselves more aggressively in foreign policy."

She paused to translate the next paragraph. "He will speak about the end of Japan as an apprentice nation and its fulfillment of a century of progress and growth since Meiji."

"Great. Let's go." Art tugged at her arm. "We can congratulate him tomorrow morning. Maybe it'll make him more cooperative."

"No, wait," she said. "Listen to this! He's invoking the spiritual founder of the nation, Amaterasu, the Sun

Goddess, as well as the traditional Boy's Day reference to Musashi and the samurai tradition." Sally turned to Art, her eyes afraid, her voice a whisper. "Led by the powerful Matsuzaka Group, Japan is now poised to assume its predestined position—"

She flinched as the metal object ripped through the page and thunked into the bright red ball of the Rising Sun emblem directly behind him. Spinning around, she could see the pointed tips of the spur-like throwing star glistening in the light.

"Down!" she yelled, and jerked hard on Art's arm.

They fell to their knees on the sidewalk as a second star whooshed over their heads. Art heard a tired voice whisper hoarsely and looked over his shoulder to see the old woman, slumped across the wooden counter of her newsstand, a metallic object embedded in the side of her throat. Like thick blotters, the newspapers sucked up the blood.

"Son of a bitch!" Art's face was white and drawn. "We've got to get out of here."

As she rose, Sally glimpsed a shadowy figure dressed in black dart behind a neon sign yards away. She whirled. A third throwing star struck her shoulder bag just as she ducked behind the newsstand.

Catching up to her, Art grabbed her hand. "What in hell is going on?"

Sally hurriedly scanned the doorway signs. "In here," she said, without turning. The pink neon winked at them as they entered.

Sakuragi. The Cherry Tree.

Another crowd, dimmer lights, the sweet smell of alcohol and sake. In one corner, a small band played popular Japanese music. A few couples tried to dance in the center of the floor, squeezed together by the overflowing mob. A roar of laughter exploded to their right.

"Over there," Art said, plunging into the cigarette fog. They knocked an elderly man aside as they struggled through the throng. Art shoved onto a small wooden bench and pulled Sally down with him. The kimono-clad hostess who had occupied the opposite end of the bench found herself seated on the floor. She scrambled to her feet, angrily grabbed the neck of a large sake bottle, and raised it above her head.

Someone caught her arm and shouted, *"Gaijin!"* She spun away.

The throwing star lodged in Sally's leather handbag glimmered menacingly as Garrett gingerly extracted it.

"What the hell's this?" he asked.

"Shuriken," Sally gasped. She glanced at the deadly object and shuddered. "At first, I thought they were meant for someone else. Ginza is a popular playground for the Japanese mafia."

"Shuriken?" Art scanned the crowd. He could detect no forced movement, but then he wasn't exactly sure he knew what he was looking for. He pulled out a handkerchief and wrapped the metallic object, taking particular care to cover the sharp points.

"Japanese throwing stars. Tipped with a deadly poison that attacks the central nervous system," Sally said, also scanning the crowd. "They were perfected in the seventeenth century by Tokugawa's ninja, black-hooded agents who spied on disloyal *daimyo* and assassinated those they considered potentially disruptive."

"Christ. What the hell are we looking for?" Art asked.

Sally glanced over his shoulder, left and right. "Dressed in black," she repeated, "from head to toe." She held his arm tightly, her knuckles white.

"Somebody may not want us at Matsuzaka tomorrow morning," he said, carefully slipping the throwing star into his coat pocket. "One thing's for sure, though."

"What's that?"

"As soon as we get out of here, we're heading for Eisenstadt's office. He's going to be involved in this whether he likes it or not."

Art craned his head. "Can you find a back door? I think we'd be safer outside."

Sally squinted as she searched for the distinctive green-and-white emergency exit sign.

"What do you have in mind?" she asked.

"I'm not sure yet. But it's clear to me that we've got to

find somebody above Katoh, somebody with enough clout to force him to tell us the truth."

They pushed their way back through the crowd, angling toward the green light Sally had spotted. At the same moment, the kimonoed hostess, armed with a fresh bottle of hot sake, was inviting a solitary figure clad in black to join her in the traditional celebration of *Tango-no-Sekku*.

When he viciously brushed her aside, she raised the heavy bottle and smashed it over his head.

"Baka!" she yelled. "The stupid foreigners I can excuse . . ."

12

Their heels clicked like castanets on the deserted street as they walked along the Sumida River toward Tsukiji. A soft roar of traffic could be heard in the distance. The air was very still.

Katoh dabbed at his neck.

"Just another week," Fukuda said, wincing as the smoke from his cigarette curled into his eyes. "What do you hear from Washington?"

Major Nakamura stopped, unfolded a cryptic telegram from Kobayashi's negotiating team, and passed it to Fukuda.

Fukuda scanned the message. "Very good," he said, flicking away an ash. "Kobayashi is holding firm. We take responsibility for all of Southeast Asia in return for cutbacks in defense support payments from Washington. I see we've also raised the issue of nuclear weapons, but the Americans are balking at that."

The Major nodded. "That would take away their sole excuse for renewing the Security Treaty," he said. "They question our resolve."

"Baka!" Fukuda's exclamation echoed in the vacant stalls lining a narrow alleyway. As the three men entered the fish market, a gray pigeon flapped out from beneath the tin roof, breaking the stillness. Fukuda watched it disappear over the tiled rooftops beyond the river.

"They question *our* resolve?" He took a final drag on his cigarette and tossed it into a pail of discarded shrimp shells and fish tails.

"You know the Americans," said the Major. "They believe they are still in control."

428

Fukuda scowled. He brushed a hand over his head. "Kobayashi will continue to push?"

"But, of course."

"Yoshi."

The Bucho turned to the MITI man. "Tell the Major the news from Moscow."

Katoh shook his head. "The Russians are not budging. Regardless of our attractive offers, they remain adamant." He paused, licking drops of sweat from his lower lip. "We have proposed a vast array of hard goods, from drilling rigs to earth-boring equipment. It's still not enough. 'We keep the Kuriles,' they say."

"Chikusho," Fukuda grunted, nudging the Major's shoulder. "I wish we could turn all our missiles loose on Moscow. The Soviets are nothing but great turds of wild desert beasts!" He slammed a fist against a nearby pillar.

"Perhaps the Moscow team is waiting for a word of encouragement from Katoh-san's new minister," the Major said.

"Or perhaps Katoh-san is losing *his* resolve." The Bucho's words cut through the dark night like a sword. He stopped at one of the fish stalls and spun the MITI man around by his lapels.

"Listen, you with the weak stomach and evaporated discipline! How can we be sure you won't break down and give away our position to the Soviets? You've already endangered us by your weakness with Garretto-san."

Katoh shivered slightly as sweat soaked through his collar. It clung to his neck with a damp chill. "That's nonsense!" he said. "You're putting words in my mouth." His voice echoed inside the shed. He stumbled backwards into a porcelain fish bucket which scraped across the concrete with the sound of fingernails on slate.

The Major stepped forward to mediate. Fukuda brushed him aside.

"The decision to include a high-level contact from MITI was a matter of some debate to begin with. You know that. We could have done all this without you."

Katoh braced himself against a wooden counter. A sliver

of moonlight fell through a crack in the tin roof, casting a single stripe across his face.

"You can trust me," he said. "You have from the beginning. You can until the end."

"Trust!" Fukuda shouted, "I begin to doubt you are worthy of it."

The MITI man drew himself up against a weighing scale, tipping a pan out of its hooks but catching it before it clattered to the floor. "This project was conceived in harmony," he said, his voice calm and steady. "Executed with loyalty to a common goal. The goal of supremacy. Cultural supremacy. *Our* supremacy. None of us has wavered from that goal. My hesitation with Garretto-san was based on a desire to see our plan succeed, but when it appeared in danger—"

"Baka!" Fukuda shouted. He pulled out another cigarette and sucked it alive. "You crumbled when you received word from Kitagawa that Garretto-san was coming to Tokyo. You telephoned me in panic, at my office, which I have told you never to do."

He blew a cloud of smoke at Katoh's face.

"And when Garretto-san turns up with a Pentagon expert, a lowly *woman*, and makes an offhand reference to May 15, which everybody knows about because it's in all the papers, you melt! Since when has this project been conceived in cowardice, Katoh-kun? Answer me that!"

Katoh drew himself erect, staring straight into the Bucho's black eyes. "Who secured the construction permits for the subterranean cavern at Ise?" he demanded. "Katoh Shohei. Who falsified the transfer documents to give Matsuzaka possession of illegal nuclear fuel? Katoh Shohei. And whose department served as a lightning rod when your stupid microimagizer was found in Sunnyvale? *Mine!*" His voice struck out in the darkness. He ignored the perspiration streaming from his face and stuffed the handkerchief in a hip pocket.

"We have planned this project with the precision of a military exercise," he continued, pointing to the Major. "To propel our country to the pinnacle of power where it rightfully belongs, and which it has been denied since the beginning of modernization, in Meiji. Each of us has worked hard to succeed with a plan that has involved not only intricate political manipulation domestically, but may also cause a complete reordering of our international allegiances." He paused, took a deep breath. "And MITI is the sole agency of the Japanese government that is a buffer to the outside world, Bucho-san. You know that. That's why I insisted from the beginning that our plan be executed *within* the framework of our international responsibilities."

Katoh stopped and drew a coatsleeve across his tightly pressed lips. With the Major silent nearby, he felt his confidence growing.

"But *you!*" he accused. "You had to resort to the lowest form of petty thievery to obtain the optical chips for Japan's greatest corporate power!"

"We merely bent the rules in an industry already characterized by questionable behavior," Fukuda snapped back. "Who could have ever guessed that an impotent midget named Micro Optix would develop the optical chip technology first? A sheer accident. We were way ahead of both IBM and Texas Instruments."

Katoh was undeterred. "When the chips were installed in our reconnaissance missiles, you immediately thought of nuclear blackmail as a means of coercion, despite your assurances to the contrary when this project started. No, you said, the mere fact that these missiles exist will be sufficient to bring the American cowards to their knees."

"As a safety valve, Katoh-kun! The Americans know our military weaknesses. How could we be certain they would buy our bluff? The strategic targeting was a stroke of genius. *Ne*, Nakamura-san?"

The Major said nothing.

"And then," said Katoh in a sharp whisper, "then you wreaked havoc and destruction in the government district by fomenting political riots the likes of which this country has not seen in over fifty years! And you accuse *me* of endangering our plan?"

Fukuda's eyes were black bullets. He glared at the MITI man. "Enough!" he said. "The fact is we would never be where we are today had I not pushed, and pushed hard, to keep us ahead of schedule. We would have lost valuable time waiting for the November by-elections instead of pressing for cabinet changes now, when they would do us the most good."

The Major stepped quickly into the ribbon of moonlight that separated the two combatants. His bald pate glowed like a second moon, equally round and full.

"Yoshi," he said quietly. "Ordinarily I would welcome such spirited competition, but we no longer have that luxury." Turning to Fukuda, he said, "Katoh-kun is right. We could never have met our schedule without MITI's covert assistance."

Fukuda's eyes never left the bureaucrat's face. Smoke from his cigarette trailed upward, disappearing in the blackness underneath the shed.

The Major continued in tones of soft mediation. "The Bucho is also right. Your caution has been perceived as a sign of weakness, of indecision, of disloyalty." He watched the MITI man, unblinking. "But we know that is not the case."

"It *is* a question of loyalty, Nakamura-san," said Katoh. "But who has the higher loyalty? Loyalty to the faction that inspired this plan or loyalty to the nation?"

"I know, I know," said the Major, his voice soft and reassuring. "But we must preserve harmony, so close to our goal."

Fukuda sucked on his cigarette, watching. He knew he was not to be denied success at this late stage.

"Besides," the Major continued, "we're still on schedule. Especially now that the Bucho has arranged for our American friends to have a little . . . accident tonight." He glanced at Fukuda.

Musashi's words sang in his ear, like a call from the gods.

Timing of the void is born in timing of the cunning.

"I trust we have heard the last of our colleague's moaning," Fukuda said.

The MITI man shifted uneasily again. He looked at the Major.

"I'm sure we have," Nakamura said, nodding. "I'd hate to see him meet with the same fate as the Americans." He glanced at the bureaucrat, his eyes glowing like coals.

He turned to Fukuda. "Tomorrow night?" he asked.

Katoh swallowed. "Yasukuni," he said, nodding.

"There he is," Art said. "Let's go."

They crossed against the traffic in front of the government building, dodging a taxi, cutting around a delivery truck crammed, front to back, with rolls of unmatted tatami, and sprinting through a row of cars jammed to a standstill in the Friday morning rush hour flow. Sally almost slipped on the rain-slick pavement.

They reached the broad canopy fronting the MITI headquarters just as Katoh Shohei mounted the first steps. Art took him by the right arm, Sally by the left.

"Sorry to disturb your morning," Art said. They pulled him briskly toward the street corner. "I think we ought to take a little walk before your day begins."

"Nan desu ka?" he said, turning his head rapidly from right to left. "Garretto-san," he whispered. The color drained from his face.

"This way," Sally said. "And please close your mouth. People might talk."

He jerked his left arm free.

"Easy, Katoh-san," Art said. "We're not alone." He gestured to a waiting car parked across the street.

Katoh glanced over his shoulder and saw the unmarked Plymouth sedan with its distinctive blue license plate, the *kanji* "gai" unmistakable. Foreign. Diplomatic. Official.

His shoulders slumped. "Where are we going?" he asked.

Sally took his arm again. "Just for a short walk," she said. "Hibiya Park is nice in the morning."

"We're going to relax our grip," Art said, as they stepped onto the opposite curb, "and we'd like you to behave normally. Just your usual morning stroll with the *gaijin*."

Katoh saw the green Plymouth edge into traffic. It trailed slowly behind them.

"What happened?" he asked, looking up at Art. His eyes were colorless, like prisms without light.

"That's what we'd like to know," Sally said. "We have an appointment with Mr. Fukuda this morning, as you know. But we got the feeling last night somebody didn't want us to see him."

Katoh swallowed, looking straight ahead. "What do you mean?"

Art directed him by the elbow down a pebbled path that paralleled the roadway. Looking back he saw the circular thumb-and-forefinger sign from Eisenstadt in the Embassy car.

"Something happened last night?" Katoh asked, his voice a pitch higher. He felt the nerves going out of control again, so he made fists at his side, trying to steady himself. But it was hopeless.

Sally saw the perspiration begin to form on his temples. She leaned in to whisper in his ear.

"Ninja," she said softly, and watched him flinch.

"Ninja?" he squeaked. His lips barely moved. He looked into Sally's eyes. "That's impossible."

"Is it?" Art asked. He pulled the handkerchief from his coat pocket and slowly unwrapped the throwing star, holding it in the palm of one hand.

"Shuriken," Katoh whispered, his eyes wide. He stared at the deadly object for a second, then glanced up at Art. "But—"

"But, nothing. There's someone else following us now who would like to see you."

Katoh spun on the gravel, his head dropped immediately as he saw the black limousine. A maroon Imperial crest topped each front fender and in the back seat was the unmistakable form of the Crown Prince, flanked by two bodyguards.

Katoh Shohei shuffled over to the waiting car. Art and Sally watched as he bowed deeply and repeatedly to the revered figure. A rear window slowly opened. There was a brief conversation. Katoh straightened and bowed again. He remained bent from the waist as the window closed and the sleek limousine eased quietly away.

Katoh rejoined the foreigners. "How did you—"

"Katoh-san," Art interrupted. "We'll ask the questions from now on, if you don't mind."

Katoh swallowed.

"It . . . wasn't my idea," he stammered. "I was against it. I was against the whole concept of violence from the beginning." He looked at Garrett as they stopped on the path underneath a broad cryptomeria tree. "You must believe me."

"What wasn't your idea?" Sally asked.

"Your accident last night," he said. "I perceived you to be a threat to our plan, but Fukuda took the action. Had I known he would resort to *ninja* . . ."

"This plan," Art said, stopping briefly. "Does it have anything to do with my optical chips?"

Katoh nodded. "That was Fukuda's idea, as well."

"And you're just an innocent observer, I suppose?"

"Innocent, no. Observer? Well, my role was perhaps not as active as the others. Come. There is no reason for me to hold back now."

As they walked, they talked. The mist collected in droplets on their hair, on their clothes, on the chrysanthemum blossoms that lined the path. They looked strangely magnified in their jewelled enclosures, like porcelain flowers studded with pearls.

Katoh told them about Fukuda's scheme to infiltrate Micro Optix and capture the optical chips, about the missile conversions, the riots, the continuing negotiations in Moscow and Washington.

"You must understand, Garretto-san," Katoh said, stopping momentarily and looking Garrett in the eye. "The motivation for this plan came from the purest of intentions. This was no fanatical plot by disgruntled military officers. It was the culmination of thousands of years of cultural continuity, cultural tradition, cultural . . . supremacy, if you will. Regardless of what happens now, our time is definitely coming. You must not forget that."

"The ascendancy of the East," Sally said, half to herself.

"What was that, Miss Hendricks?"

"I said, the rise of the East. Many take the industrial and political decline of the West for granted," she said. "They do not simultaneously accept the notion that Asia may yet again dominate world affairs."

He nodded. "You are very wise. It may take ten years, it may be another fifty. But we firmly believe it will come."

"Outgrowing the apprenticeship?" Art asked softly.

"Exactly, Garretto-san. You see, our culture is not based on the same value system as yours. In the West, universal values are sacrosanct. Peace. Truth. Freedom."

He folded his arms across his barrel-like chest, and faced Art.

"In Japan, we embrace particularistic values. Conformity. Loyalty. Harmony. Threads that have sewn the fabric of our society together for nearly two thousand years."

Katoh reached down and clipped a small, maroon chrysanthemum from the rainbow of colors at his feet.

"This is the symbol of our Imperial tradition," he said, twirling it in his fingers. "Our elected politicians wear a stylized velvet miniature in their lapels, symbol of their unwavering loyalty."

"Loyalty to the tradition?" Art asked.

Katoh shook his head. "Loyalty to the people, who are the embodiment of the Imperial tradition today," he said. "The problem is that allegiances can be distorted, cultural goals blurred. That has happened to Fukuda, I am afraid. His loyalty ultimately embraced a single faction, even a single man, as his allegiance grew further away from tradition. I began to see that only too late."

"Too late for what?" Sally took the delicate blossom from Katoh's hand, held it to her nose and smelled the sweet freshness.

"Too late to stop him, of course, once everything had

been set in motion. I am a pragmatist, Miss Hendricks. As you know, MITI is Japan's window on the world. Our global relationships are dependent upon the continuation of a harmonious international order. Fukuda didn't agree, but without a hierarchy, Japan is nothing." He paused as he searched for words, staring at the chrysanthemum. "My country deserves greater global power as evidence of its economic achievements and cultural strengths. But there is no point in sitting atop a trash heap."

The crowds began to thin out, leaving them almost alone.

"You said Fukuda's loyalty centered on one man. Is that Prime Minister Tanaka?" Art was frowning now.

Katoh shook his head. "No, his chairman. Matsuzaka Yukio. His *oyabun.* Chairman Matsuzaka supported this plan from the beginning, supported it with the power of the Matsuzaka group. You see, Matsuzaka-san sponsored a young man for the Diet many years ago. His name was Kobayashi. They shared common ideals."

"The same Kobayashi who has just taken over as Foreign Minister," Sally said.

"Correct. When Matsuzaka started his Domestic Institute of Competition, Kobayashi pushed through the necessary legislation. He later became Director General of the SDF." Katoh paused. "That is equivalent to Minister of Defense."

Art suddenly snapped his fingers. "The Mitsuya Incident! Of course! When those young military officers were plotting to end civilian control."

Katoh nodded. "It is hard for westerners to understand. Kobayashi-san is Prime Minister Tanaka's *oyabun.* Our key players stay out of the public spotlight. They work behind the scenes, manipulating events through their factions, practicing the art of invisibility. *Kuromaku,* we call it, like the bunraku puppeteers."

"Or like ninja?" Sally said.

Katoh lowered his head, closing his eyes. "Or like ninja."

"But surely Mr. Matsuzaka's loyalty is to your Imperial tradition," she said.

Katoh looked up. He shook his head again. "The Emperor, represented by our present government, remained loyal to the United States when your country was no longer loyal to us."

Sally frowned. "You mean, the trade war?"

Katoh shook his head. "Only in part. Before that, when Washington snubbed Tokyo in favor of Peking. The soybean shock. The yen shock. The oil shock. And then the ultimate humiliation." He paused.

"Vietnam," said Sally.

Katoh nodded. "Loyalty, Miss Hendricks, is a fickle lover." He did not smile.

Art looked at his watch. "We don't have a lot of time," he said. "We're due at Matsuzaka in a half-hour."

Katoh Shohei put a hand on Art's arm, aware that he was breaking the cultural tradition of touching another person. "Surely you are not still thinking of going to see Fukuda?"

"We thought it might shock him into cooperating, as it did you."

Katoh was silent for a moment. "He is not expecting you after last night. He won't receive a report from the ninja, and will assume the mission to have been successful. The assassin will not call because he is probably dead himself; he would commit suicide to atone for his failure. Even so, Garretto-san, Fukuda will not allow the ninja's failure to deter him. He will tell you nothing."

"Then you will have to escort us to the missiles. We're taking those optical chips back."

"I am obligated to His Majesty to do whatever you ask."

Art glanced down at Sally. She met his eyes and nodded slowly.

Katoh glanced at his watch. "But you are right, Garretto-san. We do not have much time."

Art frowned. "What do you mean? If we skip our meeting with Fukuda this morning, we can confront him with the evidence when we return."

Katoh shook his head again. "It's not that simple. You see, we are scheduled to rendezvous tonight."

Sally turned to face the MITI bureaucrat. "Where?" she asked.

"At Yasukuni."

"Yasukuni Shrine?"

Katoh nodded.

Until we meet again at Yasukuni.

"A victory celebration already?" she asked.

Again he nodded. "That was what was intended. May 15 is only a week away."

"Then we'd better get going," Art said.

14

It was almost eleven when they surfaced on the rooftop of the American Embassy at Akasaka to board the waiting helicopter. Eisenstadt had had to bring a machine up from Yokosuka, a half-hour to the south, brief the pilot, arrange for fuel, and clear their route to Ise through domestic airspace with the Foreign Ministry.

"A helicopter to the National Shrine?" he was asked. Eisenstadt simply told them in his best Japanese that the demands of high-ranking visitors from Washington had to be met. They knew how it was, didn't they?

They did. Politicians were egotists, regardless of national origin.

The flat blades of the small Sikorsky whirred impatiently, streaking the clear bubble top with trails of water as the rain fell harder.

"Let's get moving," Art shouted above the roar of the engine.

Eisenstadt nodded and tossed a thumbs-up sign to the pilot. Garrett grasped Katoh's elbow. Ducking their heads, they ran under the moving blades and clambered up into the machine. Sally was right behind them. The pilot lifted off as soon as he saw Eisenstadt secure the door.

Engine noise made conversation difficult during the two-hour flight, and the poor weather made for a bumpy ride.

As they banked, dropping altitude over Nagoya, Art glanced down at Katoh. The MITI man's face, red from nervousness earlier, was now a pallid white.

The pilot cut sharply left, out across Ise Bay. Within minutes they could see the National Shrine below.

"That it?" Art shouted.

Sally shook her head. "That's the shrine," she yelled back. "Matsuzaka's just beyond."

Katoh glanced down at the pure cypress temple beneath him and saw the concentric rings separating the inner and outer shrines. He shut his eyes and visualized the three sacred treasures of the Imperial Throne stored within. The Mirror. The Jewel. The Sword. And he thought how close he had come to losing them.

"There!" Katoh pointed to a small clearing in the grove of *hinoki* trees.

The pilot nodded and slowly lowered the helicopter through the trees. When the runners had settled into the grass, he cut the power. The engine whined down.

Sally was the first to see the warning sign.

TRESPASSERS WILL BE SHOT. SURVIVORS WILL BE SHOT AGAIN.

She tugged at Art's arm. A look of disgust crossed his face as he glanced at the *kanji* while Sally translated.

Crossing the grove, Katoh waved at the shadowy figure at the edge of the void and then threw a concealed switch. He motioned for them to stand back by the helicopter as the ground began to vibrate and the passageway below yawned open. Then he rejoined them.

Out of sight of the guard, Eisenstadt slipped a revolver from its holster on his hip. "Okay, let's go," he said.

"Please," Katoh said, putting his hand on the American's arm. "You won't need that."

The defense attaché stared into the MITI man's eyes. "I hope not," he replied. He sheathed the weapon.

Katoh led them into the wooden elevator cage and started the descent. With four people squeezed in, three of them *gaijin*, it was a tight fit.

As the brilliantly lit cavern came into view, Art could see the rocket, white and gleaming and launch-ready on its moorings. His eyes traced the full length of the tall missile, focusing on the *Hi-no-Maru* sphere at its apex.

"Christ," he muttered under his breath.

Footsteps approached as the four visitors emerged. The

chief technician, clad in antiseptic white, was followed closely by his small crew.

"Nan desu ka?" the chief asked. He glared at Katoh and eyed the *gaijin* suspiciously. "What is the meaning of this? Fukuda did not advise me of a second meeting here prior to launch."

Katoh Shohei stepped forward. "There has been a change in plans," he said. "These Americans are from the Pentagon in Washington. Our government has agreed to a renewal of the Security Treaty," he lied. "There will be no need for a launch."

The chief technician said nothing. His eyes darted to the pistol at Eisenstadt's waist, then flickered back to Katoh.

"That is . . . impossible," he said. "Why has the Bucho not informed us?"

"Fukuda Bucho has been busy with last-minute changes," Katoh said. "He and the Major are at the Foreign Ministry now. I have been dispatched with the Americans to deactivate the rocket."

He held out his hand. "Give me the code card."

The chief technician retreated a step. He glanced again at the *gaijin*. Impossible, he thought. The Bucho would have called. There would have been communication. Besides, a woman? It couldn't be.

He reached into the breast pocket over his heart and withdrew the red plastic card. His eyes shifted to the control box on the near wall.

"Domo," Katoh said, extending his palm. "I assure you this has the Bucho's assent."

The chief glanced back at the MITI man. *"Naruhodo,"* he said, lowering the card toward Katoh's hand and bowing deeply.

Katoh returned the bow.

As Katoh Shohei's upper torso began to drop in traditional response, the chief technician spun suddenly and crossed to the control panel, inserting the red card into a narrow slit.

"Stop that bastard!" Art yelled. "He's going to launch the rocket!"

Katoh jerked up, incredulous that an underling had dis-
obeyed.

Eisenstadt whipped out his revolver and dropped into a
crouch. The other technicians scattered.

"Tomatte kure! Stop!" Sally shouted.

Eisenstadt fired.

Holding his left shoulder, the chief whirled and faced the
visitors. "Impossible!" he said. He reached out with his
right hand and punched the launch code into the panel.

Eisenstadt fired again, and the chief slumped forward as
the bullet pierced his chest.

"No!" Art chopped Eisenstadt's arm before he could
shoot again, but it was too late.

At that moment a siren began to whoop above them.
Numbers flashed on a large digital screen. The countdown
had begun.

180 . . . 179 . . . 178 . . .

Wisps of white vapor began to seep from beneath the
massive rocket.

Art grabbed Katoh by the lapels. "We're got less than
three minutes to deactivate this thing!" he shouted.
"What's the cutback code?"

Katoh Shohei swallowed. "There . . . there is no cutback
code," he said.

"Bullshit, Katoh!" Art shook the MITI man, hard. "This
is no time to play games."

163 . . . 162 . . . 161 . . .

Katoh brushed Garrett's hands away, straightening. "I
am no fool," he said. "You think I would play games now?
Fukuda never programmed a cutback code. Obviously, he
thought it would be unnecessary."

145 . . . 144 . . . 143 . . . 142 . . . 141 . . .

Art spun toward Sally. "You and Chuck get back." His
eye searched the far wall. "Over there! Into the control
room."

Sally grabbed Art's shoulders. "I'm not leaving you,"
she said.

Garrett ripped himself away. "Chuck," he said.
Eisenstadt grabbed Sally and hustled her toward the control room.

Turning back to Katoh, Art said, "Where's the guidance mechanism? Get one of these technicians over here, quick!"

127 . . . 126 . . . 125 . . .

The digital readout kept ticking down, its red numbers glowing eerily, as clouds of vapor rose ominously from the base of the rocket.

Katoh shouted at the technicians, huddled together against the far wall. His voice was sharp, his words curt. The Japanese command slapped them in the face. They straightened and bowed crisply. They all ran forward.

"You!" Katoh shouted, jabbing his finger in the chest of one. "Up the scaffolding with Garretto-san. Now!"

"Hai!" he replied, clicking his heels together. He was white with fear.

Garrett ran up the scaffolding steps, the technician with his bag of tools in close pursuit. He knew what to look for—oh God, did he ever, he thought—he just wasn't sure where to find it. Or if he had time.

106 . . . 105 . . . 104 . . .

His knowledge of the McDonnell Douglas TerCom guidance system told him roughly where the access panel should be. He shot two-thirds of the way up the rocket, watching the outer skin, until he came to a section about two feet square. The siren shrieked, ear-splitting and painful.

"Screwdriver," Garrett shouted. He was breathing heavily.

The technician shrugged, uncomprehending.

As Garrett yanked the kit from his hand, it opened, spilling a wrench and a small electronic drill through the grating.

Looking again at the panel, he jerked a heavy screwdriver out of the bag. Hurriedly, he began to unfasten the four corner screws that held the panel in place. When he had three out, he pulled sharply on the outer shell and bent it down, cutting the palm of his hand.

Cursing, he stuck his head into the opening. It was dark, but he could make out the complex web of videx boards and chip cards. He needed only the one key chip. The optical.

"Flashlight!" he yelled, pulling his head back out.

76 . . . 75 . . . 74 . . .

He glanced down at the digital readout while the technician rummaged nervously through his remaining tools. Perspiration ran down Art's face in small rivers. His shirt was soaked.

"Shit!" Garrett forced the technician down a half-dozen steps, and shouted at Katoh. "Get a fucking flashlight up here, quick!"

Katoh dispatched another technician up through the thickening vapor clouds to hand the first man a small torch.

Garrett snatched the flashlight from him when he returned and played it across the maze of circuitry. He yanked out one videx board, and then another, looking for the telltale chip. If he could get it out, the whole system would be thrown out of kilter. He tossed the circuits aside, his bleeding hand forgotten.

Sticking his head back inside the hole, he threw the light from side to side. Then out of the corner of one eye, he saw it. The unmistakable letters.

M.O.

He jerked the optical chip out of the circuit board and spun around. Tossing the flashlight aside he held the optical chip triumphantly aloft.

Chuck Eisenstadt and Sally Hendricks came running from the control room. Katoh Shohei slumped against the wall, a look of intense relief on his face.

Garrett collapsed against the side of the scaffolding only to spot that the digital readout was still counting.

25 . . . 24 . . . 23 . . .

He looked in disbelief. He checked the chip again. There was no doubt. The whole system *should* have malfunctioned.

"Get back!" he shouted, pushing the technician out of the way and catapulting down the scaffold. He leapt over the guardrail when he was close enough to jump. His feet hit the floor with five seconds left.

Garrett and Katoh tore into the control room on the

heels of Chuck and Sally, slamming the thick door just at the digital readout clicked its final numbers.

. . . 02 . . . 01 . . . 00 . . .

Art grabbed Sally and held her in his arms, as they waited for the roar that would signal the beginning of a new era of destruction. Suddenly the siren stopped.

It was Chuck Eisenstadt who finally broke the silence when he peered through the safety glass and saw the rocket still on its pad.

"Thank God," he muttered.

Eisenstadt nudged Art and Sally. Garrett opened his eyes and rose far enough to see that the rocket was still there. The trails of vapor had vanished, and all was quiet.

Art stood and pulled Sally up, hugging her to him. His arms were shaking.

They exited the control room, Art and Sally in the lead, Eisenstadt and Katoh following close behind.

Garrett glanced at his watch. It was nearly three p.m.

"Chuck, you stay here with this gang. At least, you can communicate with them. Sally and I will take Katoh-san back to Tokyo." He turned to face the portly bureaucrat.

Katoh nodded.

"Art, the other chips." It was Sally.

Garrett opened his bloody palm. The Micro Optix device sparkled in the bright lights.

"Right," he said. He showed the chip to Eisenstadt. "There should be another dozen of these mounted in the missiles up in that nosecone," he continued, pointing to the tip of the rocket. "We want those back at a minimum."

"Check." Eisenstadt spoke briefly with the technicians who nervously bowed in assent.

Garrett turned to Katoh.

"What about the rest of the chips?" he asked.

The MITI man shook his head. "You'll have to ask Fukuda," he replied.

15

They stood on the flat stone steps of the *hondo*, bowing to the bronze statue of Buddha smiling back at them from within.

Yasukuni's Buddha. *Hotokesama.* Japan's Buddha. *Sakyamuni.* Their Buddha. *Bodhisattva.*

Major Hideo Nakamura stood stiffly erect in his starched dress uniform, a chest full of ribbons, his two swords clinking at his side. The long, curved *katana* for combat; a short *tanken* dagger next to it.

Fukuda Kenji thrust open the folds of his dark blue *hakama* and stepped out of his wooden *geta.* He hurdled the low barrier at the entrance to the meditation hall, moved softly across the tatami and bowed in front of the Buddha once again.

He kneeled down on the white silk cushion. Tucked into a dark blue sash about his waist was the Fukuda family sword, long and curved and gleaming in the candlelight. His left hand rested atop the leather-bound grip.

The Major padded quietly across the tatami, bowed a second time and knelt beside him on a neighboring cushion.

"Word from Washington?" Fukuda asked, his eyes forward.

The Major smiled. "Kobayashi has the Americans right where we want them. They still say no to our nuclear rearmament plans, but we have rejected their position on regional defense. Net result: stalemate."

"Yoshi," Fukuda said. He felt in full control now. "And Moscow?"

"We sent new instructions to the MITI team early this morning. No compromises. The Kuriles, or nothing."

448

How sweet the cedar smelled, Fukuda thought. He took a deep breath.

"It's almost a dream, Nakamura-san," he said. "Like the Buddhist tales of old."

"But this is no illusion," said the Major. "The future always appears as such until it materializes in the present."

Fukuda held himself erect, proud. But it wasn't pride at all. He tried to think—when did that feeling prevail? At special times, of course, when his mind and his body achieved a oneness that made them inseparable.

Rare times, memorable times.

Of course, that was it. His *kendo* battles, the victories, that special feeling of accomplishment, of winning! And yet, not he, but his sword.

He had achieved oneness with his sword.

Fukuda squeezed the grip now, felt the hard leather thongs against his palm, felt secure, confident, eternal.

But it was not just accomplishment or achievement. It had to be more than that. He felt his mind becoming weightless.

Then it clicked into place like his sword in its scabbard.
Superiority.

He . . . felt . . . so . . . *superior.*

Buddha's bronze eyes stared ahead, but they did not see. They focused far, far beyond the limits of time, an invisible link between past and future, joining present to present, symbolizing the eternity of Japan's cultural traditions.

Nakamura glanced at the empty cushion to his right. *"Katoh-kun wa?"*

Fukuda leaned forward. "Late, as usual."

The Major ignited several sticks of incense from the candle that flickered at his side, jamming them into a bronzed cup of sand nearby. The sweet perfume quickly saturated the damp night air.

Fukuda clapped once. He felt so at peace with himself, so much a part of his country's past. It flowed in his veins. He could hear it.

The then.

He clapped again. The sharp, snapping sound echoed quietly in the hall. Hotokesame kept smiling, one hand at attention, fingers curved, the other at rest, nestled in his lap. His smile said, I hear you.

The now.

When he clapped the third time, he stared intently at Buddha's forehead, folding both hands, palms up, in his lap. His spine was stiff and curved, like his sword.

The forever.

They were beyond time now. They would redefine time, because Japan was timeless.

Fukuda rose effortlessly from the *zabuton*. He grasped the single candle and holding it with both hands, touched the pale blue flame to each of eleven others arranged in a semicircle at Buddha's lotus-shrouded feet. The dark interior of the *hondo* grew measurably lighter.

He pulled his sword from its scabbard, touching the tip lightly to each one of the twelve glowing spires. Twelve tiny pillars of light, statue-still in the dampness of the deep night.

Twelve beacons guiding the way into the future.

Twelve lighthouses protecting them from external danger.

Twelve missiles lofting their country back atop the pyramid of power.

Fukuda whirled on his toes, smiling up at the soft bronze lips. He wanted to kiss them, to feel their coolness against his. *Hotokesama.* Stay with us. We are almost there.

Pivoting on one foot, he flashed the sword above his head, swinging it in shorter and shorter circles. Light from the candles glittered off the double-edged blade.

Nothing is more transient than nothingness.

He snapped the sword back into its scabbard, and bowed to the bronze Bodhisattva.

Nothing is more certain than uncertainty.

He sat back down next to the Major. As if on cue, they clapped their hands together.

Once. *Perseverance.*

Twice. *Victory.*

Three times. *Survival.*

Fukuda breathed in deeply, felt the sweet incense penetrate his lungs, down into his stomach, deep into his abdomen, deeper into his bowels.

Hotokesama winked.

"Inevitability," Fukuda whispered.

The Major nodded.

Then the Bucho froze as he heard the sound of approaching footsteps on the pebbled path. He whirled on his *zabuton.*

"Katoh-kun?"

Silence.

"Is that you?" He shaded his eyes from the candlelight, but saw nothing.

Major Nakamura turned his head slowly around.

Art Garrett stepped out from under the shadow of a cedar branch. "Garrett," he said softly.

The sight of a *gaijin* in the holy inner sanctuary of the temple forced Fukuda to his feet, disbelieving. He inched forward on the tatami, his silk *tabi* digging into the straw.

"So, we finally meet, Mr. Fukuda," Art said. "Sorry to keep you waiting."

"Garretto-san desu ka?" His voice was the shadow of a whisper. He scrambled forward for a closer look. "That's impossible!"

"Not impossible at all," Katoh said, stepping forward, his eyes pointed darts. "Your violent strategy has failed, Bucho-san. The assassin missed his targets. He managed only to kill an innocent old woman."

"Nani?" It was the Major. "That can't be true." He rose now, moved to join Fukuda, his swords clinking softly, like ice cubes in an empty glass. Then he saw the *gaijin* standing by Katoh's side. "It must be true."

Fukuda rubbed his eyes, as if Buddha had created an illusion. Suddenly, he unsheathed his great-grandfather's sword, swinging it above his head in a wide arc and then thrusting it down in a violent motion in front of him, its long, curved blade sucking through the thin struts of the wooden barrier as if through paper. Fukuda touched the top half of the railing and pushed it forward. It fell to the tatami as if neatly folded, a mirror image of the bottom half.

"My God," Sally said, edging out from beside the tree. She grasped Art's arm.

"*Baka!*" Fukuda shouted. "This is nonsense! I am dreaming!"

He wheeled and turned, executing a barrage of intricate sword movements, cutting crisply through the air.

Timing is strategy. There is timing in everything.

Of course, the timing! What had happened to the timing? A moment ago, all seemed so certain, so sure.

Perceive those things that cannot be seen.

His sword. He held his great-grandfather in his hands, the link to past generations, his connection to the future.

Do nothing that is of no use.

Musashi?

The master's voice seemed to grow weaker, a whisper from the past, soft words in his ear. Fukuda held his sword high, curving into the dark reaches of the hall.

"Garretto-san?" His voice pleaded that it not be true.

Art stood motionless. "Fukuda-san," he said. He waited.

Fukuda drew in a long breath and exhaled. Soundless sound.

"The microimagizer?" he whispered.

"In part, yes."

"The Security Treaty?"

"In part, yes." Art's voice was steady, firm.

Fukuda stood effortlessly erect. His breathing was long and slow. He could hear the blood surge through his veins.

The Major's face was passive, his shiny head a canteloupe in the candlelight. "So you know?" His eyes burned forward, blazing at Katoh.

Art nodded. "Yes," he said. "We know. But we don't understand."

Let the people hear but do not let them understand.

"Two thousand years," Fukuda said. "Two thousand years of cultural refinement unparalleled anywhere, Garretto-san. In less than a generation, Japan has outperformed the largest and most powerful economic system the world has ever seen."

Art took a step closer, watching Fukuda's blade, resting his foot on the first stone step.

"We are not unaware of that, Fukuda-san. We know we have lost much of the competitive drive, the resourcefulness, the initiative, that gave us our earlier achievements," he said, his eyes locked in a stare with the Bucho. "But the last chapter hasn't been written yet. We can recapture that discipline again."

Fukuda snorted. "Disipline? What do you Americans know about discipline? It never existed until we Japanese applied it to our modernization efforts." He stepped closer, raising the sword over his head. "We wrote the book of discipline, beginning with the first chapter," he said, his voice hissing with the heat of steam, "and we'll write the last chapter, too."

"Art, be careful." Sally tugged on his arm.

"Maybe not, Fukuda-san," he said quietly. "That chapter's still up for grabs."

"What do you mean?" Fukuda's arms began to quiver under the weight of his sword.

"Kobayashi-san has been contacted in Washington," Katoh broke in. "He's returning to Tokyo for consultations. The Security Treaty talks have been temporarily suspended."

"*Chikusho!*" Fukuda spat the word out, flicking his sword forward. It pierced the tatami in front of him and stuck, glowing, in the candlelight.

"And Moscow?" he asked, his eyes riveted on the curved blade.

"We telexed the team an hour ago," Katoh said. "They are to do nothing until they receive further instructions."

Lunging quickly to his left, he pulled Nakamura's dagger from its scabbard. Holding the *tanken* in his right hand, he slid silently into a kneeling position directly behind the split barrier, his back to Bodhisattva's sightless gaze. The dagger sparkled like a mirror.

"Our plan may be aborted," he said. His voice was hushed. "For now. But our time is coming, Garretto-san. The Americans have been warned."

Sally tugged again at Art's arm. He took a step back.

"We'll see. If it happens, it will be legitimate, and not

the unnatural consequence of a fanatical elite." He put an arm around Sally's back.

"Fanatical elite?" Fukuda exhaled slowly, the dagger motionless. "It is obvious you do not understand. Japan *is* the elite. Our survival is predestined."

"Perhaps," Art said. "Perhaps not. Any manifestation of global power can only be temporary. The bronze statue behind you is evidence of that."

"Survival," Fukuda whispered. "Which we will achieve through perseverance. As Musashi said, 'Practice day and night, and your spirit will broaden.' "

Sally's soft voice hung in the night air like a cloud. "Musashi also said, 'What I could not achieve, let no imitator presume to attempt.' "

"If you can persevere, your opponent will be forced to give in."

The Bucho's words pierced the dampness. The soft mist was a transmitting vapor, an ether, a bond to the millions of souls enshrined at Yasukuni, a message to the millions beyond, waiting, living, dreaming for Japan's resurgence.

In a blur, Fukuda brought the sharp dagger down into his abdomen, so fast they never saw his arm move. His next words were soundless, a gargle of spirit, as he pulled the knife quickly across his lower stomach, from right to left, with both hands, and then vertically up into his ribcage in the traditional, ceremonial ritual of *seppuku*.

Blood spurted in a great gush from the gaping slit, the rich, thick fluid dark purple, almost black, in the haze of candlelight. It soaked into the straw, oozing down onto the stone steps.

Art flinched visibly, hugging Sally to him. She turned her head.

"Death with honor," Garrett whispered. "Atonement." His lips barely moved. He understood now.

Fukuda Kenji's body slumped forward, a hollow void. His soul joined the silent millions at Yasukuni in their eternal vigil. Major Nakamura slid silently across the tatami, bringing his own sword down. The thin blade cut through the Bucho's neck as easily as if it were young bamboo.

The Bucho's head rolled off his body in slow motion as blood sprayed across the Major's crisp uniform in scarlet stripes, drenching the motionless figure of the smiling Sakyamuni.

He had achieved oneness with his sword.

The Major crumpled to the tatami, his sword limp and useless in his hands.

Art's gaze focused on Fukuda's face, whose hateful eyes were empty now but whose smile endured.

We will write the last chapter, Garretto-san.

The words echoed in his mind, like wind in a tunnel.

Katoh slowly ascended the smooth stones, kicked his shoes off and walked to the Major. He removed the sword from his grasp, setting it aside on the tatami.

Kneeling, he whispered into the Major's ear. "They have the chips."

The Major nodded, gazing at the Bucho's blood-soaked form. A solitary tear fell onto the tatami and disappeared, colorless, in the river of red.

16

Art and Sally walked hand in hand through the cryptomeria and the chrysanthemum of Hibiya Park. They crossed the footbridge that led over the moat to the Imperial Palace.

Sally's eye caught a carp streamer that remained from the Boy's Day celebrations. Its tail was torn into tatters, but its mouth yawned wide against the stiff breeze that blew in from the Japan Sea, bringing clear skies and a warming sun.

"Amazing how so few could do so much," Art said.

Sally smiled. "People forget that Japanese society is still basically feudal," she said. "Governed by an elite bureaucracy, as in Tokugawa, and divided by factions that mask a fierce domestic rivalry."

The aged slats of the wooden bridge creaked under their feet. When they reached the other side, Art noticed a grove of young bamboo off to their right.

He tugged on Sally's hand and they walked through the supple shoots that whispered in the wind. Art reached out and stroked one, mint-green and smooth as silk.

"Bamboo," Sally said. "Like so many Japanese traditions, it twists and turns and bends out of shape, but it never breaks." Her voice was quiet. "It survives."

Art arched a young shoot back and let it go. It snapped upright instantly.

Sally knelt down and pulled a sprout from the black soil. She twirled it thoughtfully in her fingers. Shading her eyes from the sun, she looked up at Art.

She stood and handed him the sprout. "This bamboo preceded the computer chip and will outlive it, too."

He sniffed it. It was tender and fresh, a replica of centuries. He draped an arm around Sally's shoulder, leaned down, and kissed the top of her head.

"Some things have to be eternal," he said quietly.

They walked on in silence. Sally hooked a thumb in Art's hip pocket as she put her arm around him. Art gazed across the garden at the bronze gates leading to the Imperial Palace, near the stone ramparts of old Edo Castle.

Suddenly he stopped and pulled her to him. "If you can arrange a shorter sabbatical, I'll join you," he said, whispering into her ear.

Her face lit up with a soft smile. She wrapped her arms around him. "It's a deal," she said.

Both turned their heads when they heard the crunching sounds and saw a tiny Japanese boy walking toward them on wooden *geta* no larger than toy boats. He wore a black samurai costume; a small *kendo* sword was tucked in at the waist. His eyes were mere slits as he squinted against the bright sun.

The child stopped abruptly. His eyes flashed open. He stood, weaving from side to side on his frail wooden platform. Then he pointed up at Art.

"*Gaijin!*" he squeaked, as his parents raced forward, red-faced, bowing repeatedly. They pulled him back.

Art knelt down and drew an imaginary six-shooter from his hip, aiming playfully at the child.

The boy shook himself loose and drew his sword, barely an arm's length away.

Art cocked his thumb and fired, blowing an invisible trail of smoke from his upraised finger. He smiled.

The boy stood, unfazed, holding his sword in both hands above his head. He took a step forward.

"*Ken-chan!*" his mother shouted. She ran forward and snatched him away. "*Baka!*"

"Ken-chan," Sally whispered, watching them retreat.

The Sword Master.

Kensei.

The sky is everlasting,
And the earth is very old.
Why so? Because the world
Exists not for itself;
It can and will live on.

The wise man chooses to be last
And so becomes the first of all;
Denying self, he too is saved.
For does not fulfillment find
In being an unselfish man?

GLOSSARY

Arigato gozaimasu Thank you very much

Baka Fool, idiot, imbecile
Bakufu Military government (under the Shogun)
Banto Clerk, attendant
Banzai Hurrah, hurray (victory cheer)
Boku I, me (informal)
Bucho Director of a division, department head
Bunraku Traditional puppet theater

Chikusho Damn, damn it
Choko Sake cup
Chotto Briefly, just a moment

Daijobu All right, okay
Daimyo Medieval feudal lord
Deshi Apprentice, disciple
Dohyo Sumo wrestling arena, or ring
Dojo Fencing hall, exercise hall
Domo Thanks; much obliged
Dozo Please; by all means

Ekiben Box lunch sold at railroad stations

Futon Full-sized bed cushion used for sleeping

Gaijin Foreigner, outside person
Gambaru To persevere, persist, stick it out
Genkan Entryway, vestibule
Geta Traditional wooden clogs or sandals

459

Hachimaki Headband, frontlet
Hai Yes; certainly
Hakama Men's formal pleated robe
Han Feudal clan, fief, feudal domain
Haori Men's formal half-coat; worn with *hakama*
Harakiri Suicide by disembowelment; *seppuku*
Haramaki Woolen stomach band
Hatamoto Bannerman, retainer, vassal
Higasa Sunshade, traditional paper umbrella
Hisashiburi Long time no see
Hondo Main, or inner, temple; sanctuary
Honto Really; indeed

Itai Pain, hurt
Iya Unpleasant, distasteful
Itte'rasshai Please come again, return

Jisatsu Suicide, self-destruction

Kacho Section chief
Kamameshi Lunchbox served in a ceramic pot
Kamikaze Divine wind, suicide corps
Kampai Cheers; a toast
Kanban Signboard, shingle
Kanji Ideographs used in Japanese writing
Katana Traditional samurai sword
Keiretsu Conglomerate, group of affiliated firms
Kendo Traditional fencing, swordsmanship
Kensei The Sword Master, or Sword Saint; the historical
    name of Miyamoto Musashi, Japan's most famous samurai
    warrior
Keyaki A dark brown hardwood
Kirisame Light rain, drizzle
Kiseru Traditional tobacco pipe
Kobun Protégé, follower, adherent
Koi Carp
Kotatsu Footwarmer; a latticed wooden frame over a bra-
    zier or heater, usu. submerged in floor
Kotowaza Proverb, maxim

-kun Mr. (informal)

Kuromaku Wirepuller; mastermind; working behind the scenes (lit. black curtain)

Kuzumono Trash, garbage

Maa Well, I should say, indeed

Majime Serious, earnest

Mashiko Distinctive pottery made in the folkcraft style, known for its simplicity and beauty

Mawashi Sumo wrestler's loincloth

Mikan Tangerine, mandarin orange

Misoshiru Slightly salted soybean soup

Mompei Women's workclothes gathered at wrist and ankle

Mochiron Of course; naturally

Moshi-moshi Hello (telephone response)

Mugicha Traditional tea leaves mixed with grain

Nani What, which; What!?

Naruhodo I see; yes, of course

Nashi Nothing, without

Ninja A traditional samurai who mastered the art of making himself invisible and engaged in espionage activity on behalf of the Shogun

Noren Shop curtain, cloth sign

Obi Wide belt or sash worn with kimono

Ofuro Traditional bath, wooden bathtub

Ohayo gozaimasu Good morning

Okaenasai Welcome home; welcome back

On-giri Obligation, duty; the traditional feeling of indebtedness stemming from a favor or benefit

Oshibori A steamed face towel

Oyabun Mentor, master, boss

Ryokai Understand, comprehend

Sakaba Bar, pub, tavern

Sakeyake Red-faced from drinking too much sake

Sakoku Closed country; isolation, exclusion

Sakura Cherry tree, cherry blossoms

Sensei Teacher, master
Shakuhachi Traditional wooden flute
Shikata ga nai It can't be helped; inevitable
Shiken jigoku Examination hell, ordeal
Shimaguni Island country; insularity
Shuriken Poison-tipped throwing star
Soba Noodles, noodle soup
Subarashii Splendid, wonderful
Sumi Black ink
Sumimasen Excuse me; I'm sorry
Sushiya Raw fish restaurant
Sushizume Overcrowded, packed like sardines (sushi)

Tabi Traditional silk socks, worn with geta
Tadaima I'm home; I have returned
Tanken Dagger, short sword
Tofu Soybean curd
Tokkuri Small, round sake bottle
Tokonoma Alcove, honored place
Torii Temple archway, gate

Umai Delicious, savory

Wakaru Understand, grasp
Wasabi Grated horseradish, eaten with sushi

Yatto Finally; at last
Yoshi Good, all right, fine
Yukata Informal kimono, unlined cotton bathrobe

Zabuton Traditional sitting cushion
Zaibatsu Prewar financial clique, or oligarchy
Zannen Unfortunate; too bad

Buy these books at your local bookstore or use this coupon for ordering:

Avon Books, Dept BP, Box 767, Rte 2, Dresden, TN 38225
Please send me the book(s) I have checked above. I am enclosing $_____
(please add $1.00 to cover postage and handling for each book ordered to a maximum of three dollars). Send check or money order—no cash or C.O.D.'s please. Prices and numbers are subject to change without notice. Please allow six to eight weeks for delivery.

Name _____

Address _____

City _____ State/Zip _____

Toys 1-84

"A MILE-A-MINUTE TALE OF ARMS SALES, REVOLUTIONS, SEDUCTIONS AND ASSASSINATIONS"

The New York Times Book Review

THE TRADE

WILLIAM H. HALLAHAN

An ex-CIA agent involved in the international arms trade is led from Cologne to Paris to London to Amsterdam in search of his partner's killer. Instead he falls into a neo-Nazi conspiracy leading to World War III—and into the arms of a seductive, lethal beauty.

Hallahan "graduates to the Ludlum-Follett class of writers with this crackling good thriller."

Publishers Weekly

"A dandy thriller...keeps the reader's interest right to the end."

Detroit Free Press

Avon Paperback   **57737-2/$3.50**

Available wherever paperbacks are sold or directly from the publisher. Include $1.00 per copy for postage and handling; allow 6-8 weeks for delivery. Avon Books, Dept BP, Box 767. Rte 2. Dresden. TN 38225.

Trade 11-82